A spec

ROGER HANNAH

WHAT IF?

A Second Chance At Life for Elvis

RK Hannah Publishing

Published by
R K Hannah Publishing
Wesley Chapel, FL 33544

United States Copyright Office: TXul-242-823

ISBN: 978-0-9718280-0-1

Creative Coordination and Publishing
by
AUTHOR'S PUBLISHING
CONSULTANTS

Clearwater, Florida

Photo Art by: Corrie A. Ladd

Printed in the United States of America
February, 2007

A huge thank you to Priscilla and Lisa Marie, and to all the fans for their dedication and hard work in keeping Elvis's memory alive.

A special thank you to my loving wife and many friends and family members who helped to inspire me to write this story, but the greatest thank you of all is to Elvis himself!

As an Elvis Impersonator having studied Elvis's Life History, I have come to love and understand his feelings. For this reason I have written him a second chance.

PREFACE

As a child, I never realized that I would someday become a legend in my own time. Looking back on how excited I was when I cut my first record, I wish I knew then what I know now. There seemed to be no escape from the pressures and demands from everyone that surrounded me. If only I could go back in time, there are so many things that I would change.

For one, I would not have allowed "The Colonel" to have full control over me. Even though he was good for me in so many ways, he made it impossible for me to live a normal life.

I must now find a way to change the present. A Second Chance at Life. *What If*. . .

CHAPTER 1

Months before August 16, 1977, I had conversed with numerous well-known doctors, friends and family members about dreams I was having, dreams that I would die in the same month that my mother had died. These dreams are what gave me the idea of how to escape from the prison I had built around me, and the drugs I took to escape from unhappy memories and everyday pressures. I knew deep down in my heart that my life could be happier. I needed to get off the myriad of drugs that consumed my body and controlled my erratic behavior. I was living in a shell with no way out, unable to walk the streets, shop markets or even go to the matinee.

My dreams allowed me to plan the greatest acting scene I had ever played, but at the same time, I knew I would have to accept a new and very different way of life.

My plan was to have my family doctor that I had been seeing for many years, I will not mention his name, give me a pill that would slow my heart rate down to an almost comatose state. It would appear to everyone that I was deceased. The danger of this was the poor physical condition I was in and the duration of being comatose. I would have to lie 'in state' for several hours. Afterwards I would be given an injection to bring my heart rate back to normal, and so the plan began. . .

. . .

After I arrived at the hospital, my father, my personal doctor, and a close friend that I knew I could trust explicitly were waiting for the injection to take effect. Dad and my friend had left the room to get coffee when I opened my eyes to see doc taking my vitals.

"Welcome back, you're doing great. How do you feel?" he asked, while pressing his cold stethoscope against my chest.

"Fine," I replied, "it's as if I just awoke from a long, deep sleep."

"You feel strong enough to walk around? No dizziness?"

"I'm ready to get out of here. Everything work like we planned?"

"Yes, everything went as scheduled," the doc replied.

I slowly raised myself up, and doc replaced me with my lifelike, waxed figure. It was so lifelike that when my father returned, even he did not know which body was which.

I had gone into the next room to change into my new identity of long hair and a full beard. In the meantime, dad had returned and I over heard him talking to the waxed figure thinking it was me.

Those involved in my plan had to make sure everyone else believed that the wax figure was really me. Since it fooled dad, we then knew this would work.

I had secretly opened an account with a bank in south Florida under the name of Johnny Raye, which I had chosen for my new name. Doc owned a cabin in that area which was situated on a private lake. Doc rented the cabin to famous patients on numerous occasions. It was a place for patients with problems similar to mine to have time to "rehabilitate" themselves. It was what the doc ordered and exactly what I needed.

Those involved in my scheme knew it would be years before they would see me again, if ever. I didn't want to make leaving hard on them, or on myself, so we said our goodbyes and I left. Prior arrangements had been made to have a motorcycle parked outside the hospital. Garbed in my new appearance, I walked out of the hospital without even a sideways glance from anyone, hopped on my bike, and headed to Florida with the wind whipping through my long hair. I started to laugh, at first to myself, then out loud. I couldn't believe we had pulled off this stunt. I had always been a glory seeker and this was the ultimate high.

The following day I arrived in Florida, tired and hungry, but feeling exhilarated from my newfound freedom.

The cabin was about a mile from the main road and about three miles from the nearest neighbor. As I drove up the long driveway, I stopped to admire the beauty of what was to become my home for the next several years. Vivid reds and purples, sunny yellows, and snowy white flowers adorned each side of the driveway. Various shaped evergreens encircled palm trees of all sizes. The grass was a succulent green, mowed, and trimmed to perfection. It was obvious the landscaping service took pride in their workmanship. It wasn't Graceland, but it was breath taking. Driving closer, I could see the deep, blue water of the lake behind the cabin. It glittered and sparkled like diamonds under the hot Florida sunshine. I stopped and parked my bike on the circular drive.

The cabin itself was made from hand-cut logs. A full-length porch stretched across the front. I found the key under the flowerpot, as doc said it would be, and unlocked the door to my new home.

I stood in the foyer a moment allowing my eyes to adjust to the interior's darkness. From outward appearance the cabin seemed small, but I was surprised at the vastness of the interior's open concept and design. The dining area, kitchen, and den were all in one large area, separated only by large, rustic, column posts. Wrought iron chandeliers hung from log ceiling beams with matching sconces on each wall. The back wall was encompassed by a stone fireplace. A foot high hearth was centered between two floor to ceiling windows. A tan leather sofa with matching chairs was centered in the room to allow you a full view of the lake and surrounding area. Solid wood tables were placed intricately to add to its richness. The floors were inlayed with rustic tile and stone in the kitchen, foyer and dining room. The kitchen had a snack bar with high-back, swivel chairs. Black appliances enhanced the light, oak stained cabinets. A solid oak table with seating for twelve and a matching cabinet filled with glassware and whatnots filled the dining area. The master bedroom was completely furnished in antique oak furniture. The king-size bed faced French doors that opened onto a three tiered deck. Stone steps led to the gazebo by the lake. The master bath's tub and double sinks were all in black with polished gold fixtures. A black tiled double shower stood separate in one corner. Across the hallway were two other bedrooms completely furnished as well.

Doc told me he had a housekeeper named Jessie Mae, who was extremely trust worthy. Jessie cleaned on Saturday mornings so I needed to disappear before she arrived so as not to run into her. Doc had told Jessie Mae that a friend would be staying there for a few years, and needed total privacy.

CHAPTER 2

During the first five years of getting my body and mind to heal, I learned a lot about fishing, and I knew all the soap operas on television by heart. I managed to maintain my voice, pick a guitar, and even write a few songs. Having always been accustomed to having people around me, I was lonely and starved for human contact. The loneliness led me to think I had made a mistake.

Deciding it was time to get back into public life, I started first by going to the movies and burger joints. I no longer needed a disguise as my hair and beard had grown long, and so far, no one had recognized me. At first, people did look at me curiously, but after seeing me a number of times they became friendly and accepted me as a harmless loner.

One Saturday afternoon I returned to the cabin from fishing and discovered that the housekeeper was still there. Enough time had passed, and knowing that she would not recognize me, I sat down on the hearth of the fireplace and asked if she was Jessie Mae. She acknowledged she was as she observed me with her penetrating dark eyes. I introduced myself to her as Doc's friend, and that she could call me Johnny. We shook hands and I told her I was happy to finally meet her. She said that after five years of cleaning up after me, it was about time we met. I explained that I went fishing on Saturdays and sometimes to a movie and that she was always gone by the time I returned.

"Mr. Johnny, what type of work do you do?" She asked.

"I'm a song writer," I replied. "I needed a place that was quiet, and this was perfect for me."

"Well, it's good to meet you Johnny, but I've got to leave early. I'm cooking dinner for some friends tonight, but I'll be back next Saturday."

I smiled in return. It was nice having someone to talk to besides the old man at the movie theater.

I didn't know how close I could get to Jessie Mae. I still had fears of recognition to overcome. Having watched the news, I knew that there were people who thought I was still alive and that several had claimed to have seen me. I'd come too far to blow it now.

. . .

The years slowly passed and a close friendship developed between Jessie Mae and me. During this period of my life, I had taken a part time job at a small diner in town washing dishes and cleaning up. I finally felt that I was getting my second chance at life. I missed singing before an audience, and I really missed my daughter, Lisa Marie. That was the one thing I very much regretted. I often wondered if she was happy and in good health. I wondered what kind of life she had without me around. Then I'd think, she's the daughter of Elvis Presley. She was famous in her own right and had plenty of money. Priscilla was a good mother, and I knew she would see to it that Lisa Marie would be well taken care of. I knew somehow, someday, I'd get to see and talk to Lisa, but for now, I had to stay away no matter how much it hurt.

I decided to quit working at the diner because one of the waitresses's told me how much my voice sounded like Elvis's when I talked and especially when I sang. She had overheard me sing while I was cleaning up after a long day. I'd always laugh and tell her she must be hard of hearing and that no one sounded just like Elvis, but she started telling everyone she believed I was Elvis.

Jessie Mae told me she supervised workers in a near-by orange grove during the week. I asked if she could hire me on. From our conversations, I detected that most of the workers were Mexicans, as well as black men and women. I figured they wouldn't be asking questions, so the following day I quit the diner and started work in the orange groves.

The workers liked Jessie Mae and worked hard for her. They didn't pay attention to me at first, and I was glad. It just felt good to be around people. After a week or two, a couple of the black men heard me singing as I worked and began singing along with me. At lunch they would sit in the shade of the orange trees and sing gospel music. Eventually they asked me to join them. Those moments were the highlight of my day.

One afternoon they asked if I'd sing "Peace In the Valley." As I sang, the other workers gathered around to listen, some joined in on the chorus. We sang a number of songs before Jessie Mae chased us all back to work.

Jessie Mae pulled me aside and said, "Mr. Johnny, "I need you to pick more oranges because you're not filling as many baskets as the rest of the crew."

"Yes ma'am," I replied. "I'll do better."

The next morning before lunch several of the guys, Samuel, Joseph and Eddie, started filling my basket with oranges. That way it would look like I was keeping up with the rest of the crew so Jessie Mae wouldn't get mad. I now knew I had some real friends that gave friendship without asking or expecting anything in return.

I felt great. I was still over weight, but working in the groves had toned my muscles. For the first time in years I felt real happiness.

Another time while we were singing, Jessie Mae pulled me aside, and said, "Mr. Johnny, I've known you going on nearly ten years now, and I've heard you sing. You don't belong here any longer. It's time you get back part of your life."

Somewhat surprised by her comment, I asked, "What life?"

"You know what I'm talking about, Mr. Elvis, I've known for a long time who you are."

Wise beyond her years I knew it was foolish to lie to her. "How did you know?"

"Not everyone eats fried peanut butter and banana sandwiches, and not everyone can gyrate those hips like you do when singing. Besides, you talk and sound just like him, and you've been in hiding for about fifteen years. Johnny, I don't know if you're aware that there's a lot of Elvis Impersonators out there singing. They're enjoying life dressing and singing like you," she laughed and continued, "I think you'd make a great Elvis Impersonator."

"Jessie Mae, it takes money to put a band together."

"If you'd get out more you'd know what's going on," she smiled. "They now have music called Karaoke, it's all on C. D's and more and more bars are doing it. Now I don't condone drinking, but some of my friend's children were telling me all about it. I know it would be a good place for you to get back into singing. Let me explain to you how it works . . ."

That night I thought about what Jessie Mae had told me and decided she was right. I spent the night planning what I would do, and the next morning I said my good byes to all, shook hands with Samuel, Eddie and Joseph, and hugged Jessie Mae tight. Tears filled our eyes.

"Don't you go get all sentimental on me," she cried.

"Jessie Mae, listen to me. I know your house needs a lot of repairs. I asked you one time before, and I'm asking from my heart now, please come and live in the cabin and bring Samuel and Joseph with you. I know they've been staying with you, and there's plenty of room in the cabin for all of you. Besides, I need someone to look after the place while I'm away, and I can't think of anyone better than you. Jessie, you can keep up the inside, and Samuel and Joseph can do the yard work. What do you say?"

"What about the doc?" asked Jessie Mae.

"I purchased the cabin from doc under the name of Johnny Raye back in March, of 1977. The deed is filed at the courthouse. Soooo, what's your answer?"

A big smile spread across Jessie Mae's face, "I guess I'd better get to packing."

I hugged her again, hopped on my cycle and told her I'd stay in touch.

CHAPTER 3

I wanted so much to see Graceland, so I headed for Memphis.

On the way, I rode through Birmingham, Alabama. On Highway 78, I spotted a billboard with a picture of an Elvis Impersonator by the name of David Lee. The sign stated he was hosting an Elvis contest at a local Karaoke bar located just north of Birmingham. The winner would be paid five hundred dollars.

I thought that this just might be what I was looking for, and besides, I needed the five hundred if I could win. I stopped at a local service station and asked for directions. It seemed everyone knew where the bar was or at least David Lee.

I followed the directions the attendant gave me, found the bar and an old motel nearby. The motel wasn't much of a place, but it looked clean so I stopped to get a room. I needed to clean up from my long ride and before going to the bar.

The lady at the reservation desk of the motel looked me up and down. "If you're looking for a room that will be cash in advance please?"

I handed her the money.

"You can have room six. We don't allow parties or loud music."

"Don't worry ma'am, I'll be so quiet you won't know I'm here." I wonder what she'd do if she really knew who she was talking to, but I can't say as I blame her considering the way I looked. I had on an old pair of faded jeans with holes in the knees, and grease from my bike on my pants legs. I wore a red and black plaid shirt the pocket half torn off. It ripped when I fixed a flat on my bike. My black western boots hadn't been polished, and the dust from traveling didn't help.

I found room six. It wasn't fancy, but it was clean. A television on a stand was in one corner and a table with two chairs in the other. The bed looked comfortable, but I laughed at the bedspread. I remembered mama having one similar to it when I was a child in Tupelo, Mississippi. Red roses were stitched in the middle of black and white squares. An old vase lamp with a fringed shade stood on the night stand next to the bed. The carpet was red shag with a few dark spots that looked like it had been scrubbed but the stain wouldn't come out. The bathroom was small and smelled of lemon disinfectant. Like I said, it was old, but it was clean.

I was tired after having ridden for so long. I flopped across the bed and instantly fell asleep. So different than years before when I couldn't sleep without the aide of pills.

I woke around five o'clock and jumped in the shower. The hot water felt good on my aching body. Getting old, I thought. I dried off and looked through my bags. I found a clean pair of jeans and a red, long-sleeved, cuffed shirt. My jeans were faded but at least they didn't have holes in them. I figured it would be alright to wear for the night. I needed a shave, so I trimmed by beard. I needed a hair cut, but I decided I'd better leave it for now so I brushed it straight back. I looked in the mirror and I felt I was dressed good enough for the bar.

I hopped on my cycle and found where the bar was located. To my surprise, it actually was called 'The Bar'. As I pulled up, I noticed how old the building looked. It had been painted a light brown with red trim. A lighted sign flashed Karaoke every Wed., Fri., and Sat. Nights. Neon beer signs hung in windows. This looks like a place from the '60's, I thought. A real honky-tonk. It was like the motel room, something from the past.

Everything seemed to be working out except for my being nervous about being here. I wondered if maybe this wasn't such a good idea after all. Well, I had come this far, and all I had to do is look around. If it looked like it's not what I wanted to do, I could leave. I took a deep breath and opened the front door.

The place was dimly lit. The old wood floor squeaked beneath my boots. I looked around the bar room and noticed round tables scrunched together to get as much seating space as possible, leaving a small space for a dance floor.

I went to the long "L" shaped bar. It was made of mahogany wood, trimmed with black vinyl around the top edge and down to the foot rest. A large mirror filled the wall behind the bar. Bottles of whiskey and wine were lined up like glass soldiers on the wooden back bar.

To the far end of the room was the stage where the Karaoke equipment was set up. Behind it hung a banner that said "Elvis Contest" written in bold, black letters. I stared at the banner for a few minutes and got flash backs from shows

9

I had performed at in various cities and towns years ago. A lot of memories flooded back from that banner.

To the left of the stage was a group of Elvis Impersonators dressed in various colored jump suits. A few guys were dressed in blue and red costumes, but most were in white, and made similar to what I used to wear. How strange this all began to feel. I didn't know what I'd expected, but I wasn't prepared for this. I felt foolish dressed like I was. With my long hair and beard I look more like a hippie from the '60's, and 'I AM ELVIS,' and I'm looking at a bunch of guys dressed in nice jump suits, and they're the impersonators.

I asked a woman sitting at a table to my left if you had to be dressed like Elvis to enter the contest. She had said no, but it would help to look like him, and then laughed at my appearance. Feeling foolish, I was about to leave when a young man who had over heard me talking to the lady came and shook my hand.

"Hello. I'm David Lee. Pay no attention to her. If you're here to enter the contest you'll do just fine with what you are wearing. Go over to the table with the rest of the "Elvis's" and fill out a Karaoke slip."

"Thanks," I replied with a smile.

As I approached the table, one of the guys in a white jump suit approached me and introduced himself. "Hi, my names Chance. If you're looking for a slip to fill out I'll get you one."

"Thank you very much," I replied, as I took the slip from Chance.

"You're welcome very much. Write a fast song at the top and a slow song at the bottom," he instructed, as I was unsure of what to do.

"What songs are you going to sing?" I asked in return.

"Jailhouse Rock" and "Can't Help Falling In Love."

"Those are two great choices," I commented.

"What about you, have you made your song choices?"

I stared at the slip. "I really have no idea right now."

Chance looked at me with a puzzled expression and asked, "Have you ever sung Karaoke before?"

"No, I haven't."

"Well, where have you sung before?"

"I used to sing with a band, but it was many years ago."

"Well, just relax and be yourself. It's easy to sing, and once you do it, you're hooked. Just read the words as they appear on the TV screen on the stage."

"Thanks again for the information," I told him, as he walked away.

David Lee took the microphone and announced to everyone in the contest to draw a number from the hat to find out what order they would be singing. When it was my turn, I drew number six. The same as my motel room. I wondered if there was something to this. No, I smiled. I'm no longer superstitious. I filled out my slip and handed it to David Lee. I had decided to sing "Don't Be Cruel" and "Love Me Tender."

David called for the first singer to come up on stage. His first song was "Don't Be Cruel." I didn't know if it was right to duplicate another singer's choice of songs so I asked David if I should change my selections.

"No need to as there will be others singing the same songs. Just relax, sing from your heart and you'll do just fine," he said encouragingly.

By this time I was really nervous, so I told David to change the song to "Burning Love."

David looked at me curiously, and asked, "Are you sure? Burning Love is a tough song to do. I mean, no one ever picks this song, but if you think you can do it, it would be perfect for this crowd and the judges."

"No sweat!" I answered feeling a little perturbed. Then I caught myself, I'll have to be more careful in the future of who I now was, not who I had been. I smiled at David, "This song is one of my favorites, and I'll do it!"

I joined Chance and some of the other singers. The first and second singer's finished. I had expected them to be better. I heard that David Lee was tough to beat, but because he was hosting the contest he would not be competing. I had also heard that Chance would be tough to beat, and that he was the last singer of the evening. So far I felt I would do well except for my appearance. I knew the way I was dressed would be a drawback to my scores as dress appearance counted for ten points. I had to perform my best and capture the audience.

Finally, it was my turn. David Lee called my number and introduced me as Johnny Raye, a newcomer on the "Elvis" circuit. Still nervous, I walked onto the stage. The crowd stared as if to say, "you're kidding me," or "he's going to sing Elvis!" Just wait till I'm through, I thought.

As the music started, I closed my eyes and let myself drift back in time. I began to sing "Burning Love." My body responded to the music. My leg began to twitch. The crowd stared in amazement. Within minutes the audience was screaming, "Elvis! Elvis!" They went wild. During my second song, "Love Me Tender," I walked out among the crowd. They were still screaming. Several even took pictures.

I can't explain how I felt. I only knew it felt great to be back performing. I finished my songs and walked off stage. The crowd rushed me. Several people wanted my autograph. David Lee came over and complimented me, "Man that was awesome, if I didn't know better; I'd say you were the real Elvis."

That statement caught me off guard. Maybe I'd made a big mistake, and thought it would probably be best to leave, but the crowd finally calmed down.

David Lee asked me to sit at his table.

Chance approached me, "Man, you knocked them dead, great job! Are you sure you've never done this before?"

"No I haven't," I answered honestly. "It was my first time, but I've been hoping I could get started and maybe make a living as an Elvis Impersonator. What do you think? Is it possible?" It was hard to keep a straight face.

"Well," he said looking thoughtful, "I've been doing this for a few years, and so has David Lee, and we have both done very well. I think you'll do great, but one thing you need to do is clean up your appearance and have someone make you a costume. This is good advice, I'm not trying to be critical," he smiled.

I asked him where he had his costume made. He informed me a seamstress across town made his, and he gave me her number. His suit resembled the one I wore for the Hawaiian concert. It seemed so strange to be considering ordering a costume designed like the one I used to wear.

At that moment, David Lee called Chance to sing. I knew he'd be good, and I was right. "Jailhouse Rock" was a success with the crowd. His next song was "Can't Help Falling In Love." He was going to be tough to beat as the crowd was very pleased with his performance.

When the contest ended, all the contestants stood around nervously waiting for the results to be tallied. People were telling me how much they enjoyed my performance, and that I sounded just like Elvis. In fact, they said when they closed their eyes; it was as if they were hearing Elvis himself.

After what seemed an eternity the final scores were tallied. David Lee called the third place winner. I held my breath. "Mike Carlson, come on up! Second place winner, Chance Smith, come on up! First place winner," and he hesitated a moment to keep the crowd in suspense, Johnny Raye."

Chance hugged me first. Laughing heartily, he said, "Man you're good, when I grow up, I want to be just like you."

David Lee hugged me, "Awesome man, awesome!"

The audience screamed for an encore.

"How about it, would you do one more?" David asked.

"Sure, what would you like to hear?"

"How about "Suspicious Minds?"

By the time I started the second verse, David and Chance had to keep the girls from climbing on the stage. After my encore they rushed me out the back door. The three of us stayed outside talking until the crowd settled down, but when we went back in, out of habit, I decided to stay close to the door. The rest of the Elvis Impersonators came over to congratulate me. It seemed I'd made a good impression on everyone and found two good friends all in one night.

David had asked if I had a place to stay. I told him I did that I'd found a room down the street, and thanked him for asking. It was late and I decided to leave, so I said, "See you later!"

"Right, see you later!" They responded.

I rode to my room feeling great singing "You've Got To Follow That Dream." As I unlocked the door, the bed looked inviting. I realized I was tired and needed to get some sleep.

The next morning I rehashed the previous night's contest. I thought about Chance's costume and knew I'd have to get one made for myself. My winnings didn't add up to enough to purchase a new costume, but I figured if I could save enough, I could get several made later. I decided, however, I definitely needed new clothes and went into Birmingham to shop.

I located a men's clothing store, and with the help of the salesman, I purchased new shirts, pants, a white sport's coat, and a 14kt gold necklace.

Next I found a hair salon near the men's clothing store. It was a busy time in the shop, but one of the hairdressers who had just finished working on a client, smiled warmly.

"Hi, my name's Judie and what are you in need of today?"

"Hi! I returned her friendly greeting. My name's Johnny. I need a shave, my hair died, cut, and styled like Elvis's."

"I had a cancellation, so you just sit right here and I'll make you real pretty!"

She was fast and efficient, chatting all the while she worked. When she was finished I looked in the mirror at my reflection. "You didn't lie, you did a great job! I feel human again."

"I'm an Elvis fan, and I was at the Elvis contest last night. I saw you perform. You're good. I'm glad you won!"

"Thanks. You might say I just got lucky."

"No! Judie replied. You were very, very good. Was it your first time?"

"Yes, did it show?"

"No, I figured it was because you weren't dressed as an Elvis Impersonator."

"Well, I'm just getting started." I smiled, and hoped I would not have to continue to defend myself.

"Are you going to sing Karaoke tonight?" She chatted while brushing the remains of cut hair from my shoulders.

"Yes, I've got some people to thank. Will I see you there?"

"Uh huh! But I have some friends I'd like to bring," she said coyly. "I want them to hear you sing."

Laying a fifty dollar bill on the counter, I thanked her again, and returned to the hotel. I changed into a black shirt and pants, and decided to wear my white sports coat that I had just purchased. I went to 'The Bar'. People stared and smiled, but said nothing. I knew they did not recognize me. I looked around and spotted David Lee in the corner.

"Hey David, I'd like to thank you for your help last night!"

He stared at me, paused for a moment, and said with a low voice, "Johnny?"

I laughed at his shocked expression, "Yeah it's me."

"Man you look sharp!" David replied in amazement.

"Thanks, do you think this will work until I get a costume?"

"Yes," he nodded. "You don't owe me any thanks; you earned that win on your own. I still can't get over the way you brought down the house. People asked all night where you went. They wanted to hear you sing some more."

"I left because I was afraid they'd tear my shirt off."

He laughed, "I thought that they would too! Are you going to stick around?"

"I thought I'd hang around and talk to you awhile. If you don't mind?"

"Good. Sit here!"

We talked all evening. He informed me of a contest they were having in Panama City, Florida. Five thousand dollars to the winner. I asked him if he would be going, but he hadn't thought about it.

"I haven't had supper yet," I invited, "can you take a break and go next door and get something to eat?"

"Not right now, you go ahead. My wife brought me a barbeque sandwich and fries."

"Alright, I'll be back in a little while because I'd like to hear more about this contest."

"Go eat and I'll see you later. Heed my words, don't order the barbeque pork sandwich, it has a tendency to attack you later on."

"Hey, I appreciate that," and I left to feed my growling stomach.

The cafe was small but crowded, and as I walked in the waitress hollered out, "I'll be with you in a moment Elvis!"

Again I was caught off guard and hesitated. I thought she knew me, and then I remembered; I was dressed like me.

I sat in a booth, and as she came over, she smiled and asked, "Could I help you young man?"

I looked up at her, and laughed, "Baby, I'm far from being a young man, but it sure sounded good."

"You're as old as you feel, and besides, you look pretty good to me!"

"Thanks! I'll have a burger, an order of fries, and a large glass of sweet tea, please ma'am."

"Coming right up honey! You can have my number too, if you want it?" she asked brazenly. "I get off work tonight at nine o'clock."

"Well, darling, I'll keep that in mind." While I waited for my food, I laughed when I saw David Lee came in.

"I changed my mind, I need to take a break," he grinned.

I invited him to join me, and the waitress came back and asked, "What are you having today, David?"

"Bring me a salad and a bowl of your home made vegetable soup."

"You know the contest I was telling you about, Johnny? You should go! Gary Jackson, a well-known K. J. around the Florida area is hosting the contest. He has contacts in Vegas, the kind of people that could help you. I mean this sincerely; I think you are good enough to make it in Vegas."

"David, I'm in my fifties!"

He looked at me, "Really, I thought late forties. With your talent and looks you could get by for another ten to fifteen more years. You'll never know unless you go for it."

"I guess you're right, but I hope I'm retired by then. So David, what about this contest?"

"I could call Gary for you and get you signed up."

"Just me? What about you and Chance entering? Hey, that gives me an idea, why don't the three of us go? It would be a lot of fun, and besides, I think the two of you stand a good chance to win."

"You really think so?" Excitement sounded in his voice. "Yeah, I'd like to go, let me call Chance as soon as we're done with our meal."

After we finished eating, we went back to 'The Bar.' I sat and watched the Karaoke singers while David called Chance. Judie came with her friends as she promised. She told me she was new at singing Karaoke, and was a little nervous, but you couldn't tell by the way she sang one of Patsy Cline's hits.

David talked with Chance and told me Chance was on his way over so the three of us could discuss this further. When he arrived, he walked past me without saying a word.

"Where's Johnny?" he asked David.

David laughed, "Look behind you!"

Chance turned, looked at me, paused for a moment, "Johnny, is that you?"

I grinned at the shocked expression on his face. "Yeah, it's me."

"Man did you ever clean up good. You look at least ten years younger," he commented while shaking my hand and staring at me in astonishment.

"Well thanks a lot, but I'll take that as a compliment, I think," and grinned at him.

"What group did you say you sang with before?"

"Oh, a small band in south Florida. No one you'd know," I replied cautiously. "We just played around. That's when I decided to come here and try to make it as an Elvis Impersonator."

"Well, you're not going to have any problem! It was all Lee and I could do to keep the crowd off of you last night. Man they went wild."

"Yeah, maybe too wild."

"No, that's what you want; believe me, that's good."

"Let's discuss the three of us going to the contest in Panama City," I said, to change the subject.

"Well, I'd like to go, what does Lee say about it?"

"Lee said he wants to go, and if we do, I'd like to get there a day earlier than the day of the contest."

Chance motioned for David Lee to come back to our table. You could see the excitement in Lee's eyes. "Are we on or not for Panama City?" Lee asked.

"I guess we're going," Chance responded, "but I need to tell my wife of our decision. She's taking classes for her degree, and right now she's too busy to come along."

"I've got to find someone to work and cover for me while I'm gone," David said, already thinking of a replacement. My wife can handle the equipment, and I'll need to get a bartender. It's too much for just one person to handle."

"Yeah, I'm lucky," Chance said. "I have a sub who's available any time, loves to sing, and knows my equipment!"

"Well lets plan on leaving Wednesday afternoon," I responded, "that'll give us time to get there, rest, and check things over."

David called Gary Jackson, and told him to add three more names to the roster and then we finalized our travel plans.

Judie sauntered over to where we were sitting and asked if I was going to sing for them.

Before I could answer, David Lee said, "Yes, he is, right now!"

"Well, okay, I guess I am."

"What are you going to sing?"

"How about "Loving You"?" I grinned at her.

"Coming right up, my man!" David jumped up to set up the song.

Lee introduced me to the crowd, and asked if they would please stay in their seats and try not to scream too loud. As I was singing, the girls started gathering around the stage, but were quiet except for a few ooo's and awe's.

I finished my song. Lee set up another titled, "That's When Your Heartaches Begin," then another, "Are You Lonesome Tonight." As I finished the last song, the ladies were asking for autographs, pictures and kisses. Needless-to-say, I enjoyed all the attention, but then I always did. This is going to work out just fine, I thought.

I told Lee and Chance that I'd meet them here at "The Bar" around noon on Wednesday, and gave them the number to reach me at the hotel if anything changed.

"I think I'll go back to my room and get some sleep."

"Sleep!" Chance laughed, "What's that?"

"Hey, I've got a few years on you two, and I think I'm going to need it to keep up with the both of you!"

They both laughed and said, "Okay, we'll see you Wednesday."

Back in my room, I looked at my watch and was surprised that it was already after midnight. I took off my boots, turned on the television, lie across my bed and fell asleep thinking about our plans for Florida.

I awoke early the next morning. No pills to wake me up, no pills to put me to sleep. That's really something. I can't get over how much better I've felt these last fifteen years. I spent many nights back in the late 70's in tremendous pain from quitting cold turkey to get off the 'pills' I had taken over the years. So many times I wanted to give in, but I knew I didn't have any more chances. Sometimes I look back and can't believe I made it, but by the grace of God, I did. I made myself a solemn promise, and I've always been true to my word, that I'd never take anything stronger than aspirin again.

CHAPTER 4

Wednesday came quickly. I checked out of the motel and met Lee and Chance at 'The Bar' as planned. The guys were waiting outside and were saying good-bye to their wives when I arrived. David and Chance introduced me to them, Tara and Michele, respectively.

David was sitting on his '63 Harley. He had it refinished in light blue with black saddle bags and chrome wheels. Man it looked sharp! Chance was on a '65 Harley sports model, refinished in red with chrome wheels. His saddlebags were black, but trimmed out with fancy silver buttons and buckles. It looked like something out of an old movie. My old bike was a '60 Harley that I'd had for years. I was actually surprised they didn't question me about it. I had it refinished in black with gold emblems, chrome wheels & covers and gold saddle bags. It was definitely out of the past, but it's the one thing from my past I felt I could keep, and so far, no one asked questions.

"Knock them dead!" their wives cried out, as the three of us headed out of the parking lot.

I thought how lucky to have wives who believed in their husbands dreams and supported them in their Elvis performances.

Once we were on the interstate, we sang and laughed as if we didn't have a care in the world. I hadn't felt this good since I was a teenager starting out on that old Mississippi hay ride. We continued on our trip. People yelled and hollered out, "Elvis's," "Three of them!" We'd wave and laugh as we rode by.

Arriving in Panama City, we decided to ride the strip. Before long, we had girls running and screaming after us. We almost didn't make it to the beach, but as we drove into the parking lot, it was full of bikes. And the beach, well it was full of bikinis. Several girls were wearing nothing but strings.

"Is that legal?" I asked," as I stared at the scenic view that just walked past us, "because it sure wasn't when I was young."

"Where have you been hiding?" They wanted to know.

I grinned at their expressions.

To the left of the hotel was the beach hut. It looked just like the ones you'd see in the movies. It was constructed of large carved wood posts with hand rails. Palm leaves were intertwined as a roof covering. In the middle was the bar with various liquors to make any type of fruit drink imaginable. Music was blaring with sounds of the '60's.

Inwardly I felt relief and a newfound freedom. I had a wild desire to run in the sand. I wanted to sing and to perform like I had never performed before. The feeling was wonderful. I was co-existing in a normal environment, something I had missed during most of my life.

David and Chance looked at me with puzzled expressions.

"Hey man, haven't you ever been to the beach before?" David was curious.

"Yes, but this is different!"

"You haven't been in prison, have you?" David asked jokingly.

"No, not as you know it anyway." I said with a smile.

"What do you mean by that?" Chance asked, looking more perplexed by the minute.

"Someday maybe I'll tell you, but not right now. First of all, I'd like to get a room and take a hot shower." I wanted to change the subject.

To save on expenses we rented one room with double beds, which left one of us to sleep on the floor. We drew straws. You might know; I drew the short straw.

After our showers, we sat out on the balcony which overlooked the beachfront. The evening was warm. A gentle breeze blew in off the ocean. A full moon offered a path of light across the water as far as the eye could see. The night air seemed so fresh, and at that moment, I felt that life was great. For the first time in a long time I saw life in an altogether different light.

I remembered the advice Jessie Mae gave me before I left. *"Johnny, just let go and be yourself. People will accept you for what you are, not what you used to be."*

She was right! Chance, David, and even the Karaoke crowd accepted me as one of them.

19

With that in mind, I looked at Chance and David, "We're going to win this contest; I feel it in my bones."

"I hope one of us wins," Chance replied, "that would be great." "I'm like Johnny, I feel it too. We can't lose!"

We heard music coming from the beach hut. "Let's Go On A Moonlight Swim" was playing. I started to sing and Chance and David joined in. Females in the room next to ours overheard us and came out on their balcony to listen. A tall, lanky brunette asked us to sing more. As the music kept playing, we kept singing. Before you knew it, the whole beach crowd stood below our balcony to listen.

Chance and David Lee had promised their wives they would only look at the girls and not touch. I had promised Tara and Michele to make sure their hubby's eyes didn't wonder too far. I think they trusted the guys, just not the women. Anyway, we couldn't go down to the beach so we stayed on the balcony. Temptation was strong, but we managed to overcome it. Several Elvis Impersonators were on the beach, and they picked up where we left off. Back in our room we laughed and were filled with excitement. I enjoyed my new found companionship.

I couldn't wait for the contest to start. I was filled with exhilaration and anxious to perform before a crowd of wild people. I guess there are some things you can't change in your life, and this, along my music, was one of them. Fifteen years in hiding, not singing before a crowd, and now, well it was a lot to handle in such a short time, but I knew I now had control of myself. I was now my own boss.

The following morning we felt rested. We sat around and watched television to pass the time. At noon, I asked the guys if they thought we should go over and meet with Gary Jackson, but first we ate a bite of lunch as Chance was hungry, and since we had slept through breakfast we all ordered cokes, burgers and fries.

We found Gary sitting at a large round table at the end of the bar with several Elvis Impersonators, as well as a few ladies. They were all laughing and seemed to be having a good time. Gary saw David Lee and Chance and headed towards us.

He shook hands with them, looked at me, and said, "You're Johnny Raye!"

"Yes. I am. What have you heard?"

"News travels fast around the Karaoke circuit," Gary said jokingly. "Friends called me from Birmingham, and said you're very good."

"He's not only good, he's awesome!" Chance stated in my defense.

These two have been out in the sun too long. I'm about average, maybe a little better, but not nearly as good as they claim."

"Well, some of the guys heard you last night, and they said the same thing," he replied, and looking me over added, "you're a little older than the rest of the Elvis Impersonators!"

"Well, maybe a little older, but I don't think I am an antique yet. Why, is the contest judged on age?"

"No!" Gary laughed. "It's judged on voice, looks and moves. By looks, I don't mean costume!"

"Who are the judges?" I was curious.

"This is a well advertised competition," Gary replied. "We were lucky to get some big names, Lisa Marie Presley, Joe Esposito, one of Elvis' old body guards, and Judd Phillip's. He helped with Elvis's production at Sun Records."

"Oh hell!" I was totally caught off guard by what I just heard.

"Why? What's the matter?"

"Oh nothing, just some pretty tough judges," I managed to say.

What Gary had just told me had me shook up. I got up and walked down to the beach and wondered what I'd do if I were recognized during the contest. Joe, will go nuts. Maybe I need to talk to him before the contest. Maybe I should just leave it be. Lisa Marie. How am I going to handle seeing her? I sure wish I could talk with her, but I know that's not possible. I'm not worried about the rest, I don't think they'll know anything, but Lisa Marie, and Joe, well they may be a problem. Then again, Joe has kept our secret all these years. Maybe I should forget this contest; I still have time to withdraw. What should I do? Why don't I just walk up to Joe and talk to him, and see if he even recognizes me. If I withdraw now, everybody's going to start asking questions.

I was still deep in thought when Lee approached me, "Hey man, what's wrong, you're shaking?"

Startled, I said, "Nothing, just real nervous about tonight."

"I was a little worried about you, Johnny, you left us in such a hurry. It was as if you'd seen a ghost."

"You know this is going to be tough with those judges," I laughed nervously.

"Hey Johnny, just be yourself, you're going to be great! Believe me, you have nothing to worry about."

I laid my hand on his shoulder. "You're right! Let's go and meet the judges in person, it may calm my nerves and take away some of the fear."

"Yes, let's go. I'm a little nervous myself."

We found the judges sitting in front of the beach hut. Gary had rejoined them. David and I introduced ourselves as Chance joined us. I looked at Lisa Marie, our eyes met. Swallowing hard, I said, "Hello, I'm Johnny."

"Hello, Johnny, a little nervous are you?" she questioned.

"Does it show?" I tried to keep my voice from shaking.

"No, Gary told me you were a little nervous."

"Well maybe a little." I looked at her. "You know you are quite a lovely lady and I think your father would be very proud of you."

"What a charming thing to say; I like you already."

Not wanting to say too much to give myself away, I turned to speak to Joe. He looked at me for a moment and said, "Hello, I'm Joe Esposito."

"I'm Johnny." We shook hands. Then I asked him, "What was it like being one of Elvis' body guards?"

Still staring, he commented, "It was exciting, never a dull moment."

I laughed at his response, "Yes, I'll bet it was."

He looked at me again, and smiled warmly. I knew then he had recognized me and was happy to see me.

"You're one of the contestants I presume, aren't you?" he asked, to ease the tension.

I nodded nervously.

"Don't be nervous. I've got a feeling you'll do just fine, just be yourself. In fact, I'm sure of it!" he said emphatically.

We exchanged greetings with the rest of the judges. We shook everyone's hands, but when I shook Joe's, he slipped me a note and on it was his number to call him later.

Gary spoke up, "I've heard that Johnny's the one to watch, he's very good."

"Thanks. I am looking forward to Friday nights contest." I turned and joined David and Chance as they headed back to our room to relax.

David must have felt sorry for me. "Hey Johnny, why don't you lie on the bed and rest awhile, that floor has to be pretty hard."

"I'll take you up on that offer, thanks.

It was evening when I awoke. We were all hungry again and decided to hit the beach hut for food and refreshments. We spent the night meeting the rest of the contestants and sitting around laughing at their stories of other competitions. It was growing late and David and Chance felt we needed to get a good night's sleep to be ready for tomorrow night. Years of abuse took a toll on my body as I tire more easily now and require a lot more sleep. Of course age doesn't help.

I woke feeling refreshed. We walked around the beach for awhile watching how much more crowded the beach was since our arrival on Wednesday. We sat around the hotel to relax and prepare ourselves for the contest.

I dozed off again and woke to Chance saying, "Hey sleepy head, it's time to get ready."

David and Chance dressed in black pants, black shirts, white belts and shoes.

"You guys sure are something; you should be wearing your jump suits."

"No," David replied, "we are going as the 'King' looked in the late 50's. Besides, we're not going to let you be the only one who looks different."

"Are you sure this is the way you want it?"

"Yes," Chance said, "David and I already discussed and planned this, now hurry up and get ready!"

Fifteen minutes later the three of us walked out the door and headed to the beach where the stage was set for the contest.

"Wow, this is impressive!" I was surprised at how much work had gone into the contest.

The stage set up was in the shape of a half moon with a white canvas, canopy top. It looked like a large opened sea shell. Hundreds of seats were placed in front of the stage. In the back ground, the ocean shimmered and glittered like tiny diamonds as the sun began to set and fall into its vast depth.

As we arrived, the rest of the Elvis Impersonators were already drawing numbers from a hat to see how we would place in the contest. I had hoped to draw last place, but I drew number eighteen. There were twenty-two contestants entered in the contest. I walked around trying to find number twenty-two to see if he would exchange numbers with me. I finally found him and he was happy to make the exchange. He didn't want to be last for fear the crowd would lose interest by then.

I didn't know it at the time, but Lee had drawn number twenty one, and Chance had drawn number twenty. We laughed when we said what our numbers were so we made a pact. Whoever won would split the money three ways.

The contest required each contestant to sing two songs of our choosing. The three of us had agreed to turn our songs in secretly, and not tell each other what each of us selected. That way, if we sang the same song, it would be because we chose to do those songs. If one of us duplicated a song, so be it.

The contest started. As the other contestants performed, we wrote down their name and number, as if to judge them as to whom we felt might be tough competition.

When number fifteen was singing, David said, "Write his number down, he did a pretty good job."

"I just don't think he has the voice quality that the judges are looking for."

"You're the only one that sounds that close to Elvis's voice," Chance encouraged me.

"No, the two of you are very good, don't cut yourself short," and then added, "you're both better than what I've heard so far."

The crowd screamed at every singer. Behind the stage, it was hard to hear, but you could hear enough to know just how well the guys were doing.

Finally, Gary called number twenty. That was Chance.

As he walked on stage, David and I said, "Knock them dead, Elvis!"

Chance laughed and smiled back at us. His first song choice was "Viva Las Vegas." The crowd really reacted to the song, and so did Chance. His second selection was, "Treat Me Nice." David and I looked at each other and agreed that so far, Chance was the best.

When Chance finished, Gary called number twenty-one. That was David Lee. Chance tapped David on the shoulder and said, "Break a leg!"

Chance looked at me, "Well?"

"Damn good, job, buddy."

David's first song was, "Hurt." The crowd was enjoying it because none of the other contestants had sung that one all night, and that seemed to make a difference to them. David's second song was "Don't Be Cruel." The audience jumped up and down.

He finished his two songs, and I said, "Man you did great, I hope I do as well."

"Bring home the bacon!" He answered.

I smiled as number twenty-two was called.

"Last but not least, Johnny Raye!"

I walked on stage, as I had done so many times in the past. I bowed to the audience and said, "Ladies and gentlemen, thank you, thank you very much!"

I tore loose with "Burning Love." I felt a warmth come over me as the crowd screamed, "Elvis! Elvis!"

Guards held back the crowd as they tried to crawl on stage. I smiled as I sang, I knew I was back!

Before I started my second song, security had to remove two women from the stage as they had managed to break through security and had managed to rip my shirt trying to get at me. Gary asked if I was okay. I nodded yes and started to sing my second song, "One Night." Several women handed me roses, and I knelt down to kiss each of them. I finished my song, and walked backwards off the stage, throwing kisses to the crowd.

The guy's were at the bottom of the steps waiting for me and yelled above the screams that I had been fantastic. I was smiling from ear to ear. I felt great! Several other contestants came to congratulate me and express their feelings as well.

We waited backstage for the results. Finally, Gary announced they had a tie for second place and they were going to leave it as it was, and not call out a third place winner. The money for second and third place would be split between the two winners. Gary then called out, "Would Chance Smith and David Lee come up on the stage please?"

As they walked up, the crowd screamed and yelled and kept jumping up and down, obviously pleased with the winning choices. Gary presented them each with a check for fifteen hundred dollars and asked them to remain on stage.

"Please, may we have some quiet," Gary said, and raised his arms to silence the audience. "And now, what you've all been waiting for. Our first place winner, like no other performer we have witnessed here tonight, ladies and gentlemen, let's have a huge round of applause for Johnny Raye!"

Tears filled my eyes as I walked out on stage. The women were still trying to get to me. I stood there smiling in my torn shirt. Everyone in the audience stood, screamed and clapped, including the judges.

Gary handed me a check for five thousand dollars. "Johnny, would you sing us another song? I know the audience would love for you to do another."

"How about American Trilogy?"

"Great choice. Let's hear it for Johnny Raye!"

When the crowd settled down in anticipation, I started to sing and a hush fell over the audience. I looked out into the crowd. Several people had lit their cigarette lighters. Arms raised high in the air; they swayed back and forth to the music. I put everything I had into that song and as I hit the high note at the end, the crowd went absolutely nuts! Chance and David grabbed me by the arm and rushed me off the stage. We headed straight to our hotel room. It was almost like old times. I needed to be careful as I didn't want to fall back into a bad pattern. The three of us hugged and patted each other on the back in excitement.

"Guys were rich! Well not rich, but some bill money anyway." It was a big plus for me as I was running short of cash.

David looked at me. "Man, you really know how to put on a show!"

"Well, we needed to win."

"Yes, but you were fantastic!"

"Okay, that's enough about me, besides, you guy's tied for second, and that was pretty awesome in my book. Let's order deluxe pizza's, I didn't eat much before the contest, and I'm as hungry as a bear."

"Me too!" Chance grinned.

I looked at him, "So what, you're always hungry."

David picked up the phone and called in our order. While we were waiting for our pizzas, Gary Jackson called to join us. David told him that would be great since we had just ordered pizza.

Gary arrived, smiled and laughed. "Hey, there are women on the beach waiting for you to come back."

"At the age of some of these women," I said, "you'd think they'd be a little less active."

"At their age? Hell, they're in their twenties and thirties. They're not old at all, and pretty nice looking too! I wish they were after me, I'd let them catch me and rip off all my clothes."

"You are crazy." I laughed at him.

"By the way," Gary commented, "the reason I came here is because I have a friend in Vegas looking for a good Elvis Impersonator. If you are interested, not right now, but whenever you feel you are ready, just call me, here's my number.

"Thanks, I'll do that. And thank you very much." I looked at David and Chance. "Why aren't the two of you in Vegas?"

"Oh no, not us," they answered.

"Johnny," Chance stated, "our wives won't leave Alabama." "But you have no ties anywhere, do you?"

"No, I don't, but I have places I want to see, and well Vegas, I'm just not ready for that yet. Gary, do you want to stay for pizza? I again changed the subject.

"Yeah, I'm starving, thought you'd never ask."

The pizza's arrived and we all dug in greedily. Gary made the statement that Lisa Marie was very impressed with my performance.

"What did she say?" My heart skipped a beat.

"She said you remind her of her father, and that you should be in Vegas."

I swallowed the lump that formed in my throat, and asked, "Is that all?"

"Yes, what else should she have said?"

"I don't know," I answered solemnly. "Gary, how long have you been a Karaoke Jockey?"

"Well, Karaoke first started in my area around 1989, didn't it, Dave?"

David nodded with a mouthful of pizza.

"Anyway," Gary continued, "I started about five years ago." "How about you Johnny, how long have you been and Elvis Impersonator?"

"Oh about a week," I grinned, hardly able to contain myself.

"A week!" Gary's mouth dropped open.

I laughed so hard at Gary's expression that David had to explain to him about me coming into 'The Bar' with a long beard, my long hair and wearing old worn out clothes and boots, and then winning the contest.

"Where did you come from and learn to sing like Elvis?" Gary was now intrigued with me and my past.

I answered, as straight as I could manage. "I sang with a band back in the late '50's and early '60's, and we did some of Elvis's music back then."

"Well, how old are you anyway?"

By this time I was really grinning. "Let's see, its 1993, so I guess that puts me in the middle to late fifty's."

"Elvis would be about that old now too, if he was still alive, wouldn't he?"

"I believe he would," said David, who was an Elvis trivia expert.

"I guess you're not going to tell me how old you really are," Gary grinned, "and it really doesn't matter when you can sing like you do."

"To set the record straight, I'll be fifty-seven in January."

"Well you look younger."

"Thanks, but all those compliments are not going to get you that last piece of pizza."

"I don't think so either!" Gary said, as we watched David and Chance dive for the last piece, and then laughed when Chance came out the winner. Look guys, there's another big contest in Dallas next weekend, and the prize money is the same as tonight's. You guys should enter!"

"We'll be there, you can count on it," I replied in response for all of us, falling back into my old ways. But it was too late to take back my response and no one seemed to mind or even notice.

"If ever you want to do a big show call me," Gary said in earnest. "I'll handle the music."

David frowned, "Hold on a minute, Johnny, next weekend! I don't know if I can get away two weekends in a row."

"Me either," Chance agreed.

"Well, it's going to be a lot of fun, and I hate to see you two miss out on it," I tempted them."

"Yeah, I know!" David thought a moment, "Well, we could ask our wives, after all, they could go with us. We'll have to work it out somehow."

"Great, I figured you both would want to go. Gary do you have the details or any information on it?"

"Not with me, but I'll fax it to David on Monday."

"I don't know about all of you, but I'm ready to hit the sack," I said, and yawned.

"Yeah," David agreed, "we have a long ride ahead of us tomorrow, and it's been an exhausting day."

Gary left and said he'd see us all in Dallas.

We were quiet on the way back to Birmingham, each of us lost in our own thoughts of last night's contest and next week's competition in Dallas. When we got to Birmingham, I told the guys I had business in Memphis and I'd call them later in the week. I split and drove north on Highway 78. It was a warm, sunny day and I was enjoying the ride.

CHAPTER 5

My first stop would be in Tupelo, Ms. I rented a room at the local hotel and called Joe.

When he answered, I said, "Don't speak! Just listen! I'm in Tupelo, and I want to see Graceland! See if you can get me a private tour late tomorrow! Tell anyone who asks any questions that I'm an old friend of yours! Meet me at the front gate at three o'clock. Can you arrange it?"

"I'll be there, and I'll get it arranged somehow."

"Good, see you then, and remember my name is Johnny Raye!"

"Are you sure this is what you want? Aren't you afraid someone will recognize you?"

"I've had plenty of time to think on the way here, and I know what I'm doing, okay!" I said, as I hung up the phone.

I showered, shaved and rode over to the old house. I pulled up front and parked my bike. Tourists were standing in line for the last tour of the day. Several people noticed me. I could hear them whisper among themselves about me being an Elvis Impersonator. I was wearing a long sleeved black shirt, and pants, and my white boots. Several people wanted pictures taken of me with them standing in front of the old house. I laughed at the hypocrisy of the whole situation.

I wanted time alone inside, and so I waited until the last tourist went through. I entered slowly. Nostalgia hit me like a rock. Memories came flooding back. I remembered the old pot bellied stove, and mama cooking fried green tomatoes, turnip greens, and the best beef stew ever. On cold days, she would fix me a hot bowl of grits, and fried peanut butter and banana sandwiches. I felt her presence and tears fell freely as I remembered her and daddy working so hard so I would have nice things. In the back yard, I looked for my old tire tree swing. It was gone now, as well as the tree.

I walked through the museum. Displayed behind glass were some of my jump suits and jackets I wore for different movies and specials. I looked at them and laughed at how skinny I was then. It sure felt good to walk around without people knowing who I was, although I have to admit, the response I received in Florida renewed my spirits.

I got on my bike and decided to ride around town. I drove past the old school. Things sure had changed. I guess nothing ever stays the same, but it would be nice to back up sometimes. I returned to the motel to get some sleep as I had a long day planned for tomorrow.

I awoke feeling refreshed, ate a hearty breakfast and headed to Memphis. I rode around town killing time. Finally I worked my way around to Graceland. I drove up Elvis Presley Boulevard and parked across from Graceland. My heart raced as I stood in front of the gates that now prevented me from entering what was once my safe haven and prison for so many years. Emotions ran rampant; first, anger, at not being able to enter without permission; second, relief that I was free to live my life as I chose.

George was still the security guard. He had aged considerably, but I knew it was him. He buzzed the office and told Joe that Johnny Raye had arrived. About five minutes passed. I was getting antsy, and then Joe drove up in a limo. He opened the back door for me to get in. The gate closed silently behind us as we drove up to the house.

Joe asked me several questions, but I couldn't answer. I just kept swallowing. He tried to get some response from me, but he knew I was having a tough time with my emotions.

"You're looking good," he commented to break the ice.

Finally, I was able to speak. "Thanks, how are you doing?"

"Wait right there," and he came around to my side of the limo. He opened the door for me to step out. "I thought you deserved to come back here for the first time in years in the style you so rightly deserve."

"Thanks, Joe. That means a lot to me."

I stood and looked around, and then followed Joe through the front door. It was like I had stepped back in time. Everything seemed to be as I left it over fifteen years ago. I shook Joe's hand and hugged his neck.

"Joe, I've got to say it was good seeing you in Florida. I didn't think you would recognize me."

"I almost didn't," he whispered back. "The more you talked to me, the more I knew it was you. And, by the way, great performance!"

"Thanks. Hey look! My old piano! Does it still sound as good as it used to?"

"Try it and see."

I sat down and started to play a few chords when George came in the front door and said, "I'm sorry sir, you are not allowed to play that piano."

Joe looked at George, "It's alright George, we were looking at making a movie, and Johnny wants to check everything out."

"Okay," George said, "By the way, you play jus' like Elvis. I remember when Mr. Elvis would sit there and play for hours in the winter time, and I'd come up and look through the window and listen. Course he always pretended he didn't know I was out there, but I knew he did," he cackled. "Then he'd act surprised and say, "George, come on in out of the cold."

Before George could finish, I interrupted, "And then he'd ask you in for a cup of coffee, no, hot chocolate wasn't it?"

With a puzzled expression, George asked, "How did you know that?"

Realizing I had slipped up, I replied, "I guess I must have read it in a book somewhere."

He walked out the door and shook his head in bewilderment, "I don't remember that ever being written in any old book, but I guess it must have been. How else would he have known?" he mumbled. "Guess I'm getting old and my memory ain't as good as it used to be," and quietly closed the door behind him.

"Wow! That was close, Johnny, you need to be more careful, you know how this house has ears."

"I want to see my bedroom!" I got up from the piano and headed upstairs. Joe unlocked the bedroom door and explained that it had to be kept locked to keep out nosey tourists that might sneak away from the tour to try and see it.

Memories flashed quickly before my eyes. Some good, some not so good, especially those of my last night here that left me shaking where I stood.

"It hasn't changed a bit, has it?" I said softly.

"No, they'll never change anything in here."

We went to the kitchen, and then to the jungle room. I looked at my recording equipment. It was still set up, as though waiting for someone to switch it on. So I did.

I found some of my old tapes on the shelves. I held one up to Joe, "Karaoke music they call it now. How about that Joe, we were doing Karaoke back then and didn't even know it."

Years ago I had made tapes where we just recorded music on them, no vocals, and then I'd rehearse the words before recording a new song. I put in one of the tapes, "I'll Remember You," filled the air. It was a song I had written after Priscilla and I separated. I picked up the microphone and started to sing. The next song was, "Just Ask Me." As I was singing my third song, "Are You Sincere," Lisa Marie walked in.

"What are you doing?"

Joe spoke quickly, "I let him in."

"Joe, I'll handle this. I'm sorry Miss Presley. I asked Joe for a special tour, he's going to handle some personal affairs for me, and I talked him into letting me see Graceland, without anyone else around. I'll just put everything back, it won't happen again."

"Well, no harm done, I guess." she said. "I over heard you singing, "Are You Sincere" and "I'll Remember You." "Don't let my mother hear you singing those songs; they're some of her favorites. Daddy wrote and sang those to her around the time of their divorce. They've not been recorded yet, for sale anyway. By the way, where did you find the words?"

"Oh, they were here on the shelf with the tapes," I answered quickly.

"Is Don't Cry Daddy on the tape?" she sounded wistful and somewhat sad.

"I think so, I'll check, why?"

"I'd like you to sing it to me, as my daddy used to, right here in this studio."

"I'd love to sing that song for you," I said huskily, trying not to show any emotion,

I inserted the tape and started to sing, tears stinging my eyes, and then slowly trickling down my cheeks. I saw her sad, tear streaked face and stopped.

"I'm sorry," I said, "This song touches me pretty deep, maybe another time."

"Yes, me too," she agreed. "Get Joe to show you the rest of the grounds."

"Before we go, I'd like your thoughts about possibly doing a Christmas Special here at Graceland? It would be good for Graceland, and I'd love very much to perform here. What do you think, Joe?"

Before he could answer, Lisa Marie spoke quickly, "Yes, you may be right. What a great idea, but let me talk to mother, and we'll let Joe know." Her eyes sparkled with excitement. She turned to leave and then looked back, "I'll be in the main office, why don't you see me before you leave?"

After she left, Joe said, "That was a close call "E!"

"Joe, my name is Johnny. 'E' could be the worst name you could call me. Forget the sixties; think about who you are talking to now. You called me Elvis earlier."

"Yeah, Johnny, I'll watch it, if you will?"

"Fine, Joe, now how about we visit the grave sites before we leave?"

On the way, George stopped us and said, "Lisa Marie would like to see you, she's in the main office."

When we walked in, Lisa Marie said, "I've thought about your suggestion regarding the Christmas Special, and I think you are right! It would be a tribute to my dad, and I think you would be perfect for the show. Mother and I have agreed that it would be a big boost for Graceland. I'll set it up the 22nd and 23rd of December. Mother said we can advertise it several months in advance, lot's of publicity. I bet we could fill the front lawn and around the block."

"Outside?"

"Yes. Why not? There's no other place big enough to handle thousands of people."

Once again Joe interjected. "She's right; there could be as many as fifty-thousand people. I'll help all I can, Lisa."

"Thanks Joe, mother will see to it that you do," she grinned impishly. "We'll need all the help we can get. I want this to be a show no one will ever forget. And besides, I think my dad would be pleased with this idea. She looked in my direction. "How much pay will you require?"

"For you, whatever you feel it's worth, as for me, I'd just love to do it!"

"How will I get in touch with you? I need to get a contract prepared."

I looked at her. "If you don't mind, your word is good enough for me, and I promise you won't be disappointed. I want to do this more than anything in the world; shall we shake hands on it?"

"You know, my daddy always told me, you're only as good as your word. You've got a deal," as she extended her hand to me.

We shook hands, hers feeling so soft in my rough ones, but it felt so good just to have that brief touch after all these years.

"I'll be leaving shortly. Joe knows how to get in touch with me."

"Will I see you in Dallas for the contest, I'm judging again?"

"Yes, when I leave here, I'm headed that way."

"Good, I'll see you there," she said, as Joe and I walked away.

We stopped at the grave sites for a brief moment. Neither of us spoke. Words were not necessary.

"Walk across the street with me, Joe. Once we were out of range of anyone hearing us, I said, "When we are in Dallas, act like you don't know me, or the other guys will think the contest is rigged."

"Alright, Johnny, be careful and I'll see you there. It sure is good to see you again. It's even better to see you in such fine form."

I knew the hidden meaning behind his words. He was right. I had come along way from the lifestyle I once lived. I thanked Joe for everything and headed towards Dallas.

CHAPTER 6

The visit to Graceland was much better than I had expected. I only wanted to go home for a visit, but I came away with much, much more! A Christmas Special! Yes! I'd say this was a great homecoming!

After riding for several hours, I stopped to take a break and decided to call Chance and David Lee. I lucked out. I was able to get in touch with both of them. I told them I had left Memphis and would meet them at the Casino in Vicksburg, Mississippi, located just north of the I-20 Bridge. David had said he knew where it was, and that they would arrive sometime tomorrow around noon. I had lots to tell them, and said so. I hung up the phone and laughed. I could just see those two stewing over what my comments meant. I knew it would bug them, and drive them nuts trying to figure out what it was.

The following morning, I waited at the front entrance to the Casino. I'd only been there a few minutes when I saw David and Chance pull into the parking lot.

"What's going on?" David asked, as he shook my hand.

"Yeah, what happened in Memphis?" Chance was anxious to know.

"Come on, I'll tell you all about it over breakfast."

As we ate, I explained the arrangements to do the Christmas Special at Graceland on National Television.

"I don't have the details yet, but I'd like to try and arrange it so you both can participate in this with me."

The excitement was overwhelming for them. They shot a hundred questions at me all at once. I had to tell them to hold on and that they would know more when I knew more.

As we rode out, I was thinking about Dallas, and remembered I had performed there before. It was many years ago, and I'm sure Dallas had changed a great deal since then. We arrived at the Dallas Inn, late that night, and again, money was tight, so we shared one room. We drew straws for the floor, and, of course, I 'won' again.

The next morning, we ate a good breakfast and then went over to "Six Flags. The lady at the ticket office directed us to the Amphitheater located at the south end of the park. On the way, David Lee saw some of the guys that he had met previously at one of the Elvis competitions.

David made introductions and asked them to walk along with us. One of them, named Rick, asked David if he had made the Panama City competition.

"Yes, I did," David replied. "Chance and I tied for second place."

"Did you meet the guy that won first place?" Rick asked.

"Yes, and you did too!" replied, David.

"No, I wasn't there, but I heard about the winner," said Rick, puzzled at why David was laughing, "and what's so funny?"

"Rick, this is Johnny Raye, he's the one who took first place in Panama City."

"Sorry man, I didn't catch your name at first, but I've heard about you from some friends in Memphis. It's good to meet you."

We reached the Amphitheater. We found Gary setting up the sound equipment. The Amphitheater encompassed an area the size of a football field. Bleachers surrounded the center arena with three levels, ten rows to each level.

We walked to the stage so Gary could meet the rest of the group. As usual, he was excited and cheerful; a man who thoroughly enjoys what he loves the most, his music. I know exactly how he feels; I feel the same. I really enjoyed being around Gary. Other than his curiosity about my age, he never questions anything else about me.

"I spoke with Gus at the Silver Dollar in Vegas," Gary said. "He's still looking for and Elvis Impersonator. Have you had time to call him?"

I shook my head no. "I plan on doing so by the first of the year."

"Don't wait too long as Gus may have someone else by then."

"That'll be all right, I'm not sure that's what I'm looking for at this time."

"Rick, have you met Johnny yet?" Gary asked him.

"Yes, I have. I'm just wondering if the rest of us should even enter after all I've heard about him," he replied.

"I'm sorry man, if you and the rest feel this way. I'll drop out of the competition?"

"Not necessary," arrogance crept into his voice. "I think I'm pretty good myself, and maybe as good as you."

"Well, I hope you are, then maybe the crowd will rip your shirt or suit," I responded, and laughed at the memory of my last contest.

Rick turned to David and asked, "They ripped his shirt?"

"Probably would have ripped more if we hadn't rushed him off stage," David retorted.

"Damn, that's good," said Rick, privately wishing he'd get the same reaction.

I looked at Chance and David, "You two want to go on a ride or get something to eat?"

"Eat!" yelled Chance, "I'm starving to death!"

"You're always hungry," we all said.

"Hold up a minute," Gary hollered to us, "I'm hungry too!"

The food stands were busy and we had to wait in line, something that I had trouble getting used to, but worth it to have my freedom. It turned out to be fun. We signed autographs and had our pictures taken.

We finally ordered. I wanted a foot-long hot dog and soda. So did the others. Chance, well he ordered two hot dogs, fries, a soda, and a candy bar. We looked at him at grinned.

"Oh hell, I'm starving," Chance said, with a mouth full of fries. Then along comes Gary who ordered a burger, fries, and a soda. I found out later that was about the only food besides pizza in his diet.

Gary left to check on his sound equipment. The three of us headed back to our room to get dressed. I decided to wear a pair of white pants, and a long sleeve black shirt. I debated on my white sport coat and then decided to wear it.

For a change, I wanted to really look the part. I wore my gold eagle chain, and rings for each finger. No one had noticed my rings. Joe had kept them for me all these years and returned them to me while I was in Memphis. Chance and David Lee wore their white jump suits with the red, white and blue eagles on their sleeves and pant legs, and a large eagle on the back. We called a taxi to carry us over to Six Flags. The guys were afraid the cycles would get their costumes dirty and mess up their hair.

Women stood at the front gate of the ticket office and yelled, "Shake it

Elvis, shake it," when we arrived.

Again, they wanted pictures. We were finally able to get through the crowd when a guy with a six-passenger, electric cart gave us a lift over to the Amphitheater.

Numbers were already being drawn by the time we arrived. David and Chance joined the group of Elvis Impersonators. I had privately asked Gary to place me last. He saw me coming and walked over and discretely handed me number thirty-two.

"Looks like you're last!"

Just then a little girl that looked to be about five years old approached me and asked if I would please sing "Puppet On A String" for her. She told me it was her favorite Elvis song.

I smiled at her and said, "Honey, I'd be happy too!" "What is your name?"

"Alyssa," she answered shyly.

I signed her program. I wrote her name down on the palm of my hand so I wouldn't forget it. Her mom thanked me and they left to take their seats.

Gary had us give him a list of our songs earlier so he could get them programmed into his equipment. He was busy checking the music and making sure the discs weren't scratched. I went over to him to let him know that I had a change of songs. I wanted to substitute one song with "Puppet On A String." Gary told me it would not be a problem. He would do it, but not to tell anyone as it could get out of hand if everyone wanted to make changes.

Once again, I stood around with the other guys and listened to the singers. This competition seemed better than the last. As far as voice quality, I knew my voice wasn't what it used to be, but everyone still thought I sounded original.

David did a great job singing "Hurt." He finished his second number leaving the crowd screaming for more. He smiled as he came off the stage. He knew he did a good job. Chance and I congratulated him on his performance. He responded with a big smile.

Two more singers performed, and then it was Chance's turn.

"Give it your all, buddy!" We told him.

He picked up the microphone, and started doing his body moves. The crowd responded enthusiastically. "Viva Las Vegas" warmed him up, and by the time he did "Polk Salad Annie," the crowd screamed for more. No one had sung that song all night, and the crowd loved it! By the look on his face, you could tell he knew it too!

Gary called number thirty-one. It was obvious that this guy was doing everything he could to compete, including jumping on tables. His performance looked more like a singing gymnast than as an Elvis. I wasn't that wild in all of my movies put together.

When number thirty-one finished, Lee patted my back and said, "You're next," as Gary called my name and number.

"We need the money, so let's bring home the gold," David quipped.

"I'll do my best, partner."

"We warmed them up for you, now knock them dead!" Chance added.

I had decided on "Puppet On A String" to be my first selection and then "Don't Cry Daddy." I took the microphone and asked Gary to wait a minute before he started the music.

I looked at the judges and spoke slowly. "A little girl named Alyssa, asked me to sing her favorite song. It may be against the rules, but I'd like to sing this to her personally. Alyssa, will you come up here with me please?"

Her mother brought her to the edge of the stage. I lifted her up, took her little hand in mine, and led her to the center of the stage. Her little face glowed with excitement.

"Are you nervous?" I asked her.

She nodded her head yes, but you could tell she was not the least bit afraid.

Gary started the music. I knelt down on one knee, put my arm around her, and started to sing "Puppet On A String." Half way through, she leaned over and kissed me.

The audience went wild yelling, "Elvis! Elvis!"

As I finished my first song, I asked Alyssa if she would like me to sing her another. She nodded and grinned impishly at me.

"Ladies and gentlemen, Years ago, I used to sing this song to someone who is very special to me. Tonight, I'd like to sing it to Alyssa. Also, this song is also dedicated to another special young lady who is in our audience tonight."

As I began to sing, Don't Cry Daddy, the crowd screamed so loud that Gary had to turn the music up louder in order to be heard.

When I finished, I walked Alyssa back to her mother who was waiting for her at the end of the stage. Women wept openly, overcome with emotion. Several were trying to get on stage. Security guards were ready for this and had the stage surrounded. I reached down, kissed a few women who were trying desperately to get to me, and then walked back to the center of the stage.

I turned and saw Lisa Marie standing. Tears trickled down her cheeks. She mouthed the words, "Thank you!" The crowd was breaking through security. Chance and David helped escort me away from the area.

When we were a safe distance away, David spoke, "Man, I've never seen or heard a performance as awesome as this, except from the King himself!

Fantastic, Johnny!"

Chance patted me on the back. "You should hear the jealous comments from some of the other guys that said it wasn't fair for you to have brought that little girl on stage."

Rick spoke up and said, "To hell with everyone else, I thought it was brilliant. I've never witnessed anything like it! A brilliant performance Johnny!"

"Thanks guys."

Gary called all the contestants back onto the stage to announce the winners. Once again, David and Chance tied for second place, and I was announced as the first place winner. The crowd rushed the stage; security struggled to hold them back. Gary thought it best if the three of us left right away. He'd meet us later at the hotel.

We reached the front gate, and asked the lady in the ticket booth if she would call a taxi for us. Within five minutes the cab arrived and drove us back to the hotel. We changed clothes. Too wound up to relax, we decided to go to the lounge. A celebration was in order.

The bar's customers were sitting around waiting for Karaoke to start. We sat at a table near the front, close to the Karaoke Jockey. (K. J.) He was late getting started and apologized for the delay. He explained he had attended the Elvis competition and that he had a hard time getting through the crowd.

"It seems the crowd was trying to find you," he said softly looking in my direction, so no one else could hear.

"Look, don't mention I'm here," I whispered back.

We ordered a round of drinks and sat back to listen to the Karaoke singers. The first singer for the night was a lady dressed in a red western shirt, black jeans, and black boots. Her blonde hair was shoulder length and she appeared to be in her middle to late forties. She caught my attention as she was very nice to look at!

I listened attentively as she sang a country song. When she finished, she walked by our table.

I stopped her and asked, "You did a great job, what was your name again?"

"It's Karen, and thank you for the compliment. You guys sure did a great job at the competition."

"You were there?"

"Yes," she replied, "we left right after your number for fear of being trampled." She had a beautiful smile that made me want to know her better. "You really made quite an impression on the crowd."

"But not on you?" I asked, and then was sorry I said it by the look that came over her face.

"Oh yes! But I'm not going to act crazy about it!"

"Well thanks, I think!" I felt a little disappointment from her response.

"Are you going to sing us a song?"

"Maybe later," I said, "but not right now." She nodded and walked back to her table.

The guys had turned in a song and Chance was singing when Joe and Lisa Marie walked in. They were staying at the same hotel. They had tried to find us, and since we were not in our room, they figured we'd be in the lounge because that's where the music was. Lisa had come to thank me for singing "Don't Cry Daddy."

"I felt my father's presence while you sang," she said. "I haven't felt like that since I was a little girl. You know, you remind me so much of him."

I couldn't say a word.

Joe spoke quickly, "We brought you guys your checks! You know, winning is becoming a habit with you three!"

"Yeah, but it's a good habit, and that's what we are here for, right guys?"

"Yeah, my day is coming." Rick said dryly.

"Sure, if you would learn to do the songs you sound the best on, and stay away from the others, you'll do just fine," I replied.

"You better listen to him," Chance chimed in. "He helped us and we have tied for second place twice now."

"Okay Johnny, I'm listening," Rick said.

"Some other time," I responded.

"Johnny, you're still planning to do the Christmas Special at Graceland, aren't you?" Lisa asked.

"I wouldn't miss it for the world."

"Then Rick started asking at the same time, "What Christmas Special?"

"Hold on and I'll tell you in a minute," I answered.

Lisa rose to leave and told me she would see me tomorrow before I left. She informed me she would call my room in the morning. I stood and watched her walk away.

I turned to the guys, and said, "As you know, I'm doing a Christmas Special which is scheduled for Dec. 22nd. and 23rd. at Graceland. Don't worry, you guys and your wives will be special guests. I looked at David and his solemn expression made me ask, "Aren't you happy for me?"

"Oh yes!" he said, "I'm just stunned at the thought of it."

Gary arrived, laughing and excited about the crowd making such a fuss over me. "They're still looking for you at Six Flags. I sent a bunch of them to the haunted house in the park, and told them you were hiding in there."

"Guess who's doing a Christmas Special at Graceland?" Chance said, as he pointed his finger at me.

"Am I doing the music?" Gary was excited with the idea.

"Buddy, I wouldn't think of doing this without you."

"Graceland," he said, "man that's awesome!" "Hold onto your hat, big guy, because I've got something to tell you. Paul Steadman, the owner of Steadman's Supper Club and Hotel in Dallas, saw the contest tonight. He is on his way to speak to you about us performing in his night club, three nights a week!"

"Is Steadman's a big place?" I asked.

"It's *the* largest in Dallas! He also owns the controlling interest in the Dallas Victorian Inn. And get this, a meal at his supper club costs about fifty dollars per person, and that's probably for a hamburger steak," he giggled at his own humor. "Speak of the devil, here comes Mr. Steadman now."

Gary made the introductions. We shook hands and I asked him to join us. It was obvious he was a business man as he wanted to get down to brass tacks right away.

He spoke quickly, and said, "I was at the competition and heard your performance tonight, Johnny! How would you like to sing at Steadman's Supper Club?"

"Well, that depends on how much you are paying?"

"How about one-thousand dollars per night for you and five-hundred for Gary."

"Mr. Steadman, I thought you said you'd like us to work for you!"

"Okay, Johnny, fifteen hundred for you and five-hundred for Gary."

I could tell Gary was getting nervous, and I could see he was happy with the deal and was afraid I would blow it.

"Well let's see, I figure you'll probably make and extra ten-thousand per night, so how about two-thousand per night for me, and a thousand for Gary."

"That's pretty high, Johnny," Mr. Steadman said, but he grinned at my boldness. Disappointment was written all over Gary's face. You could tell he thought it was over for us, but I wasn't done yet. I had been screwed over in the past, and I vowed that would never happen again.

"But you are right," Mr. Steadman responded, "I will be making an extra ten thousand per night."

"You know," I continued, "the Silver Dollar in Vegas is offering much more?"

"How much more?"

"Well, their offering a suite for me and a room for Gary on the top floor, plus three-thousand per night."

He glanced at his watch, and said, "All right, I'll offer you the same thing," but that's my final offer."

"One more thing," I added, I promised Lisa Marie Presley that I would do a Christmas Special at Graceland on Dec. 22nd and 23rd. I can't miss those shows."

"Well, that would work out; I like to change out my entertainment every few months."

"When would you like me to start?"

"This coming Wednesday night would be good."

"How about Friday, I have some personal business in Alabama."

"Good enough. I'll look for you at the hotel by Thursday. That'll give you time to check things over and get settled in. By then I'll have your contracts drawn up and ready for your signatures, and get the advertisement handled."

We stood, and shook hands.

"Gentlemen," he nodded, "nice meeting all of you." "Gary, give me a call tomorrow," and he left.

During this whole ordeal, no one else had said a word. I think they were stunned at what they had just witnessed, but the minute Mr. Steadman left, they hurled a dozen questions at me, all at once.

"Hold on guys," I'm tired. "David, you asked me if I ordered a costume. No, actually I ordered several."

"Wow, I've got to see these."

"You will," I responded. "Look, you guys can hang around, I really am exhausted and need to get some sleep, this old man just ain't what he used to be," I laughed.

"Hell, if sleep makes you better, I'm going too," Chance piped in.

Everyone decided to call it a night. Gary said he'd stay in Dallas to handle arrangements.

I walked over to Karen's table. She was with a few of her friends. Judie, my hairdresser, was with them.

"What are you doing here?" I asked Judie.

"We came to see you perform at Six Flags.

"Did you enjoy yourself?"

"Yes. Very much."

"Good," and turned my attention back to Karen. I had told her that I would be leaving and going back to Birmingham for a few days, but I'd be back in Dallas by next Friday. I looked into her big blue-gray eyes, and asked, "I'd like to see you again sometime?"

"Well, we're leaving tomorrow also."

"How about 'The Bar' in Birmingham, say, Wednesday night?"

"Okay," she blushed and smiled back, "I'll see you there."

I left and went back to the motel room.

As soon as I walked in the door, Chance asked me, "Well?"

"Well what?"

"Did you score with the blonde?"

As I laid my pallet on the floor, I said, "I didn't try to score, I only told her I'd like to see her again, she seems genuinely nice."

"And?" Chance just had to ask.

"I told her I'd see at 'The Bar'. She said that's Crazy Lee's bar, whatever that means."

"Friends call me Crazy Lee most of the time," David answered.

"Huh!" I said. "So you're crazy, I knew when I met you, you were a little strange!"

Lee threw a pillow at me and Chance burst out laughing. "Thanks," I grinned, "I need the extra pillow," and rolled over to get some well deserved sleep.

CHAPTER 7

Morning came early for all of us. I was tired and sore from sleeping on the floor. David and Chance were tired from staying up half the night talking about the contest, and how their lives had changed since they met me. Showers helped to relieve the stiffness, and rejuvenate our energy. Anxious to get going, we again hopped on our bikes and headed to Birmingham.

Tara and Michele were waiting for us when we arrived. They wanted to know everything about Dallas. I was tired and needed sleep, so I told David and Chance to fill the girls in on everything that happened, and what lay ahead.

"Tara, do you have a spare bedroom where I can crash for awhile?"

"Yes, the guest room's upstairs, the second door on the right. Make yourself at home, and if you need anything just holler. The bathroom has plenty of towels and toiletries, so you should be set, Johnny."

"Thank you baby, good night everyone." I laughed, as I heard the excited chatter coming from the kitchen.

I was glad to have escaped the fifty million questions that David and Chance were trying to answer.

I rose early, everyone else was still asleep. I left a note where I was going, and headed to town. Gary had told me to check out an antique car dealership in Birmingham, and talk with the man who rebuilds old cars. He had a 1963 Cadillac convertible, candy apple red with white interior that looked like new. I had seen it when I drove past the last time I was in town.

I pulled into the car lot and spotted the convertible right away. I parked and walked over to admire the classic beauty before me. A guy in dirty jeans and a tee shirt approached me.

"Hi, I'm Zeke!" he said shaking my hand. "Well Elvis, this car seems to suit you. Would you like to take her for a spin?"

"Yeah, I would, but my name's Johnny!"

I took the car for a test drive around the area with Zeke bragging about the engine, the body, and everything else he could think of for a sale.

"Save the sales pitch," I said. "I'll take her, but first I have to go to my bank for a loan."

"You won't need to do that, go back into our finance department, and talk to Brian. He's our finance manager. He'll take care of your needs with no inconvenience to you."

I found Brian sitting in his office, and gave him all the information he needed. A short time later, after a few phone calls, and signatures for a one year loan, I now owned, at least on paper, my Cadillac. I found Zeke, and told him I would be back later to pick up my bike. He told me to go ahead and park it on the side of the building so it wouldn't be in the way.

"You wouldn't want to sell your bike would you? I'd give you a fair offer."

"No. Not right now. I've had it a long time, and I don't want to part with it, and probably will never sell it."

"If you ever change your mind, you know where to bring it."

"Thanks, if I change my mind you'll be the first one in line," I said, as I shook his hand and left.

I drove to the costume shop to pick up the jump suits I had ordered. The seamstress had finished them the day before, and as I entered her shop, I could see them hanging in the back room. The jewels and studs sparkled under the florescent lighting.

"Are those mine, I hope?"

She smiled, "Yes they are, and I'll get them for you."

Her talent with a needle was excellent, and I was more than pleased with her work, and told her so. In fact, they were intricately designed, each bead hand sewn, and she had followed the pattern to the minutest detail. She covered them in vinyl bags, while I counted the money I owed her. I had paid five hundred dollars down and I owed a balance of fifteen hundred. I handed her the cash, thanked her again for her excellent workmanship and left.

From there, I stopped at the shoe repair store. It was owned by an elderly black gentleman who made customized leather boots and shoes. A craft that was rare to find these days. I ordered a pair of shoes, black with white across the top, and a white pair of boots, both pair in soft, quality leather, to be ready by Wednesday. He charged me two hundred for each pair, and I paid him with four one hundred dollar bills.

My money was dwindling fast, and then realized I had forgotten to have scarves made to give to the women in the audience during my performances. I thanked the man and headed to the costume shop.

The seamstress looked up as I entered, a worried expression on her face when she saw it was me, and asked, "Is something wrong with the costumes?"

"No, I forgot to order scarves to hand out," I answered.

"No problem, I'll have them ready for you early Wednesday afternoon, all we have to do is decide what style you want. I'll get my pattern book."

Of course, I again had to pay in advance. I had spent most of my money. I guess I'll have to talk to David or Chance, and borrow from them until I get paid at the club. I picked out the pattern for the scarves and left.

I returned to David's house feeling good about my day's purchases and all I had accomplished. Tara saw me drive up in my nice shiny, red Cadillac. Zeke had cleaned the whitewall tires, polished the white leather interior while I handled my finances. She sure looked pretty sitting out front for everyone to see.

Tara yelled out, "David, come and see this and hurry!"

David rushed out of the house, his mouth hung wide open. "Man, where did you find this beauty?"

"Across town," I answered, smiling all the while. "Not only did I pick the car up today, just feast your eyes on these," as I pulled my suits from the trunk.

David's eyes shone like bright headlights. "Those are real diamond studs?" he asked. "No wonder they were so expensive."

"Go try one on for us," Tara piped up, happy for me.

"Maybe later. Right now I'm going upstairs to clean up."

"I've got to call Chance and tell him to get over here," David said, as he went to get the phone, "he has got to see all this."

"I'm also having a pair of shoes, and a pair of boots made," I said proudly. "Not bad for a day's work, huh," I added, as I went inside.

It only took a few minutes, before Chance and Michele arrived wondering what was going on. David had moved the car to the back yard.

"What's up?" Chance had a puzzled expression on his face.

"Look out back, and see for yourself," said David, excitedly.

They walked to the back of the house, and Chance stopped dead in his tracks. Stunned at what he saw, he finally found his voice, and said "Cool, man this is awesome, where did you get her?"

"It's Johnny's," David said proudly. "He bought it across town at Zeke's. He owns an antique car dealership."

"Let's take the top down and take it for a ride," Tara said eagerly.

"Yeah, Johnny won't mind," Michele added.

I was still showering when I heard a knock on the door.

"Johnny, it's me, Tara. Chance and Michele are here, and we want to take the Cadillac for a ride."

"Sure, baby, David has the keys," I hollered out in return.

"See you when we get back," she yelled excitedly.

While they were out joy riding in my Cadillac, I finished my shower, and stretched out on the sofa to watch T.V. I started thinking about how well things were working out for me. My mind wondered back to Jessie Mae. I wonder what she's doing, as well as Samuel and Joseph. I decided to call and find out. I dialed her number; her gruff old voice brought a smile to my face, as she answered.

"Hello Jessie."

"Johnny, is that you?" she inquired, excitement in her voice.

"How did you know it was me?" I teased.

"Well," she said, with that old familiar cackle, "I figured when things were going good for you, and you knew what direction you were headed, you'd call me."

We talked for quite awhile, and I filled her in on everything that happened since I left, including my new purchases.

"I'm very happy for you, but what about your daughter? Have you talked to her?"

"Well, as I've told you, I've seen her, and I'm doing the show at Graceland."

"But you haven't told her who you are?"

"No not yet, the time isn't right."

"Well don't be in a hurry, the right moment will present itself. I've got to go, Johnny, I need to get back to the groves," she sounded a little more tired than normal. "Now you call me again, and take care."

"I will, and don't work so hard," I scolded.

As I hung up, I felt something was wrong from Jessie's voice, but the guy's and their wives had returned and had pulled into the driveway. I dismissed my feelings as they came in all excited. Their hair all wind blown from their drive around town.

"Johnny, I heard about your new costumes and I'd like to see them," Chance wanted a peek preview.

"They're on the bed, go and take a look."

"Wow," I heard him exclaim, as I went to join him. "Now that's a costume," he added. "Who designed them?"

"I did!" I grinned proudly.

"Well how about designing me one?"

"Okay," I retorted. "Do you have a thousand bucks?"

"Yes, I do, why?"

"Good," I answered, "I need to borrow it, I'm near broke again."

"Well, I can see why," David said, coming into the room, "I can loan you some money"

"Thanks, I do need a thousand. Could I borrow five hundred from each of you until next week?"

"No problem, Johnny, I've got my contest winnings. David left to get it."

"Me too, Chance said laughing, "Michele's got mine, or I should say "hers" in her purse. We were on the way to the bank when David called us to come over here."

"Johnny, are you sure this will be enough?" David had returned.

"I think I can make it for now until I get paid from the club," I answered and thanked them. On the way downstairs, I asked, "What time are you guy's going to work tonight?"

"I'm going to stop by the club around seven o'clock. My sub said he'd work one more night for me, and I just want to check and see how everything is going," Chance answered, "then I'll meet you guys here and we can all leave together and go to 'The Bar'."

We had decided to wear our "Elvis" jump suits and have some fun for the night. We had pre-arranged to walk in 'The Bar' together, arms raised high, saying thank you, thank you very much. We took everyone by surprise, and all the people cheered. A huge banner hung on the far wall behind the stage that read, "Welcome Home Big Winners - Elvis Still Lives." If only you knew, I thought, as I read the banner.

We sat at the table in front of the stage. The regulars and several new faces wanted pictures and autographs. Several made comments about my new costume. Karen was sitting with Judie, and she came over to say hello and how much she liked my jump suit. I thanked her and asked her if she would sing a country song for me. She said she would reciprocate, but only if I would sing "Puppet On A String" for her.

David started his Karaoke for the night, but told the crowd that the "Elvis's' would be doing a few songs first, and then have Karaoke for everyone after that. David called Chance to come up and sing first, as Chance had to leave early. He stopped at his bar. His sub wasn't feeling well, so Chance told him he'd be back at ten o'clock and his sub could go home then.

I asked Karen if she and Judie would like to join us at our table. She thought it sounded like fun, and went to get Judie. We talked about the competition in Dallas and the little girl who wanted me to sing "Puppet On A String," and what a big hit it was having her on stage with me. It really added to my performance, and the audience loved it.

"Isn't that your favorite song?" I asked Karen.

"Yes it is. And you didn't plan it?"

"No, the little girl really did ask me. The other guys didn't think it was a song you could win the contest with, but I didn't care, all that seemed important at the time was the little girl. It just turned out to be a great idea."

When Chance finished singing, David said he'd sing next. He thought I needed a little more time with Karen. I knew I really didn't need to get involved with anyone, but it felt good to have a female to talk to and be with rather then the guys all the time, and she was pleasant to talk to, and look at.

David sang three songs and called me to come up on stage. Before I started, I thanked the crowd for their support and loyalty. I had noticed a few of them had too much to drink and were getting a little loud, so I asked them not to scream or get too wild. Most of them knew me by now. They had heard me sing before and honored my request. Several came over to the table and complimented me, but it wasn't that big of a deal anymore. I was now being treated as a "regular." I was now a part of the Karaoke family.

I walked back to the table and asked Karen to come outside and see my new car. "Wow!" she exclaimed, "It's beautiful." Flashing her gorgeous smile at me, she asked, "Can we go for a ride?"

"Jump in and I'll get Judie," I smiled back.

The three of us rode around town for about an hour. I had put the top down. People passing by waved and yelled, "Hey there's Elvis!" It was great just to laugh and enjoy the warm, beautiful night, but mostly the company.

When we returned to "The Bar," David spotted us and quickly asked Karen to come and sing.

"After your song," Karen, "I've got to go, but I'd like to see you again."

She smiled and said, "I hope so."

"Sing from your heart," I said, as she walked toward the stage. While Karen was finishing her song, I told David and Tara that I was going back to their place to relax and watch T.V.

"Is Karen going with you?" asked Tara, a mischievous smile on her face.

"No, not this time, it's too early for that yet," I grinned back at her.

"The time is right, and I bet she'll go if you ask her."

"You may be right, but I'm not ready. She's the type of woman who wants someone more stable and settled than me. Maybe the day will come, just not now."

"Here's the key for the front door, just leave it under the mat. We'll be home after we clean up."

I wished everyone a good night and left. I really had a lot on my mind, and I knew right now I needed to be alone to think things through.

I was headed for the door when David hollered out, "Johnny, wait up! I couldn't help but notice you look very worried, is there anything you want to tell me or maybe talk about?"

"No. I'm all right; I just have a lot on my mind."

"Yeah, Johnny, I'll bet you do. If I were the 'King' I'd have a lot on my mind too!"

I looked at him questioningly, as he said, "Good night, I'll see you tomorrow." He patted me on the shoulder, and walked back to the stage.

I began to wonder if I had made too many errors. What if he knows? Will he tell anyone else? No, I thought. He was just making a statement, I hope, or was he?

I went back to the house and stretched out on the sofa to watch TV. When the news came on, the reporters mentioned that there had been numerous Elvis sightings. They further reported that a few of these same people had seen "Elvis" perform in Dallas. The 'Elvis sighters' said it had to be the real Elvis. No one else could be that good.

Apparently, several of the Elvis Impersonators in Dallas were interviewed and told the reporters that they would have won, if it wasn't for Johnny Raye, the first place winner. Oh great, now the news media would be looking for me for my comments. Now what am I going to do? I start at the club on Friday. I thought. I decided to call Joe for advice. He had seen the news too.

"When you are interviewed, tell the reporters, yes, you are good, and you're glad they think you are Elvis. Say that you believe these guys were just making excuses because they weren't good enough. Because the fact is, there were second and third place positions. Why did they not place in those positions if they thought they were that good?" He stated.

"Good idea," I agreed with him. "By the way, I'm playing at Steadman's Supper Club for the next three months."

"In that case, I guess I'll have to take some time off and come and see you perform."

"Great, I'll see you later then, and thanks Joe."

The next morning was Wednesday. I got up before David and Tara, took my shower, and once again dressed in black pants, black shirt, white shoes and white sports coat. I quickly went out the back door so I wouldn't wake anyone.

I started the Cadillac and let the top down. As I was backing up, Tara came to the back door dressed in her bathrobe, yawned a few times, and asked, "Where are you going so early this morning?"

"Good morning sleepyhead, I'm going to town to pick up my shoes and scarves."

"Okay. But hurry back I'm going to cook breakfast."

"Not for me, I'll eat out."

"Are you sure?" she asked, and yawned again.

I smiled. "Thanks for the offer, but yeah, I'm sure. See you later," I hollered, as I finished backing out of the driveway.

I enjoyed my drive into town. It was a glorious October day. The sky was pale blue. Puffy white, billowy clouds floated softly in the air like giant marshmallows. There was hardly a hint of light breeze. The sun felt warm on my face, indicating it would be a scorcher by noon.

Several neighbors were mowing their lawns before the afternoon heat set in. One of them waved and hollered out, "Nice car Elvis!" I smiled and waved back.

My thoughts drifted to David, Chance, and their lives. They were settled down, had beautiful wives who supported and believed in their husbands in whatever they did. I wondered if the guys realized how fortunate they were. I thought back to when I was married and had a beautiful wife and child. I never took the time then to think how lucky I was in so many ways. My biggest problem was career pressure. Many people contributed to my problems, and I blamed so many people. I realize now how much of it was my own fault. I let too many people take control of me and run my life.

I parked in front of the shoe repair shop. It wasn't open yet so I sat in the car and waited. A few passers-by looked at the car and smiled in admiration. One lady asked, "She's a beauty Elvis, what year is it?"

"It's a 1963 model," I answered, smiling back.

The owner of the shop arrived. "Elvis, this is some car you have here."

"Thank you very much," I responded to the compliment.

"Come on, let's go and get those shoes and boots you ordered, and see if they fit. You're early; I didn't expect to see you until this afternoon. Good thing I worked late last night to get them finished."

He picked up both pair and brought them to me. "I hope these soles aren't too thick! I know you Elvis's like to move around a lot, so I made them light and flexible. Here, sit over in that chair and try them on."

I tried both pair. They were a perfect fit, and were soft, and very comfortable. I knew I couldn't find anything like this in a regular shoe store, and I knew they were worth more than he charged me, so I gave him an extra hundred dollars.

"Now that's the Elvis I know," he grinned.

I thanked him and left.

Just then, Chance drove past. He had taken Michele to work because her car was in the repair shop. He stopped.

"Hey Johnny, thought that was your car parked out here."

"Hi Chance, I'm on my way to pick up my scarves, want to go with?"

"Yeah, I've got time to kill. Let me park my truck and I'll join you."

We drove to the costume shop, and Chance mentioned he had been here before, but didn't order anything because it was too expensive. I had told him that was true, but the quality of work was excellent, and you pay more for the best.

Mrs. Morrison, the seamstress, had already opened her shop. She was in back busily sewing when she heard us enter.

"Good morning," she said. "My goodness, we have two "Elvis's" today."

"Good morning to you," I greeted her warmly.

She had a pleasant personality and a genuine, warm smile. Her blouse had pins sticking everywhere, and a tape measure wrapped around her neck. She obviously had been sewing for quite awhile before we arrived.

"Came to pick up your scarves, right?" she questioned.

"Yes ma'am."

"They're ready and boxed, let me go and get them for you. Just wait right here, I'll only be a minute."

She returned carrying three, long narrow boxes. Her eyes twinkled with merriment. Each box contained separate colored scarves. One box all black, one all in red, and one white. Each scarf was folded neatly. She had made them about five to six inches wide, and long enough to wrap around your neck. All were made from satin material.

She took out a black scarf from the box, and held it up for us to see. She had stitched a large "E" on one end and Johnny Raye in small letters on the other end, all in gold thread. The red and white ones were the same except she substituted silver and black thread on them. They really were impressive. Chance thought they were great. As we left, I thanked her again and told her I'd be back for more when I ran out.

I drove Chance back to his car, took out a black scarf, and said, "Here, take this with you and give it to Michele."

He laughed and said, "Thank you, thank you very much," and drove off to go home and get some sleep since he'd been up all night.

I finished my errands, and drove back to the house. Tara was still in her bathrobe, and David had just woken when I walked in the back door.

"You didn't happen to stop by "The Bar" on your way home, did you?"

"No. Why?"

"Our day manager called us a little while ago. Apparently the news media stopped by and was asking about your whereabouts."

"Channel Six wants to interview you." "What are you going to do about it?" asked David, while he was eating.

"Nothing," I said and then added, "I found out that someone from Steadman's Supper Club started the rumor. I guess it's good for business." "Now," I grinned at David, "not to get into your business, but since it's such a beautiful day, why don't you take Tara to the park for a picnic?"

Before he could answer, Tara said, "Good idea, Johnny, I'll get dressed and pack sandwiches, chips, and fruit for lunch." She gave me a kiss, as she hugged my neck.

"Thanks buddy, but I was going to hang around with you today."

Tara shot him a dirty look.

"But Tara and I do need a day off," he quickly added to avoid a lecture.

"That's good, because I'm leaving for Dallas. I've got a lot to do before Friday night."

I went to the bedroom packed my bags and loaded my car. David and Tara came out to say good-bye and to wish me luck. This time it was David who hugged my neck. "Love you man. Be careful."

"I love you my friend," and hugged him back. "Tell Chance I'll see all of you at my last show in December."

"For what?" he asked, his brows rose in question.

"Don't the two of you plan anything, I'm already planning for you," I commented.

"Okay," he shook his head, "just let me know beforehand."

"I will," I promised, as I got in my car, "and don't worry about the cost; I'll work that out too. I'll send you and Chance the money I borrowed next week when I get paid. Thanks again for everything, and thanks for picking up my bike at the car dealership for me. Are you sure it's not an inconvenience to store it here for awhile?"

"Not a problem, big guy. We're glad to help out.

"Then I'm out of here!" I hollered out, as I backed out of the driveway, anxious to get started with my plans.

CHAPTER 8

It felt good to be on the road again. I stopped at a pay phone outside of Birmingham and called Gary Jackson. He said the news media was waiting for me outside of the hotel lobby, along with twenty or thirty Elvis fans.

"I think they believed the news reporters," I laughed.

We chatted for a few minutes, and then I told him I'd call him back before I got to Dallas with a plan on how to avoid the media.

It was a long drive to Dallas, and it gave me time to think. I reached the Dallas city limits around midnight, and stopped at another pay phone to call Gary again. He told me the reporters would be at the hotel around nine o'clock in the morning, as it was late, and they got tired of waiting. I let him know I was on the outskirts of the city, and I would be there in about fifteen minutes.

At the hotel, the valet parking attendant laughed, and said to me, "Sir, everyone has been waiting all day for you."

"Well, they should have waited a little longer," I grinned, "and don't park the car yet," as I had spotted Gary walking out of the hotel lobby towards me.

"Wow, where did you get this little beauty?"

"In Birmingham at that antique car dealership you told me about. She was still there." We talked about the car for a few minutes, and then I asked him, "Do you have everything set for Friday night?"

"Yeah, if you want to we can go over to the club and check everything out?"

"Let's go. I'd like to check everything out while no one's around to interrupt us. I knew he wanted to take a ride in the Caddie.

We had to go through the service entrance because the club closed at eleven o'clock every night, and the only ones there were the employees cleaning up. Gary showed me where my dressing room was so I could hang up my costumes.

Two waitresses came in to see what was going on and introduced themselves. Sandy, a little blonde, about five-feet, two, looked to be about thirty years old. Denise, had long sable brown hair, about five-feet, five, and appeared to be the same age as Sandy. Both girls had knock-out bodies. They were dressed in short red, pleated, mini outfits, with white cowgirl boots and hats to match.

I told them who I was and turned to introduce Gary. I burst out laughing when I saw his face. His eyes were as big as saucers, and he looked like he was about to step on his tongue.

"Ladies, this is my music man, Gary Jackson."

"Hi," they both said, smiling sweetly at him.

"Uh, uh, hi," he finally managed to say.

We walked into the main dining hall. Huge, glass crystal chandeliers hung from the ceiling. Room dividers were spread open to allow enough seating, comparable to an auditorium. Because of the size of the room, speakers were placed on the sculptured support posts so everyone could hear. Over a hundred round tables with seating for at least ten were covered with taupe colored linen cloths and napkins to match the décor of the room. Centered on each table were crystal vases filled with water that held a large, rosebud shaped, floating candles. Each place setting had crystal wine and water goblets with solid white dinner settings, and gold ware placed appropriately.

The massive, oak stage was at least thirty feet in length, and twenty-five feet deep with a rounded front and steps on each side. Above, stage lights hung from metal grids to support their enormous weight.

This club was the number one hot spot in Dallas. Many entertainer's had performed here. For new comers, it was awe inspiring to be there, let alone to entertain. We walked on stage where Gary had set up his equipment.

"Would you sing us a song, please?" asked Sandy.

"Sure, we want a sound test anyway," I answered.

Gary put in the disc, "Loving You." As I sang, Sandy and Denise looked like they could eat me up! I started to laugh and walked to the edge of the stage.

"How does it sound?"

"Sounds wonderful!" They exclaimed in unison. "Would you sing some more songs for us? Please!"

"Not tonight." I smiled at their enthusiasm.

I was about to leave when some guy walked in, stomped over to Sandy, and asked sarcastically, "Hey stupid, what are you still doing here, don't you know I've been waiting for you?"

Sandy's face paled. She stammered out, "We were just listening to Johnny sing."

"Who the hell is Johnny?" he spat in her face.

"I am!" I retorted back, "and you are?"

"I'm Sandy's husband, so keep your eyes off her!" he growled.

"Hey man, now that's hard to do!" I felt my blood begin to race.

"He's not my husband, he's my boyfriend," Sandy said defensively.

He grabbed her by the hair, yanked her to him, and said, "Let's go, smart mouth."

I jumped off the stage and snarled at him, "Hey, why don't you grab my hair, hot shot!"

He looked at me and took a swing. I dodged his fist, grabbed his arm and pushed him to the floor.

I then grabbed a handful of his hair and asked, "How does this feel, tough guy?"

I let him go, and as he was getting up, he took another swing. Anticipating he would try again, I was ready for him. This time I locked arms, putting my leg behind his, and again threw him to the floor.

"Stop, please stop!" Sandy cried. She helped Jimmie get up, looked at me sadly, and said, "Thanks Johnny."

They walked toward the back door and Denise said, "He's always beating on her, and when she gets home, he'll really beat the hell out of her."

"But why?" I asked, Denise.

"Because you stood up for Sandy," she said sadly.

"What about you?" I thought I'd better ask, "Do you have a boyfriend waiting?"

"No, I'm the type who uses men, and then throws them away."

"Sounds to me like you're someone who's been burned one too many times. Come on, let me by you a cup of coffee, and then you can throw me away," I grinned at her, as my body began to relax.

She laughed, "You better watch out, I just might keep you."

"Ha!" You're too rough for me. Come on let's go and get that coffee."

"I'm ready, when you are," she grinned, "I'm finished for the night anyway."

The employees that had gathered around to see what was going on went back to their cleaning. Gary was still sitting on the edge of the stage, grinning from ear to ear.

"Just what do you think is so funny?" I asked him.

"You. I thought you might need some help there for a minute, but for an 'old fart', you obviously knew what you were doing."

"Watch it. I might have to show you how it's done, "I grinned back.

"Nah! I'm a lover not a fighter," he winked at Denise.

"You coming with us?" I asked.

"No, I'm going to do some fine tuning, and then I'll head back to the hotel. See you tomorrow," he waved, and walked back to his equipment, as we headed out the door.

"Johnny, there's a breakfast place down the street, its open all night. Let's take my car," she suggested.

"Mine's right here."

"I figured that, but my baby needs to go for a spin." She got her keys out.

"Sounds good to me, where are you parked?"

"Right over here," she said, as she unlocked the doors to a brand, spanking new red Porsche with black interior.

"Wow, this is your car, you must be rich?"

"My last name is Steadman, get in," she grinned. "Don't worry, my father doesn't own me, he just spoils me rotten."

"Oh, that explains it!"

It was a short ride to the restaurant. When we walked through the door, everyone behind the counter hollered, "Hello Denise!"

"Sounds to me like you come here often."

"Two coffees, Mary!" she told the waitress. "You might say I've been here a few times," she commented. Sitting in a booth, Denise said, "Johnny, I'm glad you stood up to Jimmie, Sandy's boyfriend. He's always knocking her around, and everyone else is afraid of him."

"Why?"

"I don't know, I guess it's because he's so big and he acts so tough." "But," and her voice became serious, "if he ever tried to hit me, I'd kill him."

"Why does she stay with him? She could get someone a hell of a lot better than that?"

"I guess they go way back, or something, and then he always tells her the next day how sorry he is, and that he won't do it again. Each time the beatings get worse and I'm scared one day he'll kill her."

We finished our coffee. "Want another cup?" she asked.

"No, I'm tired from the long drive," and laid money on the counter to pay for the coffee.

"My place or yours?" she asked me coyly.

"My place, if you please," I smiled, as we got in her car.

She drove us back to the supper club so I could pick up my car. "Sure you don't want me to come up, Johnny?"

"No," I smiled. "I need my sleep, and I've got a feeling if you come up there, I won't get any."

She smiled mischievously, "You got that right!"

I turned to leave when Gary came running toward us, yelling, "Denise, Johnny, wait! A neighbor of Sandy's called the club looking for Denise and said it was an emergency. They said it sounded like there was a big fight at Sandy's house, and they're really worried about her."

"That son of a bitch," Denise cried, as she was getting ready to drive off.

"Wait, we'll go with you, come on Gary," I said, as we hopped in her car.

We barely shut the car door, when she sped out onto the street.

We arrived at Sandy's in record breaking time. Sandy's neighbor was outside waiting, and ran to us talking rapidly, as if she herself was in danger. "Jimmie just left; I don't know if Sandy is all right or not."

Denise asked her if she had called the police, but the woman shook her head no. "It doesn't do any good," she spoke softly. "She won't file any charges to have him arrested."

"Thank you ma'am," I said. "Go inside now, we're here and we'll take care of everything."

Gary and I knocked several times on the front door. No one answered. I tried the handle. It was unlocked. I entered first to make sure Jimmie wasn't there. I glanced around and spotted Sandy lying on the floor of the living room. Her mouth and head were bleeding. Her face was swollen, and her eyes were already turning black and blue from Jimmie's fists. She appeared to be unconscious.

"Oh my God!" Denise said, as she ran over to us.

Sandy cried out as we gently lifted her from the floor to sofa.

"Her leg may be broken, and it looks like broken ribs by all the bruising in that area. Probably a concussion as well," I said. "Denise, call '911', this girl is in bad shape!"

It seemed like hours, but it only took a few minutes for the paramedics to arrive. We explained to them that Sandy's boyfriend had beaten her. They said this wasn't the first time they had been here. The paramedics quickly administered first aid and prepared Sandy to be taken to the hospital. Sandy was still unconscious.

"Will she be all right?" Denise asked, tears flowing from her eyes.

"It's hard to tell, her vitals are strong, but we don't know if there is any internal damage," one of the paramedics commented, as they lifted Sandy into the ambulance. "Any of you a relative?" he asked.

"No, but I'm her best friend," Denise replied.

"Would you like to ride in back with her? We need some forms filled out, and there will be additional paperwork at the hospital."

"Gary, why don't you follow the ambulance in Denise's car, I'm going to stick around here for awhile," I whispered to him. "I'll meet you at the hospital later."

"Are you sure you don't want me to stay with you?" Gary asked in a hushed voice, so no one else could hear.

"No, if there are no witnesses, then it will be my word against his."

"Johnny, don't kill him man, just make him wish he was dead," Gary said, as he climbed into Denise's car.

I glanced at Denise, our eyes held for a moment; she nodded her head, and threw us her keys. She then turned, and held Sandy's hand. They closed the doors and sped off to Mercy Medical of Dallas with Gary following close behind.

I walked back into Sandy's place, turned off all the lights and unscrewed all the bulbs in the lamps. That way, when Jimmie returned and reached to switch on the light, there wouldn't be any electricity. I sat on the sofa to wait. All criminals return to the scene of the crime, and this one was no different.

Fifteen minutes passed when I heard a car pull up. I peeked through the blinds, it was Jimmie. My blood rushed through my veins. My fists clenched and unclenched. I was ready. Keep your head clear and keep yourself under control, I thought. The door opened.

"Hey bitch, I'm back, and I've sobered up! Hey, what the hell did you do to lights? Guess you didn't learn your lesson. Looks like I'm going to have to give you more of what I gave you earlier," he bragged.

I let him get within a few feet of me, and snarled, "Hello, asshole!"

"Huh!" was all he muttered, as my fist hit his face before he even knew it was coming. Sandy's beaten body flashed before my eyes. I kept hitting him, until I was exhausted.

When I had finished teaching Jimmie a lesson he'd never forget, I picked up the only lamp that hadn't been broken, and screwed the bulb back into the socket. I looked down at Jimmie, and gave him one more swift kick in the ribs.

"That one's for Sandy!" I hissed, and walked out the door.

I stepped onto the unlit porch. I glanced around, but didn't see anyone. The neighbors had gone back to their homes, and except for a barking dog down the street, all was quiet. Staying in the shadows, I headed down the street for several blocks until I felt it was safe to hail a cab. At the hospital, I found Gary and Denise.

Gary looked at me, "Before someone sees you, and starts asking questions, you better go to the men's room and wash those hands, they're still bleeding."

I found the men's room to be empty. I ran cold water over my hands. Because of my anger at Jimmie, and my concern over Sandy, I didn't realize until then how sore and swollen they were. The cold water felt good, and it did help stop the bleeding. I'd have to wait until I got back to the hotel to put ice on them to reduce the swelling.

I returned to Gary and Denise. "Are you all right?" she asked, genuine concern in her voice.

"I'm fine, how's Sandy?"

"She's going to make it, but she won't be able to get around for quite some time. The doc said she has to stay here for observation, to make sure there's no internal problems," Denise said, looking tired from all that happened.

"Can we see Sandy?"

"No, they're monitoring her tonight, and they want her to rest. She regained consciousness a little while ago, but they've given her something for pain, and to help her sleep, so I'm going to stay here for the rest of the night in case there's any change."

"Okay, I'll be back in the morning. Gary, I'll ride back with you." "Ahh, just one thing," I whispered, "in case anyone asks either of you, I rode with Gary to the hospital."

"You got it," said Gary.

Denise whispered, "Is he alive?"

"I don't know. At least he was when I left."

"Leave my car at the hotel. One of you can bring it back with you when you come in the morning," Denise said. I kissed her cheek and we left.

Neither Gary nor I spoke a word on the way to the hotel. I guess there wasn't much left to say. Gary parked the car and we walked to our floor.

"If anyone asks about my hands, you accidentally slammed them in the car door." He nodded in agreement and went to his room.

I was grateful the manager had arranged to have my things brought to my room and put away. I was exhausted now, and desperately wanted to sleep, but first I had to scrub the dried blood from my clothes. When I finished, I took a hot shower, and fell across the bed into a deep sleep.

CHAPTER 9

It was early the next morning when I woke to the sound of someone knocking. I grabbed my bathrobe and opened the door to two police officers. They showed their identification, asked if I was Johnny Raye, apologized for waking me, and said they needed to ask me a few questions. I told them to come in, sit down, and make themselves comfortable.

I needed time to get my thoughts together. I stalled their questions by asking if either wanted a cup of coffee. I quickly made a pot and puttered around until it finished brewing.

"I'll take a cup with cream," said the one who went by the name of Captain Williams.

I sat on the end of the sofa, and faced both officers. "Okay, officers what's this all about?"

"The younger officer spoke first, "A Mr. Jimmie Stamps has filed an assault and battery charge. You've been named as a possible suspect. We also know about the beating he gave his girlfriend. He'll do time if we can get her to file charges. We've already talked with the paramedics and they confirmed that you were at her place last night, and you were the one who found the girl. Is that correct?"

Choosing my words carefully, I responded, "Yes. I was with Denise Steadman, Sandy's girlfriend, when Denise received the message that Sandy had been beaten. I admit I had a run in with Jimmie Stamps at Steadman's Supper Club earlier in the evening, and you can verify that with their employees, but that was it. Denise rode in the ambulance with Sandy, and Gary and I followed in Denise's car. That's all I know."

"We've already talked with Gary and Denise, and they confirm your statement," said the Captain.

"Are you officers going to arrest him?"

"Oh we will, as soon as he's out of the hospital," said the younger officer.

"Hospital," I acted surprised. "What happened? He's not anywhere near Sandy is he?"

"No, she's safe for now, we saw her this morning, but she was not awake," said the Captain. "She sure is a mess, she's lucky to be alive, and as for Jimmie, it seems someone gave him a taste of his own medicine."

"Good for them," I commented.

"That brings us to why we are here. This Jimmie character said that he thought it might have been you that beat him up, said it was dark and he didn't see your face, but he knew it was you!"

"Me!" I feigned surprise.

"I have to ask this," the Captain inquired, "did you go back to the house from the hospital?"

"No sir, I came straight from the hospital back to the hotel. You can verify that with Gary, he drove me back, I didn't even have my own car."

"We already checked," said the Captain as they stood to leave. "Sorry to have disturbed you since you got in so late from the hospital, but we had to do a routine follow up."

"I wonder why he thought it was me." I pretended innocence.

"We don't know, but whoever it was did a good number on him? They broke his right leg, his left arm is severely fractured, three or four cracked ribs, a broken nose and his face looks like a truck hit him, for starters," said the younger officer watching my reactions.

"Serves him right!" I replied

"We just thought you'd like to know," said the captain.

"No. Not really!" And that was the truth.

We walked to the door, and the captain turned to me and said, "Ice will help the swelling in those hands."

"The younger office asked, "How did you hurt your hands?" "Car door," I said, "you can…"

"Yeah, we know, we can verify that with Gary," the captain interjected. "By the way, we'll see you tonight at Steadman's."

"Oh you're coming to see my show tonight?" I asked, wanting to verify it was for the show and not to check on me.

"Yes, it seems our wives are dying to see your performance, I just hope we can afford it."

"Hold on a minute, maybe I can help." I wrote on the back of their calling cards, "Denise, special guests of mine, treat them well, half price." "I'll pay the rest," and handed the cards back to the officers. "When you come through the front door, tell Harry you have something for Denise, from me, and wait for her to seat you, okay."

"Thanks, Johnny," said the captain.

"What about Jimmie Stamps?" the younger office asked the captain.

"Oh forget about his complaint," the captain replied. "We don't have sufficient evidence to arrest anyone for his assault, but we'll arrest Jimmie when he's released from the hospital for the assault on his girlfriend."

"I'm sorry I wasn't much help, Captain Williams," I said, still feigning innocence.

"You were a big help," he laughed, as they headed down the hallway.

I showered and dressed. I was starving and decided to eat in the hotel restaurant. I no sooner sat down to order breakfast, when a woman approached me.

"You're Johnny Raye?" she questioned.

"That depends on who wants to know," I answered evasively.

"Hi, I'm a reporter with Channel Six News in Dallas. I'd like to talk with you if I may?"

I looked her up and down, "Five-foot, five, one hundred and twenty-five pounds right?"

"Right, how did you know?"

"Just a lucky guess."

She pulled off her outdated glasses for a moment, leaving me to peer into beautiful, hazel green eyes.

"What is it you want to know so early in the morning?"

"Well, some say you are the real Elvis, are you?"

That question momentarily caught me off guard. I didn't expect her to hit me with that one right up front. "Well, I wish they were right, but no, I'm not, I'm just better than most Elvis Impersonators. "And as for the three guys that told that story," I added, "they were just jealous," and winked at her.

She was busy writing little notes, and since I wanted to eat, I asked her if she wanted to join me for breakfast. She thanked me as she didn't have time for breakfast and was hungry.

"Well, my first performance at Steadman's is tonight, are you coming?"

"Yes, I'm writing a story about you."

"Not about me, lady!"

Ignoring her presence, I turned my attention to the scenery outside. We had a window seat, and the view was spectacular. A small waterfall had been built to channel the creek that ran next to the hotel. Fancy colored rocks were brought in and layered in steps which allowed the water to flow softly over them. Lights were scattered in and around the falls. Foliage and bright colored plants were placed intricately. Funny how, as you get older, you start to take notice of the beauty around you. It doesn't seem important when you're young.

"Are you listening to me?" she asked.

"Ah, yes, sorry, what did you say?"

"Look, if you'll just answer a few questions, I'll leave you alone."

"Fine, but not while I'm eating!"

We had already ordered, and the waitress had brought our food.

"Where did you get those clothes?"

"What's the matter with my clothes?" her cheeks turned a slight pink.

"Well, that long dress, and that blouse, it looks like something my grandmother would wear."

Her face turned a bright shade of pink. "Look, I'm not here to discuss the way I'm dressed, besides, have you looked in the mirror lately? You look like something from the 50's."

"I hope so," I said, having a little fun at her expense. "Like Elvis, right!"

"Yeah, well, I guess you're supposed too!" she sounded offended, her face now a bright red.

We ate in silence for a while, when out of nowhere she asked, "Where are you from?"

I quickly spoke to evade that question, and asked her a question instead. "You are coming to the show tonight, right? Why don't you come to see me in my dressing room after the nine o'clock performance? And, please wear something a little more sexy."

"Anything else?" she asked, sarcastically.

"Yes, instead of pinning your hair up, wear it down!" I stood up to leave.

"I'll bet you have a good looking body hidden beneath those baggy clothes." I threw a twenty dollar bill on the table. "I've got to go, I'll see you after the show tonight," and left her sitting there with her mouth open.

I drove to the hospital to see Sandy. Denise had gone home and changed clothes and was back, but so was Captain Williams. Sandy was awake and he was having her sign papers charging Jimmie Stamps with assault and battery.

I asked Denise, "Did she sign the complaint form?"

"Yes, she did. Johnny, the captain asked me if you were with me last night and I told him, yes, all night," she whispered to me.

I laughed and told her that the captain had stopped by my hotel room this morning asking questions. "Don't worry about it, our stories check out."

Captain Williams finished with Sandy. The exertion of just signing those papers tired her out. "See you tonight, Elvis," he said, as he headed out the door.

I told Denise about the cards I had signed for the captain, and specifically about the fact that I paid the balance for their tickets, as it was important to me. She nodded without question.

Sitting gently on Sandy's bed, I took her hand, "Don't try to speak. Just listen! When you get out of here, you are going to stay with me until you are well." She tried to talk. "No," I said, "Just listen!" "I've already talked with my maid, Louise; she will help me take care of you whenever she can. All you have to do is concentrate on getting well, so you can get out of here, and that's an order."

Tears welled up in those poor little slits she had for eyes, and slowly slid down her cheeks. Emotion choked my words, but I finally managed to say, "I've got to go now, but I'll be back tomorrow to see you." I bent down and kissed her cheek. "You get some rest," I ordered gently. "Denise, I'll see you tonight at the club."

"I'm going to be leaving here in a little while; I just want to make sure Sandy's comfortable before I go. See you later, Johnny."

Before I left the hospital, I went by Jimmie's room. He saw me and fear replaced the placid look he had when he saw me standing in the hallway. I stared him in the eyes, and said menacingly, "When you are out of the hospital, and you serve your time, I want you to get the hell out of Dallas or I'll pay you another visit." I then left and walked down the hallway, where I ran into Captain Williams.

"How's Jimmie?" he inquired.

"He doesn't look too good this morning," I said, and kept on walking.

I drove to the club to see Mr. Steadman. We still had to finalize the deal. He was in his office when I walked in. We talked for a few minutes, and then we went over the contract. "Three thousand each night I perform," I read out loud. Everything seemed to be in order so I signed the papers. We shook hands and I left.

It was almost two o'clock. I found Gary checking his equipment. When I approached him, he asked how Sandy was doing. I told him she'd make it, but that Jimmie was looking somewhat poorly. I asked him to wake me up around five o'clock. I left for the hotel to rest.

When Gary came to get me, I was already in the shower. After I dressed, he and I drove across the road and parked at the back entrance of the club.

A large crowd had already gathered at the front. "Looks like it's going to be a sell out performance," I noticed the line getting longer.

"Yeah, Mr. Steadman is going to make a killing tonight."

When we got to my dressing room, a pretty little gal dressed like a Dallas Cheer Leader, handed me my scarves and towel. Gary couldn't stop talking to her. I finally had to tell her what I wanted her to do on stage, and sent her out so I could change into my costume. I had decided to wear my red jump suit with my white boots.

At seven o'clock, Mr. Steadman thanked everyone for coming and hoped they enjoyed their meal. "And now, what you've all been waiting for," his voice boomed into the microphone, "Mr. Johnny Raye. Let's give him a warm Texas welcome."

Gary started my intro music. I walked out on the stage, as I had done a thousand times before to the sound of the crowd clapping and cheering, and the women screaming.

Years before, large crowds always helped me to stay high and give my all. That hadn't changed. I could feel the excitement pulsating throughout my body. I was ready to give my best.

I jumped right into my first song, "Burning Love," followed by "Don't Be Cruel," to keep the momentum going. I then slowed things down, and did "Can't Help Falling In Love." During this song, I walked to the edge of the stage, kissed several women and handed out a few scarves.

I turned and asked Gary to stop for a moment. I asked the audience for total silence. "This next song that I'm going to do, I used to sing to my little girl or at least Elvis did. Although she's not a little girl any more, she's here with us tonight. I'd like to bring her up on stage and sing this song to her. Ladies and gentlemen, as a special treat for you tonight, Ms. Lisa Marie Presley. Kitten, would you come up here, please?"

The crowd was stunned at first, and then clapped with delight while Lisa Marie joined me on stage. I asked to have a stool brought up for her. The lights went low, only a spot light shone on us. Gary started the music and I sang to my daughter, "Don't Cry Daddy."

After I finished, I kissed her on the cheek, and she said, "Daddy used to call me Kitten when I was a little girl."

"I know. You don't mind do you?"

"No, it sounds good to hear it again." She then kissed my cheek, thanked me, and walked off the stage. It took a full five minutes to quiet the audience so I could continue.

"Ladies and gentlemen, Elvis wrote this song for Priscilla." I announced, "She's also here with us tonight, and I'd like to dedicate "Are You Sincere" to her. Gary, music please!"

The crowd looked around to find where she was sitting. As she stood up, I started to sing. I was half-way through and saw her wipe her eyes. When I finished, she walked on stage, and kissed my cheek. I placed a scarf around her still slender neck.

She looked at me through her tear filled eyes, and whispered, "Where did you get the words and music to that song?"

"Ask your daughter," I smiled, and whispered back. She walked off the stage, and again, we had a standing ovation.

Gary restarted the music and I sang several more songs. I ended my performance with "American Trilogy." I walked off stage, and from my dressing room, I could still hear the cheers from the audience. They wanted an encore, but tonight I decided not to do one. I felt they already had a special treat with Lisa and Priscilla.

Gary walked in, "Great performance, big guy!" Laughing and dancing around the room, being his normal cheerful self, he commented, "The crowd really enjoyed the show," he grinned, finally sitting down in a chair.

"I sure hope so, that's why we're getting paid these big bucks," I responded back with enthusiasm.

I looked into the mirror and saw Priscilla standing in the doorway. I turned toward her. "Did you enjoy the show?"

"Yes, very much." she replied softly. "Lisa Marie told me that you were playing the music to "Are You Sincere," when you were in the studio at Graceland, but I know there are no words written down to that song," she said with a puzzled expression on her face.

"Yes there is," I answered quickly. "There's a picture of you and Lisa Marie on the shelf, and when I picked it up to look at it, the glass fell out. Behind it was a yellow sheet of paper with the words written on it. I'm sorry, but when I was done singing, I put it all back behind the picture. When you go back to Graceland, you can look for yourself."

She looked at me strangely, "You act so much like him, and Lisa Marie said you seemed to know your way around the recording studio."

"Well, being into music like I am, I'm fairly knowledgeable with musical instruments and equipment," I quickly tried to dodge her questions.

"Well, when you come to Graceland for the show, don't go in there, okay!" She walked away without waiting for an answer.

She never heard me say, "Sure Cilla, no problem."

I turned and looked at Gary, "Forget what you just saw and heard, all right!"

"Sure man, no problem," but you could tell by the look on his face that he didn't quite know what to make of what he had just heard.

We walked out together, and I headed towards the kitchen to get a pitcher of water to bring back to my dressing room. When I returned, I stopped dead in my tracks. Standing in front of my dressing table was one gorgeous woman. Not to mention the fact that she was totally naked. She looked like a perfect 38-24-36. Her breasts looked as firm and round as honey dew melons. No hair anywhere, except for the long, chestnut brown hair that hung down her back to the top of her round, bare butt. She had a shape most women would die for.

"What do you want?" I finally found my voice.

"Your autograph," she purred like a kitten.

"Lady, it looks like you're looking for more than that!" and re-opened my door. Gary was standing outside in the hallway talking to some girl. I grabbed him by the shirt and said, "Go get Denise, and hurry!"

He took off running. A few seconds later he returned with Denise.

Shaking her head, she asked, "What did you get yourself into this time?"

"Nothing yet, but take a look in my dressing room."

Denise peeked in and laughed. "Hey, I don't want her. She's definitely not my type."

Gary, looked in, "I'll take her."

"No you won't," I said seriously, "get her out of here!" "She is trouble with a capital 'T'!"

About five minutes later, Denise brought her the woman fully dressed. "Unashamed, the woman said, "My husband is going to be soooo mad that I didn't get your autograph."

"Lady, if your husband wants my autograph, tell him to come and get it."

As Denise was escorting her down the hallway, another woman walked towards us.

"I'll take care of this one, Gary grinned."

The girl that Gary was with walked away and told him he could have them all, but he wasn't going to get her.

I watched the woman as she approached. She had long blonde hair, and a sexy little shape. She was wearing a light blue, knee length dress. The bodice was cut low, which didn't leave much to the imagination. Her spiked heels were dyed to match her dress, making her look taller than she actually was. The closer she got, the better she looked. It was then that I noticed those beautiful, hazel-green eyes.

"The news lady!" I exclaimed, shocked at the transformation. "Here for that interview?"

"No, not tonight, I just wanted to say thank you for the advice you gave me this morning," and then added, "I went out and bought myself a new dress, and had my hair highlighted." "Do you like what you see now, sexy enough?" she twirled; quite pleased with the way she looked.

"Sexy, very sexy! Sure you don't want to do that interview?"

"No, I have a hot date tonight, and I owe it all to you," she chatted excitedly.

I mumbled to myself, "Big Mouth."

"What was that?" she looked back at me.

"Oh, nothing! By the way, I didn't catch your name."

She smiled sassily, "I guess it's because I didn't give it," and turned and walked saucily down the hallway, fully aware of mine and Gary eyes on her.

When she was out of ear shot, Gary, who had been grinning this whole time said, "Man, I hope you don't blow your next performance, you've blown everything else."

"Oh shut up, I don't see you doing any better!" and shut my door to get ready for the next show. I could hear him laugh all the way down the hallway.

I finished my last song for the night, and was on my way back to my dressing room thinking it sure would be nice to not have anything else happen tonight. No sooner did I think that, when the news lady showed up again.

"I thought you had a hot date?"

"So did I until my date's wife showed up on the arm of another man. I don't need that kind of trouble. Johnny, I'm sorry I was rude to you earlier. I was trying to get back at you for this morning," she looked a little sheepish.

"No, I'm sorry. I shouldn't have said anything about the way you were dressed. It wasn't any of my business to say anything."

"No, I'm glad you did, Johnny, I like the new me much better."

"In that case, me too!"

We went into my dressing room. I went in first, just to make sure there were no surprises waiting for me.

"Is it too late for that interview?"

"Yes, it is, but not too late for a drink, how bout it?"

"Sounds good," she said, making her self comfortable.

"I'll quick change out of my costume," and went behind the screen.

"Oh, well I guess I'd like to keep my clothes on," she laughed.

"You heard the story about the woman in my room?"

Still laughing, she said, "Yes, everyone in the dining room has heard it by now. I'm curious, why did you throw her out? I heard she was very pretty."

"Two very good reasons. First of all, she had trouble written all over those large breasts; and secondly, she's married, and like you, I don't need that kind of trouble." I had finished changing and walked out from behind the screen. "I'm ready if you're ready."

She stood up wrapped her arms around my neck and gave me one long kiss. I returned the kiss, her lips tasted sweet as I held them between mine. I slid my hands slowly down her back, and finding her firm butt, pushed her closer to me. She stopped kissing me, and tilted her head back.

Breathless, and lips wet from the kiss, she asked, "Are you ready to go?"

I looked in her passionate hazel-green eyes, "Well, I was getting there."

Laughing, she withdrew from my embrace, "Let's go before we get into trouble."

We walked across the street and I asked the parking attendant to get my car. Gary came by with the same girl that earlier had given him the brush off.

"Guess everything has a way of working out, huh?" he grinned.

"Guess so, my friend, see you tomorrow."

"I really don't care for a drink, Johnny. Would you mind putting the top down and just drive somewhere quiet and peaceful?"

"Sounds good to me!"

We rode around on I-35, and enjoyed the warm night. Eventually I found an old country, dirt road, turned onto it and discovered it ended at the top of a hill. We parked and were amazed at the spectacular sight of the city lights of Dallas, as they glittered and twinkled below us. I sat back and relaxed. A full moon, a beautiful night, and a beautiful, sexy girl at my side. What more could a man want/ She slid over to my side of the car. I pushed the seat back to give us more room. We sat and held each other for a few minutes, not demanding anything from each other, just enjoying each others company. She started talking about her life, where she grew up, family, and old flames. She had just asked me about my life, when a set of head lights from another car pulled up behind us. We turned to see who it was.

A young trooper approached us. "What are you two doing up here?"

We both laughed at the irony of the situation.

"We're trying to have a romantic evening," I replied.

"Aren't you two a little old to be parking? I've got enough teenagers to watch without trying to keep up with the two of you," he tried to be serious. By this time we all laughed.

"Relax son, just because you get old, doesn't mean that life is over, hell, it's just begun," I said. My little news reporter giggled.

"How about we go and get a room?" she looked at me mischievously.

"A room," said the young trooper, "How about a home!" He shook his head, got back in his car and left.

I started the car and headed back to town. "How do we do this?" she asked, having grown quite serious. "I mean, it's been twelve years since my divorce, and I haven't had a serious relationship with anyone since."

"Well, if I remember correctly, I'm supposed to ask, your place or mine, and you tell me which one we go to," I joked.

"Okay, let's make it your place, I have a room mate."

"You're serious aren't you?" She nodded her head yes. "My place it is," I said, and put my arm around her shoulders.

It was one o'clock by the time we got to the hotel.

"Wow, this is a nice suite," she said, kicking off her shoes and wiggling her toes in the plush carpet.

I fixed her a drink, and poured myself a coke. I took off my shirt and laid it across the sofa. I took her hand and led her to the bed.

"Wait," she said. Like all women, she had to go to the powder room first. I got undressed and had just crawled under the covers when she walked out of the bathroom totally nude.

"I hear you like naked women in your room," she said, coyly.

"Come here," I commanded, looking into those hazel-green eyes, and kissed her passionately.

We began to make love, slowly at first, exploring each others bodies, and then with a frenzy, until our passions were fulfilled. Afterwards, we lay in each others arms. Neither of us spoke. The last thing I remember was looking into those hazel-green eyes, and her body curled next to mine.

The sun shone bright through the windows onto my face, arousing me from a deep, relaxed sleep. I reached my arm out only to discover that the other side of the bed was empty.

She walked out of the bath room already showered and dressed, and said, "Good morning sleepy head." She walked over and sat next to me. I could smell the freshness of her body from the shower. "By the way," she grinned, flashing those sexy eyes, "My name is Kristi Walters."

"It's a beautiful name for a beautiful lady."

She bent down, and kissed me, "I still need that interview."

"How about tonight?"

"I'll let you know," she answered, as she walked to the door. She turned, blew me a kiss, and left.

I had just finished my shower and was getting dressed when Gary dropped by.

"You going to see Sandy today?" he inquired.

"Yes, Denise is supposed to pick me up by ten o'clock."

"Speaking of Denise," he said, "she heard about you leaving the club last night with the news lady, and she's jealous. Said something about you not giving her the time of day, and you falling all over a news reporter. It's a female thing, I guess."

"Will you quit laughing," I said, thinking of the humor in it. "You sure seem to get a kick out of my life."

"It has been interesting."

Gary and I were discussing the show when there was a knock on the door. It was Denise. "Come in," I yelled out.

"Are you sure?" She peeked her head around the door. "I don't want to be a third wheel."

"What do you mean? Gary and I are the only ones here."

"Oh, I thought the news lady was here," she commented sarcastically.

I grinned and decided to have a little fun with her, "She was, but she left about and hour ago."

She looked at me, "And what's wrong with me? You know I like you, and you won't give me the time of day."

"Look honey, there's nothing wrong with you. In the week that I've known you, look what we've been through. I consider you a close friend. You're someone I can depend on. Doesn't friendship mean more to you than a casual relationship?" I asked.

Meanwhile, Gary was rolling his eyeballs, thoroughly enjoying my predicament. I shot him daggers, which only seemed to intensify his humor.

"No," she pouted, "it doesn't."

I took her into my arms, held her for a few minutes and said, "Look, you're young and pretty. You have a body that drives men wild, but all they want is your body. Be honest with yourself. You don't really want that, you told me so. Now cheer up, and let's go see our friend at the hospital."

Smiling, she asked, "Gary, you want to come with us?"

"Sure, why not."

As we walked out the door, she whispered to me, "I'll get you yet. Just one night is all I want."

"Maybe some day," I laughed.

She linked arms between us and started to hum a tune.

We arrived at the hospital as Jimmie Stamps was being handcuffed and wheeled out by Captain Williams and two other officers.

"Hey Johnny," said the captain, "My wife and I really enjoyed the show. It's all she's talked about. She wore the scarf you gave her to bed. The other guys and their wives had a great time too. You sound so much like Elvis, that it was hard to believe it was you singing and not the real Elvis."

"Thanks again. I'm glad you enjoyed the show, come see us again," and walked over to where Jimmie was sitting.

"Oh, we will, she wants to go again next week."

I glared at Jimmie. He flinched as I put my arm on the back of the wheelchair. I laughed at the reaction, and said, "If I were you, when you get out of jail, I'd leave town, no, make that the state, you may not be so lucky next time."

Jimmie looked at Captain Williams, "See, I told you it was him!"

"He's not admitting to anything. It sounds to me like he's just giving you good advice. Officers, let's get this character behind bars where he belongs," the captain said, shaking my hand.

We turned and left, Denise grabbed my hand, her body was trembling.

"What's wrong, honey?"

"Nothing, I just wanted to hit him for what he did to Sandy."

Gary looked at me, "Man, you really did do a number on him. If I was him, I'd leave the country."

The elevator took us to the third floor. The nurses had propped pillows behind Sandy so she could sit up. She looked so small and lost in that hospital bed. "Good morning sunshine," I said, as I leaned over to kiss her cheek.

"You're looking better today," Denise said trying to be cheerful, "and pretty colorful too," she added with humor. It was almost a week since Sandy's beating, and her bruises had turned from black to purple, to blue and yellow. "Where's your flower's?" Denise looked around the room.

"I had them sent to my home," Sandy answered. "Guess what?" she tried a feeble attempt at smiling. "The doctor said I'm being released today. He said since there were no internal injuries, and my bones have started to heal, and as long as there is someone around to take care of me, I can recuperate at home." "I told the doctor I'd be in good hands," and Sandy grinned at Denise, as if they shared some secret.

Gary went to get a wheelchair, and I went and arranged for Sandy to leave while the nurses and Denise helped Sandy dress. Gary brought the car to the front entrance. With a lot of groans from Sandy, we were finally able to get her in the back seat. What a sight we must have been. The three of us scrunched in front, and Sandy wrapped in bandages stretched out in the back seat.

CHAPTER 10

Denise had called the club and told everyone there that we were bringing Sandy home to my suite. It was quite an ordeal getting her out of the car without causing her much discomfort. We had arranged for a wheelchair to be at the hotel when we arrived. When I opened the door to my room, a number of employees from the club were there to greet Sandy.

"Welcome home!" they yelled.

Sandy started to cry, she was so surprised and so happy to see them. Mr. Steadman had trays of food sent over to make it a real party for her. The well wishers sat around and chatted for a while, but you could tell that Sandy was in pain and tired from all the excitement.

The guests finally left, and Gary went to check on the equipment for tonight's show. Denise took the night off from work and stayed with me to help with Sandy. Sandy had a cast on her right leg from her upper thigh to right below her knee. The bone in her thigh was cracked, but not broken. A plastic cast ran from under her breasts to right below her waist. She would need to wear it for several weeks, as it offered support for her cracked ribs and bruised spine where Jimmie had kicked and puncher her.

Sandy told us the doctor said the X-Rays showed severe bruising to the lower vertebrae in her back, but nothing was broken. The body cast would giver her support, and keep her immobilized to allow healing, but she would be as good as new as long as she took it easy. Most of her pain was from being sore and stiff where she was bruised. She was very lucky.

We put Sandy to bed, which was no easy chore. You'd think we were killing her with all the moaning and groaning she was doing.

"Denise, I'm going to lie down for awhile on the sofa, wake me between five and five thirty, or if you need help with Sandy."

At five thirty, Denise shook me and said, "Wake up, you old fart!"

I grabbed my pillow and hit her with it.

She laughed. "Sandy is awake and feeling much better. Her pain medicine is working. She's insisting on coming to the first show to see you tonight."

"Tonight! Isn't it a little soon for that?"

"Sandy said she's going if she has to wheel herself over there, and I believe she'd do it too," Denise laughed. "We've got it all worked out. Some of our friends will help me get her to the club. In the meantime, I'll clean her up and apply make-up on her face to help cover the bruises, and I can fix and style her hair. One of the other waitress's has an evening dress she's bringing over that should fit over her cast. A pair of sunglasses, and she'll be set."

I shook my head in disbelief, and went in to take my shower.

I dressed and was ready to leave. I looked at Denise and Sandy and asked if they needed anything, but they shook their heads no. Denise had already given Sandy a sponge bath and was working on her hair.

"You sure you're up to this?" I asked Sandy, as I kissed her and Denise's cheek.

"We're fine," they said, "see you later."

I walked over to the club and immediately went to my dressing room. Kristi was waiting for me.

"Hello," she smiled, and flashed those gorgeous eyes at me. "How is Sandy?" she asked with genuine concern.

I had told Kristi about Sandy when we were parked on the hill.

"She's better, and should be up and walking around in a few weeks."

"Johnny, I felt so good today when I went to work and no one recognized me. Then my boss had to spoil it by asking me for the article on you."

"Okay, Kristi, you want to do the interview now? I've still got thirty minutes before I go on stage. Fire away."

Q. Where are you from?

A. South Florida, my parents have passed on. I have no brothers or sisters.

Q. When did you get into music?

A. I've loved music all my life. I used to sing with a group back in the sixty's. We did gig's on Saturday nights, in and around the south Florida area. Pretty much for nickels and dimes, but we did it because we enjoyed it. Back then, making people happy with your music was worth more than money. That's not the way it is today."

"Thanks Johnny. I can complete my story with what you've given me. By the way, my boss is coming tonight to see you perform. I bragged so much about you that he wanted to come and see you for himself. Will I see you tonight after the show?"

"Not tonight, I'm caring for a sick friend."

"Sandy?" she asked. "I hear she's staying with you."

"That's right. Is someone making more out of it than there is?"

"No!" she said emphatically, "Just the opposite, everyone thinks you are great for helping out."

"I'm sorry for sounding so sharp with you just now, it's just that I hate it when people pass judgment about something they don't know anything about or understand." "Are you staying for the show?" I asked changing the subject.

"I wouldn't miss it for anything."

"Good! Denise is bringing Sandy to watch the first show, it would be good if you spoke to Sandy, but watch out for Denise."

"Why?" she asked innocently.

"Because, she's a little jealous of you."

"Oh!"

"Gotta get ready, baby."

"What is it you guy's say in show biz, break a leg?" she asked.

"Yeah, break a leg," and I shuddered, as I thought of Sandy.

I changed into my white costume, grabbed some scarves and met with Gary on stage behind the curtain.

"What's the girl's name that holds these for me?"

"For the tenth time, big guy, its Candy," he answered.

"Candy?"

"Yes, Candy," he said again.

"Give her these scarves for me, will you?"

"Sure, are you ready?"

"It's not going to get any better than this," I laughed.

Mr. Steadman made his announcements and Gary started the music. As I walked on stage, I decided to do several of my Karate moves instead of breaking into song right away. It worked perfect; the crowd was wild right from the start. Numerous women approached the stage, jumped up and down and screamed on the top of their lungs. It looked like several husbands were not too happy with them. I spotted Sandy sitting in her wheelchair, and she hollered her cheers along with Denise and Kristi.

I signaled Gary to start my first song of the night, "All Shook Up," and followed with "As Long As I Have You." After the first set was over, I went out into the audience to sign autographs and pose for pictures. I talked to Sandy and Denise at their table. Sandy cried and laughed at the same time.

I smiled at her excitement. "Did you enjoy the show?"

"Of course, can't you tell?"

She reached out for me to hold her. I bent down and gave her a hug. She kissed my cheek and said, "I love you, you've been so wonderful."

"Thanks baby, you're pretty remarkable yourself. Now, and this is an order, get your ass back to the hotel, and get some sleep! Denise, would you please take her back!"

"Yes, I will, we're going right now, but first this," she kissed me, long and tenderly, with the promise of more to come. "I love you too," she said, "I just can't help it, you turn me on."

I laughed, pulled away from her embrace. "Now get out of here both of you!"

Kristi had moved to another table, so I walked over to see how she enjoyed the show. "Hi, Johnny, you were absolutely terrific!" She introduced me to Mac, her supervisor, and several of her co-workers from Channel Six.

"Enjoying yourselves and the show?" I asked.

"We sure are." Mac replied. "I've heard so much about you from Kristi that I had to come and hear you for myself. We all feel you're good enough to be the real Elvis," he said eyeing me closely.

"Thank you, thank you very much, but don't use that in your report."

"You don't like to be in the lime light very much do you?" Mac asked.

"No, I don't. It was good meeting all of you. Kristi, I can finish the interview after the second show."

She looked at me, paused for a minute, and then said, "Okay, I'll be there."

"Excuse me, but there are women over there that are motioning for me to sign autographs," and I walked away.

I went to my dressing room to rest before the next set. Gary and his girlfriend were standing in the hallway talking. I stopped for a minute to compliment him on the great job he was doing with my back up music.

"Nothing to it man, you're doing all the work," he said.

"No Gary, that's not true. We're a team."

"Do you realize that each show we've done has been a complete sell out? I talked with Mr. Steadman earlier, and he said he had to turn people away or we'd be over the seating capacity.

"Great, I hope it stays that way for the next three months." I was happy to hear that.

I opened my dressing room door slowly and peeked in before I entered. Gary laughed at my hesitation to enter the room. You never know, that naked woman could come back and I wasn't taking any chances.

I took off my white jump suit, set out my red one for the next show, and stretched out on the sofa. I no sooner closed my eyes, when Kristi came in and sat next to me.

"Need a back rub?"

"That would be nice. Do I need to put my pants on?"

"No, not unless you feel uncomfortable," she replied.

I rolled over on my stomach. She got up, locked the door. Walking back to me, she lifted her skirt, straddled my butt, and massaged my back.

"Turn over!" She commanded.

I did as she said. She started to kiss me and move her hips up and down.

"Are you wearing underwear?" I questioned her.

Laughter filled the air. "No, I'm not!"

"Oh me!" I said, as she pulled off my underwear. My body responded to her touch. I closed my eyes and groaned with pleasure as our bodies joined and became one. I had to admit, this was a great way to relax.

After we had satisfied our sexual desires, I told her I wished we could be together all night. But, unfortunately, I needed to hurry and take a quick shower, as I was due back on stage for the second show.

While dressing, I said to Kristi, "You know, this is only going to make it hard on you and me, when I have to leave Dallas."

"I know, but, like you, I just want to be friends, and there's no reason why we can't express our feelings every now and then. Is there?"

"No, but that type of relationship between two people is hard to find."

"Johnny, I know you are not making love to me just for my body. You treat me with respect, and when we make love, I feel good about myself. I haven't told you this before, but I once was a Dallas Cheerleader. All the men who met me were only interested in my body, not me as a person. Once they got what they wanted, they treated me like I was dirt. I was young and foolish, and thought that being friendly was the way you got ahead. One day I finally woke up and realized after two years of a rotten marriage, my husband only wanted me as an adornment, someone pretty to show off to his friends. He even went so far as to bet my body for fun in a poker game. Can you imagine the humiliation I felt when I found out from one of his drinking buddies? That was the final straw. I filed for divorce, and hid my appearance with non-flattering clothes and hair-do's, that is until the other day when I met with you. You've made me feel good about myself again, and it made me realize that I do have a beautiful body. I can show it off and be proud, not ashamed. Let men look, I've learned to say 'no' to their type."

I kissed her cheek, "Kristi, I have to get back on stage, don't leave, okay?"

"I'll be watching you," she said. "You turn me on and make my body feel like it's on fire."

"Well don't burn up," I laughed, and left.

I gave Gary the signal to start the music, and was ready for my second show. As I started to sing my fifth song, "Anything That's Part Of You," a big, heavy-set woman hollered up to me, "I bet you wouldn't want any part of this old fat body!"

I stopped the show. "Honey, bring it right over here, let's see just how much I can hold." Suddenly, the room that only moments ago was filled with a screaming crowd, was now deathly still. All eyes focused on the woman who approached the stage. I turned to Gary and said, "Loving You!"

I asked a gentleman at the front table to let this woman borrow his chair for a moment. He obliged, and a security man helped seat her next to the stage. She sat down and smiled.

As I looked at her, something in her face reminded me of my mother. "I'm going to sing this one just for you," and my voice filled with emotion.

As I started singing the lyrics, "*I will spend my whole life though, loving you, just loving you. Winter, summer, spring time too, loving you, just loving you,*" she stood up, and I knelt down and placed a scarf around her neck and kissed her. I continued singing when her husband came and stood by her side.

I finished singing, and said, "See, you are loved by the one that counts the most." Everyone stood and clapped as the couple returned to their table.

"Let's burn some love, Gary," I said. The music blared to "Burning Love," and the crowd resumed their screaming. In fact, security had to block the stage to hold the women back.

I finished my show, did a couple of encores, and went straight to my dressing room. Kristi came back with tears in her eyes. "See how you are, you care about people just like the real Elvis did. You love the excitement on stage, and you care how the audience feels. I understand and like our relationship. I'll love and respect you, and will be there for you when you need me. Your friendship means a great deal to me, and don't worry, when you leave Dallas, a part of you will remain in my heart. I love you, Johnny, don't ever change. And by the way, Sandy and Denise desire you too," she laughed. "They want and need your affection and understanding. It's not you physically they hunger for; it's your love and kindness that you so willingly give. When a woman cares that much about someone, it's only natural to have some physical attraction. Let them know that friendship is all you're looking for, not a permanent or sexual relationship."

"Maybe you're right," I agreed, and walked her to her car and kissed her good night. "You really are quite an extraordinary woman."

I entered my hotel room and saw that Denise had fallen asleep on the sofa. I gently picked her up and carried her to my bedroom and put her on my side of the bed. I covered her with the sheet and noticed that Sandy was uncovered. As I walked around the bed, the light from the alarm clock on the night stand was shining on Sandy's naked body. I tried not to look at her breasts or below the cast as I covered her with the sheet. Then I noticed that she had placed a towel across her bottom.

I smiled and said with a low voice, "Thank you Lord!"

I remembered when I was young. I would not have let that bother me. After I became famous and women threw themselves at me, I wouldn't refuse them. That was the past. I want to change my life. It's hard, when you know someone is there for the taking. I don't want to slip back into my old ways. I never want to hurt another woman. I want to settle down with a woman I can share the remainder of my life with. My thoughts then turned to Karen. I think she is attractive, and she's my age, but I've got to settle my personal life before I can promise her more than I can give her now. I thought. I walked over to the sofa, stretched out, and fell asleep.

The next morning I awoke and realized, it's Sunday, stay in, and sleep all day. Then I remembered, Denise and Sandy were here and decided to get up and make coffee.

Denise came out of the bedroom, "I fell asleep on the sofa. How did I end up in your bed?"

"I carried you."

"Oh really. Why didn't you undress me?" She teased.

"You know why, so don't even go there."

"I see you covered Sandy up with a towel," she commented.

"No, she covered herself, being the nice girl that she is," I teased back.

"And I'm not?"

"Do we have to discuss this so early in the morning?" I asked, evading her question.

"No, I was just trying to get you going, you know I was only teasing," she laughed. "Any way, Johnny, I'm the one who covered Sandy with the towel. I knew you'd need to use the bathroom, and you wouldn't go in if her bottom was uncovered."

"In that case, I'm sorry, come here," I said, as I put my arms around her, "you really are a thoughtful person, Denise."

"Just keep holding me, and I'll let you know in an hour or so, okay," she grinned mischievously.

"I need a shower; do you think you could check and see if Sandy is covered?"

"Sure, I'll check now, and then I need to go home and clean up too."

"Oh, have I thanked you for staying with Sandy last night? I asked.

"Hey, she's my friend too, you know."

Denise opened the bedroom door, and peeked in. "The coast is clear," and headed for the front door.

"Are you coming back later?"

"I'm going to visit my granny today; I'll stop by after that."

"Good, I'd like for all of us to have dinner together. I'll see if Gary wants to join us," I added as she quietly shut the door.

I turned on the TV and had just sat down to drink my coffee, when Sandy called out, "Denise, bring me a cup of coffee, please!"

I got up, poured Sandy a cup and brought it in to her. "Good morning Sandy, Denise left, she's going to visit her grandmother this afternoon."

"So you're stuck with me today?"

"Yup, Louise, my maid, fell and broke her hip, and since Denise left, it's me and you, baby. But don't worry; I've got nothing to do but sleep!" I teased her.

"Who's going to help me with my bed pan?"

"Bed pan?" I stopped dead in my tracks.

"Yes, Johnny, bed pan, you do know what that is don't you?" she teased.

"Right, I'm afraid I do," I said, realizing I hadn't thought about that end of things. "Let me know when you have to go okay?"

"Johnny, I need to go now!"

"Right now?"

"Yes, the pan's under the bed, and if you don't hurry, I'm going to wet your bed."

"How are we going to do this?"

"Just put your right arm under my waist, and your left hand under my leg with the cast. When you lift me up, I'll slide the pan underneath me. Ready, Johnny?"

"Well, uh, well, I ah," I stuttered, not quite sure of what to do.

"Maybe you can close your eyes," she suggested, "but I don't know why, it's not like you haven't seen a naked woman before."

I finally got her situated on the bed pan. She yelled for me when she finished. She laughed as I took and emptied the bed pan.

"It's not funny, honey."

"I know, but you are!"

When I came back, she was lying there uncovered.

"Do me a favor?" she asked.

"Sure baby, what?"

"Will you roll me on my side? I'm tired of lying on my back."

I helped her roll over and covered her up. "Are you comfortable?"

"That feels better, thank you. Johnny, do you think I'm ugly or something?"

"No Sandy, why would you ask such a crazy question?"

"Well, here I am, naked, and you don't even want to look at me."

"Sandy, it's not that I don't want to look, because if I did, it would make it harder for me to be a gentleman, besides you're in no shape to do anything."

"I know it's hard on you, but I'd love it if you found me desirable. When I'm better, I'd love for us to make love one day, but I'm not going to ask because I know you don't want too," she said. It would be easier for you if I had someone else to help me, but all my family lives in south Texas. Besides, you have so much going on, I feel like I'm going to be a burden to you."

"Sandy, I feel I am partially responsible for what happened to you. I told you I'd take care of you until you're better, and I'm going to do just that. Let me tell you something. Maybe you'll understand me better when you hear what I'm about to say. Years ago, I knew a man who couldn't keep his hands off beautiful women. He was rich and famous. Women threw themselves at him and he used them for sex and good times. All except one, he loved her. They married and later had a little girl. But women were a dime a dozen. They were there for the taking, and he took, until he lost his wife and child. After she left, he realized what he'd lost, but his work kept him away, and the women, well, the women were always around. He definitely was in the wrong. So, what I'm trying to say is, I don't want to be like that. I don't want to hurt anyone, and I certainly don't want to hurt you. These women deserved better, and so did his wife and child."

"Johnny, was that someone you?"

"Yes, it was me," I was surprised at her awareness. "You see, if we make love once, then we'd do it again, and then you'd expect more of me than I'd be willing to give, it could destroy our friendship."

"Johnny, I never want to lose our friendship or trust, believe me. If we made love everyday, I would never hold it against you or even blame you for anything. I know you are much older than me, which is another reason our relationship would not work. Denise and I talked about this. We both only want you because you're such a caring person. You give so much of yourself. And when you are on stage, it's like, wow, we have to have you no matter what. So, don't turn away from us. We are your friends, and I will forever be in your debt for helping me. Denise and I will always be there for you if you need us for anything. So relax, let us love you 'our way', okay?"

I laughed at her philosophy. "I'll try! The problem with this whole situation is you and Denise are doing to me what you say men have done to you," I said, and walked into the living room.

I could see myself slipping back into my past, the last thing I needed to do. It wasn't good for me to be around so much temptation, although I should have expected this when I first started singing at the club.

Sandy called for me again and asked if I was hungry. I told her I was, and that I'd call room service and have breakfast sent up to us. I ordered eggs, biscuits, bacon and fries.

Breakfast arrived. I propped Sandy into a sitting position, and put a tray across her legs so we could have our breakfast together. Seeing her naked, didn't seem to be a problem for me right now.

While we ate, we talked about what she was going to do when she got well. When we finished our breakfast, Sandy asked, "Johnny, would you mind carrying me into the living room, I'm tired of lying in bed.

"Sure, be happy too!"

"First, I'll need a bath. Will you help me wash?"

"Yes, I believe I can handle that."

After our talk, I think we became closer friends. I understood her desires as a woman, and she understood my fears as a man. I really think I may have over reacted because of my past, my old life style. It's only natural that I would desire beautiful women, especially if they are naked. After all, I am a man. I think the way I handle a situation, will make the difference. Whatever happens, happens. I'm going to accept it, and direct my life toward my real desires, a woman I can spend my life with or so I thought.

Sandy grew impatient and asked, "Well, are you going to move me?"

"Just wait a minute, okay? I'm going to prepare a spot for you on the sofa so you'll be comfortable.

"Hurry up, pokey," she giggled.

I fixed her a spot and went back to the bedroom to get her. I put my left arm under her bare butt, and my right arm behind her back for support. She wrapped her arms around my neck and I gently carried her to the sofa.

"Comfy," I asked, as I fluffed the pillows for her.

"Yep, but you forgot one thing."

"What's that?"

"My bath, silly."

"Oh, yeah. Sorry, I'll get your stuff, and together we'll give you a bath.

I brought towels, a pan filled with hot water, her scented soap and wash cloths. "How do you want to do this?"

"I can do my upper half, but you'll have to do my lower half because of this body cast."

She finished scrubbing her face and arms, as well as her breasts. I did her shoulders and back, up to her cast. I gently washed the exposed part of the leg that was encased in the cast. Sandy grinned all the while. I washed her other leg. I started at her feet, and slowly worked my way to her thigh. My desires were aroused which only seemed to enhance Sandy's humor, and add to my discomfort. Okay, little girl, I thought. We'll see who teases who, and who has the last laugh.

I took the washcloth and began to rub between her legs, with slow, sensual strokes. Her mouth parted and she closed her eyes as her hips began to move to the rhythm of my rubbing.

"What's the matter, Sandy, not so funny any more?" I teased, and stopped.

"Johnny, don't stop now."

"Oh yes, I'm finished and you no longer smell," I laughed and started to clean up the mess.

"You're cruel," she whined.

"Yes, I am, but you asked for it."

"I'll get you back."

I covered her up and sat in the lounge chair to watch television. Hell, I said to my self that was more fun than I thought it would be, and laughed quietly. It was cruel to get her all excited and then stop, but I believe it did her more good than harm. I decided to take a shower.

When I finished dressing, I checked on Sandy. She had dozed off. I decided to call Gary to see what his plans were until Wednesday's show. He told me he was going to Memphis to prepare for the Christmas Special at Graceland. I told him I thought that would be great and wished I could go with him, but I had made a commitment, and I was going to stick to it no matter what.

Gary volunteered to stay and take care of Sandy, if I really wanted to go to Memphis that bad. I laughed and told him to drive careful, and we'd talk when he got back.

I returned to Sandy and apologized for my behavior that morning. She said she deserved it for laughing at my discomfort. "I could see your p.j.'s rising," she flashed her pixie smile at me, trying her best not to keep laughing.

"Oh really," I joked back, "maybe I should have waited until Denise comes in tomorrow, and let your bath wait until then."

"No, I wanted you to give me my bath regardless of how you feel, and I did enjoy my bath. For the first time, in a long time I enjoyed a man's hands on me. It was fun, and I wasn't afraid."

I looked at her, smiled and said, "No one is ever going to hut you again, you believe me don't you?"

"Yes, I do," as a tear slowly slid down her cheek.

We watched TV and dozed on and off throughout the day. Denise came by after supper.

"Feeling better?" she asked Sandy, when she saw her lying on the sofa.

"Yes," much better, thanks."

"How was your day?" I asked Denise.

"Great!" "Granny is getting up there in years, but she wants to come and see one of your shows. I'm bringing her Wednesday night. I bet you two had an interesting day," Denise grinned.

"Sandy winked at her, "Uh huh, very interesting, because I got a bath from you know who."

"Oh really," Denise's eyebrows raised slightly in question.

I spoke up, "Nothing happened, Denise, so get your mind out of the gutter."

"That's right, it didn't, but it was still fun," Sandy teased.

"I'll bet," Denise glared at me.

"Look, I'm going down to the bar, you two find something else to talk about while I'm gone!"

I hadn't had a drink of liquor in fifteen years, but tonight, I ordered a Crown and Coke in the hotel lounge.

John, the bartender looked at me and asked, "Problems have we?"

"No, I just feel like having a good drink."

"In that case, one Crown and Coke coming up!"

As John set my drink down in front of me, he said, "We've heard what you're doing for Sandy. That's real friendship. We also heard that you made sure Jimmie wouldn't be coming around anymore."

"For some reason people were afraid of him and I don't know why," I commented, and then added, "he's afraid of men, he can only beat up women."

"Well, the story is he has a couple of guys that 'take care of' anyone who messes with him, so I'd keep my eyes open if I were you. Just a little friendly bartender advice."

It was quiet for a Sunday night, so John and I talked about my shows and how I was doing at the club. I was about to leave, when two bikers came in and ordered a drink. One of them asked the bartender if he had seen Jimmie Stamps.

John, looked at me and then back at the bikers, and said, "No, Jimmie's in jail for beating up his girlfriend."

"Oh yeah, what happened?" the other inquired.

"It seems, Jimmie put Sandy in the hospital, and then someone put Jimmie in the hospital, only he's in a lot worse shape than she is."

"No way! Who could beat him that bad? Had to be more than one, cause Jimmie was damn tough."

I spoke up and said, "Excuse me, but Jimmie was a pussy!"

"Who are you?" asked the larger of the two.

"The name is Johnny Raye."

"Oh, you're the Elvis Impersonator everyone in town's been talking about."

"Guess so!"

They came closer to where I was sitting. "Why do you say Jimmie was a pussy? He was our friend."

"Well!" I spoke slowly and deliberately. "Any man that has to beat up a woman to prove he's a man, isn't much of a man in my book."

"Is that so!" The smaller of the two replied, "I've seen him beat up two men at the same time, now that's one tough son of a bitch."

They had already downed one beer and were working on the second. "So," said the other biker, "then it must have been a big man, or two, cause one man couldn't have done it by himself."

"Really," I said dryly, "one man did!"

"Who, and how do you know that?" asked the other biker.

"Me," I said. "Jimmie was like a baby, crying and begging from the pain, and I hate people who think their tough, then cry and whimper when things get tough. What do you think of that?" I stood up and faced them.

"You say Jimmie was whining and crying like a baby?"

"Yeah, big time!" I replied.

They looked at each other and asked the bartender what they owed for their beers.

"It would be a good idea, for all involved, if you left this thing with Jimmie die," I said.

"Jimmie's in that bad of shape?"

"Uh, huh, and I'd hate to see anyone else hurt that bad."

"Jimmie wasn't that good of a friend," said one of the bikers.

"Then I guess I won't be seeing you two again, right?"

"Right man, we're outta here!" and they left.

John and I looked at each other and laughed. John poured me another drink, compliments of the house, which by then I needed another.

"For a minute I thought you were going to have to take care of those two," said John.

"I didn't like their manners," I said dryly, and we both laughed.

I finished my drink, went back to my suite, and found Denise and Sandy talking and laughing.

"Where have you been? Sandy and I thought you got lost."

"Having a drink," I answered.

"What, a coke?" Sandy laughed, and then said, "you've got coke in the refrigerator."

"No, I had a Crown and Coke."

"Wow, this morning must have been pretty hard on you," Sandy started to giggle. "A little early for a drink, isn't it?"

"No, it isn't, and in answer to your other statement, I feel just fine about this morning, nothing to it."

"Sure," said Denise, laughing along with Sandy.

"I'm sorry, I told about our bath this morning." Sandy tried to sound contrite but failed miserably.

"I figured you would!"

"Look, let's forget this morning, let's go for a ride, it's a beautiful evening."

Denise and I managed to get Sandy dressed, and into the car. We rode around for a while, and spotted a carnival that had come to town. Denise and I wheeled Sandy around the carnival grounds. We played games, and I managed to win a big stuffed dog for Sandy and a large giraffe for Denise. I wanted to go on some of the rides, so Denise handed Sandy her purse and we went on the tilt-a-whirl. We rode four times until Denise said she'd had enough or she'd get sick. We ate cotton candy, and stuffed ourselves with sausage dogs piled high with fried onions and green peppers. Sandy was having a ball and so were we. I felt young again. In some ways I think Denise and Sandy were good for me. It was so much fun for me to not have to buy a night of fun.

It was getting late, and the park started closing their rides. We grabbed the stuffed animals, and were on our way back to the car, when several people recognized me from the club.

"Johnny?" A lady asked shyly. "I was at your show the other night, and I didn't get a chance to have my picture taken with you. Would you mind doing it now?"

"No problem, be glad too." Before I realized it, a half an hour had passed. I must have signed at least twenty autographs. Denise and Sandy were getting a kick out of watching me. It felt so good to be around people and be able to have fun without getting mauled by a group of fans.

We stopped at a Chinese restaurant on the way home. We weren't that hungry after having pigged out at the carnival, but egg rolls sounded good. While there, Denise saw some of her friends. They came over and told us they were going dancing at a small club not too far from the restaurant, and asked if we'd like to join them. Denise and I wanted to go. We looked at Sandy.

"Don't even think of bringing me home, I don't ever want this night to end," she said, her eyes twinkled like jewels from all the excitement and fun she was having.

We finished our egg rolls, and followed Denise's friends to the dance club called the 'Two Step'. As I parked the car, a couple of guys came over to admire the Cadillac. I explained where I had purchased the car. They said that you don't see many of these any more, and thought she was a real beauty. I thanked them as I wheeled Sandy into the club.

The club had hired a country band for the night. The music was loud, but they were good. We barely sat down when Denise grabbed one of her friends and hit the dance floor. One of the girl's at our table whispered to Sandy and asked if this was the Elvis Impersonator that was playing at Steadman's Supper Club.

Sandy proudly told her I was their date for the night. She wanted me to sing them a song, but I told them if they didn't mind I'd rather sit and listen for a change. She nodded and understood.

We had been there about an hour, and were enjoying the band when Denise rejoined us. "How about dancing with me?"

Before I even had time to respond, she grabbed my hand and pulled me unto the dance floor. I was grateful for a slow tempo. Denise curled into my arms.

When the song ended, one of the band members spotted me. He was the band's lead singer.

"Ladies and gentlemen," he announced, "we have a special guest with us tonight, Johnny Raye!" "Let's see if we can get him to come up and sing for us? Johnny. How about it?"

I asked if they could play "Can't Help Falling In Love."

The lead singer picked up his guitar and said, "Hit it guys." They started to play, and as I sang, everyone kept dancing. We finished that number when someone requested, "Suspicious Minds?" The band nodded and started playing. The crowd moved closer to the stage. They didn't scream, but they enjoyed the music. For me that was a pleasant change. I finished, and jumped from the stage, and went back to the table enjoying the applause.

"Thanks Johnny," said the lead singer, and told the audience they could see me perform at Steadman's on Wednesday, Friday, and Saturday nights.

"Johnny that was so good, I could listen to you all night," Sandy smiled.

"I hope not," I said, "I'm tired and about ready to go."

"Actually, I am too," she agreed. "I just didn't want to spoil your fun," Sandy said yawning.

"In that case, I'll go look for Denise." The last I'd seen of her, she was dancing. I walked around and found her sitting at a table with a couple of guys.

"Ready to go?" I tapped Denise on the shoulder.

"Yes, I'll be there in a few minutes."

One of the men at the table said, "You can't go, we just bought you a drink."

"So," she said saucily, tossing her hair over her shoulder, "I didn't tell you to!"

"Well then you can just repay us," one of them said, drunkenly.

Seeing where this was headed, I took money from my wallet.

"Here, take this," and threw a twenty on the table.

"No, we don't want money, we want her.

"You can just kiss my ass, buddy!" Denise said, as she stood up and glared at him.

"We plan on doing just that," he smarted back.

"Denise go back to the table with Sandy, I'll take care of this."

The guy on the left stood up, and said, "Look old man, we've already told you, she isn't going anywhere until she drop's those drawers, and gives us what we paid for."

I looked at Denise again, "Did you hear what I said?"

She nodded yes.

"Then I suggest you get out of here and now. Take Sandy and wait for me by the car?"

I looked back at the two men. "I bet the likes of you two knows Jimmie Stamps!"

"That's right, what about it?" one of them asked.

"Jimmie liked abusing women as if he owned them; I just figured you had to be friends, seeing how you think alike."

"That's right, that's what women are for, to lay on their back and give men pleasure," he laughed.

"Your friend Jimmie thought the same thing, but he doesn't think that way any more."

"Oh yeah! How do you know what Jimmie thinks?"

"Believe me, I know, he's now serving time. I guess you might say we had a 'heart to heart' talk before he was arrested. Jimmie couldn't see reason then, but while he was in the hospital, he said he'd change his ways."

One of the guys spoke up, "Look, we don't want any trouble, I saw Jimmie in the hospital too, and he looked like he was beat half to death. Said something about Elvis did it."

"That's right, so what do you say you take this twenty, buy yourself a couple more drinks, and forget the whole thing."

Taking the twenty, they both sat down and sipped their drinks. I left and met Sandy and Denise at the car. By now I was very tired. It had been a long day. I just wanted to go home and forget both incidents. Things sure had changed, and I wasn't sure it was for the better. I don't envy anyone growing up with the attitudes I had encountered tonight.

When we got back to my room, Denise said she was going home. She thanked me for protecting her.

"Johnny, I shouldn't have stopped at their table and sat with them."

"No, you shouldn't have, but you didn't know they were such jerks, now go home."

"Anyway, thank you again," and she kissed my cheek. "See you tomorrow," she said, as she closed the door.

I asked Sandy if she wanted a cup of coffee, but she said that she was too tired, and she just wanted to go to bed. I lifted her from the chair, and laid her on the bed. I helped her take off her clothes, managed the bed pan without any incidence, and tucked her in.

"Thank you for one of the most memorable days of my life."

"Your welcome and good night," I answered, kissing her on the forehead.

Yawning, she asked, "Do you want to sleep in bed with me?"

"No, I'm heading to the sofa. I'll see you in the morning."

Sandy had already snuggled into the pillows, and was asleep before I shut off the light. I lay on the sofa, and drifted into a fitful sleep.

Denise came in early, all cheery and smiley.

"I came to help Sandy with her bath and the bed pan. After last night, I figure I owe you one, besides, you look like you need a reprieve."

I was glad to get a break from the bath, and especially the bed pan.

"As soon as you're done with Sandy, I'll take my shower."

Denise finished Sandy's bath, and I carried her to the sofa. When I had picked her up, she had allowed her bathrobe to slip open and expose her bare breasts. I quickly covered her as Denise propped her pillows. Sandy was still tired from yesterday, and was soon dozing.

I went into the bathroom undressed, and started my shower, the hot water felt good, when Denise hollered, "Johnny, I need to use the bathroom, I'll only be a minute."

I rinsed the shampoo from my hair and thought Denise was probably gone when the shower door opened, and there stood Denise butt naked. She stepped in and shut the shower door.

"Johnny, don't turn me away!" She wrapped her arms around me and kissed me longingly, excitement exploded from her body. I thought about pushing her away, and remembered what Kristi had said about Sandy and Denise. At first I was angered by the intrusion of my privacy, but that soon dwindled as my body responded to Denise's hands working magic on me.

We played for a while, soaping each other's bodies, and then she began to play in earnest. She started kissing me all over, never letting up with her butterfly kisses. Her touch was so thorough, but so light, it left you wanting more. There wasn't enough room in the shower for us to be comfortable, so grabbing towels and hastily drying off, we went to the bed. We made love for an hour, each exploring the other.

When we finished, she asked, "Johnny, was that worth waiting for?"

"Not bad!" I grinned at her.

"I know it wasn't fair to trap you," but I wanted to find out if those moves you do on stage were as good in bed." "I won't do it again, but I was right, you're even better than your moves," the seriousness was gone from her voice, and replaced with a teasing tone.

"You could have waited until Sandy moved out. You know she's probably awake by now and is going to ask why you were in here so long."

"Oh, she knows, we planned this together," she giggled.

"I should have known the two of you were up to something. Now, get out of here so I can finish dressing."

I had time to think while I dressed, and decided it would be best for all if I took a couple of days to visit with Chance and David Lee. I packed my bag, and walked into the living room area where Denise and Sandy were smiling from ear to ear.

"Look, I need to talk to both of you, and now is a good time."

"Look, our friendship means a lot to me, and I'd like for it to remain just that, friendship. Making love wasn't what I had in mind. I know that the two of you have been hinting to do so since the night you first saw me perform at the club."

"I've watched how both of you get involved with someone that looks exciting. Here I am with two beautiful women, and until earlier, have been able to remain cool about it. Sandy, it's not easy looking at your nakedness every day, touching your private parts while I bathe you. I want to make love to you so much that I can hardly stand it, but I won't. I respect you enough as a friend to be able to look at you, say yeah it looks good, and then go about my business. I know that if we made love it would destroy our friendship."

"Denise, I enjoyed making love with you this morning. It fulfilled my desires for you, and gave me relief even though I hunger for more. You look good enough to make love to everyday, but when the 'new' wear's off, then it becomes just what it is, sex. A good friendship can last forever. When you 'love' someone a great deal, making love to that person whether it's everyday, once a week, or even once a month, the feeling is always strong and filled with joy."

"What I'm trying to say is our friendship means a lot to me. What Denise and I shared this morning was strictly sex, nothing more. I only hope we can get past it and still remain friends."

"Johnny, I'm so sorry for trapping you," Denise apologized again. "I don't regret it," she said seriously. "Our friendship hasn't changed, so please don't be mad at me," she pleaded in earnest.

"I'm not mad." I answered. "I'm just afraid this could get out of hand."

"Look Johnny, Denise and I know that when you leave here, you may never come back. This is hard to explain, but it's your sweetness we desire. You, yourself. Granted you turn us on the way you sing and move on stage, but it's not your body we desire. Denise and I know the real you, and that's the person that turns us on, and the one we want to make love to." "Does any of this make any sense?" Sandy asked.

"Yes, I guess it does. But, when I leave Dallas, I'd like to come back some day knowing I have three beautiful friends here."

"Three?" Denise asked, and looked at Sandy quizzically.

"Yes, you two, and Kristi."

"Oh, I forgot about Kristi," Denise admitted.

"Look, I've decided to go to Birmingham, and see some friends. Besides, I need to get away."

"Go Johnny, we'll be fine," Denise said, and Sandy nodded in agreement.

I called David and Chance, and told them I was driving up for a couple of days. I said good-bye to the girls and left, but before I left Dallas, I went to the club and met with Mr. Steadman. I told him about my idea of having three Elvis's the last Saturday night of my scheduled tour and that he could advertise "Three Elvis's," and that it would go over big.

"We have a complete sell out every night you're here, why do I need more Elvis's?"

"What if I promise it would be a show everyone would remember and besides, no one in Dallas has ever done this before," I responded.

"Just how much extra will this cost me?"

"I tell you what, how about dinner for four, and two hotel rooms, and a thousand dollars each per show for the other two Elvis's. We'll do two shows. Now, that's pretty cheap."

"Cheap," he said, "I think I'm losing money now. This time of the year business is slow, but you do make up for it on Wednesday, Friday, and Saturday nights."

"Mr. Steadman, three nights a week you turn better than twenty thousand dollars."

"Has Denise been talking to you again?"

"No. It's not hard to figure out from what you charge, and what your seating capacity is. Mr. Steadman, that's a lot of money."

He tapped his finger together in thought. "Tell you what, Johnny, I'll agree to this, but we better turn more profit than usual. If we don't, I'll only pay five hundred dollars toward the deal, now that's fair, isn't it?"

Now it was my turn to think for a moment. "Only five hundred, huh, that's only if we don't have a complete sell out, and people standing in line to get in to see the show?" I smiled, and said, "Mr. Steadman, you've got a deal," and I shook his hand.

"You know Johnny, you're quite the salesman." "Thank you sir, you won't regret it."

CHAPTER 11

It was after midnight when I arrived at David and Tara's. David had left early from work. When I drove up, he was already home. We shook hands and hugged. It felt good to be there, in quiet surroundings, compared to the turmoil I'd been through in Dallas. David told me Tara was in bed as she had to be at work early the next morning.

We sat and talked for awhile, and then we decided to head over to see Chance, as Chance's hours at his bar were from ten o'clock to five o'clock in the morning. His club stayed open to accommodate the workers who worked the late shifts. It gave employees a place to unwind and relax since the other clubs were closed by then.

Chance was cutting up with the audience when we walked in. He spotted us right away. He grabbed his microphone and announced, "My dad and brother just walked in."

David was quick to respond, "I'm the brother, the old man behind me is the dad," and everyone laughed at our humor.

"But," I added to their comments, "I taught them everything they know, which, come to think of it, isn't much!"

One girl in the crowd yelled, "Now we know why he's crazy."

"No," I said, "David Lee is the one that's crazy. Chance just doesn't know any better." Chance jumped from the stage, and gave me a big ole bear hug as he welcomed me home.

"Chance, sing a duet with Crazy Lee," someone suggested.

"Okay, but 'my dad' can sing too!" Chance answered, as he tossed his long black hair, his boyish grin spread from ear to ear.

"Not tonight Chance. I'm just going to listen."

Lee and Chance sang, "Don't Be Cruel" and "Jail House Rock." They were really hamming it up and the crowd was thrilled. They yelled for more, but Chance told them later. He called up his next singer, a tall, long legged blonde with a husky voice. You could tell this wasn't her first time singing Karaoke. She was relaxed and enjoyed what she was doing.

Chance took a break and joined us, "Well 'old man', you enjoying yourself?"

"I sure am. It feels good being on the outside looking in for a change."

"How's Dallas?"

"Dallas is great, but you and David will be able to find out for yourselves in about two weeks."

"What? What have you cooked up now?" Chance asked, moving forward on his seat so as not to miss a word.

"Listen to this," David said. "Do you want to tell him?" Lee asked me, deliberately holding Chance in suspense.

"Well somebody tell me something, you've got my curiosity running again." Chance said.

"Well," said Lee, "Johnny has arranged for us to do a show at Steadman's Supper Club with him in two weeks. And, get this! It pays a thousand dollars for the night, plus hotel rooms, plus dinner for four. We can take the wives with us and it won't cost us anything extra," David said excitedly.

"Yeah, buddy it will!" Chance laughed. "If Michele and Tara find a shopping mall, it'll cost us plenty. Wow, this is great, Johnny." "Two weeks, huh?" he grinned. "Hey, don't you have your Christmas Special in Memphis then?"

"Yes, but it's the following week-end. I want to share some of the glory with you two. You've helped me, now it's my turn to repay the favor by helping you."

"You don't owe us anything, Johnny," Lee replied. "Your friendship is enough," he added, as Chance nodded in agreement.

"I'm going to try and arrange to have you two sing a couple of songs with me at Graceland for the Christmas Special."

"Johnny, why are you doing this?" Chance asked, and then said, "Man, that cuts down on your money."

"The sooner you find out it's not the money, it's the music, and pleasing your crowd with your singing that's important, it's all you need. The money will come, but first, have fun and enjoy your life!"

Chance called another singer to come up and then rejoined us. I continued, "Look guys, I want to share with you what I've experienced in my life, and show the two of you that you have more now than I ever had."

"What do you mean?" David asked, looking puzzled by my statement.

"You both have steady jobs, nice homes, a family to come home to and spend the rest of your life with. Me, I have 'a job', and friends, but that's it, no place I can really call home, and no one to share it with if I did. Beautiful women surround me, and yet none of them are what I need, only what I desire for a night. To tell you the truth, I'd trade places with you any day," I finally finished.

"What are you really trying to tell us?" asked Chance.

"It's like this, if you become famous or rich, your life will change drastically. Unless you control it, like now, for instance, I'm helping you to get ahead with your careers as Elvis Impersonators. The main key to success is not to forget what you have when fame hits. When you help perform with me in Dallas, and you share the limelight with me at Graceland for the Christmas Special, women are going to chase after you. Temptation will be strong, and you're both young. It's hard to fight it. Nothing is more important in life than the people you love. To lose them, is to lose everything. I've been there, done it. So, promise me that you won't let this break up your marriages."

David and Chance looked at each other, and then stared at me. "You're serious aren't you?" David asked.

"Yes, I am, and after Dallas, and the Christmas Special in Memphis, I've decided to perform in Vegas at one of the casinos. I'm going to see about getting you to perform there also, that's if you're interested. It's now the big time. You have lots to think about, just let me know."

It was getting late, actually it was early morning. We decided to leave. I told Chance we'd get together for dinner as I wanted to talk with their wives about this.

"We can talk to them," he said.

"Yes, you can and they'll tell you just what you want to hear. If I talk to them, they'll tell me the truth."

"You're right!" he answered.

"Tomorrow guys, I'm very tired," and stood to leave.

"Wait, where you going?" someone hollered out as we headed for the door. "Yeah, we want to hear the 'old man' sing. Yeah, the teacher."

I looked at Lee and Chance, "All right, just one."

"Chance, we'll probably need help to get him out the door, call security," Lee laughed.

I chose to sing, "Treat Me Nice." At first, I just stood there. Then, like always, my leg started shaking and my body found its own moves. My love for music had not dwindled. If anything, it was stronger. The crowd responded, and women began to gather at the foot of the stage. I was about half way through the song when I stopped and headed for the door.

"Hey, don't stop, don't leave," the crowd yelled.

"This will work," Lee said as we hurried out the door. The women were mad, but at least they didn't get out of hand.

We jumped in my car and on the way home Lee made the comment that he and Chance would have to learn more Elvis moves. I told him practice makes perfect, and from what I had seen tonight, they had good moves of their own.

"Do you really think you can get us a job in a night club?"

"I'm going to try. If you set yourself up to perform in three or four clubs two months a year at each one, you'll make money and still have time between performances to spend quality time with your families. Right now, you're performing in your home town. People know the both of you, they see you all the time, therefore, they don't get as excited seeing you perform. But, when a crowd sees you for the first time, new moves, new voice, the crowd's will love you. I'll prove it to you when you come to Dallas."

It was daylight when I pulled into the driveway. Chance's hours at the club reminded me of when I slept during the day and stayed up all night. I don't know how I used to do it. Now, I can barely stay up past midnight. I guess with age, there are a lot of things that change.

Tara was waiting for us when we walked in the kitchen. "Do you guys know what time it is?" she asked, trying to suppress a smile.

"Yes, we do, and I'm sorry for being gone so long, but the night got away from us." David answered apologetically.

I looked at Tara. "It's my fault, Tara."

"Yes, it is," and then she hugged my neck, and laughed. "How have you been, Johnny?"

"Fine, and you?"

"Great, but you two look like you're hungry, how about if I fix breakfast. You two look like you could eat a horse. Within minutes we were sitting around the kitchen table eating, fried eggs, bacon, grits and home made biscuits.

Tara left for 'The Bar' to check on last nights receipts, and to open up for the cleaning crew. She promised she'd be back early. In the meantime, David and I went to our bedrooms in desperate need of sleep.

I awoke four or five hours later. Lee was still asleep so I showered and went downstairs. Tara was already home and watching her favorite soap opera.

"Hey baby, I'd like to take you and Michele to dinner tonight, someplace special with a nice atmosphere, and good food."

She looked at me and asked, "Okay, Johnny, where are you taking the guys to now?"

Laughing at her wisdom, I responded, "Well, this time, you and Michele get to go."

"Where?"

"I'll tell you tonight!"

"But what about our bar?"

"Diane can handle it while you're gone. It won't be for a couple more weeks yet. That will give you time to prepare. I want to talk to the two of you about something else, anyway."

"What?" she asked.

"Tonight," I said.

David finally woke up, and joined us in the living room. Tara told him his plans for the remainder of the day were, lawn needed mowing, and trimming, garbage needed to be hauled to the bar's dumpster, and the car needed to be washed and waxed, plus vacuumed out thoroughly.

David looked at me, "You still think I've got it made!"

"Well, I may have over stated the matter a little." I laughed.

"Or a lot!" he grimaced. '

"David, I'll mow the lawn, but I don't care to weed eat, you can do that." I found the mower out in the shed, and had just started to mow when Tara came out. Putting her hands on her hips she instructed, "Don't you mow over my flowers, and watch out for my bushes too!"

"Yes ma'am, I'll be careful," I answered her, trying hard not to laugh. I could see David out of the corner of my eye. He was laughing his ass off. "Shut up or I'll leave it all for you to do," I hollered over the noise of the mower's engine.

"Oh, you asked for it, big mouth, now you're getting a taste of the good life."

He was right. By the time I'd finished the front yard, I was ready to hang it up for the day. Unfortunately, the back yard was larger than the front, and it was hot, and we were working up quite a sweat.

"How about a break?" I asked.

"Yeah, good idea, let's sit on the porch where it's shady.

Tara brought us two tall glasses of sweet tea.

"This sure hits the spot, Miss Tara," I told her.

Pointing her finger, and trying to remain serious, she said, "Good, cause you missed a spot over there," and went back inside.

Lee looked at me and patted my shoulder, "Guess you're part of the family now!"

Sipping our tea, I asked Lee, "Did you and Chance get the money I sent from Dallas?"

"We sure did, but you didn't have to send the extra hundred."

"That was for interest, besides, you never know when I may need to borrow money again. Not to change the subject, but have you seen Karen?" I asked, trying to sound nonchalant.

Lee grinned, "She's been coming in regularly on Monday nights."

"That means she'll be there tonight?"

"Yes, she should be," he kept grinning, "you really like her don't you?"

"Let's just say there's something about her that keeps me interested."

Tara looked out the screen door, "You two aren't getting much done out here."

"Slave driver," I retorted.

"The sooner you two finish, the sooner you can have a slice of fresh baked apple pie with ice cream."

"Let's get to it," I said, turning to David, but he was already running down the steps.

We finished with the lawn chores and went in for our pie. Tara had fixed us each a plate of sandwiches, chips, pickles and another tall glass of sweet tea with apple pie for dessert.

"See David, I'm right, the rewards are fantastic."

"Uh, Huh," he said still eating his pie, "I guess you're right."

That evening, Tara and I picked up Michele at her house and the three of us went to Michaels Supper Club.

Once we were seated, Michele asked, "Okay, what's up, what have you got planned for our husbands?"

"I guess I may as well tell you right away! In two weeks, I'm doing my last show in Dallas, and arrangements are being made for the four of you. . . ."

When I finished telling them about all the plans, Michele said, "Wow! That's great! What's the big deal?" she asked. "Did you think that we wouldn't want our hubby's to go?"

"No, I knew the two of you would love the idea," I hesitated for a moment.

"Johnny." Tara asked, "There's more isn't there?"

"Yes, I'm doing a Christmas Special for Graceland the following weekend, and I'm working on getting David and Chance a spot in the show. If it all works out, they will be on National TV. A lot of people, some of them very important, will be watching. This could be a big break for them." I watched the expression on their faces.

"My God, that's fantastic," said Michele, beaming.

Tara looked at me, "Johnny, you hesitated for a minute before telling us the rest of the news. You're afraid of something. What is it?"

I took a deep breath and continued, "With success comes money and fame. Fame is what bothers me. You see, with the fame, will come beautiful women chasing after David and Chance, along with offers to take them to bed. I'm just concerned whether or not the two of you can handle that pressure. You may not think it's a big deal now, but believe me, it's hard on the wife, and it will be even harder on the guys. Temptation will be at their finger tips. My question is, can you handle all this and still control your feelings and emotions? You'll have to be able to laugh off sexual remarks by saying, he goes home with me, he sleeps with me, hands off, etc."

"If you get mad and blame your husbands you'll ruin their careers and possibly your marriages. If all this is going to cause trouble between you and them, and it's more than you can handle or control, I'm not going to help them. I'll call off the whole deal right now. So, ladies, what's your answer? I know this is a lot to think about, and digest all at once, but I have to know."

Michele looked at me, and said, "I can handle it, and I know Chance loves me enough to stay faithful to me."

Tara spoke, "Well, I trust David, and I believe he'll be faithful to me. David and I have worked hard to get him this far. It's a life long dream come true. Yes, I know we can handle this."

"I don't want you to think I'm trying to discourage you, but I want you to hear what happened to me in Dallas. One night, I went into my dressing room. Standing in front of my dressing table was a beautiful naked woman. She had a body that could make a man melt in his jeans. She said she was waiting for me. Had a crazy story that her husband wanted my autographed picture, no matter what. That's the kind of thing that can happen. Do you get the picture?"

"Guess I'll just have to guard the door to David's dressing room," Tara laughed.

"I think it will make me want Chance even more," Michele said and then added, "Do it!"

We placed our order. It was unanimous for prime rib. While we ate, the girls made jokes and laughed about women chasing their husbands. They said they were somewhat used to it from shows their husbands had done. I called for the waiter to bring our bill.

"You're Johnny Raye, aren't you?"

Looking totally surprised, I answered, "Yes, I am."

"I hate to ask this, but I have a picture of you in my car, and if you wouldn't mind autographing it for my wife, I'll run out and get it."

"I'd be happy too," I said, perplexed at his knowing who I was.

When he returned, I asked, "Were you in Dallas to see one of my shows in order to get this picture?"

"Actually, I wasn't, but my dad and step mom live in Dallas. They went to see you perform, and said you were a great entertainer. They sent me this picture."

"Well thank you, and the next time you talk to your parents, tell them thank you too! What are their names?" I was curious if I might remember them.

"Bill and Nancy Jordan," he said proudly.

Recognizing their names, I choked on my drink. When I was able to speak, I said, "If I see or talk to them next week, I'll tell them we met."

"Well, my wife and I are big Elvis fans, and we are planning a trip to Memphis to see you perform at Graceland for the Christmas Special."

I told him that was great, and I'd look for them. As we got up to leave, the waiter's wife came over and thanked me for the autographed picture. When we got to the car, I doubled up from laughter.

"What is so funny?" asked Tara.

"Yes, and what made you choke on your drink?" Michele wanted to know. As soon as the waiter mentioned his parent's names, you got a real funny look on your face."

It took a few minutes to quit laughing long enough for me to tell them what was so humorous. "You know the story I told you about the naked woman I found in my dressing room in Dallas?"

"Oh no!" they both said.

"Yep," the naked lady is none other than Nancy Jordan, his step mother."

This time the three of us burst into a fit of laughter.

"I was going to tell you, word travels fast when people get to know you, but in this case, forget that comment."

It was pre-arranged that I would drop the girls off at "The Bar" when we finished our meal. When we arrived, David and Chance looked like they had been waiting anxiously for our return.

Without hesitation, Chance asked Michele, "Well, what do you think?"

"About what?" she asked coyly.

"Michele, about Dallas and Memphis?" he said, running his fingers through his hair.

"Oh, I don't know."

"Tara, what did you think?" David asked, as beads of sweat broke out on his upper lip.

Tara looked over at Michele, "Oh hell, let's not keep them in suspense any longer. Okay, guys, we can handle this, and we are thrilled to death."

The guys grabbed and hugged their wives close.

"I can hardly wait," said Chance.

"Thanks Johnny," said David.

I looked around the bar, and then asked if Karen had arrived. "Yep, she's standing at the end of the bar talking with Judie, and a few friends," David pointed in her direction.

I left David and Chance to talk things over with their wives, and found Karen. She was wearing a tight pair of black jeans, black cowboy hat and boots, and a white western shirt. "Hi Miss Karen, you sure look good tonight, I said, smiling warmly.

"Thanks, you look pretty good yourself." "By the way," she continued sardonically, "how's Dallas, making a lot of money?"

"Well, I'm doing all right. I get the distinct feeling you're angry with me?"

"Why should I be angry, I hardly know you?"

"I guess it must be me, I suddenly feel a cool breeze," I was disappointed in how this was going.

Judie heard what was going on, and spoke quickly, "The last time you were in town, you left in a hurry without saying anything to anyone."

"Well, I was chased out the door by a bunch of girls."

Judie laughed and Karen said, "Yeah, you were."

"Well, excuse me ladies," and I walked back to the table where Chance, Michele and Tara were sitting.

"You didn't stay very long," Chance commented.

"I guess the last time I was in town I didn't give Karen enough attention, guess I'll have to give her some time to cool down." David called Karen up to sing. She was going to do a fast song, but at the last minute, David changed it to "Crazy," by Patsy Cline. As she was singing, I got up to leave, and told Tara I'd see them back at the house. I told her I was leaving in the morning, and needed to get a good night's sleep.

I said my good-byes to Chance and Michele, and was just walking out the door, when Judie stopped me. "You're not leaving are you?"

"Yes, I am, I'm leaving for Dallas tomorrow, and I need to get some sleep."

"Look," Judie said, "Karen's not mad at you. She just wanted to say good-bye to you the last time you were here, but you left on the run. If you leave now and don't say good-bye, she'll really feel hurt this time."

"Then I guess I'd better stay until she finishes, and we walked back to the bar to wait for her to join us. "Good job, Karen," I complimented her when she came and stood next to me.

"Thank you," and then asked if I was going to sing.

"No, not tonight, I do enough singing in Dallas. Sometimes I just like to listen."

She looked at me solemnly, "I'm sorry if I sounded sarcastic earlier."

"That's all right, I guess I deserved it. Judie, what are you going to sing?" I asked, changing the subject. You do a great job with Patsy Cline's hits, do one of hers."

There were three more singers and finally it was Judie's turn.

Karen asked, "When are you leaving for Dallas?"

"In the morning."

"Then I'm glad I got to see you tonight," she smiled.

"Me too!" I smiled back. "Karen, I'm doing a Christmas Special at Graceland in a few weeks. Do you think you and Judie could come if I get tickets for you?"

"Oh yes!" she answered excitedly. "We'd love to come."

"Motel room reservations are filling quickly, so I'll reserve a room for you with double beds, how's that sound?

"Terrific!"

"When you arrive in Memphis, I'll send for you, and have you and Judie brought to the house. Unfortunately, there will be a lot of people around, so I probably won't be able to spend a lot of time with you, but I'll make sure you get the best seats in the house so I can see you from the stage."

"Where are you staying?"

"At Graceland. I'll talk with Lisa Marie and try to arrange for a private tour."

"Gosh, I can hardly wait, but don't worry if you can't get us a tour."

"No, I want you two to enjoy yourselves, and if I have time, I'd like to show you around Memphis."

"Oh, if you could, that would be perfect!"

"Did you ride with Judie or did you take your car?"

"I rode with Judie, why?"

I looked at her, "Karen, could I take you home; it'll give us a chance to talk, without all the noise."

Her eyes locked with mine, as if searching for answers to questions that had not yet been asked.

"Yes, I'd like that very much," she responded softly. "I'll tell Judie what my plans are."

Judie didn't want us to leave yet. She had another song to sing, so we told her we'd wait.

Across the room, a table of girl's had been watching us throughout the night. Two of them approached our table. "You're Johnny Raye, aren't you?" one of them asked. We've heard you sing at different clubs, and we're hoping you'll sing for us tonight, please."

"I think you'd better," Karen smiled at me.

David heard their request, and called me to sing. I handed Karen my car keys, told her where I parked, and told her to have the engine running and I'd see her in a few minutes. She laughed, and headed outside. Judie finished her song, and I kissed her cheek. I told her she had a good strong voice, and she was improving every time I heard her.

I walked on stage, David switched on the strobe light. I had chosen to do "All Shook Up." The music started, a hush fell over the crowd. All eyes were on me. I began my song, my voice blending with the bass. I began to move, short shakes at first, and then I cut loose. I was all over the stage. The women were yelling so loud David had to turn up the volume. I was almost finished when I noticed a couple of women climbing on the stage, yelling "Elvis!" "Elvis!" Instinct took over. I threw the microphone to David Lee, jumped off the stage, and headed for the back door, the women in hot pursuit. Karen was waiting with the motor running, as I asked her to do. I ran and jumped into the car.

"Let's get out of here, and quick." Stomping the accelerator to the floor, we peeled out of the parking lot, laying a good strip of rubber.

I glanced over my shoulder and saw David and Chance trying to block the doorway. Karen and I whooped, and hollered like two young kids, and then laughed uncontrollably. We finally settled down, and Karen pulled over to the side of the road. The night had grown chilly so I put the top up on the convertible.

"Do you want me to drive?"

"No, I'll keep driving, you have a long drive ahead of you, besides, I love how smooth the car handles."

"She sure does," I smiled, and sat back and relaxed.

"Where to, Johnny? I know you're leaving early in the morning, but I'd like to drive around a little longer if you don't mind?"

"I'm not ready to call it night yet either and you're doing the driving."

She thought for a minute and said, "I know where there's a cozy, little all night diner that serves the best coffee and desserts, but its several miles out of town," she looked at me for a response.

"Let's go. If you like it, that's good enough for me."

It took better than half an hour to get to the diner. Karen was right. The place was cozy. The building was tubular in shape with neon signs around the roof line. Inside, the décor was from the 50's. Old fashioned booths with cushioned seats, lined the back wall. Each booth was equipped with song selectors that were wired to the juke box. Three plays for a quarter.

The place was dimly lit. Only one other couple was there, and they were talking quietly between themselves. We chose a booth towards the back, ordered our coffee and decided to skip the pie. Karen didn't want to gain weight, and quite seriously, neither did I. She pulled two quarters from her purse, and told me to pick out a couple of songs. Of course, I selected 'my' songs, "Love Me Tender," and "Can't Help Falling In Love," and several others to add to the atmosphere.

"How did you get into singing Elvis songs and then decide to be an Impersonator?" she asked, curiosity getting the best of her.

"Well, you might say I was born with it. I've loved music all my life, and singing Elvis songs just feels good."

"You know, Johnny, some people are talking, and saying you are the real Elvis."

"Oh yeah, like who?"

"Well, for one, Judie," she grinned.

"And, what do you think?"

"I don't know," she smiled. "You act like him, in a lot of ways."

"Oh, did you know him?" I teased.

"No," she blushed, "but I've seen all of his movies!"

"Yes, so did I and I learned a lot from them."

"I didn't think about that, I guess you would learn a lot from his movies, if you want to be good at impersonating him."

"Enough about me," I decided to switch the conversation before she asked too many questions. "What about you? All I know about you so far is you are very pretty, and you sing great."

Blushing, she answered, "I own a woman's dress and casual clothes shop, just down the street from Judies hair salon."

"That's how you two know each other."

"Yes, she only charges me what it costs her for hair supplies, like hair spray, and special shampoo's, things like that, and I give her a good discount on the clothes she buys from me. It works out good for both of us."

"Why aren't you married? You are an attractive woman, or is that too personal to ask?"

"No, I was married a long time ago, it didn't work out. It seems my ex husband liked to play around, but not at home, and I haven't met anyone since my divorce interesting enough for me to date."

"Yeah, sometimes some of us men don't know when we have it made."

"Oh, I bet you play the field especially in the line of work you're in! All those women chasing you," she teased, but I sensed a hint of seriousness in her voice.

"Ahhh, there's a big difference, I'm single!" I teased her back.

"What if you were married, would you then?"

"No, if I find the right woman, I'll retire from this business. There is too much temptation in this business, and I don't believe too many women would put that much trust in a man who has women trying to rip his clothes off half the time."

"Has that happened to you?"

"Oh yes, one lady in Dallas a few weeks ago came into my dressing room between shows. . ." I told her about Nancy Jordan. "And, I had to get Denise, the daughter of the owner of the club to remove her from my room." "Hell, her husband was waiting in the dining room."

Karen was having a fit of giggles. "Was she pretty?"

"Wow, like a model. If she was rated, she'd score a ten and a half."

"Well it looks like you handled that one."

"I was lucky, the other day I wasn't . . . ." "Never mind, I've talked enough about me, we were talking about you remember!"

"What about the other day, come on tell me?"

"Only if you promise not to get mad?"

She nodded in agreement.

"The other day a woman joined me in the shower. I gave in to that one, I'm only human."

"That's nothing to be ashamed of," she laughed. "It's only natural you didn't throw her out, you're a man, and men are weak when it comes to situations of sexual resistance!" she teased.

"No, I don't think so."

"Well, I believe if that happened to a woman, she would scream, and run his butt out, unless she knew him, or maybe if he was you!" She teased again.

"You may be right, but I don't think so," I said warmly, enjoying the easy banter between us.

Two women had come in and had sat directly behind us. We were so involved in our conversation neither of us knew they were there until a female voice spoke up startling us, and said, "I wouldn't throw him out if he was good looking, but if he was ugly, I'd beat him to death."

Karen and I looked at each other and burst out laughing.

The other lady said, "I'd like to find a man in my shower even if he was 'half' ugly."

"I took Karen's hand and said, "I think it's time we get out of here."

We drove to her house and parked out front. "I enjoyed having coffee together. I'll call you in a couple of days to give you the details for the show, and I'll see you in a couple of weeks in Memphis."

"I'll be there." She responded.

I slid my arm across the seat behind her neck, and slowly bent forward and kissed her. She wrapped her arms around my neck, and I held her close as we kissed.

While I was still holding her, she said, "I'm looking forward to Memphis; I believe it will be an exciting week-end."

"I believe it will be too," I answered, huskily, lost in the warmth of her eyes.

"Please, drive careful back to Dallas," she whispered in my ear.

"I will."

I didn't want to let her go. I kissed her again, this time I held her lips within mine, and enjoyed the feeling of her body in my arms.

She finally pulled back, and said, "Johnny, I like you, and I don't want you to leave, but, if you don't go now, I may never let you go."

"Mom, but you drive a hard bargain."

We laughed, but the passion had subsided. We said our good-byes as I walked her to her door.

Alone with my thoughts I reminisced over the time I shared with Karen and how easy it was to talk with her. We think alike, and she is very understanding. Maybe when I see her in Memphis we'll get to spend some quality time together, and I don't mean for coffee either.

David and Tara were still at work, so I sat and watch TV. I must have fallen asleep right away. The next thing I knew it was morning, and Tara was shaking me and wanting to know if I wanted breakfast.

"No baby, I'll get something on the road, and if I leave now, I can be in Dallas by nine o'clock tonight. Gary should be back from Memphis, he went there to check things out for our show."

"The guys can't wait to do the show with you in Dallas," Tara smiled sweetly, "and I can't wait to go."

"I like them too," I said fondly. "They're the kind of friends you don't find just anywhere."

"They love you too, that's all we've talked about."

I went upstairs to clean up, gather my personal things together, and put them in the trunk of my car. I finished loading everything and then handed Tara an envelope.

"What's this, Johnny?" She asked, peeking inside to see what it was. "Johnny, there's five-hundred dollars in here."

"Yes, take and split that with Michele and go to Karen's dress shop and pick out something new for Dallas."

"I can't take this money," she looked at me wide eyed.

"Yes you can, and you will. I insist! So kiss me good-bye, and tell David he forgot to wash your car," I joked.

"Okay, but you drive careful, and thanks Johnny, we love you."

"I love y'all too baby, see you in Dallas.

David heard us talking and ran to the door still in his pajama bottoms, "Be careful driving, man," he waved.

I waved in return, and headed to Dallas.

CHAPTER 12

It was close to nine-thirty before I arrived in Dallas. The bell hop at the hotel brought my luggage to my room, and I was about to follow when I heard laughter coming from the lounge. The voice sounded like Gary's. I peeked in and there he was sitting at the bar with a couple of women, laughing and carrying on like he didn't have a care in the world.

Seeing me standing there he asked, "Hey big guy, how was your trip to Birmingham?" How's Chance and David Lee?" He slid from the stool to shake my hand.

"They're fine, and they said to make sure I say hello to you from them. How was your trip to Memphis?"

"Man, this is going to be awesome. Lisa Marie is not cutting any expenses on getting everything set up. They've ordered five hundred heaters to be placed sporadically around the lawn. Fifty ten-thousand watt speakers are being hung from trees and placed along the fence line. Shit, you'll be heard throughout Memphis. The power company was there special wiring direct from the power poles to handle that much electricity. It looked like there was enough wiring all over the place to wire the whole city. There was a crew, building the stage platform when I left. It's going to be under roof, in case of rain or snow, that way the equipment will stay dry, as well as you. The last minute details will be worked out when you arrive, type of lighting you want for certain songs, stuff like that. It's unbelievable."

"Great, it sounds like we're in for a good time," I was pleased with what I had just heard. "How's Lisa Marie doing?"

"She's doing fine. I overheard her and Priscilla talking. She told Lisa Marie something about the words to the song you sang our first night here at the club, "Are You Sincere." She told her you are not allowed in the studio anymore. What happened? Did you steal a song from the studio?"

"No, you might say I borrowed a copy of it. Lisa Marie knows I have it. I sang it to her mother to bring back some old memories, guess I brought back too many." And then in the next breath I asked, "Have you seen or talked with Denise and Sandy?"

"Yeah, about an hour ago, they left to go to some bar. Sandy got her body cast taken off today. The doc said her ribs were healing nicely, and as long as she takes it easy, she won't need to wear it. She's hobbling around on crutches now because of her leg, said that she can have her leg cast taken off in about another month. Her face looks a lot better. The swelling is gone and her bruises are fading. Oh, and I forgot to tell you, Kristi went with them."

I rolled my eyes and said, "That's three women I'd avoid being around tonight. Well, look, it's been a long day and a longer drive. I'm going to my room. I'll talk to you some more about Memphis tomorrow, and thanks Gary for checking on everything."

I hung up my clothes, and crawled into bed. Some time during the night, Sandy must have come home and crawled in bed with me. I awoke and found her lying next to me, watching me sleep and waiting for me to wake up.

"Good morning sleepyhead," she purred like a kitten. "What are you doing home already?"

"Gary said you got your cast off?"

"I did, see," and she threw back the covers and exposed her naked body.

"Look Sandy, I . . ."

"Quiet!" she interrupted. "You told me when I got my cast off you'd make love to me, well, the cast is off, and I'm going to love you all morning long." Her fingers, were already exploring my body, and were working magic where ever she touched. "Lay back and relax," she said as she rose up, and carefully sat on me, so as not to hit me with the cast on her thigh.

Sandy's breasts were small and firm. Her butt was well toned, like that of a well trained athlete. Her skin was soft as cotton, and silky smooth from the oils she had rubbed on. She was exploding with excitement. "Raise your hips!"

I did as she said, enjoying the pleasure of the moment. She grabbed my underwear, tearing them in her haste to get them off of me. She pinned my hands within hers to the bed without changing rhythm as her hips moved slowly up and down, satisfying my ever growing needs. She rolled over onto her back and asked me to make love to her. I entered her body, my mind floated back to when I bathed and rubbed her with my hands, wanting to take her and make love to her with such hunger, and now I was. She screamed in total satisfaction. Our tired bodies were drenched in sweat as we lay catching our breath.

She cuddled in my arms. "I've been going crazy waiting for you to wake up, remembering what it felt like when you bathed me, my heart pounding like a drum, and getting a kick out of watching your pants rise with desire. I've never felt this good, and I don't want it to end."

"Sandy, this was good, and yes, I'll admit I hungered for you as much as you've hungered for me, but remember what I said about our friendship. You're falling in love with me, and I can't let you do that. You know I'm leaving. It will hurt me knowing I hurt you."

Wrapping her self around me, she said, "Johnny, hear me out. Make love to me again, and don't hold back. When we're through, I'll be just what I am now, your friend. Yes, I love you, but only as a friend. You won't leave me hurting. You'll leave me feeling like a real woman who has been made love to by the best in Dallas. I need to feel loved, not used. Her lips found mine. I held her tightly to me, and made love to her one more time, for the last time, ever.

We decided to eat lunch in the hotel restaurant. I was hungry for a big old fashioned burger, fries, and a chocolate shake. Sandy ordered the same without the fries.

"Johnny, do friends make love?"

"Well, we just did, and I think of us as friends. You should be friends before you love someone. I mean, some friends love each other enough to marry, and some just remain good friends."

"Well if you ever decide to get married, look me up. I'll marry you, if nothing more than for the great sex. You're a great lover," she wrinkled her perky, little nose in amusement.

"Well thanks, but it takes two, and remember, the next time you make love to someone, make sure you're friends first, not an overnight pickup."

"I've learned my lesson, believe me. No more Jimmie Stamps in my life! I'm going to make sure no one gets me unless they are my best friend, you can bet on it."

"Good girl. When can you go back to work?"

"I talked to Mr. Steadman, since I need the money to get back on my feet. He's going to give me a job as a cashier until my leg heals and I can go back to being a waitress. I start back tonight."

"Did the doctor approve this?"

"Yes, because all I'll be doing is sitting on a stool collecting money. In the mean time, can I stay with you one more week? I'm going to look for a new apartment. This time, my own place, by myself. That's new for me as I've never lived alone before."

"Great!" It's good to see you making positive decisions. Isn't it strange that it's almost noon and we haven't seen or heard from Denise?"

"No, she giggled, I told her not to come or call."

"You did?"

"Uh huh. I told her I planned on having you all day to myself, and that two and a half hours wouldn't be long enough."

I laughed at her humor. "What are you trying to do, get it all in one day?"

"Well, sort of. I figured once would be it and you wouldn't want me again. I thought I'd get all I could, and get you out of my system."

"Oh, I see. Well if you don't mind, I'd like to go back to my suite to relax and watch TV." Sandy wanted another round in the bed, but I told her no, she'd wear it out.

We met Gary in the hallway and he joined us. We still had things to discuss about the Christmas Special. I poured us each a soda, and we sat at the table to talk so Sandy could watch her chick flicks.

"I took my girlfriend with me to Memphis," he grinned, "and she left me."

"What?" I started laughing knowing this had to be funny.

"Well," he began, "we stayed at a hotel, and we were in the lounge when some girls overheard us talking about what we were doing at Graceland. They asked if I could take them with us to see Graceland, so I did. After the tour, one of the girls wanted to try my pants on."

"Try your pants on?" I asked.

"Yeah, but with me in them!" and we both burst into a fit of laughter.

"I have to ask, Gary, did you?"

"No, I didn't, but don't think I didn't want to, but there were just too many people around for us to disappear. Anyway, my girlfriend got mad for even bringing them and she left."

"She'll call you."

"I don't think so," he grinned. "Even if she does, I'll tell her to forget it."

"Are you sure?"

"Yeah, I'll find another one."

"Well that shouldn't be hard."

"No, cause I've got another one coming over tonight."

"Oh yeah, who is this one?"

"One of the girls from the club."

"Who," asked Sandy, tuning in on our conversation?

"Tammy."

"She is pretty," Sandy answered honestly, "but she's a real home body if you know what I mean."

"Not really," he answered.

"Well Gary, from what I know of her, Tammy doesn't date a whole lot; she's pretty much a loner. Stays home and watches TV all the time, or so she says."

"Good, that means I won't have to take her out dancing every night, just to bed."

"Be careful," I laughed, "Or the next thing you know you'll be married."

"Oh, no I won't. Not me, I like the single life too much!"

"Bring her over some night when we don't have a show at the club, and we'll all watch TV together.

"Yeah, Sandy added to the fun, "I'll pop a big bowl of popcorn."

"You two will giver her bad ideas," he was grinning"

"No we won't, but if you want to keep her to yourself, that's all right.

"Hey, let's do something today," Sandy said.

"Today, I thought you were going to keep Johnny in bed all day?"

"I thought so too," she pointed her finger at me, "but he couldn't handle it."

"You know about this too? Gee Sandy, why didn't you just run an ad in the local paper, or hang a sign on the door, and make sure everybody knows. "Enough, anyway," I continued, "I think anything over two hours of sex is called lust, and lust isn't good for your health."

"But it sure is good for the body and mind," Gary answered, and laughed.

"Gary, have you seen Denise or Kristi, since Sandy told Denise to stay away today?"

"Before he could answer, Sandy said, "They ran into a couple of guys last night, and they're probably still with them."

Exasperated at what I had just heard, I said, "Don't they ever learn! So where did you three go?"

"To the bar called the Two Step, remember we went there that night you got into it with those two guys who knew Jimmie, and were giving Denise a bad time and didn't want her to leave."

"I should have guessed. I hope she didn't run into those guys again!"

"No, at least I don't think so. They weren't there when I left. Denise and Kristi were acting a little jealous cause I was spending the day with you," she giggled.

"By the way," Gary asked, "Did you see Karen when you where in Alabama?"

"Karen, who's Karen?" Sandy wanted to know.

"Thanks, buddy! She's a lady I met in Birmingham a few months ago."

"Well, what about her?" Sandy persisted, wanting to know everything.

"Well nosey, if you really want to know, I'll tell you. She's a very nice lady, and she's my age, very pretty, and well built. For some reason there's something about her that makes me want to spend all day with her, and not for sex either. I guess it's because we have so much in common. I feel she may be the one I may chase after some day."

"Well why didn't you bring her back with you?" she asked, wanting to know more.

"I guess I'm not quite ready to settle down yet, and I don't think she's the type of person who just wants to be friends. I need to get my life straightened out first. If she turns out to be the one for me, then I want it so we'll both be happy with our lives."

"That's sweet of you, Johnny; you really care about her feelings, don't you?"

Yes, I do! But first I have to find the time to really get to know her."

"How about in Memphis?" Sandy suggested, trying to be helpful.

"Oh, that reminds me, I have to make hotel reservations for her, and her friend, Judie."

"You're staying at Graceland with Lisa Marie, aren't you?" asked Gary.

"Yes, but since you're staying at the hotel, I'll book a room for them at the same place. Do you have the number of the hotel handy?"

"I think so," Gary said, "let me check my wallet." After looking at a dozen pieces of paper, he handed me a torn slip, "Yup, here it is!"

The hotel needed a credit card, I had applied for one, but I hadn't received it yet, so I used Gary's, and then paid him back in cash. I called Karen and gave her the name, telephone number and room number of the hotel. I told her it was booked under my name.

I laughed and said, "Make sure there is no naked woman waiting in the room."

"If there is," she asked, what do you want me to do with her?"

"Send her to Gary's room!"

"Yeah," Gary said, "I take care of all the light work."

"Johnny," Karen continued, "I'm really looking forward to this."

"Good, I am too, see you in Memphis!"

"That's not fair, Sandy whined, Denise and I want to go, but we can't, we both have to work that week-end."

"By the way Gary, Chance and David are coming to Dallas on Friday and Saturday of our last week-end at Steadman's. They've agreed to do the two shows on Saturday with us, and possibly Memphis too."

"Cool! That should be fun, and a good way to end our commitment at Steadman's."

"I've been thinking about this. I don't think Mr. Steadman has any entertainment during the holidays, I wonder if he'd like David and Chance to do his shows during that time and maybe longer. I think I'll go talk to him, do you want to come with?"

"I do," Sandy jumped at the chance.

"Yeah," Gary answered, grinning at Sandy.

The three of us met Mr. Steadman in the bar; he was handling details for tonight's dinner. Looking up from his paperwork, he asked, "You three look like you're up to no good, what's up?"

I was the spokesperson since this was my idea. "Do you have any entertainment scheduled during the holidays?"

"No, no I don't. Actually I did. I had a jazz pianist scheduled, but he's having some kind of surgery and had to cancel, and you're leaving for Memphis, and everyone else is already booked. Why, got someone in mind?"

"Yes sir, I do. David and Chance, the two guys I have coming to do our last show with me. They may be available."

"Johnny, just how good are these guys?"

"Well, they were good enough to tie for second place in the Elvis competition that was held here in Dallas, and they'll furnish their own music. You wouldn't be paying two people. Would you want them to do one show or two per night like I do?"

"I'd prefer the same arrangements as we're doing for you, two shows a night, three nights a week."

Grinning, he asked, "What do you think will be a good offer?"

"Well, $2000 per night, plus a suite at the hotel, and since they're furnishing their own music, you'll save a $1000 per night."

"Sounds fair to me," he laughed again, "I can live with that, but I need to know which one is interested, so I can advertise ahead of time."

"Sure, I'll call them later and let you know."

"Thanks, Johnny."

"No, thank you, Mr. Steadman."

Back at the hotel, Gary said he'd see us later. Sandy and I went back to my suite. I asked her to call Denise and Kristi to have them come over.

"Oh, do I have to? I was hoping for another round of sex."

"Don't you think this morning was enough? I mean two hours, Sandy! I'm still tired," and winked at her. Then in a more serious tone, I asked, "Honey, I need a favor from you?"

"Sure Johnny, anything."

"When David and Chance get here in a couple of weeks, I'd like it if you and Denise would be friendly with their wives. Take turns taking them around, and do a little site seeing, go shopping, you know, make them feel welcome. The guys will be busy with Gary and me, rehearsing, working out a routine, that sort of thing. They'll be too busy to spend time with them. I want their first visit to Dallas to be fun, and enjoyable. Besides, if one of the guys wants the job at Steadman's, the only way it will happen is if their wife is happy and likes it here. And, I want you two 'horny toads' to behave yourselves."

"Well, I don't know, she tapped her finger against her cheek, "that depends, are they cute?"

"Well their wives sure think so, and they are good performers, lots of personality. I want to help build their careers to where Vegas Casino's will pay top dollar to get them."

"Won't that hurt you?"

"No, I don't plan on staying in this business more than a few more years. I'm not worried about me. These guys are younger and very good friends, like you, Denise, and Kristi. I want them to do well. They have many years ahead of them. They can make it big with the right break, which is what I'm trying to do for them."

"What do you need from Kristi?"

"A news story. Wait until they get here for more details, okay? I'm going to use the phone to call David and Chance. Can you use your cell phone to find Kristi and Denise?"

I called David's number, but no one was home. I then dialed Chance, and Michele answered.

"Hi, baby, how you doing?"

"Johnny, hi, we're doing great, how about you?"

"I'm fine! Michele, the reason I'm calling is I need to speak to Chance or David right away.

"Well Chance is at the store, he's being sweet, and doing my grocery shopping for me. He's been gone for over and hour, so he should be home any minute, and probably with a car load of groceries."

I laughed, "I can just imagine from the way he eats, he's always hungry."

"I know. My grocery bill takes most of my check."

"Well, when he gets home, it's urgent that he calls me right away."

"I'll tell him, and love you, take care."

"Love you guys too," I returned the endearment.

Sandy was able to locate Denise and Kristi. "I told them to bring beer and pizza with them, so they'll stop and pick it up on the way."

The phone rang. It was Chance calling me back. "Hey big guy, or should I say, dad, what's up?"

"Hi, son," I laughed, joking along with him. "Listen, I have a job for you or David, at Steadman's. The pay is $2000 per night, free hotel suite, and meals for two. You'll be doing two shows per night, Wednesday, Friday and Saturday nights, starting on Dec. 19th, through the first of March. I need for the two of you to decide which one of you wants the job. The one who take's it, will miss out on the Christmas Special at Graceland because he'll be performing at the club. Look, talk it over with David Lee, and let me know in a couple of days what you two decide. Don't delay. We need to allow time for advertising."

"Wow, that's quite a break, and damn good money."

"Yeah, it is, any other details or changes will have to be done directly with Mr. Steadman. I've got to run. I have other details to work out. Take care and call me soon."

"I'll get a hold of David right away, and don't worry, Johnny, we'll work it out."

"Love you big guy."

"Love you too!" and I hung up the phone, happy with his enthusiasm.

Denise and Kristi came bouncing through the door, their arms full of beer and pizza which they immediately plopped on the table. Denise ran to me, threw her arms around my neck, and gave me one heck of a big kiss. "Did you miss us?"

"As a matter of fact, I did."

Walking towards me, Kristi asked, "Where's my kiss?"

"Right here baby!"

"I haven't seen you all week," Kristi said acting a little pouty.

"I know, but it's only Wednesday. In a few minutes, I need to get ready to do tonight's shows, so let's get down to business. But first, let's open these pizza's, I'll explain everything while we eat."

Kristi grabbed plates and napkins from the kitchenette, while Denise and Sandy opened the beer and pizzas. I grabbed a slice of pizza with the works. "This is what I have planned for you Denise . . . ." I gave her the same information that I had given Sandy earlier.

"No problem, Johnny, we'll work it out together."

"And "Kristi, I need you to do a little news story on the three Elvis' doing a show at the club. I need you to build it up, big time! Mr. Steadman wants a sell-out, and I know you can handle this. You could do another article when the decision is made as to which one takes the job to replace me. The more confident they feel, the better they will perform. I'll have done my part to help, and the three of you will have done yours."

"Remember, friendship is the greatest reward you can ever receive. You do things for friends, and ask nothing in return. Be supportive and understanding when a friend attempts something, even though you know they're wrong. That's true friendship."

"You know, Johnny, no one has ever been as close to us as you are, you're the greatest friend we could ever ask for," Kristi said, her voice filled with emotion.

"No, believe me; the three of you have been very good for me. And quit grinning, I'm not talking sexual. Anyway, you have helped me to understand desire and fulfillment, helped resist temptation, up to a point. It's helped me to get an insight to my past life, and to see why I made so many mistakes in my earlier years, mistakes I'll never make again. You won't understand this, but I owe a lot of people. I don't mean financially; I always pay my debts. I can't explain why, but trust and believe me, you'll always be my friends, and I'll always be there for you when you need me."

"Gary knocked and came in, "I knew I smelled pizza, am I just in time?" We all laughed as he sat down and grabbed a huge slice of the pepperoni.

Denise looked at her watch, "My goodness, Sandy, we need to get ready, dad will be wondering where we are. I promised I'd come early and help with the dinner arrangements.

They quickly went to the bedroom and changed for work. Luckily Denise had the insight to bring a change of clothes with her, and they rushed for the door as fast as Sandy could hobble.

"Mind if I go with?" Gary asked. "I need to check things out for tonight," as he grabbed another slice of pepperoni and joined them.

"See you later, they hollered and left.

Kristi and I were alone.

"Johnny, can I walk over to the club with you?"

"Sure honey, something wrong?"

"I need your advice on something," she said.

"I've got to get ready, so come in here while I change, and you can talk to me then."

Kristi followed me into the bedroom. I don't know why I felt comfortable undressing in front of her, and not Denise or Sandy. I guess it's because Kristi doesn't constantly hound me about sex. She needed one night to feel loved and cherished, not to just have sex.

I was changing into my shirt, when Kristi said, "I met a man the other night, and he seems to be very nice. I enjoyed talking with him, but at the end of the night, he wanted to make out. I couldn't, Johnny, I was afraid he was like all the others, you know, want my body, and not me as a woman or friend."

"Well, let me ask you this? Did you feel warmth in your body that secretly said touch me, even though you said no?"

"No, I didn't feel that, but otherwise, I really enjoyed my evening with him."

"Well then, if you go out with him again, and he wants to make out, just tell him no. Tell him it's too soon for anything more, and that you'd like to get to know him better. Then if he acts disinterested in you to hell with him. You are much too attractive a woman to settle for anything less. If he's willing to go along with you, and if he's as nice as you say he is, he'll wait and respect you for it. That way, you'll know when you're ready, and won't feel pushed or pressured into doing something you're not comfortable with."

"Thanks, Johnny, you're right, but do me a favor?"

"Sure, what is it?"

"Put your pants on before I attack you!" She laughed to ease the moment.

I tucked my shirt into my pants, brushed my hair, and was ready to go.

We entered the club from the back entrance, but before I opened my dressing room, I had Kristi check it for me first, and make sure it was empty, of women that is!

She kissed my cheek, "Love you Johnny."

"Love you too."

I changed into my powder blue jump suit. It was designed with large, blue stones on the collar and cuffs, as well as around the belt. I walked out, and told

Denise I was ready. She gave Gary the thumbs up signal for him to begin my intro music, and for Mr. Steadman to do a quick announcement.

This time I entered the stage shaking my body, getting a feel for what the audience expected. I learned years ago, no matter how fancy the club or how fancy woman dress, something happens to them when they hear my music. Prim and proper disappears and is replaced with fun and excitement.

I held Gary from starting my first song as I enjoyed teasing the audience into a frenzy. I did this for several minutes, and then suddenly I stopped and held my hand up for total silence. Not a word was spoken, not a sound was uttered, all eyes on me, waiting for my next move. I looked out at the audience, and raised my upper lip in that infamous quirk. The women screamed, as though each felt it was done expressly for them, and I broke into song, "Burning Love."

After several more songs, one of the security guards handed my 'towel girl' a note. When she was wiping the sweat from my face, she handed it to me and whispered that it was a request from Lisa Marie wanting me to sing, "Don't Cry Daddy" to her again. I looked out into the audience and spotted her sitting with several of her girl friends.

"Gary, I have a special request from Miss Lisa Marie Presley, who has honored us with her presence this evening. Would you please put on "Don't Cry Daddy."

I began singing, and half-way through, she stood up smiled, and blew me a kiss.

"Thank you," her lips formed the words as I finished singing to her.

I did several more numbers, and ended my show. I was already tired from all the jumping around, and wanted to rest before the next set, but I decided to join Lisa Marie at her table.

I signed several autographs, and had pictures taken on the way. The crowd was pushing to get closer to me, making it virtually impossible to reach her table, so I signaled Lisa Marie to join me in my dressing room. I had the security guards escort Lisa Marie and her friends, as her friends had wanted to meet me and this was the best way to talk without interruptions. Introductions were made, and I autographed pictures for them.

"Johnny, this gives me an idea," Lisa said, "maybe we should have our picture taken together for the Christmas Special."

"How about right now?" I asked. "I have a professional photographer that takes pictures of me with people in the audience, and you look fantastic in that deep blue evening gown, it'll blend beautifully with my powder blue jump suit."

"Okay, that's fine with me."

"Why don't you girls stay here and get comfortable, we shouldn't be that long. Come on kitten, let's find the photographer." We found him in the lobby trying to drum up business, and decided that the lobby would be the best place to take the pictures.

Steadman's lobby was ornately designed with fine hand crafted furniture covered in a rich fabric of wine, green and gold. An enormous deep green marble fountain was the focal point of the lobby, and a perfect place for our pictures. Special effect lighting shone directly on the water, changing it's appearance to an almost pearl, translucent shade.

The photographer took at least fifteen different poses, and would have taken more until I said, "Stop, I'm sure you have enough now to choose from."

We decided to have him make at least five thousand prints to sell at the Christmas Special. Lisa told him she would meet with him in a few days to choose the pose she liked the best.

"Johnny, I'd like to speak with you in private," Lisa stated.

Lisa's friends, Doreen, Malinda, Misty, and Kay wanted to get a drink, and said they'd wait for her in the bar room. Besides, there were several cute guys that were sitting at the bar that had caught their attention. They thanked me for the pictures and scarves, and left to get their drinks.

"Mother keeps bugging me about the words to the song, "Are You Sincere," she said, sounding confused. "Why?"

"I told her where I found the words and music?"

"I know," she said, "but she insists you're lying. She doesn't remember any words being behind the picture frame, and why would they be there in the first place?"

"Maybe your father was afraid someone would take them, and he wanted to keep them personal.

"Well, that's sort of what I told her, but she's not buying that."

"Tell you what; I'm leaving to go to Memphis this week-end after my last show on Saturday. That will put me in Memphis sometime on Sunday, and I'll talk to her then."

"She won't be there, she's in California handling the production end of things for the show, and won't be back until a couple of days before we air."

"What did she say about me staying in Graceland rather than at a hotel?"

"That's another sore subject; just don't bring it up to her again. I've insisted you're staying at Graceland, but mother doesn't think its right. She's afraid people will talk."

"People are going to talk anyway, no matter where I stay, but if it will make it easier on you, I'll stay at a hotel. I don't want to upset your mother, and I don't want you fighting with her because of me."

"No, it's a done deal, you're staying at Graceland! Anyway, I was hoping you would play the piano for me after the show."

"Well, Kitten, it'll be late when the show ends, and all details taken care of."

"I know, but there's always the next morning. This may sound silly, but I hope it snows, Johnny. I remember one year I asked Santa for snow for Christmas."

My heart skipped a beat as memories came flooding back to that Christmas that now seemed like it was in another lifetime. I guess you could say it was.

"Anyway, she continued, my father hired someone to bring in a snow machine. It must have cost him a fortune, but money didn't matter as long as I got my wish. They made a ton of snow, our house was the only one around who had a white Christmas. The next morning when I awoke and looked outside, I literally screamed for joy. I was so happy. We played in the snow all day until it got too warm, and it all melted. That's one of the best memories I have of my father."

"You miss him very much don't you?"

"Yes, I do."

"I'm sure he misses you too!" I said, without thinking.

"How can he?" She asked, tears filling her eyes.

"Somehow, I just know he does," and held her in my arms.

I wanted so much to tell her how much I did miss her, but not here, not now, later when the time is right. So I kept quiet.

She dried her tears, and I asked her how long she would be in town.

"I'm staying with Doreen's family, but I'm leaving Saturday morning for Memphis since there's still a ton of things to be handled for the show."

"Why don't you wait until I'm finished with my last show Saturday night, you can ride with me? I bought a '63 red Cadillac convertible."

"Oh, my father used to have one; he loved riding around in it. Okay, I'll wait and ride with you. I can just see old George's face when we pull up to the security gate in that car. He's going to flip his lid."

I walked her to the lobby, and she went to the bar to find her friends.

For a change, the week flew by without incidence, which was pleasant after the excitement, and all that had happened these past several weeks. Before I knew it, it was Saturday night, and I was finishing my last show. I quickly escaped to my dressing room, changed, grabbed my overnight bag, and met Lisa Marie in the lobby. I had the parking attendant bring my car to the back of the club. We loaded our luggage in the trunk. Lisa wanted the top down. The sky was clear and filled with millions of twinkling stars, but the air was cool and crisp, so I turned the heat on high, and rolled up the windows so we wouldn't get chilled. Denise, Sandy and Kristi were there to see us off and laughed like crazy at the sight of us. I had to admit, it did look a little crazy, and for a few miles it was fun, but once we were out of the city limits, and the protection from the large buildings, the wind turned colder so we stopped and I put up the top.

I was thoroughly enjoying my time alone with Lisa. We drove through the night, she telling me about her schooling, and things she'd done, places sheds been. For the most part, she appeared to be happy and enjoying life. Graceland produced enough money for her that she had everything she wanted, except her father.

"You don't mind if I look up to you like a father, do you?"

"No," emotion filled every fiber of my body, "it makes me feel as if I was your father."

I hesitated a moment to keep my voice under control.

"It makes me feel terrific as I once lost my daughter, so I know how you feel."

"Really, Johnny, tell me about it."

"I can't right now Kitten, I'm not ready to talk about it, but maybe one day I'll tell you what happened. But, thank you."

"Your welcome," she smiled sweetly, "and slow down, I don't want to get there too early."

CHAPTER 13

It was after eight o'clock when we arrived in Memphis and were driving on Elvis Presley Boulevard. Lisa Marie had fallen asleep, and I gently shook her shoulder to tell her we were almost at Graceland. Once again, nostalgia filled my whole being. To this day, I cannot believe what an impact I had made on so many people, young and old. It amazes me how the name "Elvis" can still catch the attention of so many. It's hard to explain the feeling you have knowing you are a legend in your own time.

People were looking and pointing at seeing me with Lisa Marie. "It's Elvis. It's Elvis," you could hear them yell. They looked and acted like they had seen a ghost. Indirectly, maybe they had.

"Well, that should start some good rumors," I laughed.

Old George was on duty as we pulled up to the security gate.

"Elvis?"

"Yes George, open the gate."

As I drove through, Lisa Marie said, "Good morning, George," and giggled at the look on his face.

"Good morning, Miss Lisa," he said, still staring at me.

"Close the gate, George," I said, laughing along with Lisa Marie.

"Yes sir, right away sir."

We drove up to the main house, when I made the comment, "Well, home at last."

"Johnny, my father used to say the same thing every time he'd come home from being away so long."

"It does feel good to be here, I can understand why he missed it so much."

"I'm going to check on things in the office," she stated, "be back in a few minutes and we can eat, I'm hungry."

"Me too, after driving all night, I feel like I could eat a bear."

We walked in, and again it felt like I had walked back into time. I took off my shoes and walked over to the fireplace where it felt warm and cozy. I watched the flames dance back and forth in wild abandon; my mind floated back to a Christmas long ago.

The house was filled with people, like it was at all holidays, but this time it was different. Priscilla and I were no longer getting along, and we had just had an argument when. . . ."Johnny, oops, I didn't mean to startle you," Lisa said interrupting my thoughts.

"That's okay; I didn't hear you come in. Did you make your phone calls?"

"Yes I did, and everything is coming along fine."

"Johnny, why did you pull your shoes off when we came in?"

"Habit, I guess, I love to feel the carpet on my feet."

"Really, my father used to say and do the same thing. I guess that's where I get it from, because I like that feeling too. You know, it's funny how you are so much like him. How is it that you know so much, and act so much like him?" Lisa wanted to know, her eyes staring intently at mine.

"I'm sorry about that," I replied. "I don't mean to upset you. Let's go and get a bite to eat."

We couldn't eat in the kitchen, because the first tour of the day would be starting soon. We hopped onto one of the ground's carts and went across the street to the diner for burgers, fries and malts. It wasn't real crowded, so we didn't have a long wait. We received numerous stares and whispers, but other than that, we were left alone to eat in peace.

On the way back to the house, I had asked Lisa where we would be sleeping when I did the show. She had told me that arrangements where made for me to sleep in the guest house.

I needed to talk to Joe, and she told me I could find him in the office out back. Tour buses were starting to come in, and I needed to get out of sight before they started asking for pictures and autographs. We left the Cadillac parked out front with a guard to keep an eye on it. I said it would be fine for people to take pictures by it, but not in it.

We were headed in the direction of the office just as the first bus pulled up front. Tourists were yelling out the window, "There's Elvis, there's Lisa Marie!"

We waved and laughed as we rode past. Joe saw us coming and came out to greet us. "Well, you sure got the tourists excited today. We just got a phone call from the diner, guess there's a group over there that want autographs and pictures taken with you.

"Maybe we'll go back in a little while," I answered. "How have you been Joe?"

"Great Johnny, how's the show's going in Dallas?"

"Good, we've had a sell out every performance. I want to talk to you a little later on, okay?"

"Sure Johnny, I'll be right here taking reservations."

"How many tickets have you sold so far?"

"At last count, right around thirty thousand. By the way Lisa, the TV stations want to know if they can have an interview with you right before the show airs."

She looked at both of us, and asked, "What do you guys think?"

"An interview might be a good idea," Joe said, in a voice depicting he really liked the thought of it. "How do you feel about it, Johnny?"

"Maybe you could Lisa, but not me; there'll be too many questions that I won't feel like answering. Plus, I may say something that would upset your mother. My honest opinion is it would be best if you do it alone."

"Okay! Joe call them back and tell them I'll be available for the interview. Which reminds me," she continued, "I have a few personal things to take care of. Joe will you keep Johnny entertained for awhile?" as she hopped on the cart and rode off towards the house.

Joe and I walked toward the ticket office. People stepped out of line for autographs. We stayed for about an hour greeting tourists. It gave me an opportunity to talk about finding a club for David Lee and Chance to perform at. Joe thought Vegas would be their best place to look.

"What about that Casino you were telling me about?"

"I'm going out there right after I finish the Christmas Special, as I need the money."

"Johnny, do you realize that we'll have close to fifty thousand people on both days?"

"I know, at ten dollars a head is good for me. I promised Gary three dollars a head."

"That's changed; you will be getting fifteen dollars a head, and Gary five. We're selling tickets for thirty-five dollars each."

"Whew!" "And you've sold thirty thousand already?"

"Yes, and that's just the first night. This will be the biggest event since". . . . he paused for a moment, and then said, "since Elvis's death."

We were both quiet for a moment, each thinking private thoughts, and then I asked, "How much trouble will it be to get snow machines here? Lisa wants snow for Christmas?"

"For you, I'll find one if I have to have it shipped across the ocean. It's going to be like old times!" Joe said thoughtfully.

"Yes," I agreed, "Like old times."

Just then a reporter stopped, and started asking us questions.

"Excuse me, are you Johnny Raye?"

"Yes I am."

"How does it feel to be doing one of the largest events Graceland has ever had?"

"Great, I'm very lucky to get this opportunity."

"Do you get the feeling that you are 'Elvis' being here at Graceland?"

I thought for a moment wanting to say the right thing, "No, there was only one king, and no one can ever know how he really felt, or ever take his place. This show is a tribute to his family and his fans, and I'm very happy to be a part of it, now excuse me," and Joe and I walked toward my old jet, the Lisa Marie.

The reporter followed and kept asking questions when I looked at the security guard, and asked, "Would you please escort this reporter to the restaurant and concession stands, he wants to interview the fans.

"No," the reporter replied, "I'd like to interview you."

I looked at him and said, "This interview is over, okay!" "Guard!"

The security guard took the reporter by the arm, "This way sir."

Joe looked at me, "You handled that rather well."

I just grinned.

We stood outside the jet; I shook my head, "She's looking old Joe."

"She is old."

I climbed into the cock pit and looked around. Joe asked the security guard to hold the tourists from entering until I was through touring the plane.

I sat in one of the seats, remembering at one time my fear of flying. I'd drive a bus to wherever we were scheduled to perform, until I realized too much time was being spent on the road, so we'd fly in commercial airlines. Then that became difficult with crowds. I finally decided to purchase a plane of my own.

I sat for a few more minutes visualizing the partying that when on going to and from concerts. All the guys, my 'Memphis Mafia', as they called themselves, joked, cut up, and carried on without a care in the world. I looked at Joe and started to laugh.

"What's so funny?"

"Oh, just remembering how you used to run up and down the plane, making sure security at the airports would be ready and waiting for us. I guess back then you had one 'hell' of a time with me, didn't you?"

With a little hesitation, he answered and laughed, "Yes, we all did, but you were worth it. We really had some good times, 'E', ah, I mean, Johnny."

I raised my eyebrows in question, "Do you think I made a mistake, Joe?"

Looking at me with sad eyes, he responded, "Only you can answer that."

"Well, look at it from my point of view, I can walk around Graceland and go where I want. People only want pictures and autographs. I'm not 'locked in' at Graceland. I'm free to come and go as I please. I'm on the outside looking in, and it feels great. Let's go, I've had enough of the 'old days'."

"What if you could do a Christmas Special every year?"

"You know," I looked at him, "if this show is a big hit, even Priscilla would agree to that. It would increase Graceland's business, and I'm sure she gets good money out of it."

"She does, but the majority goes to Lisa Marie."

"At least I left her in good shape financially."

"Yes and no. Priscilla and the rest of the staff worked hard to build up Graceland to what she is today for Lisa Marie and the public to enjoy. She knew you'd want it this way. She said you'd turn over in your grave if someone else owned Graceland."

"She's right, I would! I guess Priscilla had her hands full for awhile."

"Yes, she did."

We walked out of the plane, and to my surprise, Lisa Marie was standing there waiting on us.

"Enjoying your self?"

"Yes I am very much; you and your mother have done a great job building up your enterprise."

"Yes, mother is the one who keeps things the way they were as I was too young to remember details."

"Yes, I guess you were. Well kitten, where to now?"

She laughed, enjoying the familiarity of the endearment. "I'd like to ride around Memphis with the top down on the car."

"Okay, sounds like fun, let's go! Joe have you seen my '63' red Cadillac convertible?"

"No, I haven't, do you mind if I go with, the staff can handle things while I'm gone, and if they need me, they'll beep me?"

The three of us hopped onto the cart. We laughed and kidded with each other. "Stop," Joe yelled as he spotted the Cadillac, and I hit the brakes. "I'm waiting for Elvis to step out of the car, smile and wave to the fans looking over the fence," Joe exclaimed, drawing us a mental picture.

Lisa Marie and I laughed at the thought of it. We left the cart with one of the ground attendants, and Joe jumped in the back of the Cadillac. Lisa sat up front, and, of course, as always, I drove. The temperature was about sixty degrees and sunny, but with the top down it was a little chilly, so I turned up the heat.

"This is so great, Johnny, you've made so many memories come back to life."

"No, not me, you and Joe; I'm just a tool to make it complete," I answered, as we drove out onto Elvis Presley Boulevard. We rode alongside of one of the tour buses, and someone yelled, "There he is, it's Elvis!"

"This is so great!" Lisa laughed.

We drove around town, and across the river.

"Memphis sure has changed, new office buildings, new housing everywhere. Who knows, maybe one day I'll retire here. Which reminds me, before I forget; I have a favor to ask of both of you."

"What's that?" they both asked.

"I met a lady in Alabama. Her name is Karen, and I've made arrangements for her to stay at the Colonial Inn."

"Why don't you have her stay with you at Graceland, we've got plenty of room?" Lisa smiled mischievously.

"No, we're not that close yet. I'm trying to take my time with her. She may be the one I want to settle down with someday. I don't want her to worry where I'm at or where I'm going. When the time is right, and if it's what we both want, I'll take her with me wherever I go, but now is not a good time."

"Okay, what do you want us to do?" Joe questioned, wondering what he was needed for.

"Well, when you meet her, make her feel welcome and part of the group. After all, this is going to be overwhelming for her, and if I can't get free, she'll feel lost."

"I think that is so sweet of you," Lisa smiled, "especially with all you have going on, she must be special."

"I'm not ready to put any sudden moves on her, or pressure her, I'm trying to build a foundation, but I want to build it slowly. I need her to understand show business. The 'Elvis' world."

"With all the women chasing after you, it could be hard on her," Lisa commented.

"That's right, that's why I need to get show biz out of my system, then retire and settle down, but it's going to take money to do what I want to do."

"I'm well off financially, thanks to mother and father. I can give you what you need."

"No, I can't, and will not do that. I've got to complete my dreams myself, my own way! But thank you Kitten."

We started back to Graceland. Joe needed to get back to the office and handle ticket sales. I hadn't slept, and since I was leaving tomorrow to go back to Dallas, I needed to rest. I was leaving early in the morning, so I said my good-byes to them both, and thanked them for everything.

"See you two the week of the twenty-first."

"I looked at Lisa Marie, "I can't remember when I've enjoyed a day as much as I have today," I said wistfully.

"Me too," she said, "I really enjoy being around you."

"Drive safe." they said, and I went to lie down for a much needed sleep.

I was over tired, and couldn't relax enough to fall asleep right away. Maybe it was being back at Graceland. Whatever the cause, my mind wondered from one thing to another. I rehashed the day, and realized I felt like my old self again, except for the drugs. Looking back I don't see how I could have let my life get so screwed up. I was too young to realize I didn't need drugs to keep going, that I needed control of my life, the control I have now. Sometimes I wish I could go back in time, and do it all over again, this time the right way. I'd be free to walk around as I am now. I wouldn't let drugs control me or anyone around me.

I wonder what Lisa Marie would say or do if I told her the truth. Would now be the time to tell her or would it only screw things up before the show? Maybe I should just leave well enough alone. I wish I knew the answer to that one. . . ." That was the last thing I remembered as I fell into a restless sleep. I awoke to the buzz of my alarm clock and it felt like I didn't sleep a wink. I took a shower, finished packing, grabbed a cup of coffee from the office, as some of the workers were already there, and headed back to Dallas.

134

CHAPTER 14

I left Memphis before getting stuck in the—Monday morning workers rushing to their jobs traffic. A million things ran through my mind, the finalizing of Steadman's with David and Chance, and the Christmas Special. I kept my mind focused on that to make sure I had everything covered. It seemed like at no time at all, I was back in Dallas. It was after six o'clock when I pulled into the hotel parking lot. I had taken my time driving back, as I was still tired from being in Memphis.

The bell hop took my luggage to my room, but I stopped at Gary's first to let him know I was back in town. I knocked on his door. I laughed as I looked at the sight of him. "You look worse than I feel!" I stated.

He was half asleep, and his hair was all messed up. I told him I just wanted to let him know I was here and needed to get some sleep, and that I'd fill him in later regarding Memphis. He nodded, and said he was going to go back to bed himself.

"Hard night?" I grinned.

"Yeah, you could say that, I'll tell you about it later."

I walked into my bedroom and found Sandy lying on the bed asleep with only her panties on. I grinned and walked into the bathroom for a shower, then climbed into bed. My head no sooner rested on the pillow when I fell into a dreamless sleep.

I slept for almost fifteen hours when I woke to the feeling I was being watched. My eyes opened to Sandy peering into my face.

"Good morning, you slept like a log."

"Yeah, I was tired from the long drive."

"We had fun while you were gone."

"Oh yeah, what kind of trouble did 'you' get 'me' into this time?"

"Gary, Denise, Kristi and I went out Sunday night after work, and got drunk."

"Gary got drunk, he doesn't drink."

"He did Sunday night. That's not the best part. Denise went with Gary to his room to spend the night. It seems like they've discovered they have a lot in common."

"I knocked on Gary's door before I came here, that explains his appearance and why he wanted to go back to bed," I said and grinned. Two good reasons, first of all, nursing a hang over, secondly, Denise, I'll be damned."

"That's not all. Kristi's boyfriend, Frank, has fallen head over heel's in love with her. She's crazy about him too, so she decided to trust her feelings, and they ended up spending the night together. He's already talking about proposing to her."

I laughed at what Sandy had just said. "Kristi is good in bed, but marriage, isn't that a little too soon?"

"She told Frank he'd have to wait to see how their relationship developed, but she would consider it."

"What did he say when he picked Kristi up and found she was drunk?"

"He was laughing. Said he hopes this means she's going to say yes tomorrow, which is really today." Sandy became silent, and then slid next to me, kissing me and touching me. "Johnny, make love to me, I'm lonesome, and everybody is making love but me."

"That's your fault!"

"Not anymore," she said, as she moved her body over mine. She dangled her firm young breasts across my lips. I could feel the heat of desire from her body as she removed her panties, and then ever so slowly removed my shorts. I took her into my arms and made love to her. She groaned from pleasure, and begged me not to stop until finally our bodies reached total satisfaction.

We lay quietly for a few minutes, and she softly spoke, "You really are the best lover I've ever had!"

"Sandy, I don't want to spoil the moment, but we've talked about this before. "Is your friendship turning to love?"

"No, not in the sense you mean, it's just I'm here, you're here, we're both in your bed naked." She shrugged her shoulders, "I can't help it, you always look so sweet when you're asleep, and that turns me on." "Besides, it's been a week since we've made love, and I haven't slept with anyone since we were together, so I was due for a good romp in the hay."

I laughed at her comment, "You and Denise are insatiable. I do enjoy having sex with you, but again, that's all it can be, and soon even that can't happen."

"I know, but let's not talk about that right now," she said wistfully.

Changing the subject, I asked, "Has David or Chance called?"

"Yes, David called, and wanted you to call him as soon as you returned. I didn't want to wake you to tell you, as you were in such a deep sleep."

"Good, I had hoped one of them had called."

I quickly showered and dressed, and then while Sandy bathed, I went into the living area and called David. Tara answered, and I asked her how everything was going in Birmingham. We chatted about what we had been doing and then she handed the phone to David.

"Hey big guy!" his voice boomed into the phone, "How was Memphis?"

"Memphis was great; I had the time of my life with Lisa Marie. Tickets are selling like hot cakes. The staff had to hire three part time girls to handle the volume of calls. Did you and Chance decide who's going to take the job in Dallas?"

"Chance and I hashed it over several times, and with what we have going on in our personal lives, us with the bar, it was best that Chance take the job at Steadman's. Johnny, I really want to help you at Graceland. Tara and I have decided to sell the bar, but until it's sold, I can't commit to anything for a long length of time."

"It sounds like you both gave this a lot of thought, and made the right decision. Keep in touch and I'll see you the week-end of my last shows."

I called Chance. He was just getting home from his late shift at the lounge.

"I just talked with David, and he told me about the decision you guys made."

"How do you feel about it, Johnny?" he asked, hesitantly.

"I think it's great for both of you, I'm just happy you two could work it out together."

"How about the owner of Steadman's?"

"He was happy with the whole idea and is anxious to meet the two of you."

"What about Michele?" I inquired.

"Quit worrying 'dad', I've got a sub, and Michele is taking a leave of absence from her job. What are you doing today besides worrying about me?"

"Well, Sandy found an apartment, and she wants me to go with her to look at it."

"Who's Sandy?"

"Just a good friend of mine, you'll get to meet her and Denise and Kristi when you get here."

"Three girls," he was laughing hysterically by now. "Sounds like you've been busy and it wasn't all work!"

"Yes I have, but I'm not the one with a wife to look after, so I can afford to be a little busy."

"I hear ya, big guy!"

"I'll let you go, give my love to Michele, and see you in a little over a week. Don't forget, pack enough clothes, because you'll be starting work the following Wednesday after our Saturday night debut. Catch you later."

Sandy was dressed and waiting for me to finish on the phone. "Are you worried about Chance doing the show?"

"No, he'll do great; I'm concerned whether or not this is the right thing for them!"

"Johnny, you worry too much."

"You're right, Sandy, come on, let's go see that apartment you like."

The apartment complex was in a very nice area and only a few blocks from the club. Tenants had access to a huge swimming pool, tennis court, workout room, steam room, and a club house furnished with a bar and restaurant.

"Johnny, so far I like it!"

"I do too, Sandy. It fits your style." The manager met us in the main lobby of the complex, and took us to the third floor to apartment number 315.

"Wow, this is so nice!" Sandy exclaimed. She opened the French doors and walked out on the balcony to look at the view which overlooked the pool and tennis courts. The apartment was completely furnished and offered two bedrooms, two baths, a large living room and a kitchen/dining room combination.

The manager went to make a phone call and would be back in a few minutes, which left us alone to make a decision. We discussed the price, one thousand dollars a month plus utilities. Sandy said that was not a problem. Her income from Steadman's would cover the rent and utilities, but it was her tips that she could live on quite comfortably. Her car was paid for so she would not be strapped tight with bills.

The manager returned within a few minutes, as he said he would.

Sandy smiled and said, "I'll take it, when can I move in?"

"We need to run a credit report, and I'll need your last month's pay stubs, a thousand dollar deposit, and also the first month's rent of a thousand dollars. Fill out this one year rental agreement, and depending on credit check, you can move in tomorrow."

We left and went to get Sandy's personnel belongings at her old place. We loaded the trunk of my car with her clothes, and boxed up a few pictures and personal items that were hers. She had a few pieces of fine jewelry, and packed those in her suitcase.

She looked around for the last time, shuddered, and said, "Let's get out of here, this place brings back too many unpleasant memories." She left the key on the kitchen table, closed the front door and never looked back.

Back at the hotel, I fixed us a drink.

"You're going to have one?"

"Yeah, but just a short one," I grinned.

We sat on the sofa, watched TV and fell asleep. When I awoke, Sandy was asleep with her head in my lap. I gently moved her and called the hotel restaurant, but it was already after eleven o'clock and they were closed.

I carried Sandy to bed, and I made up a bed on the sofa. The next morning, the apartment manager called to tell Sandy she could move in and to pick up the key at the manager's office.

We unloaded my car and I left her to arrange things as she wanted. I kissed her good-bye. She clung to me for a few minutes, and then said, "I can do this, I can make it, thanks to you, Johnny."

"I know you can."

She had her cell phone and had a full day ahead of her getting address changes, and everything put in her name. I told her I was only a phone call away if she needed me and left.

CHAPTER 15

The rest of the week passed quickly, and before I knew it, Chance, David and their wives were on their way to Dallas. They called from a rest stop to say they would arrive in about an hour. I checked to make sure their rooms were ready, and that all they had to do was sign the register. I talked with the bellhop and told him when they arrived to bring their luggage to their rooms, and then escort them to my room. I called Gary and could hear Denise giggle in the background. I smiled and asked Gary to come over when David and Chance arrived.

I sat on the sofa to await their arrival, and turned on the TV to watch the news. The weather forecaster finished his report, and the newscaster gave highlights of upcoming special events. I was going to change channels when the reporter started talking about the Christmas Special on the 22nd and 23rd in Memphis. She announced that over forty thousand tickets had been sold, and phones were ringing steadily with Elvis fans trying to purchase tickets before they were all sold out, according to the ticket office at Graceland.

She reported that Johnny Raye, who was scheduled to do the shows, was the same Elvis Impersonator that was starring at Steadman's Supper Club in Dallas. The news reporter mentioned that she had been to Steadman's to view the show, and said Johnny Raye gave an outstanding performance, and was the closest thing to 'Elvis' she had ever witnessed. Also, the Christmas Special would be viewed on cable television, and that a number of companies were vying for prime time advertising.

The reporters switched to other topics, and I got up to fix myself a drink. I went to take a swallow, stopped and poured it out and fixed a coke instead.

There wasn't any harm in drinking every now and then, but I remembered thinking the same about drugs, I didn't need it, so why drink it.

Just then, I heard a knock at the door. David, Chance and their wives had arrived. After all the hugs and kisses, I informed them I had refreshments sitting on the bar, and told them to help themselves. We sat around and talked about their drive to Dallas. Chance said it was much nicer riding in the car than taking the bikes, much smoother on his bottom. We laughed and joked for awhile and then the conversation got serious as we discussed the show. In the meantime, I had called Gary to join us.

I asked if they had chosen a list of songs to sing, but they said they wanted to wait until they got here to find out what I had planned first. They both had been rehearsing numerous songs and were ready to do most anything.

"Well what do you say we all walk over to the club and get familiar with the sound system and stage," I suggested, "as well as rehearse an introduction for you, and prepare a song selection."

I called Sandy. She was already at the club and would see us when we got there. I asked her to call Kristi and Denise to see if they were available.

"Already handled, Johnny," she responded to my request. "They are on their way. Oh, we're finally going to meet 'the girls' we've heard about?" asked Chance, his eyebrows rose in question.

"Yeah, and keep your eyeballs in your head," I joked with him.

"Oh, we've seen pretty women before," he responded.

Gary and I grinned at each other, each thinking, *just wait until you see these three.*

"Wow, gosh, this is awesome, this is great, it's so big," they were all commenting at once, as we entered Steadman's.

I took them into the bar area where Sandy was waiting. We made introductions and I asked where Denise and Kristi were. Sandy said she had talked with Kristi a few minutes ago. They were stuck in traffic, and should be here any minute. I asked Tara and Michele if they wanted to wait at the bar with Sandy, while I showed David and Chance my dressing room.

"Don't you mean 'my' dressing room?" Chance laughed.

We laughed, and then Sandy said, "Don't forget to check for naked women," which brought about another fit of laughter.

"Hey, this is all right, a full bath, view of the river, a sofa and a TV too, huh," Chance said, delighted.

"Well, if you're waiting for your second show, it'll help you to pass the time. Tell you what works good between shows. Sell autographed pictures. I've been selling them for ten dollars each. I have a professional photographer who owns his own shop. He prints the pictures and comes to each show to sell them. I get five dollars for each one that's sold, and on an average night, you can make three hundred dollars or more. He'll also take pictures of you with some of the customers. That price varies depending on if they want them right away or are willing to wait and have them enlarged."

"Come on, I'll show you how to get to the stage from here. Come down this hall, go around to the right, and you'll come in behind the stage. Denise or Sandy will give Mr. Steadman the cue that you're ready, he'll announce you, and that gives Gary the cue to start your intro music. Walk out, work the crowd, get them excited. I know you two have been doing this for some time now, but the crowd in an exclusive supper club is altogether different than what you're used to in a bar. There will be numerous prominent people from all walks of life watching you, but one thing's for sure, their wives will bounce and scream to the music, no matter who they are or who they are married to, and that's for real."

"Go out there with the idea you want to have fun and the audience will too, after all, that's why we make the big bucks. Tomorrow night you'll be in the audience eating a great meal and watching the show. You'll see my routine and get a feel for what you'll need to do."

We sang a few songs so they could get used to the sound system, and then I said, "Come on, let's go back and join the girls. Kristi and Denise should be here by now."

Gary told us he needed a list of who was going on first, and a list of songs from each of us so he could program them into his equipment ahead of time.

"Whew, the view in here is better than what's in the other room," Chance stared in appreciation.

Kristi and Denise had just walked in wearing black leather pants. Denise in a tight red sweater, Kristi's in black, you could definitely tell neither wore a bra.

"Jesus, David said!"

Denise and Kristi hugged and kissed me. Introductions were made once again.

"Johnny, you sure you want to leave Dallas?" Chance asked.

Michele pinched Chance, "Are you sure you want to come here, honey?"

"I'm just joking, you know that," he laughed.

"Now you two know what I meant when I talked with you in Birmingham."

"I'm in control," Michele said, "besides these three are all good friends, and I'm just teasing Chance."

"Look but don't touch, right," I grinned at her.

"If David didn't look or comment," Tara added her two cents, "I'd think there was something wrong with him, and I mean seriously wrong."

142

"Let's go back to the hotel or somewhere where we can relax," I suggested changing the subject.

"Let's go to my new apartment," Sandy squealed with delight to be able to entertain. "I've got everything arranged the way I want it, and I went out and bought supplies for the kitchen. Well let's go!"

"Kristi, do you have to meet Frank?"

"No," she replied, "he said this was important to me, and he'll see me later tonight."

"Sounds like you may have found Mr. Right."

"Yes, I think so," she said sincerely.

"Well, in that case, call Frank and tell him to join us at Sandy's."

"Great idea!" Kristi looked pleased at the suggestion, "I'll call him right away."

"You girls go together," I suggested. "I'll take the guys with me in my car, and we'll stop and pick up steaks and drinks."

Gary took his car because Denise wanted to ride along with him.

I've got all the ingredients for a salad, and I'll put the potatoes in the oven so they can bake while you guys are at the store," Sandy said quickly. "I have dinner rolls, so if you want to pick up steaks and look for dessert, we'll be all set."

We picked up the food, and by the time we arrived at Sandy's, Frank was parking his car. He seemed to be a pretty descent guy, and you could tell by the secret looks that were exchanged between Kristi and Frank, that they were falling in love. I went into the kitchen to prepare the steaks for grilling. Sandy didn't have a grill yet, so I had to use the one out by the pool and clubhouse.

Sandy had sliced the potatoes open, then layered them with butter, garlic salt and pepper, and then rolled them in aluminum foil before she stuck them in the oven to bake. Kristi prepared the salad. The guys took care of the drinks and there was plenty of beer for those who wanted it.

Tara joined me and asked if she could help just as Denise was saying, "Your friends really like you."

"No," Tara answered immediately, "we love him."

Sandy came down to see how we were doing, overheard our discussion, and said, "We do too!"

Flattered, I commented, "Okay girl's, I'm just a good friend who likes to see other people do well so let's drop the 'Mr. Good Guy' show."

"Yes sir," Denise said, and Tara and Sandy laughed, as Denise saluted me.

The steaks were almost done when several of the residents who were sitting around the pool walked over to us and started asking us questions about being Elvis Impersonators. One of them mentioned that the clubhouse bar had a Karaoke machine.

The day was sunny and warm. Even though it was too chilly to swim, we decided to eat poolside. Our group brought all the food downstairs. We were waiting for the steaks to finish when David thought it might be fun to set the Karaoke machine outside. Gary, Chance and David went to see what type of equipment it was, and what needed to be done. A few minutes later, the three of them brought out two speakers and the Karaoke player. Not top of the line, but adequate for us to use and have fun with.

"Hey Johnny, don't over cook our steaks, remember we don't like them burned like you do," Chance laughed.

"Yours are done," I grinned, "I'm just waiting for mine to be done and we can eat."

We brought two tables together, the guys sat at one and the women at the other. We had such a good time. The girls chatted about where they wanted to go tomorrow, and the guys talked about the upcoming Elvis shows. We finished eating our meal topped off with apple pie and ice cream for dessert. Everyone was full and content.

"Well," I said, "now would be a good time to practice a few songs, and prepare our list for Gary. Why don't you two work on a couple of slow songs," I suggested.

"Why," David asked, "are you trying to tell us we don't do as well on slow songs?"

"No, what I'm saying is you don't do them that often because the crowds always like the fast ones."

"Johnny's right," Chance agreed, "you and I always do a lot of fast ones, especially me."

"I prefer to do slow songs, but my crowds always request fast ones, they just seem to like them better," David said.

"Well, let's wait and see," I responded.

I grabbed a microphone. By now, there were at least twenty people sitting around the pool, some brave enough to attempt swimming even though the temperature was only sixty degrees. I asked everyone what their preference was in music, fast or slow. The majority wanted to hear us sing slow songs. David wanted to sing first. Tara asked him to do "Loving You." Michele wanted Chance to do "Love Me."

Gary was in his glory operating the equipment, and Denise went over and sat with him. The girls finished cleaning up the mess from our meal, and enjoyed sitting around and relaxing. David and Chance finished their songs.

"Gary, put "Anything That's Part Of You" on for me, okay?" I closed my eyes for a moment and let the music consume me. Slow songs are always easy for me. They bring out so much emotion and feeling. I can sing straight from the heart.

"You're right, David said. It's one thing to do good, and another to sing great."

"That's the key to slow songs. You need to sing from the heart, like it was the last time you'd ever get to sing. Feel the words, not just sing them. Close your eyes and picture yourselves as Elvis as he walked on stage, the rush he'd feel, and when the crowd screams, imagine how he felt and you will feel it too. You guys are very good, but there is a lot of competition out there. To be the best, you have to have a few tricks of your own, and that's what I'm trying to teach you."

"Gary, how about "As Long As I Have You?""

While I was singing, David looked at Chance and said, "Damn, you'd swear when Johnny sings that it was Elvis in the flesh."

"Yeah, he sounds so much like him, it's hard to tell the two voices apart," Chance agreed.

The other residents requested me to do more songs. "Gary, I know that today's your day off, but do you mind running the equipment for awhile?"

"You know I love this, Johnny."

"Thanks buddy, I know you do." I sang three or four more requests and handed the microphone back to the guys. "Let's hear you two sing some slow ones and then pep it up with a few fast ones."

They both decided to sing the same songs they did earlier, but this time the crowd went over to them and told them how great they sounded.

I told Michele and Tara, "I think they now understand what I was trying to tell them," as we watched everyone surround them. And this is just the beginning, I thought. "Are you okay with all the attention they are getting?"

Tara and Michele both nodded their heads yes.

"I think it's great, Tara smiled warmly at David, who winked back at her.

"Me too," Michele agreed, watching the excitement in Chance's eyes.

"Sandy," I stood up to leave, "it's been a great party and a great day."

I shook hands with Frank, and told him it was good meeting him and hoped to see him before I left for Memphis. He said that he and Kristi would see me in Memphis and that they were going too.

"Stick around Johnny, we're all having a great time," Michele commented.

"Tell you what," I don't want you to stop partying just because I'm leaving. The guys are enjoying themselves, and this is exactly what I was hoping for.

You can ride back to the hotel with Gary."

"You're not leaving, Johnny, are you?" Sandy asked, and then said, "I'd like for you to stay tonight."

"Not tonight, Sandy, I miss you too, but tonight I'd like to be alone."

"I understand, and thanks for picking up the steaks and dessert for me."

I said my good-byes to all, and said I'd see them in the morning.

The next day Gary took the guys to the Club to work on their songs, as well as to meet with Mr. Steadman. The ladies had made plans to shop in the morning, and then take in the sights in the afternoon with Denise and Kristi. Sandy was having her cast removed and would meet up with them later. Me, well I slept in late, lay around and watched television for awhile, and then called Joe in Memphis. I asked him if Priscilla was back from California. He told me she returned earlier then planned, and was still determined to find out how I knew the words to that song. I laughed at the thought of her frustration over the music, and told him not to worry and that all she could do was speculate and have to accept my word for it.

Before we hung up, I asked, "How's Lisa Marie?"

"She can't get over the great time she had with you, it's all she's talked about. She bought a new jet since you were here. She had her name put on one side and she's talking about putting yours on the other side."

"Why?"

"I have a feeling she's on to us, Johnny, but doesn't want to say anything."

"What if she is?"

"I don't know, Johnny, but if she does, she's keeping it to herself."

"Joe, I wish I knew for sure, I've been thinking of telling her the truth, but I don't want to lose her again. Right now I'm closer to her than I've ever been. Is Lisa Marie there this week-end?"

"Yeah," she's here, but she's flying to Dallas this afternoon. She wants to see your show tonight and tomorrow. I think she wants you to fly back with her."

"That would be great, but I'm not leaving my car in Dallas, although I might be able to get David and Tara to drive it back since they rode with Chance and Michele in their car. I'll have to ask them later what their plans are. I know I don't need to tell you this, but I'm very grateful and very lucky to have a friend like you, Joe, you're the best, partner."

"No," his voice filled with emotion, as he continued, "I'm the one who's lucky, knowing you trusted me with the greatest secret in the world. It's the best friendship a man could hope for."

"Thanks, Joe, do me a favor and keep an eye on Priscilla and let me know if she checks out the studio."

"I'll try, but with everything going on around here, it'll be hard to keep an eye on her."

"Thanks, but see what you can do."

"You bet, Johnny," and we hung up.

It was getting late, so I stopped by Chance's room to see if they were ready to go to the club. Michele was dressed, but still doing her hair. David and Tara were there waiting. I told the women they looked fantastic in their new evening dresses. They were both pleased with their purchases from Karen's shop.

The guys were already dressed in costume and were chomping at the bit to get to the club. I told them I'd meet them there. I had already checked with Gary on the equipment and made sure the song list was complete. We quickly ran through the routine one more time. Satisfied everyone was on board, I left.

I went to my dressing room, and checked to make sure all my suits and jackets were back from the cleaners. I changed into my black pants, black long sleeved shirt, and white sports coat. I thought about Lisa Marie being here tonight and wished Karen was too.

I went into the dining room to eat with our group. Sandy tapped me on the shoulder and said, "You want a steak well done, baked potato, and a salad and you'll put on your own dressing, right?"

"Well, little lady, seems you've done this before," I said in my best imitation that I could do of John Wayne.

"Coming right up cowboy, and I'll get your milk."

David looked at me totally surprised, "You're drinking milk now?"

"Yes, with my meal only, good for your health," I grinned.

"How did rehearsals go today?"

"Good," Chance replied. "You were right. We rehearsed some more slow songs with our eyes closed and concentrated on what you said. It's the first time I can honestly say I thought I sang Elvis songs that even he would have been proud of."

"Yeah," David said, "it really did make a difference." "For awhile this afternoon, I got so into it, I actually felt like Elvis."

"I knew you would if you just feel the song as you sing it."

Sandy brought my meal, "Excuse me while I eat."

The rest decided on the prime rib special with jumbo shrimp and crab legs. I finished eating about the time their order came, so I excused myself and went to get ready. Gary came in to check and see how long I'd be. I was ready, and since we had a few minutes to kill before starting, I asked him how rehearsals went this afternoon.

"Good, big improvement on their slow songs, and they really had a good time cutting up with their fast ones. Johnny, only two nights left, let's give the audience what they paid for."

Gary started the music, Mr. Steadman told the audience about tomorrow night's special treat with three Elvis's, and then introduced me. I recognized some of the people in the crowd, they had been here before. Several groups were still eating so I sang several of my slow numbers to give them time to finish, and then I changed my routine. The audience responded to the tempo, I gave them everything I had. Song after song I sang without let up. Sweat was pouring from my body. My blue jump suit was stuck to my skin. I jumped from the stage, sang slow songs to the women, and gave each a kiss and then a scarf.

I was thoroughly enjoying myself, when I turned and saw Lisa Marie at a table in the center of the room. I walked towards her, knelt beside her and sang "Memories" to her until my voice choked from the lump that formed in my throat, and the tears that slowly slide down my cheeks. Finally I was able to say, "Ladies and gentlemen, let me introduce you to Miss Lisa Marie Presley."

I took her hand and kissed it. I looked into her eyes with as much love as I could show without giving away who I was. She stared back into mine, tears running unashamed down her cheeks. Her eyes telling me what her voice couldn't.

I brought myself under control, jumped back on stage and finished the set with "American Trilogy." The audience gave me a standing ovation, many of them shed tears, and some openly cried.

"Encore, encore!" They yelled.

I turned, looked at Gary and said, "Since we don't have a dry eye in the house, I'll sing "Crying In The Chapel."

That changed the mood and brought numerous laughs and cheers. They wanted more, but I knew I needed time to rest between shows, so I thanked them, told them they were a great audience, and went to my room listening to the deafening cheers and screams of a well satisfied audience.

We now had security stationed outside my door, and no sooner had I changed into something comfortable to relax in before my next show, when someone knocked. Security announced that Lisa Marie wanted to see me.

She was alone. I asked her to sit next to me, but she stood where she was, as if frozen to the floor. "Johnny, no one can do that to an audience, and no one can sing like that except my father!"

My heart stopped beating. Her tears turned to sobs as she asked, "Are you my father?"

I knew there was no sense in keeping my identity from her any loner, so without hesitation, I answered, "Yes, Kitten, I am, and I love you so very much."

"Why did you leave me? I loved you so much. For years I've visited your grave site and asked, why, why did you have to die? Mother told me you were in heaven with grandma, and that someday I'd see you again. Now you pop up out of nowhere after all these years as an Elvis Impersonator. I had a feeling about you last week when you were in Memphis. And then tonight, tonight I knew I had to ask. You did wrong. You didn't love me enough when I was little to 'stay alive', and now you want me to be close to you, and love you like I'm just supposed to forget these past empty years without a father and start fresh. I don't know if I can do that." She turned and ran from the room crying.

"Lisa, wait!" I yelled, "Let me explain, please," but she was gone and I didn't know what she was going to do or where she was going. Right then, I didn't know what I was going to do. I sat there, numb, my head in my hands. "God, what have I done?" And I cried until there were no tears left to shed.

I looked up as the door quietly opened and then closed. Lisa stood there, her face streaked with tears. I didn't move or speak. I thought it best to let her make the first move. She walked over and sat next to me on the sofa. I was afraid to breathe, until I realized, I was already holding my breath. I started speaking to her softly, so as not to frighten her away.

"Kitten, my life was a mess, drugs every night, drugs in the morning, pills to wake me up, pills to keep me going, and pills to make me sleep. My body was literally being destroyed. I had to leave the life I was living in order to survive. I couldn't cope any longer from the pressures of everyone always wanting something from me. I was afraid for my life from all the death threats. I couldn't leave the house for fear of being killed, or having people ripping and tearing at my clothes. Kitten, I couldn't walk the streets, not even at night for fear of being recognized, and you, you had no life. When you wanted to go to the zoo or shopping, we couldn't take you for fear you'd be kidnapped."

"Why?" she asked softly, but she was listening to every word.

"What's your name?" I asked her.

"Lisa Marie Presley."

"Yes, and that was just enough for someone to kidnap you to get to me. Try and remember back, we didn't have a 'normal' life together. At times I was so drugged I didn't know if you were even around. So I devised this plan. I had to 'die' in order to live and for you to be safe. If everyone thought I was dead, they'd leave you alone and you could grow up without all the dangers of being harmed. The only time I can remember feeling free during my whole career was when I performed on stage and sitting at home at the piano singing to you, but that wasn't enough for either of us."

"I needed to get my life back and to move about freely, and be free from all the pressures. I've got that now, and by the Grace of God, I found a way to have you back in my life as well. So you see, my plan worked, but I suffered just like you, and one day, I'll tell you the whole story. I meant what I said earlier, I love you so very much, I always have, and no matter what happens, I always will. I don't want to lose you again; I couldn't go through this twice."

"You were wrong, and you did me wrong," but she took my hand, "I love you too daddy, I'm glad you told me."

"Kitten, you have to continue to call me Johnny. We can't tell anyone else or all this will have been for nothing. Can you promise me that?"

She nodded in understanding, "I'll never reveal who you are, but I want to be close to you always."

"Well, we've been close these last few months, and Lisa I don't want to be in a situation to lose you again. I did what I had to do in order to have any kind of life."

"I know," she responded, "and I think I understand." "I guess it had to be hard on you too!" She then asked, "Joe knows, doesn't he?"

"Yes, Joe is the only one left living that knows, except now you do too!"

She smiled through her tears. "That little devil, he's always told me someday, you'll see him again. I thought he meant in heaven, I never would have believed this would happen. An Elvis Impersonator, what a great cover up," and she giggled.

"Look honey, it's going to be hard on you for awhile. The news media already wants to know why we're so close."

"I know, I've already told them it's because you remind me so much of my father."

Security knocked on my door interrupting us and said that David and Chance wanted to see me.

"Tell them it'll be just a minute," I hollered.

"I'm staying for tonight's second show and tomorrow night's too!" "Oh, and I bought a new jet."

"Yes, I know, I heard you had Lisa Marie written on one side of it."

"Joe, right?"

I nodded, "Yes, I talked with him this morning." "Did you want me to fly with you back to Memphis?"

"Yes! It would mean a lot to me if you would."

"Let me see if I can get someone to bring my car, and I'll let you know later, and remember, mum's the word.

"You used to tell me that when I was little."

She washed her face, and while she reapplied her make-up, I said, "Your

150

mother must not find out for any reason, okay?"

"I know, my lips are sealed, but on the way to Graceland, I want to talk to you."

"Alright, honey."

Lisa left to join her friends for the second show. David and Chance came in to congratulate me on an outstanding performance. Tara and Michele were ecstatic.

"Johnny, you did such a great job, it's hard to believe you're not Elvis," Tara said. "David and I were talking about that when you were singing."

"Yeah, Tara's right, I've never seen you perform like that before."

"The emotion, Johnny, I don't think there was a dry eye anywhere," Michele said.

"Yeah, including me," Chance agreed. "Especially when you sang "Memories" to Lisa Marie."

I finished my second show, and our entire group decided to go to the Pancake House. While we were there, customers told Lisa that she looked so much like Lisa Marie Presley, and that David, Chance and my self looked like Elvis.

One of the waitresses, after staring at us for several minutes, asked Lisa, "Are you Lisa Marie?"

"No, I'm not, my name is Tonya. I'm always being mistaken for her, but thank you, that's quite a compliment." We laughed at Lisa's quick response.

I asked Lisa Marie where she was staying and she said she had a suite right down the hall from me. I told her we would have coffee in the morning and we left to go back to the hotel. I asked David and Tara if they wanted to drive the Cadillac to Memphis so I could fly with Lisa. They said they would rather drive than fly to save on expenses.

"Oh, Tara, cancel your motel reservations, you two can stay with me at Graceland. I have two bedrooms and only need one."

"Wow," David said, "we get to stay at Graceland!"

"Oh hell," Chance said, "and I picked Dallas."

"Tell you what, Chance, next year if we do another show, you'll be there with me."

"Thanks, but I'm happy with my job in Dallas."

We drove back to the hotel, and being tired, we all went to our rooms. I fell across the bed thinking about Denise staying with Gary. She took a leave of absence from work to see what would develop between them. I was happy for their new found relationship, but concerned about Sandy. There really wasn't much I could do anymore to help her. My thoughts drifted to my conversation with Lisa, relief that she finally knew the truth, and sad that it hurt her so, and I fell into a deep sleep.

CHAPTER 16

The following morning, the guys went to the club to rehearse their numbers for the night's show. I picked up Tara and Michele to take them to see how their husbands were doing. Mr. Steadman came in to listen. Chance was singing, and Mr. Steadman said he thought he was good, and said he'd like to keep him for a longer length of time.

"You need to talk with Chance on that decision."

"By the way, Johnny, I ran into the owner of the Casino Royale in Vegas. He's really upset with you."

"Me!"

"Seems Gary told him you were going out there a few months ago, and you never showed up. I told him you were performing here at my club, and that my business more than doubled since you were here. He said he was going to kill Gary the next time he sees him."

I laughed, "Guess I should have asked for more money."

"You probably should have," and he walked off to handle business.

I looked at Michele, "Tell Chance not to sign a contract with Mr. Steadman that you want to keep the door open for more money."

"Do you think Mr. Steadman will offer more?"

"Well you never know, unless you ask."

Lisa Marie walked in. "Hi, I thought I'd find all of you here where there was music."

"Good morning Kitten, finally got out of bed, huh?"

"Was that you who called earlier?"

"Yes it was, when you didn't answer, I figured you were still asleep."

"I was in the shower and couldn't reach the phone in time, and when I did, you had already hung up. I figured this is where I'd find you, so I finished dressing and came here."

"I'm glad you found us, how did you sleep?"

"Better than I've slept in a long time, and you Johnny?"

"Me too," I smiled warmly at her.

Tara and Michele looked at us, "Something going on you two aren't telling us?" they inquired.

"Yes there is, I've decided to adopt Johnny as my father or at least call him father."

Tara and Michele were speechless at first, and then said they thought it was a great idea.

"Besides," Tara chuckled, "he looks like the father figure."

"Thanks a lot, one of these days you two will be 'old farts' yourselves," I retorted, and laughed along with everyone else.

The guys finished rehearsing and joined us at the bar.

"Sounds like you all are having a great time in here," David said, giving his wife a hug.

"Yeah, here we are working our butts off, and y'all are in here having a grand old time," Chance grinned, and Michele socked him on the arm.

"Johnny, how did we sound?"

"Well, "My Old Dog," wasn't bad, but it sounded like he had a cut lip," I grinned at him, and then chuckled along with the girls.

"Ha! Ha!" David said. "Bet your old dog looks like you," he continued, trying not to laugh.

"Poor dog!" And I burst out laughing.

"Okay, how'd we really sound?" Chance was curious to know what I thought.

"Well, Mr. Steadman heard you singing and wants you to stay longer or at least until winter is over.

"Really," Chance looked at Michele. "I didn't want to say anything to him before talking to you, but I don't see how we can stay longer. You have too many commitments in Birmingham," she said.

"Yeah, we'll talk to him later," Chance agreed.

David looked at me, "Johnny, you still haven't told us what you thought of the rehearsal today."

"All right, from what I heard; I think it was great for two old hounds."

Chance said, "Forget it Lee, we think we did great and we don't care what these old farts think."

"Watch who you're calling an old fart," Lisa grinned, enjoying the banter between us, "I'm not an old fart yet."

Chance grinned at her, "Yeah, but you're with an old fart."

"I guess you're right," she said, trying to sound serious.

"Your day is coming girl."

Tara looked at her watch, "Hey, what are we going to do until the show starts?"

"I need to go shopping," I answered.

"Shopping?" the guys said, rolling their eyes.

"Yes, let's all go, but I only have room for six in my Cadillac. Wait, Mr. Steadman has a limo."

"Yes," Denise said, "but if I ask for it he'll tell me no."

"Well, you're his daughter."

"I know, Johnny, but if you ask, he'll let you borrow it, he's a little upset with me right now for taking off from work."

"I've got an idea, here goes nothing," and I went to find Mr. Steadman.

He was in the kitchen giving dinner instructions to the chef's, and said, "Hi, Johnny, what's up?"

"I want to take the guys and their wives shopping in town, and I figure we should ride in style since we perform for Steadman's Supper Club. Good advertising, don't you agree?"

"Good idea, tell Denise I said it's all right."

"Sure, thanks, if you think that's better than my old car,"

I turned and went back to the bar. All eyes were on me.

"Well, what are you all waiting for? Let's go!"

"See," Denise said, "he likes Johnny, I knew he'd let him use the limo."

I walked over to the garage and found Mike, the limo driver polishing the car. I told him that Mr. Steadman said it would be all right if he drove us to town to shop. He thought that sounded better than sitting around all day. We piled into the limo and headed to Dallas's Galleria Mall.

We no sooner arrived, when the girls went their own way. The guys decided they didn't want to shop and found a bar. I told them to go ahead and wait for me there as I had shopping of my own to do. I found a florist and ordered a dozen red roses for each of the girls to be delivered at the club tonight.

I still had enough time to find a pay phone and called the car dealership in Birmingham. I had previously ordered three more Cadillac's from Zeke the last time I stayed at David and Tara's. I was able to purchase all three cars for the guys for as little as fifty-thousand dollars. Zeke was trying to clear out his current inventory for quick cash sales in order to open a Cadillac dealership at a new location.

I chose a '63' blue Cadillac convertible with white interior for David and Tara, a '63' white Cadillac convertible with red interior for Chance and Michele, and a '63' red Cadillac convertible with white interior, identical to mine, for Gary. Zeke finally answered the phone and told me the cars would definitely be delivered tonight at the hotel. Zeke had talked with the delivery driver earlier; he was about fifty miles east of Dallas.

I told Zeke that the hotel management was on the alert for them. They had been instructed on what to do and would handle everything for me. I thanked him for everything and hung up. My plan was to present the Cadillac's to the guys prior to my leaving on Dallas, Sunday morning.

The guy's were still sitting in the bar engrossed in a football game when I walked in. "If you guys are going to stay here and watch the game, I still have some other errands to run."

"Yeah, we'll probably be here till the girl's are done shopping," David answered, not taking his eyes off the television.

I was looking for an exclusive jewelry store, and had stopped in several shops before I found one near the end of the mall that carried what I wanted. An elderly clerk approached me the minute I walked in the door. "Can I help you?" she inquired.

"Yes, I'd like to see what you have in Rolex watches."

"Follow me, but keep in mind they are very expensive."

"Yes, ma'am, I'm aware of that."

She pulled several from the display case both 24kt and 14kt gold. I shook my head no. I pointed to several I liked. "How about taking these out for me to see?"

"Good choice, these have twelve diamonds around the face. They are on sale. We marked them down to five-thousand dollars each, and have already sold several this week."

"Well, you're about to sell more, I'll take these four please, and can I have them engraved today? Your sign advertises you do engraving the same day?"

She verified the engraving with the store manager. "It all depends on what you want engraved on them," he said. "I do the engraving myself unless you want fancy scroll work or something different on each, then it's a two day wait."

"No, this is what I want them all to say, "Friendship, Trust and Love till the end." "Elvis Aaron Presley." The manager and the saleslady's mouths dropped open as they stared at me in disbelief.

"We're all Elvis Impersonators, and we want people to think that Elvis gave us these watches." I laughed.

"For a minute there you had me going," the manager said, "but it's your money, you can have anything you want engraved on them."

"Is there an extra charge for the engraving?"

"Usually, but since you bought four watches, I'll do it for nothing. Give me a couple of hours, and I'll have them ready."

"Could you Christmas gift wrap them?"

"Sure, but we don't actually wrap them, we have holiday gift bags that are quite lovely," the sales clerk assured me. "How are you paying sir?" she inquired.

"I'll write you a check."

She verified funding, and I left.

As I was leaving the store, I ran into the girls. Denise had called Sandy and Kristi to join them, and I burst out laughing at the sight of them all loaded down with Christmas packages.

"Hi Johnny," Kristi asked, "buying me a ring?"

"Yes, buying all of you wedding rings just in case the men in your lives are too cheap to get you one for your weddings."

Sandy spoke up, "No way!" "I'm not ever getting married, not even to you, Johnny."

"Oh really, just see if I ever give you another bath."

"I'm just kidding," Sandy said, as the others all laughed.

Lisa Marie pulled me off to the side and asked if I needed money. I told her no, that I made enough to cover all my expenses, at least I had hoped so, but thanked her anyway.

"Johnny, where are the rest of the guys?" Denise asked. In all their excitement of showing me their purchases, they finally realized the men weren't around.

"They're in the bar waiting, come on, we'll join them." It was time to leave anyway in order to have enough time to get ready for tonight's shows.

David and Chance's eyes bulged at the sight of their wives carrying all their packages.

"Uh, buy anything, honey?" Chance asked, hoping the packages weren't all Michele's.

"Oh, Michele and I were just window shopping," laughed Tara.

"Yeah, it looks like you both bought everything 'in' the windows," David commented, trying to see if anything was for him.

We found Mike standing next to the limo and we loaded the trunk with all the packages. Everyone piled in, except for Kristi and Sandy. They left in Kristi's car and would see us at the club.

At the club after we were dressed, Chance, David and I walked on stage and saw that the girls were already dressed and sitting at the table waiting for us. I saw Mike, the chauffer standing in the doorway. I asked him if he would go back to the jewelry store at the mall and pick up four gifts I had purchased earlier. I instructed him to bring them directly to my dressing room and leave them there, and not to tell anyone what he was doing.

The delivery man from the florist's arrived. I instructed him to deliver the roses to each of the girls at the table marked "Reserved for Elvis" Gary returned by then and wanted to know where the limo driver was going. I told him I had forgot something at the mall, and he was going back to pick it up for me. Sandy and Denise were dressed in their waitress outfits. Mr. Steadman asked Denise if she would help out tonight because one of the waitress's had called in sick with the flu leaving them short handed.

"Come on Gary, let's check the equipment."

"I already did."

"Let's check it again," I insisted.

"Sure," he said, wondering what the problem was.

We walked on stage, and I explained to him that I only wanted to see the girl's faces when they received their roses.

"So you don't want to check the equipment?"

"No, I think it'll be fine."

"Why are the girls so happy tonight?" David wanted to know.

"The florist just delivered the roses that Johnny ordered earlier." Chance answered. His usual smiling face looked crestfallen.

"It should have been us buying them the flowers," said David. "We just didn't think about it."

"No," I commented, "this was my way of showing the girls my appreciation, and that tomorrow won't be good-bye, it's the beginning of a close and lasting friendship, and that I will miss them. That is, Kristi, Sandy and Denise. Your wives, well they deserve to get flowers just for putting up with you two." The girls waved and blew me a kiss to thank me for the roses.

"It's already five-thirty, don't you think we need to disappear before everyone sees us?" David sounded nervous.

Gary was walking towards the table to see the flowers, and Denise, but I asked him if he would go with us. I told the guys I wanted to discuss a few items with them and it affected him too. We had entered the dressing room when there was a knock at the door. It was Mike. He had returned, and handed me the four packages. I thanked him and told him I'd take care of him later. I turned and faced David, Chance and Gary, and took a deep breath. The three of them each looked at each other in bewilderment as I began to speak. "Before our performance tonight, I've got something for the four of us. But first, I have a couple of requests."

"You bought us something too?" Chance asked excitedly.

"Yes, I answered, "I did."

"What I am about to reveal to you must never be repeated! Not even to your wives! Do not ask me any questions! Not why! Not how! Promise me now!"

"We promise," they all responded, totally mystified at what I was asking of them.

I handed each of them a gift bag and continued, "Before you open these, I want you to know that there's only four of these in the world, and they're in this room. Believe me when I say I trust the three of you and regard you as my closest friends. Please accept these gifts in the true friendship they are given, even though, as I said before, no one can ever know the truth. The signature is authentic, so go ahead and open them and accept them in the love they are given."

They opened their gifts as I opened mine.

David, who was totally surprised said, "A Rolex watch!"

Gary gasped, and Chance started to cry as I told them to read the inscription on the back of the watches. They stared at me in amazement.

"Yes, it's true. If ever you discuss this among yourselves, make sure you are alone."

Finally, David said, "I knew it! I just knew it!"

"Why are you telling us, Johnny?" Chance asked, still wiping his eyes.

"The answer to your question is inscribed on your watches."

Gary, who was quiet up until now, said, "This is the finest gift a friend could give, and I don't mean the Rolex either."

"Thanks my friend," and I smiled at him.

"Because we each have identical watches, we are bonded together; nothing can ever break our friendship, except a break in trust. Tonight, you will sing with 'The King', something no one has ever done in this capacity, but you'll know the truth. One day, when I really am gone from this earth, you can tell the story to the world, but not until then. If anyone asks you where you got the watches, tell them a friend had them made for you. Now, enough sentimentality, let's give this audience a show they will never forget."

"Chance, you are doing the first show with me, and David you can do the second show. I will call you out on stage just as Mr. Steadman calls me. Gary will play the Odyssey 2000 intro, and I will announce you. Let's do it!"

Gary went on stage first and played easy, listening music while the people finished eating. Finally it was time for us to perform. Mr. Steadman made a special announcement regarding me leaving, and the special guest performance of the two Elvis's. Gary started the Odyssey 2000 intro. Chance and I were waiting on stage behind the curtain. I came out and immediately broke into song, "Viva Las Vegas" as my first choice, followed by "Follow That Dream," and then I slowed things down with "Loving You." I signaled Gary to hold on for a moment and asked the audience for total silence.

"I have a friend; another Elvis Impersonator who will replace me, as you all know tonight is my last night that I'll be entertaining at Steadman's. I've enjoyed performing for you these last three months, and I will miss everyone very much, but I know you will enjoy my replacement, as he is a good entertainer. So let's show him as much affection as you've given me, and give him a big Texas welcome. Ladies and gentlemen, I'd like to present to you, direct from Birmingham, Alabama, Chance!"

Gary played the intro again, and Chance came out like he owned the stage. I went back behind the curtain and waited for Chance to finish his set. He was on a high, and I wanted him to stay that way. The crowd tonight was a mixture of ages, but the older crowd acted more like teenagers. All in all, the audience loved him.

Chance finished singing "Polk Salad Annie." That was my cue to come back on stage. I waited for the crowd to quiet down and announced we would do a couple of songs together. When we finished, we got a standing ovation. I told Chance to sing "Anything That's Part of You" to Michele. Gary started the music and Chance called Michele to come to the stage. She brought a rose from her bouquet for him, and he bent down kissed her, and then introduced her to the audience. He sang to her with so much emotion it brought tears to numerous people eyes.

When he finished, I ended the first set with "American Trilogy" as I always did. The lights were dimmed. I looked out into the audience, and I could see the cigarette lighters and candles swaying to the beat of the music. I blocked out everything, but the music, it was as if the music and my body were one. The applause was deafening. The audience was jumping up and down. Chance and I tried talking to each other, but couldn't hear, so we walked off together, my arm on his shoulder.

"Fantastic job "Elvis," I said.

"Thanks, tonight I did feel like you, and it's the greatest feeling ever."

Back stage, David was crying from the performance. Chance and I looked at each other, and burst out laughing.

Gary met us in the dressing room. "Chance, there are some people out front asking where you are, and wanting pictures and autographs.

"Me!" Chance said.

"You," he responded, "your fans await you."

David looked at me, "They really loved him, didn't they?"

"Yes, they did, and they'll love you too! Now I need to go change into my white jump suit."

Just then, security knocked and told me Lisa Marie was waiting to see me. She ran over and hugged my neck.

"That was the best ever and the audience loved it."

"Thank you Kitten, now I need to change."

"Go behind the screen," she said, "I'm not leaving."

David laughed, "Maybe you should leave."

"No. It's okay. She knows."

"She does?"

"Yes, she does."

Security knocked again. The rest of the girls came bouncing in, yelling and all excited about the show.

I noticed Michele looking around, and I said, "Hey baby, Chance is out in the lobby signing autographs, and having his picture taken."

I watched her face for some reaction to what I said.

She grinned and said, "That's my man."

I let out a loud sigh of relief, and knew this would work for them. They all hugged and kissed me for the roses. Was I in my glory? You bet, wouldn't you be if you had six gorgeous women kissing you?

Sandy and Denise had to get back to work. Kristi went into the lobby to wait for Frank. He had to work, but was coming to the second show. David was starting to pace, as he always did before doing a show. He said it helped him psyche himself up for a good performance.

"Are you ready?" he asked.

"Oh I think so," I laughed. "Are you a little nervous?"

"Yes," he nodded, pacing again.

"Well that's good, because I get nervous every time I step out on the stage, and yet I love it more than life itself."

"You, you get nervous?"

I looked at him and said, "There's no way or no where you can get this kind of high that you get on the stage in front of a good audience."

Lisa Marie looked at us, "I notice you are all wearing identical watches."

Gary and Chance had returned by then.

"Yes, something I picked up at the mall."

"Johnny, you'll be broke before you leave."

"No Kitten, I came with five-thousand dollars, and I'll leave with five-thousand."

"Some things just never change, do they?"

"I hope not," I replied.

"David, let's break a leg."

Tara hugged and kissed him, and the girls left to go back to their table. The second show was so over booked, tables had to be squeezed in at the back.

Mr. Steadman again announced me, and Gary started the music. I played the audience for a few minutes, and then sang "All Shook Up" which was a perfect opener for this crowd. They were already yelling and carrying on, and it was only the beginning of my last show. I followed with "Treat Me Nice" and then "Are You Sincere." I stopped and waited for the audience to settle down.

Again I asked for total silence. "I have a special treat for you this evening; let me introduce you to a very good friend of mine from Birmingham, Alabama, Elvis Impersonator, David Lee." David came out on stage, did a few Karate moves which worked the audience into a state of frenzy.

After David finished his list of songs, I re-called Chance to come up and join us. We sang "Can't Help Falling In Love." Each of us took a turn singing a verse. When it was David's turn, he jumped from the stage, went to Tara, and sang his part while placing a scarf around her neck. He rejoined us on stage, the audience getting louder. We finished singing, and the three of us bowed simultaneously, and walked off the stage together.

Security started to brace them selves as women were trying to break through to get on the stage. They were almost getting out of hand as they demanded an encore. To satisfy them, I sang "Love Me Tender." The audience calmed down, and a hush came over the club. I sang from the heart. Sweat was pouring down my face, but I didn't stop until the end of the song.

Once again I held up my hand for silence. I waved to the audience, and said,

"Good night, ladies and gentlemen, may God bless you as he has blessed me, and walked off.

Mr. Steadman returned on stage and asked the audience to give me a big round of applause for having been such a good entertainer these past months, also to welcome Chance to the club, and David for joining us.

Both guys looked at me and then Chance asked, "How do you do it?"

"Do what?"

"Turn them on and off like a faucet," David finished the question for Chance. I smiled, curled my lip, and answered, "That's why I'm the 'King'. We laughed all the way back to the dressing room.

Security was supposed to be posted at the door, but with the large audience and being so wild, they were all out front keeping things under control. I opened the door and as we walked in congratulating each other on our performance, we stopped dead in our tracks. There in the middle of the room, once again, stood a very naked Nancy Jordan.

"Holy shit!" Chance stared in disbelief.

"Hot damn!" David's mouth dropped open.

Chance began laughing, "Is this one of the extra perks that goes with the job, Johnny?"

"No, this is the same woman I told you about. Ma'am, you need to get dressed and out of here before I call security."

"I'll leave, but not until you write your name across my breasts and over my ass," and she twirled around for our benefit.

David and Chance looked at me to see what I was going to do.

"If I do this, will you leave and promise never to come back?" I poked both guys, "Either of you have a pen?"

"Forget the pen, I have a magic marker over there, you can use it," Chance said.

I signed Johnny Raye in bold letters across her breasts and ass. All the while David and Chance were laughing like a couple of hyenas. When I finished, she inspected herself in the mirror. "Thank you Johnny, my husband has bugged me continuously to get your autograph, won't he be surprised when I show him where?" She dressed, blew me a kiss, and left.

Chance finally quit laughing, "Maybe it would be better if we didn't tell Michele what just happened here."

"Yeah," David agreed, "It might be best not to tell Tara either."

"No, you two need to tell them the truth, it'll look like you're trying to hide something otherwise. I think they'll get a kick out of it."

We changed out of our suits, and met the girls in the lobby. Most of the crowd was gone by then. David and Chance walked over to where their wives were waiting and told them what just happened. Michele and Tara exchanged smug looks.

"Chance," Michele looked at him trying to be serious, "Did you two write your signatures too?"

"No, we just stood there watching."

Tara by now was in a fit of giggles. "We sent her in there."

"What?" David and Chance said in unison.

"Yeah, she was waiting here for you to return and Denise told us who she was. Michele and I thought you'd get a kick out of her."

"It was a kick all right; my eyes almost fell out at the size of those boobs!" Chance admitted.

"Tits hell," David joined him, "did you get a load of that firm round ass as Johnny was signing his name? And the way she wiggled it, sure was a pretty sight, I was afraid to blink for fear it would disappear!"

"That's enough you two," the girls laughed at their husbands.

We stood around talking and Gary and Chance were complaining they were hungry. David suggested for us all to go for coffee and dessert, but I declined, and told them to go ahead without me. I wanted to spend some time with Lisa Marie. They nodded understanding my wishes.

"Okay 'dad,' see you in the morning before you leave." Chance retorted.

"Don't make it too early," Lisa said, "I like to sleep until at least ten o'clock."

"How about nine o'clock, instead?" I asked her.

"Nine it is, but not any sooner.

Lisa and I left them and walked over to the parking lot to check on the Cadillac's. Security had parked them in back of the hotel near the guard's office. I checked the cars for any dents or scratches, and finding none, decided to take them for a test drive. Lisa drove one while I drove the other. We brought them back and took the third one out together.

"Maybe we should let David and Tara take the jet to Memphis and you and I drive these cars. They really handle great."

"We could," but then thought better of it, "no, they'll want to drive, I can see their faces now."

"Me too!" she said yawning, "it's late, let's get some sleep or I won't be up by nine."

I walked her back to her room, kissed her on the forehead, and told her I'd see her in the morning.

"Good night, I love you Kitten."

"I love you too dad, I'm sure glad we're together."

"Me too, Lisa. Me too."

When I got to my room, I realized I was tired, but not sleepy. After doing two shows I should have been, but I was really on a high from everything that went on during the day; shopping at the mall for the watches, the guy's expressions and feelings when they received them and them finding out who I really was. Then the girls with their flowers, excitement of giving the guys their Cadillac's in the morning, my last two shows at Steadman's, no wonder sleep evaded me.

I finally decided to forego sleep for awhile, and went to the lounge. John was bartending again and greeted me warmly when I sat down. "Hey Johnny, I hear you put on a fantastic show tonight."

"Yeah," I agreed, "the three Elvis's was a big hit."

The bar was getting ready to close as it was after midnight. The only other person there besides me and the bartender, was a woman sitting at the end of the bar.

"So you're Johnny Raye?" she asked.

"Yes ma'am."

"Me, and a number of my friends would love to see your show, but we can't afford to go to Steadman's Supper Club."

"I'm sorry; maybe you could come to Memphis to see the Christmas Special."

"I called, but the tickets are too expensive."

"Give me your name and I'll get you free tickets."

"That's wonderful, thank you, but we don't have the money to stay in Memphis or even afford the gas to travel."

I looked at her and asked, "Then why are you here in the bar?"

"Oh, I work in the kitchen here at the hotel, and sometimes I come and talk to John on my break. I'm waiting for my husband to pick me up, my shift is over."

"Wait here, I'll be right back."

She looked at the bartender for an explanation, but he just shrugged his shoulders.

I went to the ATM machine, took out five-hundred dollars, and gave the money to the woman.

"Maybe that will help."

She looked at me in total shock, never expecting anything like this, an said, "I can't accept this."

"Please take it. Call the ticket office in Memphis and make sure you talk to Joe Esposito. Tell him Johnny Raye gave you the money to come to Memphis, and that I'd like for him to make sure you get four free tickets and a spot near the front of the crowd."

"Up front," her eyes sparkled with excitement.

"Yes, up front so I can see you when I'm performing."

"Oh, thank you so very much, this is a dream come true," and she came and hugged my neck. She ran outside to see if her husband had arrived.

John looked at me and said, "That is the kindest thing I have ever seen anyone ever do. You made her day, but I bet she can't get off work to go."

"Who is her boss?"

"Jerry Wade, he's in the kitchen right now. You gave her money and never asked her name?"

"Bad habit of mine," I replied. "She was going to write down the names for the tickets, somehow she forgot to give them to me."

He just laughed, "Her name is Mary Cortez."

"Thanks, John, I'll be right back, hold my coke for me."

I walked into the kitchen and a teenage kid with a dozen rings in both ears was moping the floor. Things sure have changed since I was young when parents thought my hair was too long and my hips too wild. I couldn't help but stare as I asked him if Jerry Wade was around. He pointed and muttered some sound that I interpreted as 'over there'.

I found a gentleman dressed in brown slacks with a white shirt and tie. "Are you Jerry Wade," I inquired.

"Yes, and you're Johnny Raye? I took my wife to your show tonight, and I have to tell you I was very impressed with your performance. What brings you back here?" He said and shook my hand.

"Mary Cortez!"

He looked surprised at the mention of her name.

"I gave her money tonight for her and some friends to attend my Christmas Special in Memphis, next weekend. Can you arrange for her to get some time off?"

"Well that's a mighty big favor to ask."

"It is, and I'll owe you one if you can make it happen."

"Alright, I'll work it out with her and tell her she can go when she comes in tomorrow."

"Thank you sir, I appreciate it."

"Your welcome, and good luck with your special in Memphis," he said, as we shook hands.

I went to the bar to finish my coke and Mary was there along with her husband. The bartender had told her I was in the kitchen trying to get her time off for the Christmas Special.

"What did he say?" she blurted out before I even had time to sit down.

"He said, Okay."

"Thank you," she squealed, and gave me a hug.

Her husband shook my hand, and said, "You've got to be the real Elvis, only he would have been this kind to me and my wife."

"No sir, but I appreciate you thinking I am, and I look forward to seeing you in Memphis."

I laid a five dollar tip on the bar and got up to leave. I no sooner made it to the doorway when Gary walked in. "Hey, you're still up?"

"Yeah, I couldn't sleep? Where are the guys and their wives?"

"In bed, I guess."

"Denise?"

"She's in bed too?"

"And you're down here?" I kidded.

"I'm going to drink a coke and then I guess I'll go back up. Mind if I join you?"

"These cokes are on me," the bartender said.

Mary and her husband were leaving and turned to thank me once again.

"What did you give away this time?" Gary wanted to know.

"Nothing really."

John spoke up, "It may not be any of my business, but Johnny here just gave that couple five hundred dollars in cash, and arranged for her to get four free tickets to the Christmas Special, and three days off from work.

"Is that all?" Gary kidded.

"I'd say that was quite enough." John replied.

"Okay, you two, I've got to get to bed, see you in the morning."

"Wait, Johnny, I'm going up too!"

"See you in the morning, I told him as we went into our rooms---he to Denise---me to a long needed empty bed, and fell instantly asleep.

I woke before the alarm, dressed and arranged for the valet parking attendants to bring the Cadillac's to the front of the hotel. I then went to Lisa's room; she was up and getting ready. I went back to my room to finish packing and then called David, Chance and Gary's rooms to have them meet me in the lobby at eleven o'clock.

I went to get Lisa. She was ready when I knocked on her door. "Let's get some breakfast before we go." We sat in the hotel restaurant talking and enjoying our meal.

"What are you doing about the cars?"

"Already handled, I had them brought out front."

"I can't wait to see their faces; I'm so excited, aren't you?"

"Yes, I am, Kitten."

She looked at me, a serious expression on her face, "You've done a lot for Chance and David, why?"

"Well, they played a big part in getting me back to where I am today, and they've become very good friends. They wanted me to do well, and now I can return the favor. I'd like to see them both do well, they love the stage and they love Elvis. I want to help them as much as I can."

"Chance should do well here," she commented.

"I think so too, he should advance from here, and David, it's possible after Memphis that Vegas will be calling on him."

"Where does that leave you?"

"I'll do fine in Vegas. There's plenty of room for all Elvis Impersonators, but only the best get the night clubs that pay good. Besides, I'll be retiring in a few years. My voice won't hold out for ever, and at my age, I probably won't be able to move around on stage as well as I do now. No one will want to watch a sixty-five year old man on stage. People will want to remember Elvis as he was."

"No, you're wrong, you'll always be great."

"I wish that were true, but its nice having you in my corner believing in me."

Lisa was calling for a limo to take us to the airport, but I told her to hold off, as I wanted to say good-bye to Mr. Steadman, as soon as we finished eating. I knew he would want us to use his limo. I told her when she was done to go back up to her room to make sure she had everything packed.

My bags were ready to be picked up, so all I had to do to kill time until I met with everyone was to see Mr. Steadman. I walked to the club and found him working in his office.

"Johnny, I'm glad you stopped. I wanted to give you this last night, but we were so crowded and short handed, I didn't have a chance," and he handed me an envelope.

"What's this?"

"Open it when you leave here."

We chatted about some of the shows, and last nights performances. He was extremely pleased with the results of the past three months, and had high hopes that Chance would do as well.

I needed to leave and thanked him for everything. He wished me the best with the Christmas Special.

"Oh, by the way Johnny, I hope you don't mind, but I arranged to have a limo drive you to the airport."

"Thank you sir, I was going to ask if it would be all right to have Mike drive us."

We shook hands, and I left. I opened the envelope while walking across the street. To my surprise, there were ten crisp one thousand dollar bills.

I stopped at Lisa's room first. She was making sure the plane was ready when we arrived at the airport. I checked my room once more and met Lisa downstairs. We went back into the restaurant to order a coke and wait for everyone to come.

David and Tara were first to arrive. They asked if we were ready to leave as they were anxious to get on the road. Chance and Michele arrived, and a few minutes later, Gary came with Denise.

"Do you have the keys to the Cadillac?" David wanted to know.

"Yes, just wait a minute and I'll give them to you."

As I walked towards the lobby, I asked everyone to follow me.

"Now what's he up too?" someone asked.

Lisa smiled and tried not to give anything away.

I gave David a set of keys, and said, "Instead of taking my Cadillac, why don't you drive yours?"

"He looked puzzled, "I can't, mine's at home."

"No," I responded, it's out front."

David looked through the glass lobby doors. At first he didn't say anything, and then he laughed uproariously.

"You guys are not going to believe this, come here everyone and see for yourselves. Hell, forget the looking I'm going out and touching."

Everyone was talking excitedly; no one had any idea of what was going on. "David, see which key fits your car," I hollered at him. "Chance, Gary, here are your keys, try them out."

Gary immediately went to the red and white convertible. "Is this your car, Johnny?" he wanted to know, as he started the engine.

"No, mine is parked out back."

David found the key to his car after trying Chance's first. The guys sat in their cars, their wives squealed with delight.

"Man this is too much!" "Wow!" "This is unbelievable!"

I laughed. The joy on their faces was indescribable.

"Hey Johnny," David yelled over the noise of the engines, "how are you going to get your car to Memphis?"

"Each car is already set up with a tow package; my car is sitting on a trailer ready to go. You can pull it behind yours because Gary's hauling his equipment behind his."

They jumped from their cars, gave me a big hug, and said, "We love you man!"

Chance looked at me, "I don't know what to say."

"Nothing," I answered, "Say nothing."

"Johnny, it's time we left for the airport, the jet's waiting." Lisa linked arms with me.

"I've got to go, see you guys in Memphis, and David, don't you put one scratch on my car."

"Oh no, if I do, you can have mine."

I looked at Michele and Chance. Tears trickled down their cheeks. "Hey, why are you two crying, we'll all be together again before you know it, that's a promise."

"We're going to miss you," Michele wiped her eyes.

"I'll miss you too!" I said softly. "Gary, where is Denise and the others?" I asked to break up the emotional moment.

"She went to get Sandy and Kristi; they're on their way back."

"I can't wait any longer, I have to go. You'll have to tell them good-bye for me."

"Whew!" "Denise is coming with me, but Sandy and Kristi! They'll be mad as the devil for not being able to say good-bye."

"Tell you what, let me quick write them each a note, and you can give it to them for me."

I hurried to the reservation desk, wrote a note telling them each how much I enjoyed my stay in Dallas, and that I loved them dearly, and would always keep them close to my heart. I wished them both the best in life, Kristi with Frank, and Sandy to make it on her own. I told them if they ever got too lonely or in need of a friend to call me and I'd be there for them.

I handed the envelopes to Gary, and he assured me he would give them to the girls right away. The bell hop had finished loading our luggage, Lisa and I entered the limo, waved good-bye, and were on our way to the airport.

CHAPTER 17

Upon arriving at the airport, Lisa directed Mike to where the pilots were waiting. As we entered the plane, Lisa explained what the jet looked like before she had it redone to her taste. The interior floor and walls were now a soft green, accented with creams and whites throughout. She had chosen a cream colored sofa in soft leather with light oak tables, and a large screened TV, along with regular aircraft seats for safety purposes. The kitchenette adjoined the sitting area. The back of the plane contained a private bathroom and bedroom. The king sized quilt and matching curtains were cream with splashes of white. Green, white and cream colored pillows of various shapes and sizes were piled on the bed. So different than the mannish colors of browns and gray the previous owner had preferred.

Lisa still had questions as to how we had managed to execute the greatest performance of my time. So after take off, we sat together on the sofa, and I explained everything from the night I was at the hospital to our meeting in Panama City where she judged the contest on the beach. She cried for awhile, but not with the heart rending sobs that wracked her body when I first told her who I was. Instead, the tears seemed to be more of a healing of pain that had been in her heart for a long time. I only prayed that she could accept all of this, and we could develop a new relationship with one another. I knew I would have to move slowly with her and let her choose how close we would become.

Lisa had fallen asleep, whether from all the tears or the long hours of the past few days, whatever the reason, she didn't waken until we landed in Memphis.

"I'm sorry. I didn't mean to fall asleep."

"That's okay Kitten, I enjoyed watching you sleep. Lisa, you've got to remember you cannot say anything to your mother about me. If anyone should tell her, it should come from me. Promise?"

"I promise."

Joe arranged to have a limo waiting when we landed, and George was on duty when we arrived at Graceland.

"Hello, Ms. Presley, hello, Mr. Raye," good to see you again he acknowledged, as he opened the gates for us to drive through.

I asked the chauffeur to take care of Lisa Marie's things first and then bring mine to the guest house. We walked into the house together, and again, nostalgia hit hard.

"After sixteen years, I feel like I'm home again."

"Yes, but at least now you can come and go as you please," she said giving my hand a little reassuring squeeze. "Are you hungry?"

"Yeah, a little, do you have anything here to eat?"

"No, but I can call and have two steaks dinners brought to us."

"Add a baked potato and a salad, and you have a deal."

George brought us the food while I played the piano and sang Christmas Carols. "Excuse me sir," he said, "would you sing one for me?"

I started playing "Holly Leaves and Christmas Trees."

"Mr. Raye, how did you know that's the one I was about to ask you to play?"

"Because, that's my favorite Christmas song."

"Mine too," George replied."

"Here let me start over."

Lisa Marie came and sat with me.

When I finished, George smiled, and said, "Seems like old times, doesn't it Miss Lisa?"

"Yes, it does, George."

"Well you two can sit and reminisce all night if you want, but I'm going to eat my steak before it gets cold. George, before you go, how many guards are on duty tonight?"

"Oh, about five or six. Why?"

"Where do you eat?"

"We usually go across the street to the café, why?"

"You tell the cook to give each of you a steak dinner on me, okay. Have them call here and verify, and tell them Merry Christmas from Elvis."

"Yes sir, I'll tell them and thank you," he smiled and left.

"Aren't you afraid George will find out who you are?"

"No, I'm not. He may wonder and he may have doubts, but he won't say anything, and he won't ask questions. Besides George and I go back a long time and I'm glad he's still here."

"Yes, me too! When I was little, he used to run behind me when I was learning to ride my bike, and sometimes he'd pull me in my wagon all over Graceland, even in the snow."

"Kitten, George will always be taken care of, you can depend on that."

We finished our steaks, sang a few more Christmas songs, and I left to get some sleep. Pictures of Lisa and me together with Priscilla were placed on end tables and hung on the walls. Lisa Marie was right; we missed out on a lifetime. Nothing I could do now could ever change or replace the years we lost. Maybe what I did was wrong. Perhaps I could have made things different, but I don't know how I could have. I picked up a silver framed picture of Priscilla and me after our wedding. I really did love that woman. I just don't understand why I went anywhere without her. Maybe our life could have been different if she had been with me instead of me keeping her at home. Hell, who am I kidding? Our divorce was my fault. Why she stayed married to me as long as she did is beyond me. I glanced at the clock and it was already after midnight. Enough reminiscing, I needed to get some sleep.

I met with Lisa for breakfast at the main house. No tours were scheduled until after Christmas, so it left us free to use the house without interruption, or so I thought. Everyone was running in and out asking a million questions as to what goes where and who was responsible.

"I'm proud of you Kitten. You've turned out to be quite a little business woman."

"Thanks daddy," she whispered, "it helps to have a staff of very efficient people." "They prepare the itinerary for the day and I do the policing. Its fun to give orders. How did you sleep?"

"Like a baby, but before I hit the sack, I enjoyed looking at all the old pictures of us all together."

"I put them in there; I thought you'd like them."

I poured us another cup of coffee and filled my plate with food from the breakfast buffet. It was Monday. Gary, Denise, David and Tara would be arriving.

"We'll have to check out the sound system when everyone arrives. How tight is your schedule today?"

"If all goes well, not bad. Why?"

"I thought you and I could put decorations on the tree."

"What tree? The foyer already has a decorated tree."

"Nope, I mean the one we're buying this morning."

"We're going to buy a tree?"

"Uh, huh, we should be able to find one around Memphis somewhere, and there's no reason we can't shop for it ourselves. Like you said last night, I can come and go as I now please, so where can I get a truck?"

I can call the office; they'll arrange to get us one." Lisa buzzed for security, and George brought us a cart.

"George, I thought today was your day off? Lisa asked, concern in her voice.

"Yes ma'am it is, but I thought I'd come in today and help decorate the outside trees. You don't mind do you?"

"No I don't mind, but I don't want you to wear yourself out and get sick. There is a crew that's already hired to do all that," she informed him.

Georges's smile faded and he looked disappointed. "But someone will need to supervise the operation, do you think you'd like that?" she added thoughtfully.

"You'd be a big help," I commented. Can you imagine the chaos without someone giving directions? Anyway, I'm taking Lisa with me, and since you know where everything is, you'll be in charge."

"I'll get right on it as soon as I ride you two over to the office," George beamed. "The cart is parked out front."

Within minutes a pickup truck was at our disposal. Lisa and I drove to several tree stands until we found one that had what we wanted. We both spotted an eight foot blue spruce at the same time. We checked the trunk to make sure it was straight and looked for holes or gaps, and finding none, paid the man twenty dollars.

The salesman was busy helping other customers, so Lisa and I had to drag the tree about two hundred feet to where we parked. We were huffing and puffing by the time we finally loaded it onto the truck. "What about decorations?" I asked.

"We have tons at the house to pick from, and if we don't like what's there, we'll go out and buy what we want. All the outside lights have been special ordered for the Christmas Special."

I turned on the radio, found a station that was playing Christmas music, and Lisa and I sang songs all the way back to Graceland. We managed to drag the tree from the truck to the house without damaging too many branches. After a half an hour of moving the tree to several spots, and leaving a trail of needles, we final agreed to place it near the piano. I held the tree while Lisa went to look for a stand.

Minutes later she returned, "This is the best Christmas I've had since I was a little girl."

"It's the best I've ever had," I agreed. "I can't remember ever being able to take you shopping for a tree."

"Daddy, I've had time to think about all you've told me, and I think you did the right thing. A second chance at life is something you don't always get, and so far yours has worked out the way you hoped it would. And, we're together. I'm sorry for being so angry with you the other day."

"Kitten, you had every right to be angry, but let's not spoil our day, okay!"

George came in carrying a big box.

"There's two more on the porch, you going to let an old man do all the work?" he cackled.

Lisa and I ran to help him.

"I thought you were out supervising the tree decorating?" I asked him.

"I am, but I thought I'd come in and warm up for a minute. That cold air raises cane with my arthritis, besides; I knew you'd be looking for these."

"Why don't you stay here and help us put the lights on?" I asked him. But he was already taking off his jacket and digging through the boxes for lights. We finished in a couple of hours, laughing and joking over a few of the ornaments that Lisa had made when she was little.

George cleaned up the mess, and Lisa and I left for the mall. We decided 'our tree' looked bare without presents under it. Lisa made a list of who we should buy for and what they might like.

I purchased a black cashmere sweater for Lisa, and she decided on a black silk shirt for me. We found a white sweater for Priscilla, a sport coat for Gary, a blue dress shirt for Joe, red matching Christmas sweaters for Tara and David. We wanted to buy George a new jacket as his appeared to be somewhat worn. We chose a dark, brown corduroy with lamb lining and said that this should keep him good and warm, along with a pair of warm gloves to match. We had everything gift wrapped and finally hauled our purchases back to Graceland. I shoved them under the tree.

Lisa shook her head and said, "Men, have no patience," and restacked the wrapped presents artfully under the tree.

Joe stopped in to see what we were doing and to ask Lisa a few questions. "You two are going all out aren't you?" he commented, eyeing the tree and gifts underneath it.

"It's going to be a very nice Christmas," I smiled at him.

"I hope so, Priscilla will be home tomorrow."

"Good."

"I don't know about that," Lisa looked at Joe and then back at me. "Sometimes mother and I don't always see eye to eye on things, but most of the time we think alike."

"I know my being here, the Christmas Special, and then when she sees this tree is going to bring back a lot of memories for her. My point is, let's try to be understanding, and not upset her, okay?"

"Before I forget," Joe said, "Gary called."

"Are they all right? No one's had an accident?" I asked worriedly.

"No! No! They got a late start. Something about having to take several hours to calm down Sandy and Kristi. Sounds like they're a little perturbed with you."

Lisa and I looked at each other and laughed. "Yes, I'll bet they are."

Anyway, they'll be here tomorrow morning."

The rest of the evening was spent checking on the outdoor decorations. We sent George home as he was cold and tired.

Lisa called the television station to send someone out to check on the big screen that was installed ten feet above the ground, similar to what you would find at an outdoor theater. This would allow everyone to see the show live. As many people as were expected, this would help those in back to see the stage.

Next we checked on heaters, but discovered the heaters would interfere with the snow machines. A decision had to be made, heat vs. snow problem. The heaters would melt the snow as fast as it was being made. We decided to make snow eight to ten hours in advance of the show. Then Joe realized the warmth of the day would melt it. The temperature at night was in the twenties, and that was perfect for making snow, but during the day it would rise to the fifties. We needed a cloudy, cold couple of days. Our only hope would be if the weather would cooperate.

We decided to give it a trial run and to see what would happen. First we turned on the snow machines to build a good solid base. Within an hour, Graceland was being transformed into a winter wonderland. Snow was sticking to the trees; the lawn was slowly being covered. The snow on the roof of the house looked like it was ready for Santa and his reindeer.

For our own pleasure, we turned on the Christmas lights and their reflection in the snow was indeed picture perfect. You could feel the magic of Christmas in the air. The glow of excitement on Lisa Marie's face was far more important to me at that moment than anything I had ever experienced in my life.

We continued to make snow for over five hours, and then turned the heaters on to see how long the snow would last. The snow melted before it hit the ground, but to our surprise, the ground stayed covered. We shut off the heaters and decided to make snow all Friday night and on into Saturday. Of course, the weather still had to cooperate.

We were all tired and decided to call it a night as it was already after one o'clock. The guest house was warm and inviting after spending so much time in the cold air. I climbed into bed feeling lonely. Maybe it was the magic of Christmas, but whatever it was; I wished Karen was here at my side. I wondered what she was doing. I resisted the urge to call her and drifted off to sleep with the vision of her singing on stage.

I met Lisa on the enclosed patio around noon. She was eating lunch and had a place set for me. The patio area was heated and Lisa loved to sit there during the winter months. She had it decorated with white wicker furniture with blue and mauve cushions for accent. Real trees and shrubs gave the sun room an atrium atmosphere.

"The snow is beautiful, daddy."

"Yes, it is, have you looked out front this morning?"

"Yes, it's fantastic. The trees stayed covered, and the snow is almost five inches deep all the way to the concrete walls."

"Good, we just might have a white Christmas after all."

"By the way, one of the men making snow said we needed to reload two of the refrigerated trailers with ice. I told them to go ahead and reload, but they said they had to have permission from the office. I'm supposed to see to everything, but I'm not the person 'in charge'. Anyway, I told them that you were in charge of the snow machines, so you won't have any problems with them."

"Daddy," she added, "mother is here, she's upstairs."

"Is she in a good mood?"

"Well, she loved the snow and the trees. She even liked our tree by the piano, and thought it was a good idea. She was very happy when she came in this morning."

"Did she make the coffee?"

"Yes, she did why?"

"I'd almost forgotten how weak she likes it."

Lisa laughed, "Yes, some things never change."

"And be careful Kitten, you've been calling me daddy."

"Okay, Johnny!"

Just then, Priscilla walked out asking, "What things never change?"

"Johnny was just saying how weak your coffee is."

"Funny, Elvis always complained about my coffee too!"

"Oh, I'm not complaining, I'm just making a statement."

"Johnny, was it your idea to make the snow?" Priscilla asked.

"Yes, it was, it really looks beautiful don't you think?"

"Yes I do, Elvis always loved snow on the ground at Christmas; it was his favorite time of the year. Your idea for the tree next to the piano too?"

"Yes, Lisa and I thought it would be fun to share gifts after the Christmas Special is over with, probably on Monday morning."

"You're really living up the part of Elvis, aren't you?"

"Mother!" Lisa spoke sharply. "That was uncalled for! If anyone is to blame, it's me. I'm trying to make Johnny feel at home, after all, he's doing a great job as an Elvis Impersonator. And I think the show is going to be fantastic, a tribute to daddy that people will remember for a long time."

"You're right Lisa, and I apologize, Johnny. I guess I got caught up in the past for a moment."

"No problem and I accept your apology. Lisa did Gary arrive yet?"

"Yes, the office said he called this morning, he's checked in at the hotel and he'll be here later."

"Did they get the canopy room set up yet for filming and camera equipment?

"They're working on it right now. The carpenter promised me it would be finished this afternoon so the furniture can go in and I can do the press interview."

"Well in that case ladies, excuse me, I think I'll go and check it out."

I met Gary and Denise as they were coming up the driveway. I told Gary where to park to unload his equipment when Denise jumped out and hugged my neck and gave me a big kiss. "I still love you, Johnny," she teased, but she had her arm around Gary when she said it.

"Well the way you hang on to this bum, you'd never know it."

Gary laughed, "Well for being an old bum I sure drive a nice car."

"Yes you do," I grinned.

They both looked around. "This is the only place in Memphis that has snow, this is awesome, Johnny," Denise commented in amazement.

"Where are David and Tara?" I asked, looking around.

"They're somewhere behind us, they went riding through Memphis with the top down and the heater wide open. They really looked crazy, especially pulling your car behind theirs," Gary laughed.

"Well sometimes doing crazy things makes you feel good. Here they come now. I'll get someone to help you unload, and I'll ask Lisa where she wants the cars parked. Be right back." I found Lisa and talked to her about the cars, and where they should be parked.

"I don't really know," she said.

Priscilla followed us to see what we were talking about. "Wow, these Cadillac's were Elvis's favorite cars; let's leave them out front in the circular drive."

I looked at Priscilla and said, "I agree with you, they do look nice and they give the look of, let's see, how would you say this Kitten, 'the olden days'?"

Lisa giggled, and then looked at her mother, "Yes, mother, a very good idea," and winked at me. Lisa called George and asked him to come up and drop Gary's trailer next to the storage buildings where it would be out of sight, and then bring the car back.

Tara and David finally parked and were unloading my car from the trailer when I grabbed Tara and gave her a hug.

"Hi Johnny, we sure have missed you."

David gave me a big ole bear hug, and asked, "How you doing big guy?"

"Great, I see y'all had a safe trip and took care of my car."

"Yeah," Tara said, "you should see how slow we had to go to make sure nothing happened to your Caddie." "I thought we'd never get here."

I introduced David, Tara and Denise to Priscilla as she had already met Gary when he was checking out the stage structure.

"George, get some of the workers to help bring their luggage to the guest house," she directed. "Gary and Denise, you can stay there too, and Johnny, you can move your things into the house," Priscilla continued, taking charge of the situation and giving orders. Have Johnny's things brought to Elvis's room. No one has slept in there since his death. Lisa, will you take care of that?"

Lisa gasped in surprise, and said, "Sure mother, that's another great idea," Lisa looked at me and shrugged her shoulders in bewilderment of her mother's reaction to everything.

"I, uh, I'm not sure that's a good idea, ma'am," I stammered.

"Sure it is," she quickly responded.

George scratched his head, and looked from Priscilla to me and back to Priscilla, "Yes ma'am, I'll go round up some help right away."

Satisfied with her decisions, Priscilla walked back into the house.

Lisa whispered to me, "She's up to something, daddy."

"I know Kitten, I sensed that too!"

Lisa left to handle things, I suggested to David and Gary that we set up the equipment and check the sound.

"Tonight?" asked Gary.

"Yes, I think that would be a good idea."

David came and stood next to me, "Johnny, you look worried, do you think Priscilla is up to something?"

"Knowing Cilla like I do, she could be."

Lisa joined us outside. "Mother is having 'your room' prepared right now."

"What's going on?"

"I don't know, but I think she knows more than we think she does, because she's acting very strange."

"Let me know if she says anything to you?"

"I will Johnny, and I think I'll hang around the house today. Come on Tara, and Denise, I'll take you on a private tour with me." Lisa suggested.

David and Gary went to work on the stage equipment while I hopped on the cart to look for Joe. When I got to the office, they informed me that Joe wasn't in, that Priscilla had sent him on numerous errands for the day, but he'd be back tomorrow.

I rode over to the café and asked them to deliver snacks to the house. I ordered cheese, crackers, pickles, and a dozen fried peanut butter and banana sandwiches along with a variety of sodas.

"We'll take care of this, and have them sent over right away," said the manager, and then asked, Is there something wrong?"

"No. Why?"

"You look worried, you usually come in here all teasing and happy, but today you're real quiet and look troubled."

"No, I'm fine; I just have a lot going on right now with the upcoming show." I left and went back to the house.

I needed to be on my toes with anyone who asks me questions in case they are trying to trick me. If Priscilla starts to ask me questions, I'll have to act like I don't know what she's talking about. I thought.

I found Gary and David; they had the sound system set up and were connecting it to the speakers. I asked Gary to put on a disc to let David sing a few songs while I went across the street to listen. I picked up a couple of two way radios from George, and gave one to Gary. David's voice came through loud and clear. I moved to several different locations to check and make sure the speakers were okay.

"Gary," I yelled into the radio, "don't change a thing, it sounds terrific."

I brought the radios back and went to the house to join the group, when Priscilla said, "Don't you think this is a little loud?"

"It won't be if you have forty to fifty thousand people out there."

"I guess you're right, after all you should know better than anyone."

"Thank you," I said, "but if you really feel it's too loud then we can turn it down a little."

"No!" Lisa jumped into the conversation, "It's fine, now sing us a song, Johnny."

"It's a little too cold with the heaters off. The only one running is near Gary's equipment."

"That's okay, we'll go inside and you can sing and play the piano," she countered.

It was almost six o'clock and the café was delivering the sandwiches and snacks. "Oh, fried peanut butter and banana sandwiches huh?" Priscilla asked looking smug.

"Yes, David loves them."

David grinned at me, "I think they are great, you want one, Johnny?"

"No, I'll stick to the cheese and crackers, thanks anyway."

"Johnny, you promised me a song," Lisa interjected.

"Alright, let's make it a Christmas one. With all the snow on the ground, and the trees all lit, it brings out the Christmas spirit in me."

"Yes, it is beautiful," Priscilla answered, "just like old times."

"No, not quite, daddy would be off in Hollywood making a movie or on tour somewhere."

"That's not true," Priscilla said in Elvis's defense, "he was always here at Graceland on Christmas Eve and Christmas Day.

I spoke up and said, "Let's sing "Silent Night" first."

Priscilla went into the kitchen and made hot chocolate for everyone. When she returned I thanked her for her hospitality and hoped she would enjoy the show as much as we would enjoy doing it.

"Oh, I feel it will be good. In fact, very good," Priscilla stared at me.

"Johnny, how about doing "Holly Leaves and Christmas Trees," isn't that your favorite?" Tara asked innocently.

"For you Tara, coming right up."

As I sang, Priscilla walked over to the window, George was there listening. Priscilla asked him to come in, and gave him a cup of hot chocolate.

"This feels like old times doesn't it?" he asked.

"Yes, George, it does," Priscilla smiled warmly at him.

"Yes ma'am, it's so pretty outside," George responded, his mind wondered back to a time long ago, "and the car's parked out front, reminds me of the sixty's."

"Well Lisa," I spoke up quickly, "it looks like we've accomplished what we set out to do."

"What do you mean?" Priscilla asked, looking back and forth between Lisa and myself.

"Lisa Marie wanted you to feel like you did back in the sixty's, like when Elvis was here."

"Well, the two of you are doing a good job of it," she responded happily.

George finished his hot chocolate, thanked us and left. Everyone else wanted to keep on singing.

It was getting late when I said, "Enough already, I'm tired and I think we need to call it a night." I got up and walked outside.

Lisa brought my coat, put it around me and said, "Thank you so much."

"For what, Kitten?"

"For making this Christmas very special."

I kissed her. "Time we went to bed, don't you think?"

"Yes, I'm going. Do you want to sleep late?"

"That would be nice," I answered yawning.

As Lisa went into the house, Priscilla came out. She said good night to Lisa and told her she would be up in a minute.

"It sure is cold out here," she commented.

"Yes, it is. Here, take my coat."

"Then you'll be cold."

"Let's share it, think it's big enough for two?"

183

"Oh yes, if we get close enough it will be," and she put her arm around my waist and pulled me close. "I also would like to thank you for making everything so beautiful."

"Your welcome," I said cautiously.

"Lisa Marie is happier than I've seen her in a long, long time. She thinks the world of you, Johnny. It's almost like she feels you are her father."

"Yes, I get that feeling from her too. Maybe it's not good for me to stay here," I said softly.

"I don't think there's any harm in it, as long as she doesn't become too obsessed with the idea of you as her father. She loved Elvis and his death hurt her deeply. I remember when he would come home for Christmas, he'd make snow and decorate the tree's and his Cadillac was always parked right here in front on the drive, like it is now. He loved Graceland in the winter, but sometimes he'd come home, and he'd be high on his drugs for days, and then he'd go into his mood swings. I hated those days. But, when he felt good and was happy to be home, we really had a nice Christmas."

I looked at her, pulled her closer and said, "This will be a nice Christmas, and only happiness and joy shall fill the air, I promise."

She pulled me to her and kissed me long and tenderly. She looked into my eyes, and said, "You even kiss like him."

"I think right now you're just feeling his presence," I responded evasively.

"Maybe so," she answered. "I'm going to bed; I'll see you this afternoon." She went inside and softly shut the door.

I stood outside alone and fought back tears, but a few trickled down my face. I felt her hurts and pains because I was the cause of them. I remembered some of those times when I was a pure asshole. The drugs didn't help matters. How could I have been so stupid? I decided right then and there that I was going to make them both happier than ever this Christmas.

I went inside, walked upstairs to 'my bedroom'. I opened the door, a sudden strangeness engulfed me. Up until now, I had been okay being back at Graceland, but now, I felt like I needed a pill to go to sleep. I got undressed and lay down in my bed, fighting the urge for pills.

The next thing I knew, Priscilla was sitting on the side of the bed asking, "Are you getting up sometime today?"

"What time is it?" I asked, still half asleep.

"It's almost two o'clock, we thought you'd sleep all day. David and Gary said you were always up early, so I thought I'd come and get you up. I laid your house coat on the bed for you."

"Thanks, that was thoughtful."

I looked at the end of the bed; Priscilla had laid out my old white robe with the "E" on the lapel. "My robe is in my bag, I'm not going to wear his robe, that's too much."

"I'm sorry; I thought you'd like to wear it."

"No, what I'd like is to be able to get up and take a shower."

"I'm sorry," she looked somewhat contrite, and got up and left.

I couldn't believe I was showering in my bathroom, once again at Graceland. I quickly finished and went downstairs.

Lisa was already up and asked, "You must have stayed up after I went to bed?"

"Yes," I winked at her, "your mother kept me up."

"Oh no, I didn't." Priscilla countered back. "I was only outside for a few minutes."

I laughed, "Well, I was really tired. Where are the guys?"

"They're across the street acting like tourists," Lisa laughed.

"I've got to go to the office, Johnny; do you and Lisa want to join me?"

"Maybe later," I replied, "first I'd like some real coffee."

"Then be my guest and make it yourself," Priscilla quipped sounding sassy.

"I'll be over in a little while, mother."

Priscilla had no sooner left, when Lisa turned to me. "What went on when mother came outside with you?"

"Not much. She's trying to get me to say I'm Elvis. She told me about how I used to be and tried to get me to wear my old robe, you know, the one with the "E" on the lapel."

"Yeah, I remember that one. You'd better be strong; she's not finished with you yet."

"I know, I have a feeling she's just begun. Why did she still keep some of my old clothes?"

"Don't you remember? She bought the robe for you as well as the sheets and bed spread?"

"No, I don't remember who bought what anymore."

"Well, if you're done here, let's go over to the office before she comes to get us."

As we walked outside, I noticed the snow was melting. "Lisa, have you checked the temperature today?"

"No. Why?"

"Remind me later to watch the weather for the rest of the week. How are things coming along?" I asked.

"I checked earlier and all the decorations are done. They're putting the finishing touches on the stage. I met with Joe and mother; they are both in agreement to hire more security."

"What about the National Guard?"

"That's already covered along with the local police. They can only guard and handle traffic on the Boulevard., but not inside Graceland. They are going to close off the streets starting Friday afternoon and reroute traffic. This will give the people who reserved tickets the opportunity to pick them up, and also visit the museum."

"The museum, let's go see it."

"You'll like it," Tara said as she and Denise joined us.

"Yeah, it's awesome," Denise said, obvious that she wanted to see it again.

Gary looked at me, "I'm ready if you are."

Going into the museum turned out to be fun. Everyone enjoyed seeing pictures of my movies and concert tours, as well as a few of my old costumes. I can't believe I was that slim back then. I probably weighed around one hundred and seventy five pounds compared to my two hundred twenty pounds now. Course being older doesn't help.

Priscilla came in looking for us. "Look, here's your motor cycle, I mean Elvis's."

I looked at her, and said, "Yes, I've got one just like it that I'm storing at David and Tara's house in Birmingham. As a matter of fact, David and Chance each have one too."

"And look, here's an old red and white Cadillac. I'll never forget when you bought it," Priscilla said. We went for a ride around Memphis and people were following us all around town until the police had to escort us home."

I looked at her, and said, "I bet that was a lot of fun."

Everyone stopped and watched the two of us conversing. Lisa's eyes grew large, as if she was waiting for me to admit to Priscilla that I was Elvis. I knew Priscilla was trying to trick me into saying I remembered, but I played the game and won that round. I also knew she was upset that she didn't catch me at her game, but she didn't dare show it.

She looked at Lisa and asked, "Do you remember this picture of you and your dad riding the horses around the front lawn?"

"Yes, mother, I do," she answered cautiously.

David, seeing where this was all heading, said, "Hey, we're going to drive over to the casino's in Tunica, anyone want to join us?"

"No, I think I'll stay around here," I said.

"How about you mother," Lisa wanted to know, I'm going?"

"No, I think I'll hang around here with Johnny, who knows, I might get lucky."

"I think you'd do better at the casinos if it's luck you're looking for."

Lisa walked over to her mother, "Would you please cool it."

"Honey, I'm just kidding with Johnny. You just go and have fun with everyone and win some money."

Lisa looked at me. I smiled and nodded my head that I would be fine. "Okay everyone, let's load up the limo and head to Tunica."

Priscilla and I were alone. "What would you like to do today Johnny?"

"Well, there's a lot to do before Saturday, don't you have a lot of paper work to catch up on?"

"Yes I do," she sighed and said, "I guess I'll catch you later."

On the way to check things over, I met Joe. He was looking for me as Lisa had told him Priscilla was hot on my trail. He came to help me out. "Are you going to be able to handle all this?" he asked.

"I hope so."

"And another thing, why did you accept her offer to sleep upstairs in your bedroom?"

"Well, think about it. An Elvis Impersonator refusing to sleep in Elvis's bedroom. I don't think you'll find one that would refuse such an offer."

"Yeah, you're right, Johnny?" "I don't know, but I do know she's starting to get on my nerves."

"Look, walk with me over to the house."

"Why don't we ride?" he wanted to know.

"I'd rather walk. Besides the cold air will do you good, and the sun feels good too."

George approached us, and said, "Good afternoon Mr. Presley, how are you today?"

I looked at George and said, "If that's a joke George it isn't funny."

"I'm sorry sir, but Ms. Priscilla, asked me to address you as Mr. Presley."

"Well, please don't."

"Yes sir," he answered shaking his head.

Joe looked at me, and said, "You need to sit her down and talk with her."

"Do you think it will do any good, Joe?"

"It might, yeah, maybe it will."

"Look Joe, the snow on the roof and the trees, the cars parked out front! Remember when we'd come home from a long trip and it would be snowing and the Cadillac's would be sitting in the drive clean as a pin? George really did keep them clean, didn't he?"

"Yes he did. I believe he'd like it very much if you'd call him back here and ask him to clean them again."

"Good idea, Joe."

I hollered to George to come back. George turned around on his cart and rejoined us.

"George," I started the conversation, "look towards the house, something is wrong. What is it?"

He looked for a moment, and then laughed, "I'll get that snow off your car right away, Mr. Presley."

I smiled. "George, don't forget your hot chocolate tonight."

"No sir I won't, and sir, it's good to have you home, if you are him, and even if you aren't."

"Thanks George, but it was Joe's idea."

"Oh," he sounded disappointed.

"If you handle Priscilla that well, I think it'll be a good Christmas, but if you don't, I think a storm is going to hit, and I want to be far away when it does."

"Oh hush, you ole worry wart. Come on. Let's see how this movie screen is going to work."

On the way to the stage area, we ran into the television crew. The cameramen that were hired for the job were setting up their equipment to start testing. I asked one of the guys to hook up the big screen in front of the house to make sure it's dimensions did not show the canopy that was built over the front entrance of the house.

"What if it does?" Joe asked.

I told him the canopy would have to be made larger or taken down. It's only function was to keep the electrical equipment dry and lock in a little heat.

Johnny," the head cameraman said, "it's ready."

He turned his camera to the front of the house. The screen came to life before us. It looked like a giant picture hanging on a wall.

"This is great!" I said excitedly, "now zoom in on us." The clarity was crystal clear.

"This big screen was a great idea," one of the crew workers mentioned, "no matter where you are standing, everyone will be able to see the complete show."

"You getting excited?" Joe asked.

"No, not getting excited, I've been excited!"

"Johnny, there is a lot of money coming in, and Priscilla is happy about that."

"Oh really, you mean she's shown some sign of pleasure besides hounding me."

He laughed at that remark, and said, "You're going to do pretty good yourself. So far our ticket sales are over ninety thousand and people are still calling. At thirty-five dollars a person, that's a healthy chunk of bread. Plus you will receive half of the money from advertising that's been set up with local and state vendors."

"Who receives the profits, does it go to Priscilla or Lisa Marie?"

"Lisa is no longer under Priscilla's control. Lisa still owns the controlling shares, and from that money, she pays Priscilla twenty percent of the profits. Of the remaining stockholders, I own the largest amount of shares with twenty percent."

"In other words, everyone is doing fairly well from the death of Elvis Presley?" I felt hurt and anger at the thought.

Hesitantly, Joe answered, "Yes, they are, so even if Priscilla finds out you really are you, she can't afford to say anything. If everyone knew you were alive, Graceland wouldn't turn the profit it's making today."

"So what you're saying is if word got out about me being alive, Graceland would not make a profit and would have to close, but as long as I stay 'dead', Johnny Raye stands to do good from this, and Graceland will benefit for years to come."

"Sad to say, but true."

"Joe, have you discussed this with Priscilla and Lisa?"

"Oh yes, at our last meeting. We all agreed to make you happy, and let you feel like the real 'king'. That's why Priscilla has allowed you to stay in his, 'your' bedroom upstairs."

"I've told Lisa Marie who I am."

"Yes, she told me. She doesn't care about the money, she only wants to be next to you, but she let's her mother think differently."

"I see. Priscilla thinks I'm the real Elvis, but she's not going to blow it, just in case I'm not."

"Right." He nodded.

"Well, I feel like I'm being used again for everyone else's gain."

"Look at it this way, you get the second chance you wanted and everyone else gets the big bucks from your death. Elvis, I mean Johnny, your memories are kept alive and your fan's happy, because you are so well loved. It's not just for the money, believe me. Everyone still loves you. You were the best. If it wasn't for Priscilla and a few others you would have died out long ago and only be a memory today. You really owe a lot to Priscilla. We all do."

"Yeah, I guess you're right, Joe, maybe I need to approach this matter in a different way."

"I think you do."

"Thanks. I owe you a lot old friend, and you know I love you like a brother."

"Yeah, and Priscilla knows it too. You think you're the only one catching hell? Everyday since you came into the picture; she has tried to catch me off guard. So far I've been able to stay one step ahead of her, but even now, I know she's in the office watching us. I can feel her eyes on the back of my neck."

The head cameraman yelled out to me, "Johnny, we have everything ready for Saturday and Sunday. We'll be back on Saturday morning to run several checks on everything."

"Great, I'll see you then."

Priscilla drove up in the cart, and asked, "Aren't you two freezing?"

"Well, yes we are," I answered casually.

"Johnny, you can't afford to catch a cold, come on, let's go inside and I'll make us some coffee, just the way you like it."

"Let's go," I agreed, as Joe poked me in the back and gave me a 'be on your guard' look.

Joe finished his coffee., "I need to get on home. What time is it?"

"It's after seven o'clock. Man, where did this day go? I'll see you tomorrow, Joe, and thanks, I enjoyed our talk. Maybe now I won't be so nervous when the show starts."

"You'll be fine, see you later."

"Joe," Priscilla said, "the money that came in today has not been picked up yet, can you go by the office and take care of it before you leave?"

"I'll take care of it right now."

Priscilla looked at me, a determined expression on her face. "Finally, we're alone. Let's go sit together on the sofa."

"Sure, why not, after all it's your house, and who am I to tell you what you can and can't do," I responded, trying to keep my voice from sounding aggravated.

"Johnny, I've been trying to trick you, and you know it, because you are being defensive," a weak smile appeared in the corners of her mouth."

"Well, can you blame me?"

"No," she answered, flashing me a big beautiful smile. "I guess in away I want you to be Elvis, you're so much like him when he was in a good mood. "I need to ask," she looked directly into my eyes, all smiles gone, replaced with a serious expression, "are you?"

God, when is this going to end? I thought and then responded to her question, "No, I'm not."

"I really don't know why I wish you were Elvis; I guess if you were, things would be like they used to be."

"No, Priscilla, you don't want things to be like they used to be. If they were, you'd still be sad, feeling lonely and unloved. You've come a long way, since 1977. You've kept Elvis's memory alive by keeping Graceland a place for the fans to come and pay tribute to Elvis to remember him as they knew him. You turned Graceland into a multi-million dollar business."

"Now, this Christmas Special, it may have been my idea, but you and Lisa are the ones who made it happen. It's a tribute to Elvis that fans will remember for a long time to come. You ask me questions that I cannot give the response that you're looking for. The man you once knew is buried out there in the garden, and it's in your best interest, and the interest of everyone else, that he stays buried out there."

"Then you are telling me that you are Elvis?"

"No, Priscilla, I'm not. I'm just saying, quit asking me questions, quit trying to trick me into remembering the past. It's best the past remains in the past."

We talked for several hours, and before we knew it the front door opened and the whole gambling gang came in laughing and talking about all the fun they had, and how much they won. When I asked how much they came home with they all said they put their winnings back into the machines.

Priscilla laughed at them. "At least you didn't loose your shirts, I see you're still wearing them."

"How about you, Johnny?" Lisa asked, "Did you have a good evening?"

"Yes I did, it was very nice talking to your mother, and I hope we can do it again sometime."

"I agree," Priscilla commented. "It's been very interesting."

"Johnny, I see the television crew was here," Lisa was giving me that knowing look to change the subject.

"Yes they were, they have everything ready and did their testing with the big screen."

"Is it really going to do the job?"

"And more. When I stood out there and watched, I felt I was at an outdoor theater. The quality of the sound and the clarity of the picture were unbelievable. The television station uses the latest in state-of-the-art technology, and believe me when I say it's fantastic."

"I need to get with you on what songs I'll be doing," David said. "You've got me excited to get out there and perform."

"Well then, tomorrow will be our rehearsal day. We'll turn on the complete system so we get a feel for the sound. Pick out what you want in gospel and Christmas carols, the ones you're more confident in doing, and I'll work from that."

Priscilla interjected, "Wouldn't it be great if we could get a country western star to come and sing a few songs? But who could we get on such short notice?"

"Mother," Lisa scolded exasperation in her voice, "this show will be fantastic the way it is."

"I think you're right," Priscilla spoke emphatically. "The fans aren't here to see a country western star; they'll be here strictly to see "Elvis" perform. So we'd better do a damn good job, cause that's what they will be coming for!"

David quickly jumped into the conversation after seeing the expression on my face. "They will be seeing the best of the best, except for the Elvis shows of the '70's."

"No one could ever be that good," I added to David's comment.

Priscilla looked at me. "Yes, you are that good, and I'm still wondering why!"

"Johnny," Lisa took my arm, "let's go out on the back patio and look at the snow and all the Christmas lights."

"Sure. Priscilla, would you care to join us?"

"No thank you, I think I'll get ready for bed."

The rest of the group declined the offer saying they'd had a long day, and retired to their rooms in the guest house. After everyone had left, Lisa looked at me with pleading in her eyes, and said, "Daddy, you and mother are about to butt heads. She's going to get mad, and I don't want you two fighting, especially with the show to do, and Christmas right around the corner. I'll talk to mother in the morning."

"Okay Kitten, but your mother is pushing pretty hard. I did my best all evening to be understanding, but for your sake and the show, I'll try a little harder."

"Thanks, now doesn't everything look pretty?" she sighed linking her arm through mine.

"It sure does, honey."

"Did you see all the lights that were put on the wall out front?" she asked.

"I did, it looks like a piece of art work."

"That's because mother hired some upcoming student artist she met while taking art classes at the university," and then grinned at me, mischief written all over her face.

"By the way, what happened to my horse and saddle?"

"Mother has a place outside of Dallas that she goes to when she wants to ride and get away from everyone. He's there. He's pretty old now, and doesn't do much but eat and sleep. He has been very well taken care of, but I don't think he'll live too much longer."

"Lisa, I'm tired, it's been a trying day for me, and tomorrow we have to see that all loose ends are finalized."

"Okay daddy, I love you."

"I love you too, Kitten."

"Walk me to my room?"

"I would love too!"

Walking past Priscilla's room, I noticed a light shining under her door. I told Lisa to go ahead and go to bed. Since her mother was still up I thought I'd smooth things over with her. She thought that was a good idea, wished me luck and went to her room.

I knocked softly. Priscilla slowly opened her door. Before me stood Priscilla clad only in a sheer low cut nightgown, her hair hanging full and disheveled giving an almost wild appearance. "Oh, it's you, wait right here while I get my bathrobe," she said acting surprised it was me. "If you came to apologize," she cinched the belt to her robe tightly around her slim waist, "there's no need, but I accept." She slammed the door in my face.

I stood there for a moment, stunned at what just transpired not quite sure of what or how I should respond. The old me would have torn the door off and made her apologize for her behavior, but I'm not the old me, and this is no longer 'my' house. I didn't want to see Priscilla so upset. My intent was to have both Lisa and Priscilla happy, but I didn't know how to do that without telling Priscilla who I was. Maybe things will smooth over. If she's anything like she used to be, she'll forget tonight and cheer up tomorrow. Fat chance of that happening as angry as she is, I thought.

I turned and walked to my room and got ready for bed. I had no sooner pulled up the covers when I heard a knock on my door. Without thinking, I yelled, "Come in."

It was Priscilla. "Is it safe for me to enter?" her voice cracked with emotion.

"Sure, what's wrong?"

She came and sat on the side of the bed, I could see she had been crying.

"Please, Priscilla, don't cry," I said, feeling sad for her, "the last thing I want to do is upset you. I don't like to hurt women or make them cry, but all day you have been trying to get me to say I'm Elvis."

"I'm sorry, it's just that you do everything around here like he used to, and it's almost eerie. When I look at you, I see him and it's very upsetting," she continued. Lisa Marie was too young to know the details of what her daddy did, and don't tell me that you read all about him in a book, because I know better."

"Maybe Elvis and I think a lot alike. I honestly don't know. I do know that to do this show the way it should be done, I had to get to know the real Elvis, his likes and dislikes. Not just what was written about him. I want the fans to feel like he's really here, feel his presence. That's why I arranged for the snow, the lights, and the cars to be done as they are. I want this show to be as authentic as I can make it. Now do you understand?"

"Yes, I do, you're right. I'm not going to try and trick you anymore. I know in my heart who you are, and you and no one else can tell me otherwise. There are just some things a woman knows. I lived with you and loved you for too many years. I bore you a child. I survived your good days, as well as your bad days. I don't understand how or why, but I know." With that she took off her robe, and stood naked before me. "Look, because this is what you could have had if you had admitted to me that you are Elvis."

Before I could respond, she grabbed her bathrobe and walked back to her room. My heart pounded, as if I had run the Boston Marathon. I had thought she was going to get into bed with me. She just didn't realize how much I really wanted her too. Had she kept crying and got into bed, I would have broken down, but since she didn't, I managed to escape again.

The next morning I woke early, and went to see if Lisa was on the back patio. To my surprise, the whole group was eating breakfast. Priscilla had the maid come in and cook for everyone. "Good morning, how's everyone today?" I asked.

"Great," David answered first, "I just can't get over being here, this is so awesome."

"Yeah, it really is amazing, isn't it?" added Gary.

"It does feel good, doesn't it?" I replied.

"I'm glad you guys are enjoying yourselves, and mother and I are happy you're staying at Graceland. After all, you're the reason we're putting on this Christmas Special. The least I can do is thank you and show our appreciation by making you feel you're a part of Graceland."

"Speaking of your mother, where is she?"

"She's still upstairs, I think she was up late last night and she's still asleep." She then gave me this inquisitive look like her mother must have slept with me.

I smirked back at her and said, "No it didn't happen, so wipe that grin off your face."

"Okay, but I heard her go in your room last night, and she was in there a long time," she teased.

Tara, who was too quiet, said, "Yeah, its obvious Priscilla is after you, Johnny." We all laughed, and I decided to change the subject.

"What's the temperature today?" I inquired.

"I checked the news a little while ago and it's about thirty two degrees, and it's not supposed to get much warmer," Lisa was pleased to announce.

"Johnny, how do you want to handle the heaters and the snow machines?" Gary asked.

"Has anyone thought about the fact that all those people with their body heat will only add to the snow melting problem?" David wanted to know.

I thought for a moment, and then answered, "I've got the heaters and snow machines covered. The cameramen will show the outlying area of Graceland in early shots to get a good view of the snow, but during the show the cameras will be focused only on the stage, the front of the house, and the people near the front. That's all that will show on television and the big screen. The stage will be roped off and extra security will be in place."

Just then Priscilla walked in. "That's already covered, we've hired more guards and a temporary ticket office is in the process of being made at the gate. Anyone with tickets will have their hands stamped. In case of a problem, a printout of all who purchased tickets will be printed out. We've also arranged for booths to be set up to sell Elvis memorabilia. On Friday there will be road blocks set up on each end of the Boulevard in front of Graceland. No one will be allowed to travel past in cars except those who have business here, and they'll have special passes."

"Well done Priscilla, I thought I would have to handle that." I complimented her.

"No, Johnny! You were hired to perform. The snow was your idea, as well as the cars, but the rest of the responsibility lies here."

"Well I would have thought about it tomorrow, mother," Lisa added.

"Tomorrow would have been too late," her mother looked at her.

"That's okay Kitten, that's what mothers are for."

Priscilla looked at me very strangely, "You call her Kitten?"

"Yes I do," I replied, as she reached for the coffee cup in my hand, sipping it slowly.

In the meantime, David, Tara, Gary and Denise left to walk around the area to see some of the sights before starting rehearsals. Denise grabbed Gary's arm. "I've been quiet, and staying in the back ground because we're guests, but sometimes I have to bite my tongue when Priscilla starts ragging on Johnny."

"It should get real interesting when Karen gets here," Tara added, and they all laughed at the thought of that.

"Lisa why don't you join them, take the day off. God knows you've earned it. Let your mother and me handle things today," I suggested.

"Are you sure?"

"Yes, we're sure," I smiled at her.

"No one has to tell me twice to go out and have fun, see you later," and she ran out the door yelling for everyone to wait up for her.

"How did you sleep last night, Johnny?" Priscilla questioned me.

"Just like I always do," I grinned, "lying down!"

She laughed at my response.

"Very funny. Then it didn't bother you when I removed my robe?"

"Oh yes, it bothered me. It even made me think I was crazy for letting you walk out, but I managed, and I slept like a baby. Thank you."

She laughed. "Did you eat breakfast?

"No, breakfast is cold now."

She called the maid and asked her to fry some more eggs and warm up the biscuits and gravy. I poured us each a fresh cup of coffee.

"Two sugar cubes, right?"

"Yes, you remember."

I smiled and dropped in two cubes without answering.

We ate and chatted amiably. Priscilla asked if I wanted to go shopping with her as she still had to buy something for Lisa to put under the tree. In response I told her I would love to go, and then wondered if I should or shouldn't.

"Where can we go without people mobbing you?" I asked, looking for an out.

"Oh, I'm not worried about me. They only point fingers and say there's Priscilla Presley. Sometimes they'll come over and ask for my autograph, but for the most part they leave me alone."

"How about you, do you have your shopping done?"

"Uh, huh! The other day when Lisa and I went shopping. The same day we bought the tree."

"I bet she really enjoyed that?"

"Yes, as a matter of fact, she was very happy about it."

"Well, Johnny, you ready?"

"I am if you are," I sighed in acquiescence.

"Then let's go," she said as she entwined her arm in mine. Priscilla called for a limo, but I sent it back. "Why did you do that, she asked?"

"Let's take my Cadillac instead."

"Sounds like fun," she smiled, "why not?"

George waved as we went through the gate. People waved when we drove down Elvis Presley Blvd.

At the mall, Priscilla wanted to shop at her favorite jewelry store. She purchased a gold necklace with diamonds set about an inch apart for Lisa. It was lovely, but I told her that Lisa had so much jewelry now, and would probably rather have a new sweater and a pair of jeans.

We walked around until we found a store that catered to the younger 'in' crowd. With much deliberation, we finally agreed on a pair of jeans and a raglan sweater. We went to check out, but stopped first at the store's jewelry counter. Priscilla noticed a pair of diamond earrings that she thought Lisa would like.

"Yeah they are nice, but don't you think she'd like a pair with her birth stone?" I again countered her suggestion.

Priscilla, adamant about the earrings she selected, went to pay for her purchases. In the meantime, I found a pair with Lisa's birthstone that I liked, and purchased them myself.

Priscilla noticed what I did, and said, "We'll see which ones she likes the best, Mr. Smarty Pants."

"Uh, huh, we'll see," I retorted back.

We gathered up our packages, and we were ready to leave when the sales clerk recognized me from all the advertising and flyers that were posted throughout the mall. I autographed a note to her, and we finally left to go back to Graceland. On the drive home, we discussed how lucky we were not to have been bothered. Because there were so many shoppers, and being so close to Christmas, we figured everyone was too busy pushing through crowds to notice who was who. George was at the gate when we arrived.

"Just like old times sir," George commented.

197

"I wouldn't know George," and I winked at him.

"See, even George knows who you are!"

"No, George 'thinks' he knows. There is a difference."

I pulled up to the house, dropped Priscilla off with the gifts, and parked the car. By the time I came inside, Priscilla had already arranged the presents under the tree. Being as chilly as Memphis sometimes can get, we decided to eat a light lunch of soup and sandwiches, which sounded good to both of us. Besides I was tired of eating big meals and didn't want to gain any more weight for fear of not fitting into my suits.

I waited on the patio while Priscilla went to freshen up. The maid brought us our lunch, but before Priscilla sat down, she kissed my cheek.

"What did I do to deserve that?"

"That's a thank you."

"For what?" I wondered what this was all about.

"For taking me shopping. I really enjoyed the morning with you."

"Well, I did too, and it did feel good to get out for awhile."

We sat and chatted about how fortunate we were not to have been bothered so we could shop in peace. People don't realize when they see famous people that they are invading on their privacy by asking for pictures and autographs. Although, we admitted, that's the price you pay for being a star or noted dignitary.

"Years before, the fans would have torn your clothes to get at you, at least this time, only one person asked for your autograph," Priscilla laughed softly. "I guess you are getting your second chance at life."

"Oh," I responded nonchalantly, "I didn't know I was getting one."

"Oh, Elvis! You're impossible! Just admit who you are, and let's stop playing these silly games."

"What if I said I was Elvis, but I really wasn't, and what if I said I was, what would you do about it?" I knew I was irritating her, but I was enjoying the teasing.

"I guess nothing. There's nothing I could do about it."

"Why?" I asked her.

"Well, for one thing," she thought for a moment before continuing, "it would kill Lisa Marie, and for another, it would destroy Graceland. There would be no need for any of this."

"And don't forget all the money you would loose," I added, "plus all the fans." "How do you think they would feel, and what would they say?" I concluded. "It's better to just leave things like they are."

"Yes," she answered sadly knowing this would have to be the way it would have to remain. "There could be a lot of damage to a lot of people. I guess I'll never really know for sure, will I?" she asked looking deep into my eyes hoping to find the answer she was looking for. "Johnny," she said slowly, "just so you understand, Elvis will always be my first love, and I will always love him, but it's been a long time."

Several hours later the front door opened and in bounced Lisa followed by the rest of the group. She had the jet fly everyone to Dallas. She wanted to purchase something from an exclusive shop that she inhabited every time she was in Dallas, and then the group wanted to stop for a few minutes to see Chance and Michele.

"How are they doing?" I asked, laughing at the flushed look on Lisa's face from an enjoyable morning.

Gary quickly answered, "He's doing great at the club, Johnny. We saw Mr. Steadman too, and he's real pleased with his performances."

"Yeah," David said, "but we could tell he'd rather be here with us for the show."

"Well let's put our heads together and see what we can do to make that happen."

A plan was devised. Lisa arranged to have her jet waiting at the airport Saturday night. Since Chance didn't have another show until Wednesday night; that left him free to come to Memphis for Sunday's performance. Steadman's limo driver would drive them to the airport where Lisa's jet would fly them to Memphis, and Joe would pick them up at the airport in Dallas. Priscilla would arrange sleeping quarters which she said was no problem. With that settled all we needed to do was call Chance. And at that point, Lisa handed me the phone.

"I get the feeling you had this planned already," I grinned.

"We did, sort of," David said, "we didn't want to do or say anything until we talked with you first."

I dialed Chance's number, and on the second ring he answered. We bantered back and forth, and then I told him what we planned. He relayed the message to Michele, as she was sitting next to him. They both agreed the plan would work, and were all excited about coming.

"Thanks Elvis, we love ya man!"

"Your welcome, but watch what you say."

"Sorry, not to worry. Michele just went to answer her phone in the bedroom."

"Okay, see you then," and we hung up.

"He's real excited isn't he?"

"Yes, Kitten he really is, I'm glad we decided to do this."

"Looks like I need to shop some more, I need to buy two more gifts."

"Thanks Priscilla."

"Oh, it's nothing, your friends are our friends too, Johnny."

Lisa looked at me and then at Priscilla, "You two sure are happy about something."

"Johnny took me shopping, and we took his car."

"Wow," Lisa grinned, "what did you buy for me?"

"You'll just have to wait until we open gifts Monday morning," Priscilla responded, grinning back at her.

I knew I might be dropping a bomb, but I felt now was the best time to bring this up. "Lisa, do you remember me telling you about a friend of mine named Karen from Alabama?"

She nodded her head yes.

"I booked a room for her and her friend. They'll be arriving here Saturday afternoon. I won't have time to pick them up, but I thought you could arrange to have the limo pick them up at the motel, and bring them here. I can take them back after the show."

Conversation around the table ceased. Everyone's attention was now focused on Priscilla and me. "Well," Priscilla said sounding indignant, "looks like we're going to have a full house."

"Maybe it would be better if I visited them at the hotel instead."

"No!" Priscilla said, "It's all right."

"Yes," Lisa said, looking at her mother's expression. "If you want to see her, Johnny, so do we. As a matter of fact, I'd like to check her out myself," she added.

"Maybe that's not such a good idea after all," I laughed to ease the tension.

"Oh, yes it's a great idea, isn't it mother?"

"Oh yeah, right!"

David and Gary said they had already met Karen, and thought she was a nice lady, and said everyone would like her.

"Is this someone you plan on keeping around, or just someone to sleep with?" Priscilla asked, in an aggravated tone.

Again, there was dead silence.

"Why, are you jealous?" I teased, knowing she was having a hard time keeping her temper in place.

"No, why should I be?"

"No, but if you are, I understand."

Lisa quickly interjected before her mother could say anything, "I'm jealous, Johnny," and came and hugged my neck and kissed my cheek, "but I guess I can live with it," and then laughed.

"Would all of you mind giving me a moment to be alone with Priscilla?"

Everyone got up to leave, and Lisa said, "Please, don't fight you two!"

"Why should we fight, Lisa?" Priscilla questioned.

"Because you've been mad at Johnny all week, mother, and I think it's over the fact that you think he's my father. Well, he's not, so get over it already."

"Lisa, Johnny and I have already talked about that, and I'm convinced he is not your father. I'm a little jealous. I guess I wanted him for myself. Another one of those living back in the old day memories, but he's got other ideas."

Denise and Tara looked at each other, each afraid to ask the other what they were both beginning think of this whole situation.

Gary said, "Come on everyone, let's get started rehearsing."

"Denise, Tara, Lisa, once David starts to sing, spread your selves around to check on sound, Okay?" Lisa suggested. "Let's go and leave these two to talk in private."

"Priscilla, now that we are alone," I began, "I think you are a very beautiful woman, but I'm not looking to tie myself down to anyone at this time in my life. Let me tell you this so you understand. Karen is a lady I've met. We've hardly even dated let alone had sex. She's a very nice, sweet lady, and someone that I want to get to know better. I know she is not the jealous type, and she accepts me for what I am, and the way I am. That means a lot to me."

Priscilla answered, "I can understand that. I still love 'Elvis', but I've grown. My ideas of a relationship are much more mature then that of the young school girl you fell in love with. Had I been older or more mature back then, maybe things would have worked out differently. Besides, that 'adoring' love I had for you died a long time ago, as well as Elvis's infatuated love for me. Back then, Elvis loved to conquer his possessions, but once he did, his passion for his possessions would dissolve. I was too young to understand, but I do now. Like I said before, I love Elvis, and always will, but now in a more mature way."

"Being here at Graceland has been a great experience for me," I answered. "Being here with you has been utterly fantastic. The feelings I've developed for you, well, I'll always carry them with me, but close friends are all we can ever be. Oh, and by the way, just for the record, you look fantastic naked."

Damn he's good, but I'm still unsure, Priscilla was thinking to herself. I've got one more trick up my sleeve, and the first opportunity I get, I'm going to use it. I've got to know the truth! Out loud, she said, "I must not have been, you turned me down, I've never been turned down before."

"Look, tomorrow is Friday, didn't you tell me the streets would be blocked off and the booths would be set up?"

"Yes. Why?"

"Well, I thought if you want me to, I'd give you a hand making sure everything is running smoothly."

"I'd like that," she mused, "let's go into the living room and you can sing to me before you go out to rehearse."

I put my arm around her waist, and the two of us walked into the living room together. Just then, Lisa and the rest of the group, walked in. "What happened, I thought you were going to recheck the sound and do some rehearsing?"

"So did we, but the carpenters had to tear out part of the stage for some adjustments that needed to be made, and we can't rehearse with all the pounding and noise. They said they'll be done by tonight. Joe is taking care of it," Lisa informed me. She then noticed my arm around her mother. "Well you two sure made up fast."

"Made up," I questioned her, "we were never fighting."

"That's right," Priscilla added, speaking a little too sweetly, "after all, Johnny and his friends are our guests here, there was no reason for us to be fighting"

Changing the subject, I asked David if he had heard anything about the weather for the week-end. He informed me that he had heard on the local station the weather was supposed to be cold, and the temperature was supposed to drop into the twenty degree range for the whole week end, and into the first part of next week as well.

"Great, we can start making snow tomorrow night and run the machines all night into Saturday. That's a perfect temperature," relieved to know that was one thing we would not have to worry about. "We can add at least four more inches to what we already have, and when we run the heaters during the show, the snow won't have time to melt. Listen, I was just going to practice a few songs with Priscilla, and since you can't rehearse outside, let's do it here."

"Sounds good to me," David said.

"I'll fire up the piano."

David sang his choices for the show, and then I sang a few of mine. Satisfied with what we planned, we all decided to sing carols together. After a few hours, Gary was getting hungry. I told him he was almost as bad as Chance for being hungry all the time.

"I'm a growing boy," he grinned at Denise.

"Mmmm, I'll vouch for that, Denise sidled up next to him, grinning back.

202

We had a good laugh at the hidden meaning behind her words.

Our little group bundled up, squeezed into the carts, and drove across the street to the diner. Unfortunately, we arrived too late as they had closed the diner a half an hour earlier. Priscilla mentioned we could cook at the house.

"Ahhh," Lisa said, "I know mothers cooking."

"Don't look at us," Gary and Denise said, "neither of us can cook."

"Not to worry," I responded, "let's get back in the carts, I can make a mean burger and crispy fries."

"I'll help." Priscilla didn't want to feel left out."

"Sure, why not," I joked, "maybe you can learn something."

If looks could kill, I would surely have died on the spot from the look that Priscilla shot me. I had to apologize and tell her I was only kidding.

Back at the house, I donned an apron. Priscilla went to get a camera, she definitely wanted to have a snap shot of this, which she ended up taking three or four, and would have taken more until I told her that was enough. In the meantime, I heated up the grill and turned on the grease for the fries. Priscilla and the rest of the girls sliced tomatoes, cut slices of cheese and chopped lettuce and onions for the buns. Lisa helped with the refreshments.

Thirty minutes later, we had burgers with fries and served everyone in the jungle room. Someone had slipped the movie "Blue Hawaii" in the VCR. I laughed, and wondered why on earth they had to pick that one.

"Dig in," I said, as we joined the guys, "these are old fashioned greasy burgers, fit for a king."

"Hey, these are great!" Priscilla was surprised, and then asked, "Where did you learn to cook?"

"There's an elderly black lady in Florida who took me under her wing, and taught me how to cook, and a lot more. I really owe her a great deal; she's the one who encouraged me to start singing Karaoke."

"How old were you when she took care of you?" Priscilla wanted to know.

"Oh, very young," I responded nonchalantly. "Let's eat and watch the movie, okay," I smiled, trying to be tolerant of her continuous questioning.

During the movie, this didn't change much. Priscilla would make remarks, such as, "I know you just loved being in Hawaii," or "I bet you enjoyed making that scene, all those pretty hula girls swinging those hips around you?" I'd respond with some answer in the form of a joke, such as, "Well, if I did, I wish someone would have told me," and then smirk.

It was getting late, already after ten o'clock. Everything seemed to be coming along fine with the show. Our rehearsal went great. The scenery was beautiful. I felt with enough patience, I could get Priscilla to accept me as

Johnny, and stop trying to get me to admit I was Elvis. I just hoped everything would work out as planned.

We all stood on the front drive for a moment, and enjoyed being together.

"Did someone turn on the snow machines?" I asked. "It's snowing!"

"They aren't supposed to be turned on until tomorrow. I don't hear them running," Lisa answered, a questioning look coming over her pretty young face. Look up everyone, its real snow. Tara and Denise started running around, waving their arms, squealing with delight.

I looked at Lisa and said, "It's going to be a wonderful show, and a wonderful Christmas, and I'm not going to worry about a thing anymore."

Lisa hugged me tight, and whispered in my ear, "I told you everything was going to be fantastic, and you shouldn't worry so much."

The rest of group left and went to the guest house. George was making his final rounds before leaving for home. "Mr. Johnny, I think it will snow all night by the looks of the size of these flakes coming down. By tomorrow morning, all of Memphis will be enjoying the beginning of a white Christmas."

"I sure hope so George. I sure hope so."

Priscilla had disappeared inside without saying anything. That left me with Lisa. She slipped her arm around me. I hugged her close. "Stay out here for a few minutes with me, please?" she asked, her eyes exploring mine.

She was so wrapped up in the beauty of the Christmas spirit, and to tell the truth, so was I. It has been a number of years since I celebrated Christmas, and it felt good to share it again, especially with the person I now loved the most in my life.

As we stood there together watching the snow fall, she looked at me and asked, "Are you and mother going to spend some more time alone?"

"Well, I hope so," not understanding her question or where it was leading.

"Maybe you need to tell mother the truth."

"Lisa, honey, I can't, there's just too much at stake here. Besides, I don't have to tell her, she just wants to hear me say the words to confirm her suspicions."

"I know. I just feel terrible about keeping this big of a secret from her. Even though we don't live together anymore, we're still close. When this show is over, I'll be going back to my condo in L.A., and she'll probably go to her apartment there too, or to her house in Dallas. We're never here this long. It's only because of your show. Usually we just stop to stay long enough to check on our interests here and then lead our own lives."

"Who knows, maybe after the shows, I may talk with her again. I may let her know she's right without having to say it."

"That would be good, daddy, and I've kept you out here long enough, I know you're cold, cause I know I am." We shook the snow from our coats and hair, and hung them on the coat tree. Priscilla had the fireplace blazing so we joined her. The heat felt good as we watched the flames flicker and dance before us. We sat around teasing each other about what we thought was in each package under the tree, and made up silly guesses so as not to spoil the fun for Lisa.

Lisa was the first to turn in. She bent down to kiss her mother, and then me, wishing us both a goodnight.

"Would you like some hot chocolate before going to bed?" Priscilla asked me.

"Yes, that does sound good."

Rising, she went into the kitchen to warm the milk. A few minutes later she returned holding two steaming cups of hot chocolate mounded to overflowing with big, puffy, white marshmallows.

"Mmmm, that sure does look good," I said as she placed the mugs on the coffee table, and then sat next to me on the sofa.

"Johnny, it's too bad we can only be friends."

"Why do you say that?" I asked, wondering where this was going to lead.

"Well, I'm in the mood to make love."

I was glad I wasn't taking a sip of hot chocolate when she made that statement or I'd have burned my mouth. Answering warily, I said, "If I wasn't here, you wouldn't be in the mood, and I wouldn't be so tempted to make love to you, but we both know it shouldn't happen. For all I know, you may have someone special in California or even in Dallas."

"No," she responded quickly. I have friends, but no one special. I'm not interested in a relationship that leads to commitment or marriage. I just need someone who can fulfill my desires every now and then."

"That's understandable, but I believe it would be a great mistake if you and I make love. I've been over this before with other women, and I'm going to tell you just like I told them. It would ruin our friendship, and your friendship means more to me than sex."

We finished our hot chocolate, both of us quiet, each with our own thoughts.

Finally to break the silence, I said, "Come on," and I took her by the hand, "let me walk you to your room."

As we reached her bedroom, she kissed me, and softly said, with a hint of wistfulness in her voice, "Good night, Johnny."

"Good night Priscilla." I turned and went into my room.

CHAPTER 18

The next morning, Lisa knocked on my door to wake me, and asked me to come down to the patio for breakfast. It was late, past eleven o'clock. I had slept the morning away. I knew I had a lot to do, and I had promised Priscilla that I would help her with the booth placements and traffic flow. The barricades had to be arranged to block off certain sections, and guards were to be placed to prevent anyone getting into private quarters without being seen.

I hollered for Lisa to come in.

"Why didn't she wake me earlier?"

"Mother said to let you sleep."

"Where is she now?" I wanted to know.

"She's over at the office. All the workers are in and busy handling last minute preparations. But, she has a surprise for you downstairs."

"What?" I was almost afraid to ask.

"Well, I'm not telling. You will have to come downstairs and find out for yourself." She walked out the door and left me to mumble and gripe about what I might be getting myself into.

I finished my shower in record breaking time, taking into consideration all my moaning and groaning, and was dressed and walking down the steps in less than ten minutes. I had mixed feelings as to whether or not Priscilla's surprise was going to start my day out right or set me in a black mood the rest of the day. I entered the patio, and much to my surprise, sitting at the round breakfast table with all the others, was Karen and Judie. At first, I was stunned, and then I found my manners and wished everyone a good morning.

"Karen, how did you two get here so fast?"

"A limo driver knocked on our door at the hotel. He told us that the limo was waiting to bring us to Graceland. Compliments of Priscilla Presley. She wanted to surprise you, and here we are."

Happy to see them both, I kissed her and Judie, and asked, have you eaten breakfast?"

Lisa quickly, answered, "No, we've been waiting for you as it seems we all slept late." She called the maid to cook breakfast, but the maid told us that Priscilla had anticipated a big group. She prepared the meal buffet style, and we were to march ourselves into the dining room and help ourselves to the serving trays that were sitting on steamed warmers.

There was scrambled eggs, fresh baked biscuits with tomato gravy to pour over them, fried green tomatoes, sausage links, bacon and home fried potatoes. When we brought our plates back to the patio to eat, we found the tea cart sitting with fresh brewed coffee, orange juice and a bowl of fresh cut fruit.

Lisa poured me a cup, kissed my cheek and spoke softly, "I'm enjoying you being here so let me spoil you little bit before you have to leave."

"Thank you, Kitten," I was enjoying all her attention. "I will."

After breakfast, as we sat and chatted amongst ourselves, Karen laughed and asked, "Do you always sleep this late?"

"I don't usually. I'm up between seven and nine o'clock if I get to bed before midnight that is." I looked at Lisa. "It was very nice of Priscilla to have Karen and Judie escorted here by limo as a surprise for me."

"Yes it was," Karen answered, "she seems to be a very nice lady."

"She sure does," Judie added, "she must think a great deal of you to let your friends stay here at Graceland."

"Well, she respects my friends and wants everyone to have fun over the holidays. By the way, have you two had the grand tour yet?"

"No!" Karen answered. "We haven't been here that long."

"I'll show you around," Lisa volunteered. "Johnny, why don't you check on mother to see if she needs you?"

"Okay Kitten, that sounds good." I knew she wanted to check Karen out. "I'll see you lovely ladies a little later, enjoy your tour."

"Johnny," David said, "Gary and I have been talking, and we'll go with you just in case there's something we can help with."

We left the girls to go on their tour and went out the front door. Crews were working furiously to finish and clean up messes they had made. Electricians were checking wiring. Television cameramen were retesting the big screen from different angles of the areas to be filmed. Security was assigning areas to each guard. We walked through the chaos and headed in the direction of the office.

"Looks like we had a good snow fall," Gary commented, "appears to have snowed about six inches."

"Yeah," David agreed, "we already had three inches on the ground that we made, by the looks of this, it looks like it's snowed for a week."

I smiled and enjoyed the sound of the snow crunching beneath my feet. "This time of year it can't get too deep."

"Well, it could," David contradicted, "although people would walk a mile to see this show."

"Yeah, the highway traffic could get nasty; I hadn't thought of that. It's hard to imagine anything so pretty could cause a problem. "Something's wrong," I suddenly realized. "I haven't seen George anywhere, and I know this is unusual for him not to be around here for security." I stopped one of the guards. "Have you seen George this morning?"

"No sir, and you won't either."

"Why, what's wrong?" A cold chill crept down my spine.

"An ambulance rushed him to the hospital early this morning."

"What's the problem, do you know? Why hasn't someone told us before this?" I demanded.

"From what I've heard," the guard said, "George was experiencing severe chest pains, but I haven't heard anything else."

I sprang into action and told the guard to radio the office to have the limo brought to the front of the house, and to make it snappy. I quickly looked for Priscilla, but not finding her, I went back to the house. The driver arrived immediately. I told him I wanted to be taken to the hospital, and wanted to know if he had seen Priscilla. He thought she was down at the end of the street discussing the barricade placement with the authorities.

We found her there, and I hollered to her to come quickly. Seeing the anxiety on my face and hearing the alarm in my voice, without asking any questions she jumped in the limo. I quickly explained to her what was happening to put her mind at ease.

We reached the hospital in record breaking time, albeit the driver did run three red lights. Registration informed us that George was transferred to room 342. Upon reaching the third floor, we stopped first at the nurse's station to find out his prognosis. The nurse informed us he was resting comfortably and he would be fine. She told us his family was with him. She felt that two more visitors wouldn't hurt, so we could go and see him as long as we didn't tire him or stay to long.

George's bed had been raised to a sitting position. He looked quite comfortable except for all the wires attached to his chest, the I.V in his hand, and the oxygen tube. He grinned from ear to ear as soon as we entered the room.

"Why in the devil are you two here when you need to be at Graceland handling everything? He admonished us. I'm doing just fine. Don't see any reason why I'm here in the first place. Get a few chest pains and the whole family has you dead and buried. Told the doc in the emergency room I probably had indigestion."

I was back in control. "George, you are more important to us than any damn show, and you should be taking it easy. If all you had is indigestion, you would not be here. This is the best place for you to be at the moment, and don't worry about anything, we have everything covered."

"Yes sir!" He smiled at us, tears of gratitude brimming from his tired old eyes. Excuse me for my bad manners," he said, as he introduced us to his family. "This is Ms. Priscilla Presley, and this is Elvis Presley, himself."

Everyone looked at me, including Priscilla, as I began to explain, "I'm Johnny Raye, George thinks Elvis is back from the dead."

They laughed, "Yes, we know, he's been telling us that all week."

The doctor entered the room to check on his new patient. "Hi George, feeling a little better are we?"

"There's no 'we' about it doc, I'm fine, but if you're not up to par, 'we' need to trade places, and you can have this bed," George cackled at his own humor.

The doctor grinned, shook his head, and asked, "and you must be Elvis and Priscilla," he said, shaking our hands. "George talked non-stop in the emergency room about you and the show you're doing this weekend. I've heard from several sources that you are a good entertainer. I'm sorry I'll miss the show, but maybe we can get George well enough so he can be there."

"No maybe to it doc; I'll be there no matter what," George declared emphatically, alarm in his voice, "I don't want to miss this for anything."

Reverting again to my take charge attitude, and without thinking, I jumped into the conversation, "I know how you get totally involved in your work, George, but your health comes first, that means no more stress. George, as of right now, I am promoting you to head man of security. You will no longer have to work hard. All you'll have to do is stop by and check to make sure everything is going the way you want. You give the orders; the others will do the work. You'll no longer get a check each week; instead, I'm going to see to it that you get to draw your pension as soon as you come back. How does two hundred and fifty thousand sound?"

"But Elvis, I'm not ready to retire yet!"

"George, I didn't say you were retiring. I said you only work when you want to, and you'll get your retirement up front."

"That's right," Priscilla agreed, "you come and see me when you get out of here."

The doc had finished checking George's vitals and said, "That may be tomorrow. George is doing fine, but he does need to take it easy. George that means no hard work or stress, that's an order."

I shook the doctor's hand again, and said, "George has been with us a long, long time."

"He's our most trustworthy employee, and we think of him as family," Priscilla added.

The doctor smiled knowingly, and said, "Well, I've got other patients to see who seem to need me more than George, so I'll try and catch you on the television. Elvis, break a leg, cause I'll be here if you do," and laughed heartily at his own humor as he headed to his next patient.

"Hear that George? When you come in tomorrow you ride the carts, and remember, as of tomorrow you will assign jobs out, not do them," I scolded in a caring voice.

"Yes, I hear you, and I know who you are, sir!" He grinned.

One of the family members whispered to me, "His mind isn't right; the medicine they gave him makes him talk out of his head."

"That's all right, just take care of him and don't let him drive, have someone take him to and from work. If that's not possible, we'll make some arrangements to help out."

Priscilla walked around the bed, kissed George on the forehead and said, "You do what Elvis told you, okay?"

"Okay, Miss Priscilla," and he winked at her.

We wished him well, said good-bye to his family members and left. We no sooner were seated in the limo, when Priscilla turned on me with spit and fire brimming from her eyes. "George knows who you are, just like I do!" "And," she continued more softly, "you love George just as you always have."

I looked at Priscilla, ignored her comment, and said, "Thanks for having the limo driver bring Karen and Judie to Graceland, but you could have woke me up before you left."

"I thought about it, but I knew it would be best if I stayed out of your room."

"Well, thanks," I laughed good naturedly, "maybe you're right."

"Oh, and by the way," Priscilla said.

"Oh no," I thought to myself, here it comes," and groaned out loud.

"Who gave you the authority to retire George and give him a two hundred and fifty thousand dollar retirement income? We've never paid anyone that much money."

"Well then check and see how much his retirement fund is and cut the balance from my proceeds from the show!" I exclaimed, vehemently, brooking no argument.

"I'll look into it when I get back, and we'll pay it," she retorted.

"No," I said, my anger subsiding, "I'd really like to, if you don't mind."

"I know that set, determined expression on your face, but I do understand, and I'll let you know tonight or tomorrow morning what the balance will be," she agreed.

"Thank you, that will be fine," and we rode the rest of the way in silence.

I had the limo driver let me out at the security office. I asked Priscilla if she wanted to go with me, but she told me I could deal with security myself. She then told me she had already informed security to do what I thought needed to be done, that way they would not balk at me giving directions.

I smiled at her. "Now I know why I loved you so much or at least Elvis did."

"No," she shook her head, "you had it right the first time."

I ran into Joe walking into the security office. We discussed George's situation and decided to talk with Ron who was in charge when George was off duty. I informed Ron that George was retired, but that George was not ready to retire.

The three of us sat down and devised a plan. To keep George active and to let him feel useful, George could come in on the day shift for a couple of hours. His responsibility would be to check to see that enough guards were working, ride on the cart to make rounds, and then he was free to go home. The same with the second shift, that way he wouldn't be at work more than four hours a day. He could pick and choose his hours as he liked. Any major problems or crises would be given to Ron to handle. Ron was now promoted to head supervisor of the day shift. We asked Ron who would be responsible and reliable for night shift, and he suggested Richard, who had been there for several years and had a good work record. That settled, we then promoted George to executive supervisor over all.

Joe and I left. Once outside, Joe asked how George was doing, and I explained the doctor said it was his heart, and that George needed to take it easy and be stress free.

Who retired him?" Joe inquired.

"I did. And boy did I catch hell for that."

"You did?" Joe looked at me, "Have you told Priscilla the truth yet?"

"No, but she knows, and I hope it stays this way. I've come close to saying yes to her questions, but so far I've managed to skirt around them or just not answer her."

"She hasn't lost her temper with you?"

"Come to think of it, not really, she's been aggravated and frustrated, but she hasn't lost her temper."

"Yeah," Joe replied, "then she knows for sure, or else she'd be real upset with you with all the decisions you've been making around here."

"You know, Joe, you're right. I have made a lot of decisions and giving a lot of orders, and she really hasn't said anything to me about them."

"Maybe not to you, Johnny, but she sure has to me. Priscilla told me no one but Elvis would come in here, make himself at home, and do things around here like you have done without getting permission from her or Lisa first."

"What did you tell her?"

"I told her Lisa Marie told you to handle things anyway you saw fit, that Lisa trusted your judgment and only wanted whatever it took to have a great show."

"What did Priscilla say to that?"

"She said I was full of shit and that I knew who you were before you came to Graceland. Well, that pissed me off, so I told her she was full of shit and off her rocker if she thought you were Elvis, and that I didn't know anymore than she did. She got mad at me for swearing at her, but said it wouldn't do any good to fire me. That you'd intercept somehow, either on your own or through Lisa and get me rehired. I told her to get off my back or I would go to Lisa myself. That shut her up for a while anyway."

Joe and I had a good laugh, and then I told him I had company waiting for me at the house. "Come and meet this lady I met from Alabama."

"Johnny, are you nuts? You brought a girl here?"

"Yeah! Why not?"

"You're looking to get killed for real this time?"

"Joe, bring the cart before we go to the house, I'm stopping in to see Priscilla."

Priscilla was hanging up the phone in her private office when we walked in.

"Are you free for a minute," I asked.

She nodded yes.

"The situation with George is handled and I wanted to come by here and thank you for backing me up." "You're a lot sweeter than you used to be," and I grinned at her teasingly.

"I've always been sweet; you're the one who was an ass."

"Yes, you're right," and I winked at her.

"Thanks for telling me," she cried, as tears slid down her face.

"Telling you what?" I went back to teasing.

"Nothing." She kissed my cheek.

Joe looked at us for a minute, and then suggested, "Johnny, you better see to your guests."

"You're right, let's go," and walked to the door. "Aren't you coming?" I asked.

"I'll see you in a little while." I think I've got some explaining to do for the both of us."

I looked at Priscilla, "I'll see you later, right?"

"Right," she answered, giving me an understanding smile.

I left, knowing Joe would finally tell her the truth. I met everyone on the patio. They were laughing and carrying on and having one great time. "What's so funny?" I asked, needing some laughter after the morning's events.

"YOU!" They all exclaimed together.

"Me, I don't look any funnier than any of you."

"Oh, yeah!" Karen said. "We were reminiscing about the night when the girls chased you out the back door in Birmingham, and how David and Chance held them back while you made your get-a-way."

Yeah, some of them were pretty big and ugly!" I agreed. "I'm sure glad they didn't catch me.

"It was all Chance and I could do to hold back a three hundred pound woman and more behind her," David replied.

"You know you enjoyed every minute of every pound you and Chance were holding," I joked back. "Didn't they?" I asked Tara.

"Johnny, now that you mention it, I believe they did, and that explains that old cliché he's always saying."

"What's that?" I asked, my face hurting from laughing so much.

"Thin may be in, but fat's where it's at! It's all he talked about for months," she giggled so hard she was barely able to speak.

"Funny! Funny!" David said, trying his best not to laugh. "Those women really felt good. I got so excited that I wanted to go home and jump your bones," he winked at Tara.

"See," I said, "he really did enjoy it."

"Next time," David said dryly, "I'll let them get you."

"Oh please," and I threw my arms up in defeat. "That's okay, you can keep them all to yourself!"

That statement brought on another round of laughter. Things finally quieted down. I asked Karen what she thought of Graceland.

"It's beautiful," she exclaimed, excitement in her voice, "I now understand why Elvis loved being here so much, it does give you a sense of security and seclusion."

"Yes, it does, and I apologize for being gone so long this morning, but George, one of the security guards was taken to the hospital for . . ."

Lisa interjected, "What!" she shrieked, jumping up from her chair. "What about George?"

"Calm down, Kitten, and let me explain. George will be fine; he was taken to the hospital for chest pains. It is his heart, but the doctor said all he needs to do is rest and take life easy. They are keeping him over night because of his age, and to get a twenty-four hour reading on his vitals. He's hooked up to an EKG, and a couple of other wires leading to God only knows where, but the doctor said he sees no reason he can't be released tomorrow. Your mother and I went to the hospital to see him. We just got back about an hour ago."

"That's why we couldn't find Priscilla to tell her," David said, "you already did."

Lisa's eyes flashed in David's direction. "You and Gary knew about this and didn't tell me?" her voice rose in pitch.

"We were with Johnny when the guard told him what happened," David spoke softly. "Gary and I thought it best not to say anything."

"That's right," Gary spoke up, "we thought either your mother or Johnny should tell you because we didn't know how serious it could be and didn't want to alarm you unnecessarily."

"Damn," she said, sounding hurt. "I was left out of this. I wish everyone would stop treating me like a baby. Johnny, you and mother, at least one of you should have called me to tell me what was going on."

"I'm sorry Lisa, you're right. I should have sent word, but we were in such a hurry to get to the hospital to find out if George was alright, we just didn't think. It's not David and Gary's fault, it's mine."

"I'm sorry," Lisa apologized to everyone, "it's just that I'm so close to George, and I'm worried."

"Well, quit worrying, you'll see him tomorrow when he comes to get his check."

"Check, he's not quitting is he?"

"No," and I explained to her what his new position would be.

"That's wonderful," she said, with a smile on her face. "I'll bet you had your hand in that decision!" she winked at me, and then laughed, thinking of me with her mother making the decisions about George.

"Has anyone made plans for tonight?" I asked, wanting to get us all back in a good mood.

"With all the people in town for the holidays and the Christmas Special, the hotel bars are probably full of party people. We could go to one of them," Lisa suggested.

"Yeah," David agreed, "There'll be a lot of Elvis Impersonators in town. I'll bet we could walk right in and no one would recognize us."

"Even if they did, it wouldn't be that bad, probably a few pictures and sign a couple of autographs," I replied, wanting to take Karen out for an evening of fun.

"Let's go!" Everyone yelled.

"Let's get dressed and we'll leave around seven o'clock."

"Where to?" Karen asked.

"How about the hotel you're staying at, that way we'll have somewhere to escape to, just in case things get out of hand," I suggested.

"As long as you don't sing, Johnny, we won't have a problem," Tara implied, grinning.

"Don't start that again," I teased her, knowing she was thinking about our Birmingham escapade.

"What's up? Where's everyone going?" Priscilla inquired, as she entered the room.

"We've all decided to go out to a bar tonight, are you game to join us?"

She looked at me like I was crazy, and said, "If the women find out who you are, they'll be jumping all over each other trying to get to you. They'll probably rip your clothes right off your back, if not trample you in the stampede. Trust me, I know, this is a voice of experience."

"No, I don't think we'll have a problem, you and I went shopping together, and I only signed one autograph. Lisa's been shopping with me, and you and I also went to the hospital, and nothing happened. Besides, you and Lisa are noted celebrities in your own right. Right now, I don't think anyone knows me that well yet."

"Johnny, your pictures are all over town, and also in the newspaper, as well as the television," Lisa stated.

"But that's in costume," I answered her. Tonight I'm going to be dressed in western garb. You know, jeans, western shirt, boots and hat."

"If you can get away with it, then so can I," Priscilla smiled and then asked, "Where are we getting all these western clothes?"

"It's early, the girls can shop for us," I suggested. "You can join them, if you want to," I added thoughtfully.

"I don't want to be left out, I'm going too," Lisa stated, as a matter of fact, leaving no room for an argument.

I took money from my wallet and gave a thousand dollars to Karen for her and Judie, and to pick up a few things for me. I then gave each couple another five hundred and then offered to pay for Lisa and Priscilla.

"No, we won't take your money," Priscilla objected.

"Mother's right, Johnny, we have more than enough for ourselves."

"Take it, please," I insisted, "it's something I want to do."

"Johnny, thanks for the offer, but our answer is still no."

Priscilla called for the limo, while I gave Karen my size for jeans and a shirt.

"Come on ladies, let's go shopping," Tara said deciding to be the spokesperson for the group.

"Wait a minute," I held my hand up, "don't leave yet. Is that going to be enough money for all of you and the guys too?" I questioned.

"Johnny," Priscilla sounded exasperated, "Are you going to have enough money for yourself?"

"Don't worry about me. I'll have enough to last through Monday, and then after the show, Priscilla will settle up with me. Lisa, you and your mother may be recognized, be careful because people know you'll have money on you."

"Yeah, maybe Gary and I should go," David said thoughtfully, "that would make me feel more comfortable."

"Hell, let's all go," I suggested, "or we'll never get out of here."

"This should be an interesting event," Priscilla muttered.

"Here, Johnny, in that case, here's the money back," Karen handed me the thousand.

"Yeah, good idea," Tara agreed, along with the others.

"Now why did you do that?" I asked, feeling offended, as each returned the money I gave them.

Seeing my hurt expression, Karen spoke quickly, "So that you can pay for everything when we're at the store," she smiled sweetly.

We literally piled into the limo. Priscilla had asked for the stretch limo, and it's a good thing, because we were packed in like sardines in a can. Lisa gave the driver directions to the western outlet store. Fortunately, it was only a thirty minute drive from Graceland, as all of us attempted to harmonize to Christmas carols on the way. We really sounded hilarious.

What I thought would only take about an hour to shop, turned out to be three. I should have known better. The worst part of it all, the men took longer than the women. Of course, it's because the women picked out about six outfits for each of us to try on, and then they couldn't decide which ones they liked the best, so we'd have to try them on again. This all transpired after the girls each modeled for us first.

The store manager had to keep the shop open longer to accommodate us. They usually closed by four o'clock on Friday's, but since we had such a huge order, he was more than willing to extend his hours.

I decided to pick up two shirts for Chance and Michele for Christmas, as time was running short before they arrived on Sunday. I knew I wouldn't have time tomorrow to shop as the whole day would be dedicated to the show.

Finally we were ready to check out, which took another half hour. I ended up using my credit card instead, as the bill turned out to be double what we anticipated. I guess that was my fault, as I found accessories to match.

It was now six o'clock. Because of the heavy Friday night traffic it would take at least an hour to get back to Graceland to get dressed. With all our purchases the trunk was full, and to have enough room inside the limo the girls had to sit on the guys laps.

"Johnny," Karen suggested, "our motel is closer than Graceland, why don't we go there to dress instead?

"Great idea!" And for a change, we were all in agreement.

We must have looked comical, as a long line of us crawled out of the limo loaded down with packages, and all going to one room. The men waited by the limo for the girls to finish dressing. An hour later Karen came down to tell us they were ready and they would meet us in the lounge.

It was already after eight o'clock by the time we finished changing, and found the girls sitting at a table across from the bar. We slowly worked our way through the crowd. The music the band was playing was horrendously loud. In fact, Gary yelled something to me, and I couldn't hear a thing he said, and he was standing right next to me.

We counted at least fifteen Elvis Impersonators dressed in Elvis suits. The women were all over them. A couple of them had kissed David after recognizing him from flyers, when he removed his hat. He quickly put it back on to discourage any one else. The girls saw what happened and thought it was funny. They were still joking about it when we finally reached the table.

Priscilla said, "I feel like I'm starring in someone's film, dressed like this."

"All we need is a few horses, and cows," I joked.

"Speaking of riding horses," Karen jumped up and grabbed my hand, "let's get on that dance floor and ride." We danced a fast one, and thankfully the next song was a slow dance. It felt good to hold her in my arms. I gradually pulled her closer and was offered no resistance. We complimented each other on our apparel. I especially liked the way her jeans hugged her cute butt. I had picked them out for her. I had pictured what she would look like in them, only to discover the real thing was even better.

We walked back to the table to sit down when the band announced that a few of the Elvis Impersonators wanted to sing with them. After several impersonators attempted to sing, and I do mean attempted, Priscilla asked, horrified at what she had just heard, "Goodness, are they all that bad?"

"Some are pretty bad," David commented, "but there are a few very good ones out there."

"Hey Johnny," Gary started in with his humor again, "I guess you could say these guys are Elvis Imposters."

"Good one!" and we laughed at his humor.

"Why don't you sing one?" Tara asked David.

"I don't know, what do you think, Johnny?"

"I'm not sure, it could be risky, and then again, it could be fun."

"Go ahead, honey," Tara told David. I smiled at the love and support she always gave her husband. "The worst that could happen," she giggled, "is all these women will tear your clothes off, and you know I like to see you naked," and then blushed when she realized what she had said.

"Let me go with," Gary piped in, "maybe they'll attack me too."

Denise slapped him playfully on the arm, and said, "Never mind, I'll attack you later when we get back to our room."

"Later," he groaned. "What's wrong with right now," and he wrapped himself around her.

Priscilla and Lisa Marie were thoroughly enjoying themselves just watching us cutting up. "I don't remember when I've had so much fun," Priscilla said, holding her side from laughing.

"Priscilla, sometimes you just need to get out into the real world," Karen commented trying to be honest and sincere.

"You're right, Karen, but it's not always that easy."

"It is if you go out with friends, like us."

"I guess you're right, we're doing it, and getting away with it, aren't we?"

I looked at David, "Are you going to sing us a song?"

"I think I will," he stated, as a matter-of-fact.

When David's name was called to sing, one of the Elvis Impersonators named Pete, who obviously had to much to drink, hollered to David and said, "Look at the cowboy, he's going to sing get along little doggie, get along."

David glared at him, took off his cowboy hat and said, "I'm going to make that last song you sang sound like it was sung by a love sick mule."

"Oh, yeah!" Pete answered sarcastically.

"That's right, you just sit back, and I'll show you how it's supposed to be done." David's first selection was a fast song. The crowd cheered and yelled to him, and wanted him to sing another one. He decided on "Loving You." When he finished, he walked off the stage, and several girls in the crowd grabbed him and started kissing him. Gary and I jumped up to surround him until we could get him to the door. Two bouncers helped us get through the entrance and outside. The girls joined us and thought it was hilarious. We finally made it to the limo.

"Hey, all our clothes are in Karen's room," I said.

"We can ride around and come back and get them later," Lisa suggested.

After an hour we figured it was safe to return to the hotel. Karen and Judie brought us our clothes. I walked Karen around to the back of the car and told her how much I had enjoyed being with her. I told her I would send the limo for her around nine o'clock, and then I took her into my arms and kissed her. She kissed me back, her lips clung to mine. I held her tight, and told her I wished I could stay with her for the night. I looked in her eyes and saw they were filled with passion.

"What about tomorrow night?" I asked.

"That would be nice, but maybe we could be alone after you leave Graceland."

I nodded yes, kissed her again, and told her I'd see her in the morning. I got back into the limo and we left, but not before I saw the hurt in Priscilla's eyes. She tried to act like she didn't care, but she was quiet the rest of the ride.

As we pulled out from the hotel parking lot, Lisa opened the sun roof, stood up and yelled, "Viva Las Vegas." People leaving the lounge yelled "Viva Las Vegas" in return, and threw there arms in the air.

When we reached Graceland, Priscilla, Lisa, and I went into the house and everyone else retired to the guest house. Lisa kissed me good night, and then kissed her mother. "It really was fun watching you have fun tonight, mother," Lisa said smiling.

"Well, it's been a long time since I've had this much fun. Come to think of it, I don't think I ever remember going out to a bar. We'll have to do it again sometime," Priscilla said, and smiled from the night's events.

Lisa went upstairs. Priscilla wanted to know if I would like to have coffee with her. She needed a cup since the drink she had at the bar was too strong for her. We sat at the kitchen table, and I waited while she made the coffee.

"Does Karen know who you are?" she wanted to know.

"No, she doesn't."

"What about David and Gary?"

"Yes, Gary, David and Chance know, but not their wives."

"Why did you tell the guys?"

"They were starting to guess, and I wanted them to know the truth. I trust them. They've been good friends to me."

"Why didn't you tell me, why did you keep putting me off?" she turned and faced me.

"I guess I was afraid of all the questions, like right now."

"Joe told me everything, and I believe your scheme will continue to work as long as you remain Johnny Raye," she replied sadly. Lisa Marie knows, doesn't she?"

"Yes, I told her in Dallas, but I made her promise not to tell anyone."

"Well that little stinker," she laughed. "When are you going to tell Karen?"

"I may never tell her, it depends on our relationship."

"Is she the reason you wouldn't make love to me the other night?"

"No, Cilla, I just knew what you were wanting from me, and it wasn't love."

"Seeing you in that bed made me want you all over again," emotion filled her voice. "I was hoping you'd grab me and throw me on the bed and make mad, passionate love to me."

I laughed at the thought of it. "Hell, we didn't do that when we were married."

"Don't remind me," she replied. "By the way, did you tell the limo driver what time to pick Karen up in the morning?"

"No, gosh, I didn't, I forgot."

"Don't worry, I'll tell him."

"Thanks, Cilla, and thanks for not getting mad for having Karen here."

"No problem. I like her, and I think she'll be good for you. But don't do to her what you've done to your other women in the past, especially me."

"I've got a lot to do before I settle down, and I'm not making any promises. She knows I've been with other women, and I know she's been with other men. She's nice looking, has a nice shape, so I'm sure there are men chasing after her. Right now I'm just trying to keep her interested in me until we know we're right for each other."

"Elvis, you'll never be able to leave women alone."

"Believe it or not Cilla, I'm getting to old to keep up this life style. I'd like to retire and settle down someday."

"El, I hope you can, but you better get it out of your system. Music has been your life, is your life. Karen would have to learn that women are going to chase after you. I had to!"

"Priscilla, I was young and wild then. I was Elvis, now I'm Johnny Raye."

"Elvis, tonight at the bar seeing David on stage, and the women afterwards reminded me of you. If you had sang on that stage tonight, even though you're not a young kid anymore, the girls would still have wanted you. There is still magic in Elvis."

"Yeah, you're probably right," I laughed.

"What are you going to do when you leave Memphis?"

"I'm going to Vegas, and perform at some of their Casino's and Supper Clubs."

"If you do, go by yourself. Don't take Karen, you'll only hurt her."

"Do you really think so?"

I studied her face and eyes, and looked for jealousy or anger, but there was none. Her comments were honest and open.

"You know how Vegas is, the girls will be all over you."

"I plan on going out there first, say, in a month or so, and then I thought I'd ask Karen to join me, but by the look on your face, you don't agree."

"No, I don't, you're not sure of your feelings yet. Johnny, the other night, I stood naked in front of you, and you turned me down. You knew I was butt naked, didn't you feel anything?"

"Yes, but I turned you down because you knew I was Elvis, and you only wanted to have sex to trick me into admitting who I was."

"Still, you turned me down."

"Well, if it makes you feel any better I didn't want to, but I had to."

"There's your answer, Johnny. When you are in Vegas, you'll have to want to. If you fall in love with her, then you can make it work."

"That's just it, I'm attracted to her, I don't know if there's anything else.

I'm not sure how much she's interested in me."

"Tomorrow night after the show go back with her and find out," she suggested.

"I plan on doing that, but I'm not looking for a night of passion to make up my mind, Cilla. I'm looking for something much deeper than that."

"Hey," she yawned, "it's getting late and tomorrow's a big day for all of us."

I walked her to her room, and kissed her good-night. "I needed someone to talk to Cilla, thank you for being a good listener and for the advice," I said, and started walking to my room.

"Elvis, I will always love you, and if you ever need me, I'll always be there for you."

I smiled and shut the door to my room.

I woke around eight o'clock the next morning, quickly showered and dressed. I met Lisa on the patio and asked her if Priscilla was awake. She laughed and told me that she was still asleep; she wasn't used to going out drinking and probably needed to sleep in.

I called the office and arranged to have Karen picked up at the hotel around ten instead of nine o'clock. I then called Karen. Judie answered the phone and said that Karen was in the shower, so I let Judie know the plans for the day and for the evening.

"Lisa, have any of the guys been around this morning?" I asked, fixing myself a cup of coffee.

"Nope, looks like we are the only ones who can cut the late hours. Mother said I take after you for that."

"And I still think so," Priscilla said, as she joined us.

"How long have you been standing there?" Lisa asked concern written on her face.

"Don't worry Lisa, she now knows the truth."

"Thank goodness, I don't have to hide this from you anymore."

"Lisa, I respect your decision not to tell me, after all, you made your father a promise, and you kept it. I'm not angry, but I sure would like a hug."

The maid interrupted our conversation and brought out pancakes, sausage, ham and eggs. While we ate, Lisa asked her mother if she was all right with Karen being here.

"Of course, your daddy and I are still divorced, but, we'll always have a special bond between us, namely you!"

"Good," Lisa said, "I like Karen, and I think she'll be good for daddy."

"Thank you," I laughed, "I'm glad I have your approval."

I had the maid prepare breakfast for the others, and she no sooner went back into the kitchen when I spotted Gary and David with the girls coming towards us.

The sun shone brightly, but the snow was holding. The grounds workers were clearing off the drive and walkways. I spotted George riding around in his cart. Someone had enclosed his cart in plastic and installed a portable heater. I ran out and told him not to do anything but ride around. He thanked me again for the retirement income. He had picked up his papers earlier at the office.

"Just remember, you're like one of the family." I hollered to him "Oh, and something else, I'm Johnny, Elvis is dead and buried in the garden."

"Yes sir, I'm sorry about yesterday. The medicine they gave me mixed me up a little, but I won't forget again."

I re-joined the rest of the group. Karen and Judie had just arrived.

"Is George taking it easy like we told him?" Priscilla inquired.

"He is."

"Maybe we should keep him away altogether?"

"No, that would kill him for sure. I believe he needs to quit on his own. One day, when he's ready, he will."

"I don't want anything to happen to him," Lisa said.

"What's wrong with him?" Karen asked.

"He's the one that Priscilla and I went to see at the hospital yesterday."

"Oh, the gentleman who was so friendly to us earlier when we came through the gate. No wonder you're so concerned about him. He really is sweet."

"Okay everyone." I decided to get things going again. "Let's make a list of everything that needs to be done. Gary, first of all we need to recheck the sound, and the big screen. Let's check heaters too."

"Is there anything I can do?" asked Judie.

"Priscilla, do you have anything for her?"

"Yeah, what about the rest of us?" Tara asked.

"Why don't all of you come over to the office when we're done eating and we'll see what we can find for you to do. God knows there's plenty to be done."

We finished our coffee and the guys went out to check on the equipment. The girls followed Priscilla and Lisa to the office. The National Guard was already in place. Ticket buyers were already lined up at the gate. Security was already stationing them selves into position. Local police, as well as county and state troopers had secured the area and set up barricades.

Everything checked out. The set crew was finished with the stage decorations. Furniture was brought out under the canopy at Lisa's direction for her interview. She had decided on an 'L' shaped sofa and two chairs and a coffee table. Several porcelain vases filled with crimson, red poinsettias were placed around the set. The cameras were set up to make the set appear to be a large sitting room. They would also be able to capture the crowd in the front closest to the stage. The television host would interview Lisa, and Priscilla. Later, Lisa and Priscilla were to join us in song, "Silent Night" and "White Christmas," along with the audience.

The show was to start at seven o'clock, and end around nine thirty. I would perform for approximately an hour and a half. David would sing for a half an hour. After the show, I would sing a few encores for the people as a special treat, but this would not be filmed. Commercials would fill in the rest of the airtime, as well as the interview. The show would close, and security would escort everyone from Graceland. Sunday would be set up the same way except, David would split his time with Chance. At the end of Sunday's show, the three of us would join together, splitting the verses of the Christmas Carols between us. I had written all this down and hoped everything worked out as planned.

David and I rehearsed, but it didn't go well. Both of us were nervous. Gary made his adjustments, and we left to find the girls. Priscilla found jobs for each of them. Karen was helping with last minute decorations, Tara was helping with last minute ticket reservations, Judie and Denise were riding around on snack carts supplying the guards with refreshments and whatever they needed. Everything was ready.

By noon we had all gathered back on the patio. We found sandwiches piled high on a platter and a large crock of soup waiting for us. We sat around and talked for several hours, mainly about the upcoming shows and a few funny stories of prior shows. A final check was made by the crews in charge and they reported to us that all was ready and everyone was in their places. Fans were lined up along the outside walls of Graceland anxious to get in. Finally at five o'clock, Priscilla gave the signal to allow them to enter.

The girls stood on the front porch waving to the people yelling Merry Christmas. The guys were inside looking out the window. It was safer and less chaotic to keep us from being seen.

It was only a few hours until show time so we went to our rooms to get ready. Hair stylists were putting final touches on the girl's hair. Make-up artists were doing their finishing touches and were getting ready to work on David and me.

I wore my light blue suit, David wore his red suit. Gary was dressed in a black tuxedo with a red carnation in his lapel. Tara and Judie looked gorgeous in their black evening gowns. Denise had selected a green sequined gown that captured the light as she moved about.

We were waiting in the living room for the rest of the ladies. You could feel the excitement in the air. Priscilla and Lisa walked down together. Each had their hair styled in the latest fashion. Priscilla's gown was deep blue, cut low in front and back, with matching shoes. Her necklace and earrings were teardrop sapphires surrounded by diamond baguettes. The stones matched the blue stones in my suit. Lisa wore a white gown, and looked stunning in contrast with her jet black hair. Her dress was also cut low in front and back, as well as a slit on the side up to her thigh. A diamond necklace hugged her slender young neck. Diamond earrings in three strands hung from her ears. Both women looked gorgeous.

I caught a movement at the top of the stairs. It was Karen. All eyes were on her. She wore one of her own creations from her shop, a full length red sheath, with matching shoes. She had intricately stitched tiny jewels around the waist and across the bodice to accent her petiteness. Knee high slits on both sides showed the length of her shapely, long legs. A ruby red stone surrounded by small diamonds hung solely from a gold chain. Matching earrings peeked through her long blonde hair, which cascaded softly on her shoulders as she descended the stairs.

A grin stretched from ear to ear as she saw the look of pleasure on my face. I took her hand and whispered in her ear, "You were beautiful before, but tonight, you look absolutely incredible. I would be very proud to have you sitting at my side after the show, if you'd like?"

"No. I'm not interested in being on the show, I'd be too nervous! With my luck, the host would ask me questions and I'd probably stammer all over the place. Thanks, but I think I'll sit on the side lines."

"If you sit too close, the way you look tonight, I might forget the words to the songs."

Everyone laughed, and Priscilla said, "Please don't do that."

The ladies took their seats just off the stage under the canopy; Lisa and Priscilla sat on stage on the sofa. Everything looked beautiful. The snow machines were set to make a light dusting of snow. The tree lights blazed against the white starkness of the snow as it accumulated on the branches. The decorations on the stage sparkled and glittered in the back ground. It was astounding.

The crowd screamed when Gary walked out and started the intro music. Once again, my blood raced and my heart pounded. David paced back and forth, as normal, and then he got his cue from Gary and went on stage. He bowed to the crowd, and they went wild as Gary introduced him. He held up his hands for silence and then went to his seat.

Gary continued playing the intro music, and then announced, "Ladies and Gentlemen, the hour you've been waiting for, please welcome from central Florida, Elvis Impersonator, Mr. Johnny Raye!"

I waited for a few seconds, and then walked across the stage waving my arms and bowing. I stopped in front of Priscilla and Lisa Marie, and gave them each a kiss. I went to David Lee, hugged his neck and shook his hand. From then on, the crowd became the center of my attention. I moved around the stage like I was driven with exorbitant energy. I started the show with "C.C. Rider," followed with "Burning Love," then, "Treat Me Nice," and then to catch my breath, "Loving You." I gave scarves to the ladies in the front area as I sang several more songs. No one appeared to be cold. The heaters were working and everyone seemed to having a great time.

I stopped to make an announcement. I thanked Lisa Marie and Priscilla for giving me the opportunity to be chosen as the Elvis Impersonator to give tribute to the King of Rock and Roll. I then turned to them to have them stand up and take a bow. "In retrospect to the holiday season, and falling snow, I'd like to sing a few Christmas Carols, starting first with none other than "Blue Christmas."

The cameramen were doing a fantastic job of viewing the audience, and angling the cameras to capture the stage décor and the falling snow in front of the stage. During my performance, the crowd screamed, some cried, others yelled, "The King is back!"

I sang several more Christmas carols; it was as if I had turned back time. The screams were deafening, the music blared, and I loved every minute of it. I had been on stage for well over and hour. Before I knew it, Gary signaled for me to announce David. I bowed to David and gave him the stage. I walked off, pleased with my performance and the whole show in general.

David did a fantastic job. The excitement of the crowd had him pumped. He was doing several fast songs, and then switched the tempo to gospel. As David finished "Amazing Grace," that was my cue to come back on stage.

Gary handed me the microphone, and I announced, "Ladies and Gentlemen, to end a beautiful night, it would be my pleasure to have Miss Priscilla and Miss Lisa Marie join us with one of the most beautiful Christmas songs ever written, and it would be an honor if all of you would sing along. Gary, if you would please."

The music from "Silent Night" filled the air. At first only our four voices could be heard, and then slowly, one by one the audience began to participate, softly at first, and then the air was filled with the volume of melodic voices as thousands sang with the joy of Christmas. We finished with the crowd demanding more.

David, Lisa Marie and Priscilla moved to the back of the stage as I sang "Holly Leaves and Christmas Trees," and then closed the show with "American Trilogy." And to make it a real tribute to the 'king', I sang, "If I Can Dream."

Gary announced for those who wanted to stay, that I would be back to do requests, but first we had to break for interviews and commercials. The host from the television station began the interview with Lisa and Priscilla. One of the questions they asked was what made them decide to pick me to do the

Christmas Special at Graceland.

"The show speaks for it self," Priscilla spoke eloquently, "have you ever heard better, other than Elvis himself?" she smiled sweetly for the cameras.

"No, the host said, "he's got to be the best impersonator I've ever heard."

"Lisa," he now directed his questioning to her, "what are your thoughts of the show?"

"I think Johnny did a fantastic job, and the rest of the show was awesome, on second thought, make that totally awesome."

"Do you think he sounds like your father?" We had talked about that question being brought up among ourselves and she was prepared with an answer.

"Well," she said ever so innocently, "he's not my dad, but he's the next best thing to him, and I know dad would agree with me if he were today," she added thoughtfully. Lisa threw her head back for special affect, and laughed softly, "Although he is a little older than my dad," and then turned and winked at me.

He next addressed Priscilla, "I understand Johnny Raye is staying at Graceland?"

"Yes, he is, he's our special guest. Lisa and I felt that he would feel more at home here, rather than a hotel. And besides, with the show being held here at Graceland, what better place for him to stay."

"That does make good sense, and then asked, "David, I understand you and Johnny are close friends?"

"Yes, that's true."

"Where did you two meet?"

"In Birmingham at our Karaoke bar, which my wife and I currently own."

"I understand it was Johnny who asked you to sing with him tonight, is that correct?"

"Yes, Johnny is the type of person who watches out for his friends, and I'm proud to call him my very best friend, other than my wife," he quickly added.

He then turned the microphone to me, and said, "Johnny, a great performance, and it sounds like from the screams of the crowd that they really love you."

"No," I said, "they really love Elvis Presley. I'm just a symbol of what he used to be, and what he stood for. I just hope the fans here tonight and tomorrow night enjoy the show as much as I do performing for them. Please, no more questions."

"Just one more Johnny, and then I'll leave you alone.

"How did you become a singer, and an Elvis Impersonator?"

"I've loved singing ever since I was a child. As for becoming an Elvis Impersonator, that's easy. I've always admired the "King" and love to sing his songs, and since my voice sounds similar to his, I entered a contest and won. David Lee and Chance Smith are two very good impersonators. They helped me a great deal; I owe them both. The rest is history. Now if you'll excuse me, the fans are waiting," and I walked away. "Gary are you ready?" I asked.

He nodded yes in acknowledgement.

"Then let's rock and roll. David, you can help me with this one." I wanted to do, "One Night," we shared versus and had a good time cutting up with the next several songs. By now it was ten thirty. I said to the crowd, "A big thank you for being here tonight from Graceland, have a Merry Christmas, God Bless and thank you, thank you very much." David and I waved and walked into the house with an audience still screaming and wanting more. I told everyone to stand under the canopy and wave. We again wished a Merry Christmas to all and walked back into the house.

Reporters that were in the audience swarmed the house, hoping to get an interview. The television host announced that this Christmas Special was a tribute to Elvis and his many fans. He wished everyone a good night from Graceland, and would continue the report tomorrow night. Finally, hours later everyone was gone.

Inside, we congratulated each other for all the hard work, talked about the show, and about being excited to do it all over again tomorrow night. I took Karen by the arm, apologized for not talking with her sooner, and asked if she and Judie enjoyed the show.

"Johnny, this has truly been a night of magic for me. It's a night I'll never forget."

Judie, standing near-by, smiled and said, "Thank you so much for arranging for me to be here, I can't wait to get home and tell all my friends. I know they were watching."

"Are you leaving tonight?" I asked Karen huskily.

"No. Not tonight, first thing in the morning."

Everyone wandered out to the patio, still chatting about the show and still excited that everything went so well. I asked Karen to sit with me on the sofa. "I have something I'd like to ask you," I said, and held her hand. "What would you think about going to Vegas with me?"

Her mouth dropped open in total surprise. Taking a deep breath she answered softly, "There are a couple of reasons I can't go. First of all, I'm not *in* love with you. I enjoy being with you very much, and I do love you, but right now I'm not '*in love*' with you. Secondly, I have my dress shop. I've worked hard to build it to where it's at now, just like you did with your music. You love your music and you're not ready to give it up are you?" She looked directly into my eyes for the truth.

"No, not yet, but in a few months or a year or so, I'd like to retire."

"Me too," she responded.

"Sitting here looking at you, Karen, I'd like to make love to you all night long."

"That sounds wonderful," she laughed, "but Judie is with me and you have a house full. Can I take a rain check on that offer?"

"I'm leaving Graceland on Tuesday, but before I go to Vegas, I'm going to stop and see and old friend of mine in Florida. What if I send you the money to join me in Vegas after I get settled there?"

With a slight hesitation, she said, "I'd like that. But first, Johnny, I need to get out of these shoes and this dress and into something more comfortable."

"Go on up and change, I'll meet you on the patio." Everyone was already on the patio when I joined them.

"Where's Karen?" Priscilla asked.

"She's upstairs changing."

Gary came over to me and said, "Great show big guy!"

"We couldn't have done it without you my friend," I answered, "and I'd like to thank all of you for a job well done. David, you did and excellent job tonight. All the big wheels in Vegas saw you and I'm sure you'll be able to get in with a major night club out there."

"I hope so Johnny." He was pleased by my comment of praise.

Judie spoke up, and said, "I think you both should do concerts around the country."

I laughed at her serious expression. "We probably could, but I'm too old for all that traveling. I'd rather play the casinos, make just as much and sleep comfortably every night.

"I guess at my age," Judie said, "I would too!"

"For and old man, you move around that stage pretty darn good!" Lisa joked, as Karen rejoined us.

"By the way, Lisa, did you arrange for the jet to be at the airport in Dallas to pick up Chance?"

"I talked with Chance this morning," she replied, "we decided to let him sleep after tonight's show." "The jet will be ready at seven o'clock in the morning. Michele liked that idea better."

"Karen," Judie said, stifling a yawn, "I'm getting tired and we have to be up early to leave."

Priscilla told them the limo was at their disposal when they were ready to go. Reluctantly, Karen agreed. They hugged everyone, and thanked Lisa and Priscilla for their hospitality. Everyone wished them a safe trip.

Tara said, "We'll see you at 'The Bar' when we get back."

"We'll be there," she smiled. I walked her to the limo, kissed her longingly, and told her I would call her soon. "Please do." I noticed a longing on her face that I hadn't seen before. "Enjoy your trip to Florida, and good luck in Vegas."

"Thanks." I kissed her deeply once more. "See you Judie."

"You can bet on it," Judie replied.

I shut the car door, and waved good-bye until they were out of sight. Back inside, I said good-night to everyone as I was extremely tired from the excitement and the show. Priscilla and I walked upstairs together.

"Do you need help getting out of your jump suit?" she asked coyly.

"No, I can manage," I smiled and kissed her good night.

I had just started to get undressed when there was a knock on the door. I grabbed my robe and noticed it was the one with the 'E' on the lapel. When I answered, it was Lisa Marie. She gave me a hug and kiss and asked, "Daddy, how did I do on the interview.

"Fantastic, Kitten."

"I love you, it's good to have you back in my life, please don't ever leave me again."

"You can bet on it, I'll never leave you again." I then kissed her good night and she went to her room.

I slept until nine o'clock, and still felt tired, so I went downstairs in my bathrobe. Priscilla never said a word, but she did raise her eyebrows in question of my appearance. I was surprised when I walked into the sun room and found Chance and Michele sitting there.

Chance took one look at me, laughed and said, "Nice robe big guy." He then hugged my neck, delighted to be here. I bent down and kissed Michele, and told them how happy I was to have them here with us.

"It feels like old home week having us all together again." I smiled at the two of them. It had only been a little over a week since I left Dallas, but so much had happened since I arrived that it seemed like months ago.

Chance and Michele had taped the special and watched it on the plane ride to Graceland. They both were bragging about the great job we had done. I told them how successful the show was and how many fans thought I was the real Elvis.

We all laughed when I brought up the fact that one of the reporters had been heard saying, *"What if it is Elvis? Could Johnny Raye be that good?"*

David, Gary and the girls arrived and wanted to know what was so funny. After explaining to them what we were discussing, Chance filled us in on the shows at Steadman's and how well everything was going for him. I left to get dressed.

When I returned, Chance and Michele were getting settled in their room, and soon after, Chance joined us. I asked Chance to get a list of songs prepared for Gary so they would be different from what I was doing and what David had planned. I explained to Chance how we would handle the introductions and that tonight they would both come out on stage together.

"Guys, we'll need a few songs where we can alternate versus between us. Elvis songs are predominately short so we'll have to choose a couple of long ones. We can rehearse this afternoon in the studio."

"Johnny, I'll go with you and turn up the heat, plus there is a picture I would like to ask you about," Priscilla stated, giving me one of her infamous "I won't take no for an answer" look.

"Okay," I laughed, knowing what she was referring to.

"Let's go now," Gary suggested.

"Why don't you give us about thirty minutes and then come on out," I said.

It was only sixty eight degrees, so we turned the heat up to seventy five. While Priscilla made herself comfortable on the sofa, I opened the bottom drawer to my old desk, and brought out a picture of her and I together in California. Behind the picture were the written words to the song "Are You Sincere."

"In all these years, I never knew that picture was in the desk," she said.

"It wasn't, I put it in there the day that Joe was with me back in September."

"So you've had it with you all this time?"

"Yes," I replied, "there are some things you just can't let go of that easily, and the picture of you pregnant with Lisa Marie, I couldn't part with it."

"Then why did you leave it here?"

"Because, if I sang this song on stage and you heard it, just as you did, I could explain it, just as I did," I answered, sounding a little smug, and feeling a little full of myself.

She shook her head and said, "A well thought out plan, huh!"

"Well I thought so," and I went and turned the equipment on to warm up it up before rehearsing.

When everyone finally straggled in, Priscilla showed Lisa the picture.

"It's none of my business," Denise said, "but what has this picture got to do with Johnny anyway?"

Lisa spoke quickly, "When Johnny came to visit, he found it with a song written on the back. Mother didn't believe him, but here's the proof."

"Oh," Denise said, not totally convinced this was the truth.

"Chance," I said, to get off the subject of the picture, "why didn't Sandy come?"

"She's sick with the flu and didn't want to give it to you, but I think it's because her old boyfriend Jimmie is out of jail. He's giving her a hard time since he found out you're no longer around. She told me he threatened to kill her and you if she came to see you."

Anger flooded my body, "I guess I'll have to take a trip back to Dallas before I make any commitments in Vegas."

"He's got to be crazy to mess with her after what you told him and did to him," Denise said, vehemently.

"What happened?" Priscilla wanted to know.

"Lisa took Priscilla by the arm, "Let the guys rehearse mother, and I'll fill you in."

We rehearsed for almost an hour and since it sounded so good, Gary recorded us individually, and then all together. It was already three o'clock. No one had eaten all day so we went back to the house for a good, healthy country meal. We sat around for a while and drank coffee and cokes to relax.

All day the ground crew had been busy cleaning up from last night. I looked out and noticed that they had just finished. Priscilla went to dress. I looked at my watch and told everyone it was five o'clock, and that we needed to get ready and met in the living room at six thirty.

I chose to wear my white eagled suit. Chance had a royal blue suit made and thought it would be appropriate to wear for the first time on television. David chose his black suit.

Gary walked in with Denise on his arm. She looked radiant as Gary kept telling her how lovely she was. Actually, I think he was saying how 'hot' she looked. Her black dress hugged her body like a glove. It was knee length, slit in the front with double layers of pinched pleats around the hemline. The top was 'V' necked and the back was cut squared to just above her butt. She wore a roped sterling silver chain with a diamond in the center. Her earrings were silver, stringed ropes with a diamond on each strand. She wore her hair down in soft wavy curls. Her black patent leather pumps seemed to accentuate her long slender legs. I told Gary he was one lucky man as I'd never seen her as beautiful as she was tonight.

Tara and Michele came in together. Both girls were given designer suits to wear from one of the top leading women's clothing stores in Memphis. Michele's was a royal blue pants suit with large bell bottomed pants that matched Chance's suit. The high collar looked elegant with her blonde highlighted, upswept hair-do. The low cut, double breasted bodice accented her shapely figure. She had a long silver chain with diamonds set three inches apart that rested just above her cleavage. Large silver and diamond studded earrings shone brightly under the bright lights. Chance asked her who she was, and what did she do with his wife.

Tara also wore a pant suit. She chose a black sleeveless tunic top. The round collar hugged her neck in rows of beaded pearls. The back was cut out in a heart shape. The pleated bell bottomed pants flowed loosely as she walked in her four inch heels. Diamond and pearl earrings hung from her tiny lobes beneath the French coiffed twist. Strands of hair hung loosely on each side of her face. David couldn't take his eyes off her.

It was six thirty when Lisa and Priscilla were finally ready. Both looked absolutely stunning. Priscilla had chosen a conservative teal green pant suit. The collar and cuffs where outlined in satin in the same color. The suit was tailored and cut to fit her body to perfection. Her gold necklace and matching earrings had been specially made with set in stones that matched her teal suit. Her hair fell in soft waves. She looked as young tonight, as she did sixteen years ago.

Lisa looked elegant in black with her jet black hair. Her simple cut, knee length sheath clung to her body, and the back, bottom slit showed her shapely legs. The squared neckline left no room for the imagination. The gold and diamond slide sparkled brightly as it lay between her breasts. Tonight she wore her hair down and left it fall loosely around her slender shoulders. Her pumps were made of soft black patent leather with diamonds on the back of the four inch heels. It was hard for me to believe that this beautiful woman was my little girl, all grown up.

Beckman and Baileys Jewelry Store carried an exclusive line of fine jewelry. They furnished the girls jewelry for tonight as part of their advertisement. Denise, Tara and Michele were tickled that they were going to get paid for wearing the jewelry.

It was time to start the show. The snow machines had been running for the last two hours. The heaters weren't working at first, but one of the electricians found the problem and corrected it immediately.

Gary was on stage waiting for the cue from the director to start the intro music. You could hear the oooh's and aaah's of the crowd as Lisa and Priscilla were seated on the sofa under the canopy in preparation for another interview, and the others on the heated side of the stage in full view.

The director called out "5, 4, 3, 2, 1," and pointed to Gary to start his intro. That was the cue for David and Chance to walk out together. The crowd was screaming, before they ever came into view.

"Elvis! Elvis! Elvis!" The audience chanted, as the music pounded out the low notes of the bass. David and Chance moved rhythmically to the beat, each with their own style of moves.

I then walked onto the stage. David, Chance and I shook hands and gave each other a hug. I stood alone in the center of the stage waiting for the crowd to calm down.

Again, I went back in time. I turned my body slightly, cocked my head towards the crowd, lifted my upper lip in that seductive smile I loved to give, let my leg start to quiver, and then stopped abruptly. I repeated this several times, each time shaking a little more than the last until my hips and shoulders were vibrating to every beat of the music. I moved around the stage shaking every part of my body imaginable.

I was high, but not like years ago, I was high on excitement from the stimulation of the response from the crowd. The screams were deafening. I could no longer hear the music and relied on Gary to signal me when the intro would be close to ending. As soon as his arm went up, I immediately dropped on one knee, one arm out stretched, my head bowed. I was breathing heavily, sweat already poured from my body. The crowd forgot I was Johnny Raye, instead for a brief time, they saw Elvis.

Finally after a full five minutes, the crowd began to settle down, that was until I started singing "C.C. Rider." Gary had to turn the feed-back-monitor up as loud as allowable in order for me to hear myself and the music. This crowd was even more excited than last nights. I sang for a solid hour with barely enough time between songs to have the towel girl wipe my face or take a sip of water. I was physically tired, but unaware of it as I was still mentally energized.

Gary signaled me to announce David and Chance. The three of us sang together, and they did several solos, giving the crowd more show than they had anticipated. Lisa and Priscilla joined us, as they did the night before, to sing "Silent Night" and wish everyone a Merry Christmas.

They walked off the stage so I could end the performance as I always did with "American Trilogy." You could hear a pin drop. Not a sound was uttered. Several people had brought candles, others used lighters. The lights on the stage were dimmed to almost total blackness, except for the spot light on me. The electrician had worked with Gary early in the day, and they rigged a fire works display on stage that could be controlled by Gary. At the end of the song, when I hit the last note, I gave it everything I had. Gary set off the fire works, and the crowd went absolutely wild.

Security was prepared for people to rush the stage, but instead, the crowd screamed, "The king lives!" "The king lives!" "God bless the king," over and over.

The director cut to commercials and David, Chance and I joined Lisa and Priscilla under the canopy. I had no sooner sat down when the television host started asking me questions, and I knew then that something was up. He was supposed to have started with Lisa and Priscilla and then talk to the three Elvis' with generic questions.

The host said, "This was a fantastic show, and some of the viewers had called in during the performance demanding to know more on my personal background."

In defense, I replied, "There's not much to tell. As I said last night, I'm from Florida, I'm older than most of the Elvis Impersonators, that brought a chuckle from the host), and that's about it."

"What about your parents or family, are they still alive?" he persisted.

"No, I'm an only child. My parents past away when I was around twelve. I had an elderly, black nanny, and she raised me. She had sons who sang in their church choir, and they're the ones who taught me how to sing gospel."

"Where did you go to school?"

I laughed and said, "I don't think that should matter."

"How about the name of the lady who raised you?"

"Her name is only important to me, and her family, and this interview with me is now over."

Looking at the expression on my face, the host then turned to ask David and Chance a few questions, and then focused his attention on Lisa and Priscilla. While the three Elvis's walked off stage he was asking Priscilla if doing this show and having me here at Graceland made her feel that Elvis was alive.

Priscilla responded, poised and confidant, "No, Elvis's memories are kept alive because Johnny, David and Chance are what I call real Elvis fans. They not only contribute their lives to singing Elvis's original songs, they are an inspiration to others as well. Lisa and I are very grateful to have them here at Graceland, and to have given such an outstanding performance in Elvis's name. I know if he were alive today, he would be so proud and honored that so many people still love him."

"Does Johnny sleep upstairs or in the guest room?"

Lisa's eyes flamed in anger at the insinuation. "Well, naturally, he stays in our guest room. I believe it was mother's idea because it would be a great inconvenience to have him stay at a hotel. That would make things hard on everyone involved in the show's production as he has given so much input to make the show the success it was. Mother and I have enjoyed his company as well as his friends." "Besides," Lisa continued, "I think my father would have wanted it this way, don't you?" she smiled sweetly, but the smile never reached her eyes.

"Yes, I believe he would at that." He was about to ask Lisa more questions, but the station ran out of air time and the interview ended. Once the cameras were shut off, the host approached me and apologized for getting so personal. He explained that the station insisted he ask me what the people wanted to know. I told him that it was all right, and that I just didn't think people needed to know that much about my personal life; after all, I wasn't famous enough for people to know me.

"Oh, but you are," he said, "people are saying that you could be the real Elvis."

I laughed heartily, and replied, "Well, that's not all bad, if only it was true, but I'm glad the fans think I'm that good."

Security was making sure the crowd was leaving, as we went into the house.

"Johnny, I'd like to speak to you in private, would the rest of you wait for us in the sun room, please?" Priscilla asked, and I followed her upstairs to my bedroom.

"That news reporter isn't through with you," she said, as I shut the door.

"What do you mean?"

"I think he's going to be checking into your personal life, you may need to lay low for awhile."

"Maybe you're right. I'm going to Florida to see Jessie Mae when I leave Dallas."

"Dallas?" she questioned, "why are you going back to Dallas?"

"I have some unfinished business to take care of, and when I'm through there, I'll be going back to Florida."

"Well, if you need me, I'll be in California for a few days. I've made arrangements to leave Tuesday after I clean up a few loose ends. The staff will take of the rest. It's been several months of working day and night to pull this off. I guess you're not the only one that's getting older," and she laughed.

"I'll stay and help and leave on Tuesday when you do," I suggested.

"I'd like that," she responded, and smiled in friendship.

"Good, now let's join the others before they wonder what happened."

"I'll join you shortly," she said, walking to her bedroom, "I'd like to get out of these clothes and into a pair of jeans and a sweater."

"I'll be downstairs."

Chance hugged my neck, and said, "I can't tell you how grateful I am for letting me do this show with you."

"Hey, you old softy. I enjoyed having you here. You did a great job, both of you did. Look, as long as we're all together, you haven't said a word about what you'll be paid." I grinned. "What do you think is fair for helping me out?"

"Are you kidding? We don't want any money, man, just being here is the greatest gift in the world," Chance said, "and I mean that, I don't want any money."

"Me either," David chimed in with Chance in agreement. "You have given and done so much for us, we want to do this for you," he finished.

"Then let's plan on getting together tomorrow morning between ten and eleven o'clock. We'll have brunch first, it'll be our own Christmas party, and then we'll open gifts. I think Santa came early. Since I last checked, it appears that there is a present under the tree for everyone."

David asked if he was going to Vegas with me. I told him yes, but I would have to take care of things in Dallas first.

"You're going back to deal with Jimmie aren't you?" he questioned me.

"Yes, this time I'll make sure he understands what leaving town means. After that, I'm heading to Florida to visit my good friend, Jessie Mae. From there, I'll come to Birmingham to pick up my car that is if you'll tow it again for me?"

"Consider it done," he said.

"Lisa, I'd like it very much if you would go to Florida with me to meet Jessie Mae. I know she would be thrilled to meet you."

"I'd love it," she said happily.

"What do you want Gary and me to do?" Denise was anxious to get involved.

"Would you two like to go to Vegas ahead of us and check out the Casino's and Supper Clubs?"

Gary was concerned because several of the clubs singers worked with bands.

"Well, you can tell Gus when you see him that where I go, you go. We'll hire out at ten thousand a show, your cut will be thirty percent, does that sound fair?

"Hell, yes, it's more than fair, I think twenty percent will do just fine. All I need is enough to feed the machines," he chuckled.

"No, you have a lot of responsibility and thirty percent is fair. So this is the deal, ten-thousand a show, with at least a minimum of three shows a week, plus a suite for each of us. If Gus doesn't want the deal, tell him you'll go elsewhere, but I think he'll want it after seeing the Christmas Special."

"Gus is upset that you didn't show up three months ago, but I think you're right, after seeing the Christmas Special, he'll be dying to get you at his place," Gary agreed.

"While you're there, Gary, can you also find something for David?" I turned and called David to join us and then asked him, "What kind of deal do you want in Vegas?"

"As much as I can get?" he responded.

The four of us sat around discussing our best options.

"Gary, find out what the casinos are willing to pay and work from there. Play hard to get and make it look like we have many offers. It would be extremely beneficial to perform at two clubs, a couple of nights a week. That way, we could each make twenty to twenty-five grand a week. Chance could join us once he finished his job with Steadman's. We know we have to advertise and do heavy marketing of ourselves to keep the interest alive, but that would have to be done when we're in Vegas."

We sat back and relaxed. We discussed the show, the interview, and how hard it was to believe the show was over when so much went into the preparation. It was getting late, the grounds crews quit for the night, but would return early in the morning to restore things back to normal. The television station had taken all their equipment with them, but the power company would have to come and collect all their wiring and special electrical connection boxes.

Fatigue settled through my all ready tired body. I called it a night and Lisa walked upstairs with me. "Daddy, lets get together early tomorrow morning, okay?"

"You just want to open your gifts that you've been snooping at under the tree."

"Yes," she giggled, "it'll feel like Christmas morning to me."

"Alright, just don't make it the crack of dawn, how about nine o'clock?"

"That's good for me," she grinned.

"I have a feeling no one else will show up until noon by the sound of the partying that's going on downstairs."

"Your performance tonight was outstanding, I'm so proud of you," she said as I walked her to her room. I thanked her, kissed her good night, told her how much I loved her, and how much our time together meant to me, and went to my room.

Priscilla never did join us after she left me to change clothes. I assumed she had retired for the night as there was no light shining from her bedroom. I opened my door. Priscilla was lying on my bed wearing a see through negligee. I stood in the middle of the room, hands on my hips and asked, "Are you sure this is what you want?"

"If it wasn't, I wouldn't be here. I want to have you to myself one last time, besides, I deserve it."

Without saying a word, I stripped myself of my clothes.

She patted the mattress and said, "Lie here next to me."

I still hadn't spoken. She began kissing me, long and hard and then straddled by body with hers. "I'm going to make love to you, and then I want you to make love to me," she said huskily, her breathing already becoming rapid.

Priscilla had become more experienced in the art of making love compared to the innocent little school girl that I remembered so well. Finally, we satisfied each others hungers and wants. She lay her head next to mine and fell asleep.

I woke early the next morning, and quietly went in to take my shower so as not to disturb Priscilla, but by the time I had showered and dressed, she had left to go back to her own room. Lisa was waiting for me when I went downstairs.

"Good morning, daddy," she said with a smirk on her face.

"Okay, Kitten, what's that look for?"

"On my way here, I saw mother leaving your room and she was naked."

"Uh, Huh!" I responded innocently. "She was out of toothpaste and wanted to borrow mine."

"Yeah right," she giggled, "you could have come up with something better than that."

"Scout's honor!" I grinned back, "but enough of that, let's get some coffee and breakfast, I'm starving."

Entering the sun room, and looking through the window, I noticed David, Tara, Chance and Michele coming out of the guest house. It was only eight thirty. I hadn't expected anyone until much later. Priscilla was now up and went to the kitchen to ask Martha, the maid, for coffee and breakfast. She came and kissed me and said, "I really feel fine this morning, how about you?"

"I feel fine? How's your coffee?" I inquired.

"Fine," she grinned.

"Well, mother, you sure look cheerful this morning," Lisa said trying to be serious.

"Yes, I do feel cheerful," she commented, not knowing Lisa had witnessed her leaving my room. "Best morning I've had in a long time."

By then everyone had arrived.

"Boy that coffee smells good," Tara exclaimed, "I don't let anyone talk to me until I have my first cup."

We had just sat down to eat when in walked Gary and Denise. He was still half a sleep, but the minute he smelled food, he perked up.

Priscilla finished her coffee, passed on the breakfast, and said, "Wait until I get back to open gifts, I have to go to the office for an hour or so."

"That's not a problem, we'll wait," I answered.

As soon as she left, I called Joe and asked him to run to the jewelry store to pick up another ring for me.

"It'll have to be done within the hour. Can you handle that for me?"

"Sure, what one am I looking for?"

"I'm going to call the jewelry store now so that all you'll have to do is pick it up."

"I'm on my way."

I hung up and made my call. I had noticed a half caret solitaire diamond dinner ring surrounded by diamond baguettes totaling two carets that was set in fourteen caret gold. Having described the ring to the sales clerk, she placed me on hold and went to check to make sure it had not been sold.

"You're in luck," she said after checking, "it's here, and I'll have it ready for your friend to pick up."

I thanked her, and had her gift wrap it for me. She was more than happy to.

"Lisa, I have a gift for your mother, but it won't be here for another hour or so. Can you keep her at the office until Joe returns with it?"

"Sure, it won't be hard to do with all the finalizing that has to be done. I'll go over there now and get her involved in a few extra things."

The group went to the living room to sit around at wait for Santa. Gary dozed off with Denise curled up next to him. The other two couples were talking quietly among themselves. I left to go to the office to discuss the funds that needed to be cut from my check.

Priscilla was busy getting totals together for me when I walked in. Ticket sales, advertisement, sales from memorabilia and miscellaneous items totaled over twenty million dollars. Because the sales from tickets was double what we had figured, Gary was to receive a check for one million dollars. From my check a portion of George's retirement was cut for one hundred thousand to be given back to Graceland. David and Chance were to each receive five hundred thousand. The balance of my share was seven million nine hundred thousand dollars. I now had the stability to complete my plans in Vegas.

Joe returned and called me from the house. I told him to leave the ring under the tree.

"I want to see you before you leave."

"Sure," I replied, I'll get your money to you later."

"Johnny, it's not the money, I just want to see you before you leave Graceland."

"Why don't you come to the house, we'll be going there in a little while?"

"I guess I can."

I winked at Lisa and told her and Priscilla to come as soon as they could as everyone was waiting. Besides, I wanted to play Santa.

"Can you put the checks in gift card envelopes?" I asked.

"Already did and we'll be right there," Priscilla said anxious to get out of the office.

I found Joe with the rest of our group in the sun room. Joe hugged my neck and congratulated me on having done one hell of a performance. He thought it was the performance of a lifetime.

"I thought you'd stop by the house during the shows, but you didn't come either night."

"No, I was busy at the ticket booths and snack stands."

"Oh, I didn't know you had to work during the show."

"Oh yeah! I can't just sit around with something this big going on."

"Want a cup of coffee?"

"Sure." He answered, as I poured one for him.

"How do you know Johnny so well?" Tara asked, wondering what was going on.

"I met him at the Karaoke contest in Dallas," he answered nonchalantly; "I was one of the judges."

"I think there's more to it than that," Denise said dryly, "but I'm not going to ask what."

"Denise," I laughed, "your always suspicious, I guess that's why we love you so much."

"It wouldn't do any good to ask, cause no one would give you a straight answer," Tara stated smugly.

"Tara, honey," I began in a teasing voice, "if you ask me anything, I'll tell you."

"Okay," she accepted the verbal challenge, "are you really Elvis and just hiding under the name of Johnny Raye?"

I laughed good naturedly and winked at her. "Yes I am, but don't tell anyone," I laughed even more.

"See," Denise said, "you can't get a straight answer out of him."

"I don't believe you," Tara exclaimed.

"Then why did you ask if you knew I'd tell you a lie?"

"I don't know, it was a dumb question, and you gave me a dumb answer, so let's forget I asked."

"Only if it makes you happy," I replied, and everyone laughed at her chagrin. "Come on," I said jovially, "let's all go in the living room.

Priscilla and Lisa were back, Lisa's cheeks were flushed from the cold air or the excitement, or both. "Okay," I'm ready to see what's under the tree," she exclaimed.

"Patience, Kitten. First let's bow our heads and thank the good Lord for everything he's done."

"Hear! Hear!" Everyone agreed and bowed their heads.

"Dear Lord," I began, "we thank You for our many blessings, we thank You for such a good year and for many friends and family. We ask that Thee watch over us, and keep us in Thy care, that we all have a blessed and Merry Christmas, in the name of our Lord, Jesus Christ, Amen."

"Amen!" everyone responded.

"Now, we can open gifts, I'll pass them to everyone."

"Johnny," Lisa said, "here's your Santa hat, and hurry up, you're too slow."

I picked out the packages that had the rings for Lisa and Priscilla first. Handing them their gifts, I said, "On behalf of the guy's and their better halves, and myself, we'd like to thank you for letting us stay here at Graceland, and for your gracious hospitality. Also to thank you for the wonderful job the two of you did putting on the Christmas Special and for making it possible for us to entertain here. Please accept these in the love and warmth they are given."

Lisa opened hers before Priscilla had a chance to take off the bow. "Oh my gosh, this is gorgeous," and she ran around hugging everyone's neck.

Priscilla unwrapped her present, "Oh!" "I thought you were buying this ring for Lisa, I didn't have any idea that it was for me." "Thank you, all of you so very much," and she hugged everyone as tears rolled down her cheeks.

Martha made hot chocolate, and hot apple cider to sip on while we opened our gifts. Everyone was having a great time. The guys and their wives enjoyed the matching shirts and sweaters. Lisa was having a fun time with her presents that Priscilla and I bought her. She loved the diamond earrings and the birthstone jewelry equally well, which put an end to the discussion of which one she would like better. She changed into her jeans and sweater to model them for us, and was so happy with the way she looked in them that she left them on the entire day.

Lisa and Priscilla had selected a 24kt gold pocket watch etched with "Elvis Forever" engraved on the front. I was speechless, and had to swallow several times before I could mumble, thank you. I gave each a hug and kiss, as my emotions were getting the best of me. The rest of the gang pitched in together and bought me a black leather jacket to wear when riding my bike, or for when it's cold and I have the top down on the Caddie, several new shirts and pants, and a brown, suede, western jacket. They all felt I needed to increase my wardrobe, and dress in style for Vegas.

"Mom, Johnny, what a fun Christmas this has been with everyone here, and the success with the Christmas Special," Lisa hugged us both," and, well, just everything."

After cleaning up the pile of wrapping paper, I took three envelopes from under the tree and gave them to the guys, but told them to hold off for a moment. Everyone rolled their eyes, fully well knowing that along with the gifts would come a long speech. I thanked them for their friendship and great performances, their dedication to the Elvis Foundation, and what an inspiration to all the Elvis fans that were here for the show, and all over the world to keep his memory alive and meaningful. "We love you guys, Merry Christmas and may all your days be merry and bright," I finally finished, "now you can open your envelopes."

I grinned and sat down as they looked at their checks inside. They were momentarily speechless. Then, all at once they complained it was too much money, and that being in the show and staying at Graceland was payment enough. Even though they didn't expect it, they most definitely deserved it.

To stop their opposition to the money, I gave them a request. "Don't spend it all in one place!"

Once the girls saw how much money they received, they started crying and hugged everyone. I interrupted their excitement to let them all know I still wasn't done, and that Christmas wasn't over yet. I handed Joe the keys to my car.

"She's all yours buddy."

"Your car, your giving me your Caddie?"

"Yep, she's all yours. I've already called and ordered another."

Joe hugged me, and said, "I'll never let you down, and I'll always be there for you." "I hate to leave," he said, but my wife is cooking a big meal and since I've been gone so much working on the show, I promised her I'd be there. Thank you again," he was just beaming, "wait till my wife sees this."

We walked onto the porch together to talk in private. "Joe, I could never repay you for all you've done for me. I'll always be in your debt, and I'll love and cherish our friendship and trust for as long as I live, you can count on that."

"Merry Christmas, 'E'."

"Merry Christmas, Joe," and this time I didn't correct him.

Chance and Gary were complaining they were going to blow away if they didn't eat. Priscilla instructed Martha to prepare a lunch for us. I checked with Gary to see if the money was enough.

"I don't know," he shrugged his shoulders, "I haven't looked yet."

"Don't you think you should see if you've got enough to get home on?"

He peeked at his envelope, and laughed, "I believe I can get home with this."

He shook my hand and hugged my neck as he embarrassingly brushed away tears that had formed in his eyes. I couldn't help but express my amusement as Gary never gets emotional about anything, except old cars and music, his two true loves.

I wanted to discuss a few things before we headed to our different destinations, so I asked the guys to join me in the sun room where we could talk privately.

"I've been thinking, and I want to share these thoughts with you. Stop me if you have a better idea. David, what if, when you go home, you sell your bar? Or if you don't, you lease it to someone else, or find someone trustworthy enough to run it. Now that may take some time. While you're doing that, you already know of my plans for stopping in Dallas for personal business, and then to Florida to get Jessie Mae to retire before going to Vegas."

I told Gary to take some time off and I'd see him in Dallas. Although I did ask him to check on Sandy if he got there before me.

"Should I shoot Jimmie or wait for you," he joked.

"No, I don't want him dead; I just want to hurt him."

Gary snorted, "I believe he'd rather be dead than hurt as bad as you hurt him last time."

"Good, cause this time, I know he'll learn his lesson. Anyway, after a couple of weeks, I'd like you to go out to Vegas, find a house that has at least six bedrooms with separate baths, a swimming pool hopefully with a waterfall, a large den with a bar, a large kitchen and breakfast nook and possibly a sun room. Try to see what's out there. Say, something less than two million, if that's possible. When I get there, I'll handle the finances."

"Also, check on finding a maid and a gardener, and make sure they can speak English. My plan is to have a house where we can all stay and be comfortable in while we stay in Vegas."

"Why don't we just stay at a motel, and make it part of our pay?"

"Well, we could, but what about Tara and Denise, don't you think they'd be more comfortable in a house?" I countered his remark.

"See, I told you," Gary said, "he thinks of everything, so we need to follow his lead."

"Okay," David laughed.

"No, if you think we're better off at the motel, that's alright with me, let's ask the girls."

Chance spoke up and said, "I'm not going out to Vegas right away, but later I might, and if I do, I know Michele and I would rather be in a house."

"Good," David answered, "Johnny, house it is."

"I'll have to find one first," Gary added quickly.

"You'll find one, I have faith in you," I smiled reassuringly, "now let's eat some lunch."

After lunch, with many hugs, thank yous, and good wishes for the holidays, Gary and Denise left for Dallas. Before David and Tara left for Birmingham, I pulled David aside and asked him if he would pick up the Cadillac that I ordered for Karen for Christmas. I had ordered two, a white with red interior for Karen, and I stayed with the red with white interior for myself. I spoke to Zeke a couple of weeks ago, and he had promised to have them fixed and painted by Christmas Day, even though he would have to work night and day to have them ready. He charged me an extra three thousand as he would have to hire another helper to finish in time.

Anyway, I needed David to pick up the car and deliver it to Karen on Christmas Day. I hoped it wouldn't be an inconvenience, but they said they were celebrating with their families on Christmas Eve, and going to spend a quiet Christmas Day at home alone. Tara was thrilled to be a part of this. I handed her a card to put in the car, and she said she would pick up a heart shaped box of candy to go with it. I thanked them and again, after many hugs and loves, they left to go home.

Priscilla went to the office. I stretched out on the sofa when Chance and Michele walked in the living room.

"Tired big guy?" Chance asked.

"Yeah, a little, sometimes it's a let down after all the excitement, and hectic life style is over."

"Yeah, we didn't get much sleep before or since we've been here, I think we might lie down for awhile too," and they went to their room.

Lisa returned and sat on the sofa with me, cradled my head in her lap, and flipped on the television. She told me Priscilla was working at the office with security and giving out bonus checks for those who worked extra shifts for the Christmas Special. I fell asleep almost instantly, content with the closeness of my daughter. When I awoke, Lisa was sleeping and Priscilla was sitting in a nearby chair watching us.

"Didn't you get much sleep last night?" she smiled.

"Yes," I replied stretching out my stiff muscles. "I managed to get a couple of hours, but someone kept me awake most of the night."

Smiling, she questioned, "Did you want to sleep?"

"If I did," I winked at her, "I would have kicked your naked ass out of bed."

"Yeah," she laughed, and then said, "and I would have jumped right back in."

"No, you wouldn't have, you'd have been mad and wouldn't speak to me for at least a week."

"You know me too well, don't you, Elvis ?"

"Yes, Cilla, I guess I do."

Lisa awoke and wanted to know what we were discussing.

Priscilla said, "He thinks he knows me fairly well."

"Mother, don't you think he does?   You do, daddy, don't you?"

"I can't win," I laughed, "let's forget it. I'd rather love than fight."

That reminded Priscilla of my mission in Dallas, and she began to lecture me on starting trouble with Jimmie. "You know how the news media just loves that kind of trouble, and you know how that reporter is looking for anything he can find on you, it's best if you two keep your distance," she chastised me.

"I know what you're saying, but I'm not going to worry about it."

"There was a time when you would have," she said dryly.

"Uh, huh, but those days are behind me. I'm not looking to go back to those unhappy days. I'm glad I have you and Lisa Marie in my life, but I'm not backing up, it's full speed ahead from here on out. I have plans, and I've set goals for myself, and I'm going to make them happen, my way."

"Some things never change," Priscilla muttered to herself.

Michele and Chance rejoined us. We spent a quiet afternoon and evening watching television. "Miracle on 34th Street" was on, and the girls insisted we watch it. Priscilla popped popcorn, and at first we ate it, but after the third batch, pop corn ended up in our hair and wherever else it landed until we ran out.

Lisa was still tired and went to her room. Chance and Michele went back to their room. Priscilla had fallen asleep in the chair. I woke her and asked if she wanted go to the kitchen for a snack. We found left over pork chops, cole slaw, butter beans and corn bread. Priscilla must have been hungry since she ate a little of everything. As hungry as I thought I was, I, on the other hand, only ate a few bites.

We sipped on cappuccino in the sun room, and then went up to our rooms. I kissed her good night and thought she would return. I pictured her standing naked, her breasts still firm, but she didn't come back. I undressed, put on my robe and went into her room where I found her lying on top of her bed. I bent over her, kissed her, tucked her in, and returned to my room.

I lay in bed for awhile thinking of how good things had been since I made the trip from Florida to Birmingham months ago, and how much I feared getting out into the world again. I thought of the good times singing gospel songs with the guys in the orange groves when suddenly a strange feeling swept through my body that left me feeling cold. Somehow I knew it had something to do with Jessie Mae.

I got up and went downstairs to phone Jessie. After several rings I was ready to hang up when Joseph's voice came on the line.

"What's wrong with Jessie Mae?" I questioned without giving him time for formalities.

"Johnny, she's taken ill, and is asking for you. I was going to wait until morning to call, but I'm glad you called me."

"It's hard to explain Joseph, but I heard her calling out to me. What does the doctor say?"

"He wants to put her in the hospital and run some tests, but she doesn't have health insurance and refuses to go."

"Joseph, you call the doctor. She does have health insurance. She once told me her important papers were kept with her bible. Check the night stands, you'll probably find it there. The bank pay's the payments directly to the insurance company for her."

"I'm still in Memphis. Just get her to the hospital, and I'll wrap things up here. I can be there on Thursday, the day after Christmas. If anything should happen or if there are any changes, call me."

I was shaken from the news on Jessie Mae. Back in my bed, I had a hard time going back to sleep. For several hours, I tossed and turned, thoughts of taking a pill to help me sleep crossed my mind. God, will these temptations every leave, it's been over sixteen years. Then I did what the doctor's told me to do while I was in rehabilitation, focus on things I enjoy. I switched my thoughts to Lisa opening her gifts, and the pleasure she experienced this year having us together. I felt my body begin to relax and eventually I drifted into deep slumber.

I woke early and began packing my bags in preparation for the trip. Chance and Michele left for Birmingham to spend Christmas Day with their families, and then were going to fly back to Dallas to continue his shows at Steadman's. I spent the day saying thank you's and good-bye's to the staff at Graceland, and security. I spent time riding around Graceland in the cart with George. We had a long talk and discussed many things and shared memories. He never brought up or questioned my identity, he knew who I was, and I knew he knew. Out of love for me, I also knew George would not discuss it with anyone. We hugged each other good-bye, as he was going to take a few days off to spend Christmas with his family, and I would be leaving early on Thursday before he returned to work.

Christmas Day was quiet and peaceful. We ate a huge meal, and Priscilla and I sat around watching old Christmas movies. Lisa spent the afternoon visiting with her friends and exchanging gifts with them. She returned later in the evening to pack and get ready for her trip. I thanked Priscilla for everything. She volunteered to go with us to help with Jessie, but I knew she had plenty to do to finish up here. Tours would be starting up again and many preparations had to be done to get the house back in order.

We all met early the next morning in the sun room to eat our last meal together. We shared a lot of small talk as we were preoccupied with our own thoughts and plans. The limo driver had loaded our luggage and was waiting for us. I kissed Priscilla good-bye.

She hugged me tight, and whispered, "Good luck with your new life, Elvis, I wish you the best." Her shoulders shook from the sobs she had held in for so long. She turned and went back into the house.

I stood on the front stoop, and looked around Graceland one last time before I left. The snow was melting, as the days had grown unseasonably warm. All that remained were patches here and there. There still were numerous things to be taken down, workers were hurrying to finish, wanting to get done before the week-end. The stage was now reduced to a shell, and would probably be gone by nightfall. I looked at Lisa's face as she smiled encouragingly at me from the limo. Letting out a large sigh, I joined her in the back seat anxious to get to Florida.

CHAPTER 19

The plane and pilots were ready and waiting when we arrived at the airport. We quickly boarded, and three hours later, landed in West Palm Beach, Florida. We hired a limo service, and the driver drove us to the hospital where they had taken Jessie Mae.

Joseph and Samuel met us in the lobby. Joseph said the doctor was with Jessie Mae, as we spoke, and were waiting for him to leave so they could go back in with her. Samuel told me admitting wanted to talk with me when I arrived, so I headed in that direction. They needed a family member to sign her admitting papers, and Jessie told those in charge to contact me. She knew I would take responsibility for any remaining balances that the insurance company wouldn't pay. I signed the necessary papers, and told the clerk I would pay for anything Jessie needed.

"Johnny Raye, I know who you are," she recognized my signature, "I watched you on television Sunday night, you were fantastic," the admitting clerk said. "As long as you're signing papers, would you mind signing one more and autograph a note to me?" "After all," she blushed, it's not every day that we have a celebrity in here." I smiled, signed a note and left to meet the others in the lobby.

An hour later, the doctor met with us and said Jessie Mae was tired and worn out, and would need a lot of rest. "Her cancer is attacking her vital organs," the doctor informed us, when he found out I was responsible for her.

"Cancer!" I shouted, astounded at what I just heard.

"You didn't know?" he asked.

"No," I replied, stunned at what he had told me."

"She never said a word to me."

"Jessie came to me about two months ago with severe stomach pains," the doctor informed me. "That's when we ran tests and discovered her fatigue was more than old age."

"Will you operate or do chemotherapy? I asked, grasping for straws.

Sadly he shook his head no, and then softly spoke, "The cancer is too far gone, it was already in its advanced stages when she came in several months ago. Right now, it's a day to day situation. She's going to have good days, and then relapse like now. All we can do is keep her comfortable. I'm sorry, I wish there was something more we could do. You can go and see her now if you wish," he said gently. "Now please excuse me, I have other patients to see."

"Thank you doctor," I said numbly, too shocked to say anything more.

"I'll check in on her later in the morning," he continued, "and if everything checks out, she can go home tomorrow as long as there's someone to take care of her." Don't stay too long or you'll tire her out," he ordered as he walked away.

I opened her door and peeked inside. Jessie Mae was resting and appeared to be asleep. I crept softly to her bedside. She opened her eyes and smiled warmly.

"Johnny, I knew you'd come."

"Jessie, why didn't you tell me you had cancer when I talked with you on the phone?" I scolded in a loving tone of voice.

"You're a busy man these days, Mr. Johnny. You have enough going on in your life, and don't need to be worrying about me."

"I don't know why not, you know you're special to me, and that I'd find out anyway."

"Yes," she chuckled softly, "I should have known." "I saw you on television doing your Christmas Special," she giggled, and then added, "I watched you both nights. You looked so handsome, and sounded so good, I loved hearing you sing."

I held her feeble, work worn hand in mine. "Jessie Mae, there's someone waiting in the hallway that I'd like you to meet. Do you feel up to it?"

"It's your daughter isn't it?"

"Yes, it is," I said, and patted her hand. "I'll go get her."

I went back to the waiting room and told Samuel and Joseph that Jessie was talking a little, but was very weak. I took Lisa by the hand and said, "Kitten, she wants to meet you," and brought her to Jessie Mae's room.

Jessie Mae's eyes were closed, and again I thought she was sleeping. Lisa bent down and kissed her wrinkled old cheek. Jessie Mae smiled.

"I've heard so much about you, Miss Jessie," Lisa smiled back.

"And I you," she replied her voice barely audible.

"You sure are a pretty little thing; you look just like Mr. Johnny."

Lisa took her hand, "No," she said softly to Jessie Mae, "I look like Elvis Presley, my daddy."

"So you finally know child, that's good." Her eyes rested on mine.

"Jessie, there's a possibility you can go home tomorrow, so I'm going to leave to get things prepared for you at the house, and I don't want to hear any argument."

"How do you tell the 'King' no!" she yawned sleepily.

"You don't," and kissed her good-bye. Before we left the room, she was snoring softly.

Returning to the lobby, I told Joseph and Samuel that we'd see them back at the house as they wanted to stay for awhile and visit with Jessie. During the ride to the cabin, Lisa suggested staying in Florida with Jessie Mae while I went on to Dallas.

"She will love that," I smiled, proud of my daughter.

"Does she have any family?" she inquired.

"She does. She has a daughter somewhere, but she never comes to visit. Joseph has her number, he can call and let her know Jessie's ill, and give her a chance to visit with her, if he hasn't called already. Today, I'm going to hire two nurses for her care. I'll have to hire a maid, and then, I need to hire an accountant to handle my finances while I'm away."

The sun was high in the sky by the time we arrived at the cabin. The driver helped carry our luggage inside.

"Wow!" Lisa exclaimed, as she looked around, "I expected a small cabin, but this is so spacious." "No wonder you liked staying here," she added, "I love the rustic décor." "And the view," she exclaimed as she looked out the windows over looking the lake, it's fabulous."

"I'm glad you like it, Kitten, but somehow I knew you would."

Lisa continued looking through the remainder of the cabin, while I grabbed a phone directory. I called a reputable, local agency that specialized in home care. They would send several nurses for me to interview this afternoon. I found several ads in the yellow pages for certified public accountants, but one ad intrigued me. The woman who owned the company specialized in handling celebrities account's, and had been in business for over twenty five years.

251

I called her first. Carolyn, the accountant's name, answered on the second ring. After answering my numerous questions, and she giving me numerous references, we set an appointment to meet on Wednesday. I explained my situation to her, including Jessie Mae. She said she could help me out.

"How?" I asked, "Do you do nursing care in your spare time?"

She laughed at my statement, and then said, "My sister Teresa is looking for a house keeping position." She explained Teresa had been working for a family, but they had recently moved out of state. She gave me Teresa's number for me to speak with her directly. I thanked her for her help, and told her I would see her on Wednesday.

Teresa answered immediately. We chatted for a few minutes, me telling her my expectations, and she giving me qualifications and references. She wanted to come out today, and so as not to conflict with the nurses coming for interviews, I suggested she come around four o'clock.

I no sooner hung up the phone when the first nurse arrived. We talked amiably as I showed her around, and we then sat at the kitchen table to discuss employment. Betty, the nurse's name, was a soft-spoken, pleasant woman with reddish brown hair, and seemingly organized. She had brought with her, the names of patients she had cared for, dates, durations, and her training and schooling records. I liked her immediately and felt she and Jessie Mae would get along beautifully.

I explained Jessie's situation to her and described the care I wanted her to have including taking Jessie Mae for short walks, if Jessie felt up to it. Whatever Jessie wanted, I wanted her to have. I also told her that when Jessie's time came to an end, she was to remain at the cabin where she would feel the most comfortable. I did not want her to suffer.

A twin sized bed was to be brought in Jessie's room for the nurses to sleep on as I wanted round the clock care. Betty informed me that her fees would be two hundred dollars a day. I accepted without qualm, and hired the first nurse.

The phone rang and Lisa answered it so I could finish the interview.

"Johnny," Lisa interrupted, "that was Joseph." "He said the doctor is going to release Jessie to come home tomorrow morning. They will be bringing her here in an ambulance."

Upon hearing that, the nurse said, "Guess I need to get home and pack my bags, looks like I'm going to be busy this afternoon getting prepared for my new patient."

Betty volunteered to go to the hospital in the morning and ride along with Jessie to see to her comfort, and also to discuss what medications would have to administered, and Jessie's over all health care with Jessie's doctors. I thanked her and she left immediately.

Within an hour, I interviewed two more nurses, and chose a young blonde woman who was bubbly and full of energy named Sherry. She had lost her husband to cancer and had made it her life work to care for cancer patients. She would start tomorrow evening to relieve Betty, as they would each rotate twelve hour shifts. I then called the insurance company, and they were sending an agent immediately to handle the necessary forms and requirements to insure coverage.

Not having had any sleep, I lay on the sofa to take a nap. Lisa went out to explore the grounds, and I warned her to be alert to snakes and gators of which we had both.

"I guess that ends my taking a short walk in the woods."

I nodded, and said, "Stay in the open areas, even heavy shrubbery and flower beds could house predators. Samuel and Joseph check the grounds daily, but it's better to be safe than sorry." The lawn was spread with lime on a routine basis, which did help keep predators under control.

I felt like I had just closed my eyes when actually I had slept for several hours. Lisa gently shook my shoulder, "Daddy, someone is coming up the drive," she informed me. I looked at my watch and discovered it was already four o'clock.

"That must be Teresa, the housekeeper that's looking for employment."

"Well if it is," she said, she's not alone, there's another woman with her."

I opened the door and asked, "Can I help you?"

"Yes," the first woman exclaimed, "I'm Teresa, I talked with you earlier about the house keeping position."

"And I'm Carolyn," the other lady said, as she outstretched her hand to me. "I know our appointment was scheduled for Wednesday, but after recognizing your name and realizing who you were, I decided to come today. I hope you don't mind," she added, "if it's inconvenient for you, we'll keep our appointment for Wednesday."

"No, please come in," I answered. "Actually, this will be better for me as things are going to be hectic around here the next few days."

I introduced Lisa to them, and they were excited to meet her. I conversed first with Teresa, and told her I wanted the house to be kept clean on a daily basis. She would need to cook three meals a day and handle the laundry.

"I know you are used to cleaning for families, but this situation is different, as there would be more to do due to Jessie's physical condition. I really need someone who can be trusted to run the household. Do you think you can handle this?"

"Yes, I've been working part time at the hospital, and I've been wanting to quit." She laughed, "It's so far to travel everyday and my old car won't take the distance anymore. This sounds perfect for me."

"Good, what do you need?"

253

"Well," she answered honestly, my lease is up on my apartment, if I could live here, basically rent free, I would work for four hundred and fifty dollars a week."

"That sounds more than fair to me, can you move in tomorrow morning?"

"Yes sir!"

"You can drop the sir please, just call me Johnny?"

"Carolyn, my needs are simple. I need someone to pay my bills and handle my bank account."

"To save you a lot of questioning, Johnny, here are my credentials, and you'll see my company is bonded with the state of Florida."

"I appreciate that, as you will have access to a lot of money. We'll need to have your name put on my checking account, so it's important that I trust you," I informed her.

"Besides paying my bills, budgeting my money, and transferring funds as needed, you'll have to pay employees as required."

"I didn't know you'd desire that much service," she said, tapping her finger against her cheek.

"Those are my requirements, are you interested?" I asked her.

She thought for a moment and then said, "Yes, my normal fee is two hundred a week, but because of extra duties I'll need two hundred and fifty a week."

I admired her honesty and said, "Make it three hundred fifty, in case I add any extra's to your list. That way you won't have to sit and calculate time and charges."

"Fine," she smiled, "meet me at your bank at nine tomorrow morning, and we'll get my name on your checking account, and I'll bring my bond and other credentials."

"Do you want an attorney to draw up a contract or use the standard form that my company offers?" Carolyn asked.

"The company form is fine, I'll look at it and if necessary, I'll have Rhonda, my attorney, check it. Well that about wraps it up," I said.

"One more thing," Carolyn asked, "would it be too presumptuous on my part to ask for your autograph?"

I smiled, and wrote a note and signed it, Love Johnny, Elvis, Raye.

"Thanks, Johnny. I'll see you in the morning."

"Me too, and thanks," said Teresa.

"Gee daddy," Lisa commented, "you hired everyone within a few hours if it was me, it would take me a week to hire a maid."

"I learned the hard way, Kitten, if you need something fast, it's amazing just how fast it'll come together, if you work at it.

"We're going to have to make new sleeping arrangements for Samuel and Joseph. I've got it! I'll buy a camper, and set it in the back yard. Come on. Let's see if we can find one in the yellow pages. By the way, Lisa, have you seen either of them today?"

"No, I haven't seen them since we were at the hospital."

We let our fingers wander through the Yellow Pages. "Here's a dealer in West Palm Beach, and another in Vero Beach. That's only thirty five miles from here. I'll give them a call."

The dealership in West Palm Beach was closing in thirty minutes so I asked if they would stay open as I was interested in a camper trailer, and needed something immediately. The salesman said it would have to wait until tomorrow, so I called Vero Beach. They were much more accommodating.

We called for the limo and drove to 'Vero Beach Camper Sales'. An elderly gentleman from the office came out to meet us as we were looking around. He stayed with us describing details and answering our questions.

There were several models to choose from, but one fifth wheel stood out among the others. The color scheme was in a metallic gold and black design, with an expanding living area, and two small bedrooms, separated by one bath. The interior was trimmed in white as well as the kitchen cabinets.

The salesman mentioned that this was their top of the line model, but he did have lower priced models for us to look at, if we so desired. From the way he talked, it was obvious that he didn't see us drive up in the limo. "How much?" I inquired.

"Twenty-eight thousand."

"Would you consider taking less?"

"If you're going to buy tonight and not just looking, I'll sell it to you for twenty-four thousand, nine hundred ninety five, and that's my bottom line," he said emphatically.

I liked his up front attitude, so I offered him my hand, and said, "Sir, you have a deal, but with one condition. I'll pay you cash tonight, but you have to promise to have this model delivered to me by nine o'clock tomorrow morning."

He agreed, "But, because of the rush, we'll have to hire an additional driver." "I'm sorry," he added, but I'll have to charge you an additional fee for delivery, say one hundred dollars."

"Fair enough," I said.

"Good, let's go draw up the papers."

Forty-five minutes later, including insurance, the deal was complete.

"Johnny Raye," he looked at the signature I had written. "Are you that impersonator that was on television this past week-end that everybody's talking about?"

"Yes, I am."

"Well, I'll be darn. Say, would you mind signing a picture I have of Elvis from the early sixties?"

"Sure, why not."

"Wait right here and I'll go and get it, it's in the other office."

He returned with a picture of me that was taken on the Louisiana Hay Ride. I asked him how he happened to come across that picture. He told me the girl in the picture with me was now his wife. I signed the back as Elvis Impersonator, Johnny Raye, then signed Elvis below the wagon wheel on the front. We shook hands once again and left.

"It's already eight o'clock," Lisa reminded me, "we need to cook something to eat and change sheets on the beds."

"We're not going to cook. I know there's a little restaurant not far from here that has good food."

"Good," would you like to put that in writing?" she laughed.

"No thanks, I've signed enough papers for one day," and laughed with her.

The restaurant was the one I used to work in. The same waitress was still working there, and she hugged my neck and asked how I was doing when we walked in.

"You sure have changed since you worked here," she said loud enough for everyone to hear. "I watched the Christmas Special, you were very good. I told you, you could make it if you tried."

"No, as I recall, I remember you saying that there were enough Elvis singers in the world, and we didn't need another."

She laughed, and took our order.

Lisa whispered to me, "Is she an old friend or just someone who doesn't like Elvis?"

"When I worked here for a few years," I explained, "I was always singing in the kitchen, and everyone thought I should be in Vegas except her."

"Oh, a jealous woman, you better look out. Next thing you know," she giggled, "she'll be asking for your autograph, or better yet, a date."

"Real funny."

And she laughed all the harder.

"Let's hope we get served some time today!" I growled, which only seemed to add to Lisa's amusement.

The waitress finally brought our food, and she did ask if I'd come by and see her sometime. She really missed my singing in the kitchen.

"Sure," I said casually, and then looked at Lisa as the waitress walked away, "eat your burger and let's get out of here."

"Still laughing, she said, "I'm surprised she didn't ask you to sing her a song."

"Enough already," I tried to sound stern, and then found myself laughing at the absurdity of the whole situation. Back at the house, I expected to see Samuel and Joseph, but they were nowhere to be found. I knew they'd show up when Jessie came home. "I think I have everything covered and handled, don't you?"

"I can't think of anything else you could do, except rest, so why don't you rest awhile!"

"I'm going to take you up on that suggestion," and I stretched out on the sofa. Within minutes, I was sound asleep.

I awoke the next morning to the sound of the vacuum cleaner. Still half asleep, I arose to tell Lisa that she shouldn't be cleaning, that the house keeper would be here in the morning to do everything. I was shocked when I discovered it was seven o'clock in the morning, and it wasn't Lisa cleaning, it was Teresa.

"Good morning, sir, er, I mean Johnny. I'm sorry, I didn't mean to disturb you, but I wanted to have Jessie's room ready when she got here. Coffee is made, and if you're looking for Lisa, she's outside giving instructions to the delivery man. They brought out a camper. I didn't know what to do about it, so Lisa Marie handled it."

I went to see if Lisa needed help, but she had the delivery man place the trailer where she wanted it and told me to go back inside. I could tell she was upset about something, so I waited for her to come in. I noticed the delivery man leave, and when Lisa came inside, she still had that angry look on her face.

"Kitten, it's obvious something is bothering you, now out with it!"

"Johnny, this is the second trailer they brought out today and it's still the wrong one! The first one was completely wrong; this one is the same make and model, but in a different color scheme. This one has the navy blue and gray exterior, with blue décor on the interior."

"Well, then why didn't you send this one back too?"

"I thought about it, but I knew you had to have it here today, and they don't have any more models on their lot. Seems like there was a screw up in the paper work with the serial numbers. I told the delivery man that we would accept this one for now, but it would be up to you if you want to exchange it later for a different model."

"Well let me ask you this, do you like it?"

"It's nice, and it'll do the job the same as the other."

"As long as it's the same model as the other, and you like it, that's good enough for me. Has anyone called from the hospital yet?"

"Not that I'm aware of, the ambulance company has not called yet."

"Where's their number, I'll see what I can find out? Teresa, where's the number for the ambulance company? I wrote it down on a sheet of paper and put it with my notes."

"They called while you and Lisa Marie were out back. They're on their way from the hospital now. In fact, I see a car coming up the drive-way," she said, and then asked, "I wonder who it is?"

I looked out the window, "Its Samuel and Joseph. I've been wondering where they've been." I greeted them on the porch and asked them as they got out of their car where they stayed last night. They had remained in town with friends as they knew there wouldn't be enough room at the cabin.

"Come on out back. I bought a camper trailer and I'd like you to stay in it for awhile."

"Wow," Samuel exclaimed. "This sure is nice," he looked inside. "Do you know what time Jessie's coming?" he wanted to know.

"She's on her way now. I'm going in to eat breakfast before she arrives. Have you two had your breakfast yet?"

"Yeah, Johnny, we stopped at the restaurant in town and ate." "Good, then I'll see you guys later."

Teresa cooked breakfast, it was ready and on the table when we went into the house. It was a good thing because I was starved. We ate heartily, and I told Lisa it was a relief to know that sleeping arrangements for Samuel and Joseph were taken care of, as well as Jessie Mae.

"You can stay in my bedroom, and I'll sleep on the sofa, since Teresa will occupy the other bedroom. The nurse's bed!" I hollered. "We forgot to get a roll-a-way to put in Jessie's room."

Just then Joseph walked in and asked, "What's the matter Johnny?"

After explaining my problem he said, "Don't worry, there's a furniture store in town and they'll deliver."

I called information and got the name and number of the store. I talked with the store manager and told him the reason this was urgent. He told me not to worry, they had several in stock. He took my credit card number and said that he would see to it personally that it would be delivered today, by five o'clock.

"Johnny, Teresa came into the room, the ambulance is coming up the drive."

"Thanks Teresa, we'll be right there."

"We quickly wolfed down the rest of our breakfast, and by the time we walked outside, the ambulance drivers had Jessie on the roll-a-way cart and were wheeling her on to the porch. We helped get her inside, and the nurse, Teresa, and Lisa helped get her settled. She wasn't in there five minutes and she was wanting out of bed. The nurse came out to get me.

Jessie smiled at me as I walked in the room. "What's this all about, Johnny, you throwing away your money on me, now you know. . ."

"Now you just lay there young lady," I said, cutting her off in mid sentence. You're under my care now and we've got rules, so listen to me."

She looked at me, and with as much effort as she could muster, asked, "Who put you in charge of me?"

"I did," I said. "Now you lay down."

She laid her head back, and then I told her, "First of all, you can have anything you want, secondly, you can go anywhere you want, but your shadow goes with you, and when she steps out for a moment or leaves, we'll take her place until the other nurse comes on for the second shift."

"Okay," but it sure seems to me that you've gone to a lot of trouble for me, haven't you?" she asked somberly.

"Yes, I have."

"Then I guess I'll behave myself, but just for you" and she cackled lightly.

"Good, now get some rest, the ambulance ride tired you out. I'm leaving tomorrow for Dallas. I'll only be gone a couple of days, but Lisa Marie will be staying. Samuel and Joseph will be staying in the trailer out back, and some of your friends have called, they want to come out this afternoon to see you."

"Jessie Mae, in all of our many conversations, not once did we ever discuss what our plans are if one of us should pass away." I took her hand in mine, and looked directly into her eyes, "I feel now is as good a time as any."

"Johnny, let me make this easy for you. I don't want a big fuss, just keep it simple, a few friends, and if you don't mind, I'd like to have the wake here at the cabin. I'd be proud if you'd sing a few songs for me. I have a will that specifies I'm to be cremated, and I'd like it very much if you would spread my ashes over the lake."

"I thought about keeping them over the mantle, that way you could look over Samuel and Joseph until it's their time," I suggested.

"That would be okay too, Johnny, but I have a burial plot, it's all paid for. You can find the papers in with my personal belongings."

"Jessie, I've got a great idea, when I get back from Dallas, I'd like to throw a party for you, let's plan it for the following week end. Do you think you are up to it?"

"Only if you plan on singing for me?"

"That's a promise."

"Well then, I'll feel up to it," she grinned. "Johnny, have you eaten breakfast?"

"Yes. Why?"

"Because I'd like a cup of coffee, either here or in the kitchen, preferably in the kitchen. That mud they serve you in the hospital isn't fit to slap hogs with."

"I'll carry you."

"No," she laughed, "I can make it on my own."

"Whatever you want," and I called for the nurse to come back in.

We supported Jessie under each arm, and because her bones were so fragile, we placed her in a wheel chair and rolled her on the back deck, thinking she would feel more comfortable there.

She always loved sitting on the deck in the early mornings sipping her coffee, and watching the wildlife. She loved to watch the birds and ducks in the lake, especially the sand cranes. There was a pair that she had nicknamed "Gertrude and Heathcliffe" that she remembered from years ago from a skit that Red Skelton used to do on his show. "Listen to that male," she chuckled. "Making all that fuss, and strutting around for the female, and she's not paying one bit of attention to him."

We sat and shared the time together sipping coffee. Jessie said she felt at peace here. She liked the trailer I had bought for Samuel and Joseph. "You're spending way too much, and going through so much because of me," she admonished.

"Don't you worry; it thrills me to be able to do this for you. I want you to enjoy life, and be happier than you've ever been. You do whatever you want to do or go any place you desire."

"There's no place I'd rather be than right here," she said, emotion filling her voice.

"Then here is where you'll stay." I glanced at my watch and jumped up.

"What's wrong?" Lisa asked, alarm in her voice.

"I'm sorry, Kitten, I didn't mean to alarm you but it's almost nine o'clock, and I forgot I'm supposed to be at the bank to meet Carolyn. Will you call her for me, and apologize, and tell her to I'll be there at nine thirty? After a quick shower, I'll be on my way."

"Sure, I'll call her right now."

"Thanks honey, the number's in the paperwork on the kitchen counter," I hollered over my shoulder as I rushed to get ready.

Carolyn had just arrived at the bank after talking with Lisa when I walked into the lobby. We met with the vice-president to discuss what I wanted done. I filled out the necessary paperwork while the secretary made copies of Carolyn's bond and credentials. We discussed the contract, and after satisfying my few questions, I signed the affidavit. The bank gave us each a folder with the copies of our signed transactions with a copy to be sent to Rhonda, my attorney. Carolyn insisted. The checks were ordered and would be here in a week. The transfer would not interrupt accessing my funds, and with that we completed the deal.

I had prepared a list of bills that would have to be paid monthly. Carolyn would arrange a payment system where the bills would come to her directly in my name, and she would handle payments for me. This would be a blessing, since I would be away from Florida for such long periods of time.

It was close to noon when I arrived at the cabin. Jessie Mae had napped on the deck and awoke hungry for a burger.

"A woman after my heart," I laughed.

"You mean your stomach don't you!" she giggled.

The nurse had just given Jessie her medication when Teresa suggested we grill the burgers instead of frying them.

Feeling good after another productive morning, I said, "How about I fire up the grill, and I'll grill the burgers!"

"I'll make a salad and warm up some baked beans," Teresa volunteered.

"I'll help," Lisa jumped up, anxious to be a part of this.

Samuel and Joseph went to buy beer and wine. We had a party going, and kept the grill hot for the numerous well wishers that stopped in throughout the day. Jessie dozed on and off all day, basking in the warmth of the sun, and all the attention.

By evening, Jessie had grown very tired. The second shift nurse suggested we take her back to her room so she could prepare her for bed. The nurses had monitored Jessie's vitals all day to the point of Jessie becoming annoyed. We told her it was necessary, and an order from the doctor, so she relented and cooperated without any fuss.

The nurse returned after settling Jessie in bed and told me Jessie wanted to see me. "Johnny," she said, as I sat next to her on the bed, "Through the years that I've known you, I've grown to love you like a son."

"I love you too." A lump that felt like the size of a golf ball formed in my throat. "You took care of me all those years, and now it's my turn to take care of you." I winked at her.

"My own daughter hasn't come to see me in the last twenty years; she hasn't even called me in the last two."

"Would you like me to call her?"

She nodded her head yes, "If you think she'll come. I'd like to see her before I die. Here's her number," and she handed me a crinkled, worn sheet of paper with a phone number scrawled across it.

"What time are you leaving tomorrow?"

"Early in the morning, but I'll take care of this before I go. If I can't reach her, I'll have Joseph call her. I'll be back mid week, in plenty of time before your party."

She was yawning and growing sleepy. I kissed her forehead, tucked the covers under her chin, and told her to get some rest. The nurse returned, and I left to join the others on the deck. Within minutes the nurse let us know that Jessie was already asleep and resting comfortably.

"I was afraid all the excitement would do her harm," the nurse commented, "but after checking her vitals, it seems to have done her a world of good. You know, you're quite an incredible man. It's hard to find a man who would take care of an elderly woman the way you're looking out for Jessie Mae."

"If I don't, no one else will, I'm just glad I'm able to do it. A year ago I wouldn't have been able to do anything like this."

"What do you do for a living?" she inquired.

"I'm an entertainer."

"I thought you looked a little like Elvis."

Lisa burst out laughing.

"I'm an Elvis Impersonator," and laughed along with Lisa.

"Oh my, you're Johnny Raye, the Elvis Impersonator who did the Christmas Special at Graceland, right?"

I nodded in agreement.

"I'm sorry. I didn't put two and two together when you gave your name yesterday. Well, that explains Lisa Marie being here," she sounded embarrassed.

"That's a right," I tried to ease her discomfort; "I don't really care to be that popular."

"Johnny," Teresa asked, "Do you have any C. D's or tapes we can listen to?"

"I had sent one to Jessie Mae for Christmas; let me see if I can find it."

"It's in the C. D. player," Samuel said, "Jessie's played it everyday since she received it," he said rolling his eyes. "And I do mean every day."

That reminds me, Lisa, do you think we could get everyone down here for a party for Jessie next Sunday?"

"Sure, let me take care of everything, I love to plan parties? The only concern I have, is sleeping arrangements. I'm not familiar with motels here."

"If you don't mind? I'd like to help and I can take care of the room reservations, as I'm familiar with the better motels here," Teresa volunteered.

"We could have everyone brought here in limos from their motel rooms," I suggested.

"I'll need a list of people's names to invite," Lisa said, grabbing a writing tablet and pen, her mind already formulating what needed to be done. Samuel and Joseph gave her names of people from the orange groves. I gave her the names of everyone in Birmingham and told her to include anyone else she could think of.

"I'll talk with Gary when I see him in Dallas, and have him bring his equipment. Lisa, you and Teresa can plan the menu. Decorate to what ever theme you wish."

Samuel and Joseph volunteered to help hang decorations.

I turned the C. D. player on softly. I was tired and went to lie down on the sofa leaving the rest to finish planning the party. The nurse brought me a blanket and pillow.

Lisa walked in and whispered to me, "I think she likes you, she's very pretty."

"I think you're right, but I don't need another pretty woman on my mind right now."

She laughed, "You're probably the only man who doesn't."

I told her I'd see her when I returned from Dallas, and she left and joined the others who were still enjoying the remainder of the beer and wine.

CHAPTER 20

Teresa woke me the following morning. The limo driver arrived by the time I finished my shower and packed my bags. The pilots were at the airport, and the plane was ready when I arrived. I was in Dallas by eleven thirty. Gary met me at the airport, and drove us back to hotel where everyone was waiting in the lobby to welcome me back. Even the employees awaited for my return.

Everyone heard about Jessie Mae and asked how she was. I told them she wasn't expected to make it very much longer, which is why I needed to take care of things here very quickly, and get back to Florida. I let everyone know about the party on Sunday of the following week and that Lisa would be sending out invitations.

I checked in at the reservation desk. The bell hop brought my bag to my room. We went into the restaurant for a bite to eat as Chance and Gary were starving again, and so was I since I had missed breakfast.

After we ordered, I asked about Sandy. Denise said she came to work last night with a black eye, but she said she wouldn't call the cops because she's afraid he'll get out again, and beat her like the last time.

"How did he get out so soon?"

"It seems the D.A.'s office thinks the jail is over crowded, and they released him on bail," Denise said angrily.

"What about the restraining order that was placed against him from getting anywhere near Sandy?"

"It was probably dropped," Chance said disgustedly.

After lunch I called Captain Williams, and Detective Snyder to meet me at the club. Gary asked if I wanted them to come, but I told him the last thing I wanted to do was get those two in trouble.

"Maybe it would be worth it," Chance said, and then added, "all of us like Sandy; she's a sweet kid and deserves a better life."

"I agree, and appreciate it, but I'm going to need someone to bail me out of jail, you may need to be on stand by. See you later," and I left for the club.

Captain Williams and Detective Snyder arrived as I was walking across the road. We shook hands and got down to business right away. The captain said he knew why I was here. He said that the D.A. doesn't like me, and had Jimmie released from jail.

"Why? He was sentenced by the judge. How can the D. A.'s office release him?" Anger was now showing in my mannerisms.

The younger detective answered, "Because, Johnny, he was being held in the county jail. The D.A.'s office controls the county jail, and he was able to get another judge to sign a release."

"Are you aware that he forced himself back on Sandy, and is beating her again?"

"No," has she filed charges?" the captain asked.

"Hell no, she's more afraid of him than ever. This wasn't supposed to happen," I said angrily.

"Damn!" The captain swore. "I'm tired of arresting criminals, and then the D.A. cuts a deal and gets them off scott free," he said disgustedly.

"Jimmie thinks I'm gone, but I'm going to pay him a visit this afternoon."

"Do me a favor, Johnny," the captain said, "don't kill him, I can't cover up a murder."

"Look, I've worked out a plan, but I'm going to need assistance with this."

"I'm almost afraid to ask," said the captain. "This isn't going to involve us in something illegal, is it Johnny? Because I can only go so far, I won't cross the line."

"No, let me tell you my plans. I need to get my hands on some cocaine, and I know you guys know where I can get some."

The young detective smiled, "Enough to put him in the state or federal pen?"

"That's right."

"But before he gets caught with it, I'm going to beat his ass to a pulp before he leaves again. When I'm finished with him, you'll get a call on vandalism to his car. When you check it out, you'll find the cocaine and five thousand dollars under the front seat."

"The young detective said, "Not necessary to have that much money, hell, a thousand will do the job."

"Captain," I said, "this will never go any further than right here, you have my word."

"We know that, just be careful. By the way, thank you so much for the tickets to Graceland, you did an outstanding performance, and our wives were thrilled to death."

I nodded in acknowledgement and finished finalizing my plans. I wrote down the number the detective gave me to call to arrange to pick up the drugs and I left.

Since I was driving Chance's car, and not wanting to involve him, I quickly drove to a car rental agency. I told them I was a real estate agent, and I was having problems with my car and needed a rental to meet with a prospective client. I told them I would only need the car for the afternoon, and would probably have it back by five o'clock. The rental clerk wished me luck with my client and hoped I make a sale. I smiled as I left with the first step of my plan completed.

It only took an hour to make the connection. I expected to be sent to a run down area of town, but instead it happened very quickly in a local grocery store parking lot. The voice at the other end of the phone told me I was to park at the end of the lot near the entrance next to a beat up black, 1975 pick-up truck. When I shut off the engine of the rental, a seedy looking character got out of the truck. He knelt down to look under it pretending he was having truck problems. I was told to have the driver's window rolled down and wait for further instructions.

My instructions were to have ten one hundred dollar bills rolled up tight and tied with a rubber band. This made for an easy switch, and was less noticeable than an envelope The voice from below the truck quietly told me to get out and to ask him if I could be of assistance. I knelt down next to him and in less than three seconds, he had the money and I had the drugs. I was told to get back in my car and wait while he got back in his truck and counted the money. He said we were being watched by friends of his, just in case something went wrong with the deal. If everything was okay, he would drive away. That would be the signal that I could leave. Seconds later, I started my engine and left the parking lot. Part two of my plan accomplished.

I was careful not to speed. I was probably more careful than I should have been, but I couldn't take any unnecessary chances at being stopped with drugs in my car.

Finally, I arrived back at Sandy's. I drove around the parking lot a few times, and decided to park in the lot behind the building in case Jimmie was going in or out. I spotted his car parked next to Sandy's. I strolled nonchalantly towards Jimmie's car and tried the door. It was unlocked. I quickly put the cocaine, and marijuana, along with a thousand dollars under the driver's seat, and noiselessly shut the door. Even though the air was cool, beads of sweat poured from every orifice of my body. I glanced around and seeing no one, ran upstairs and rang Sandy's doorbell. Part three of my plan was now finished.

Sandy was jubilant when she opened the door and discovered it was me.

"I knew you would come," she squealed and hugged and kissed me quickly.

And then from the kitchen came Jimmies voice, "Who is it bitch?"

"Letting me into the apartment, she hollered back at him, "It's your favorite buddy."

He entered the living room and stopped dead in his tracks, his face blanched when he saw me standing there. "What the hell are you doing here?"

"I'm here to see you, Jimmie. It seems you don't listen very well, this time there will be no warnings. Your luck just ran out."

"You can't come in here and start beating on me. I've done nothing to her or to you."

"Oh yeah," I said, stepping closer to close the gap between us, "Where did Sandy get the black eye, and why are you calling her a bitch, you low life snake." The sight of him made me sick. I loathed his cocky demeanor, but hated his chicken attitude even more. His face paled even more as he saw the hate in my eyes and angered expression on my face. "You've got to be the lowest S. O. B. I've ever met. Now get your ass moving because you and I are going to take us a little ride."

"No!" he cried out, panic showing in his eyes. "I'm not going anywhere, but you are," and he ran and grabbed the poker from the fireplace. "Now," he said, feeling braver with a weapon in his hands, "I'm going to send you to your grave."

"I was hoping you'd do something stupid like this," I said, walking towards him menacingly, my hands clenched tightly at my sides.

Sizing up the situation, and looking at how the furniture was placed to use to my advantage, I stationed myself with my back to the open area, leaving me room to move, but putting Jimmie's back to the wall. This left him no where to go but directly at me, which is exactly what I wanted him to do.

He swung the poker and lunged. Anticipating his move, I ducked and grabbed the poker and shoved it into his chest, and then let go. He swung the poker at me again. Enraged, I quickly moved back, and then even quicker I jumped forward and kicked him in the groin. Those few seconds gave me the time to hit him three or four times in the ribs with enough force to break several bones, which I heard crunch each time my fist made contact with his body. He was now in a great deal of pain, his movements slowed, and his breathing labored. He cried, and yelled for me to stop.

"Stop! I haven't even warmed up yet," and with that I slammed my fist into his mouth knocking out three or four more of his teeth, and re-breaking his nose. I gave him a few minutes to try and pull himself together, and handed him back the poker.

Blood was pouring from his mouth and nose. He made a feeble attempt to stand straight, but his cracked ribs prevented that from happening. I stood with my feet apart and grinned at him hoping to stoke enough anger for him to lunge at me again. Dizzily he swung the poker, and I let him hit me in the side, a pain I needed, but wished I didn't have to have.

"Thank you Jimmie," I said, barely wincing from the attack, as he was too weak to inflict any serious damage. "I needed to show self-defense, and you just gave it to me."

With that, I kicked him in the chest, breaking a few more ribs. I took his hand, and bent his fingers back until they broke. Jimmie was almost incoherent by this time. He cried hysterically, his voice raspy, and barely audible from the pain. He begged me to stop, and promised he'd leave and never come back. I looked at his pitiful body, picked up the phone and called the police, and then called for an ambulance.

"Why didn't you kill him," Sandy sobbed openly, "he'll just get out of jail again and come back to get even with me."

"No, he won't, not this time. Trust me."

The police arrived within five minutes, and right before the ambulance. I explained that I was in town for the week-end and came to see Sandy. Her ex-boy friend attacked me with the fireplace poker, and then I showed them where I had been stabbed in the side.

"Jimmie has a history of beating women, especially Sandy. As a matter of fact, officers, he just got out of jail for beating her up and is in violation of a restraining order."

"How'd you get the black eye, miss?" one of the officers asked.

"Jimmie," she said softly, letting tears run down her cheeks.

Just then, Captain Williams came in and told the officers to bring their report to him, to arrest Jimmie, and have him placed under guard at the hospital.

"What about him?" the officer filling out the report asked, pointing in my direction.

Captain Williams, having read the report said, "Self defense!"

The arresting officers left to follow the ambulance to the hospital.

"Johnny, you'll need to come down to the station in the morning and sign a complaint against Jimmie."

"Yes sir, I'll be there."

"Johnny. Is everything else okay?"

I knew what he was referring to, and replied, "Yes sir, everything else is just fine."

Part four of my plan completed.

Sandy and I were cleaning up the mess when there was a knock at the door. Thinking it was one of the officers, she opened it and was pushed aside. There stood Jimmies two biker friends.

"Where's Jimmie?" and what the hell is Elvis doing here?"

I looked them both in the eye and said, "Your buddy Jimmie has taken a trip to the hospital again and I think you need to visit him," I said and stepped towards them.

One of them noticed the poker lying by my feet. Seeing what he was looking at, I asked, "Want this?" and I picked it up and threw it to him.

The shorter one of the two said, "Hey man, we told you once before, it's not our fight."

Walking closer, I said, "Oh, but it is."

The taller one of the two swung the poker, and I wasted no time in breaking his arm. My years of studying Karate began to pay off. Without blinking an eye, I leaped and kicked the shorter guy in the chest, knocking the air from his lungs, and cracking a few ribs. Unexpectedly, the taller one swung with his good arm and made contact with my ribs. I was knocked back a few feet when the smaller guy hit me again in the ribs. Riled by my own stupidity, I tripped the smaller guy and grabbing his leg, snapped it like a pretzel, breaking the bone into a compound fracture to the point the bone had broken through the skin.

The larger man attempted one last try to get me, but this time I was ready. I grabbed his broken arm and jerking as hard as I could, yanked it from the socket. He screamed in pain, and literally dropped to his knees. I cracked both of my hands to each side of his head, catching him directly on the ears. Grabbing his head, he started bawling like a baby, but not as loud as the guy with the broken leg. Disgusted at the sight before me, I called for another ambulance. The ambulance drivers were the same ones that had been here earlier. They had just left the hospital when they got the call.

"Busy day?" asked one of the paramedics.

"Yeah, it sure turned out to be that way." I laughed half-heartily.

Sandy and I cleaned the apartment as best as we could. Thankfully the damage was all in one room and wasn't as bad as it could have been. The worst was the blood stains. They were splattered all over the living room walls. Some had dried in the carpet. Sandy found a cleaning spray and soaked as many as she could find.

I told her to get changed for work, as I needed everything to seem as normal as possible, even though this whole situation had turned into a nightmare.

Also, I had to drop off the rental car to return Chance's car to him. That accomplished, I drove her to Steadman's.

When we arrived, Denise and Gary were at the bar waiting for Chance and Michele. Sandy started telling them about the fight with Jimmie and his two biker buddies.

"I'm expecting the police to come an arrest me for fighting with those two."

"How bad off are they?" Gary asked observing my bruised, bleeding and now very swollen hands.

"Let's just say they'll be keeping Jimmie company at the hospital for a few days."

Close to a half-hour later, two officers arrived looking for me. They asked me a few questions and then said that two guys at the hospital said I beat them up.

"Yes, sir I did, but only because they both attacked me first. They were aggravated that I sent their friend Jimmie to the hospital."

"Oh yes, we heard about that one."

"Look, I have to see Captain Williams in the morning. I'll give him a full report then. If you're going to the captain, we won't bother you anymore tonight."

"Just be sure you see him."

"Yes sir, that's a definite."

They reported to their dispatch, and then left to respond to another call.

"I have a feeling the D. A.'s office is going to be after you," Denise said worriedly.

"I have a feeling you are right."

Chance and Michele came in and asked why the police were there. Denise repeated the story to them.

"You need to talk to the judge, he asks about you every week, and he'll be here tonight," Chance said trying to be helpful.

"Thanks buddy, but I'll wait and see what happens."

"Oh, here, before I forget," I took out the keys to Cadillac and handed them to Chance. "Thanks for letting me use your car; it's parked in the side lot."

"Anytime."

We sat down to eat, Sandy was very quiet, as well as the rest of us. They were concerned about me. And myself, well I was aching from the day's activities. After dinner, Chance had his seven o'clock show. I asked him not to call me to sing as I knew I would not be able to move around on stage.

"What's wrong?" Denise asked concerned. Sandy explained how I let Jimmie hit me with the poker stick so I could say it was done in self-defense.

"Raise your shirt and let me see your side," Denise demanded.

"Let's go back to the dressing room, okay?"

"Johnny, this looks serious, you need to have this looked at," Denise was shocked at the cut from the poker, and how badly bruised I actually was.

Sandy felt of my side and I winced, "I think you have a cracked rib."

"That does it, I'm talking to Mr. Steadman and taking the night off, you re coming home with me," Sandy insisted.

"Go ahead, Sandy, I'll work for you. Daddy will probably be happy to have me back for the night."

Back at Sandy's, I lay comfortably on the sofa. She made up a cold pack and placed it on my side. She curled up next to me to watch television.

"Johnny, there's a real nice guy that lives on the fourth floor who is a paramedic. I'm going to get him and have him check you over."

"Stay put! I was thinking of going to the beach and doing the limbo." I teased.

"Oh, real funny!"

The paramedic was a nice guy, and he seemed more interested in Sandy, than my side. After checking me over, he said the rib was probably cracked, but the pain was more from the bruises. He taped me up and suggested I get an X-Ray to be on the safe side. He also recommended I alternate hot and cold compresses, and that I would probably be sore for a week, but should be fine. I thanked him and he said if the pain got any worse or noticed any other changes to go to the emergency room. He told Sandy to call him in a few days to let him know how I was doing.

"Looks like I'll be out of commission for a few days."

"Uh, huh, and I'm going to take care of you."

"No, you have enough to do."

"Don't you worry about that. All you need to do is lay back, I'll do all the work."

"Sandy, I'm shocked, is sex all you ever think of?" I teased.

"No," she grinned, "sometimes I think of other things." "Listen you, you took care of me when I needed help, now you're on my turf, and I'm in charge. So listen up! I'm going to go to your hotel room, pick up your things, and bring them back here where I can keep an eye on you."

"Yes ma'am," I replied. I slept while Sandy was picking up my things. She came back all upset.

"What's wrong I asked?

"Johnny, before I came back here, I stopped to let Denise know what the paramedic said, and what we were doing. Denise told me the police had returned to the club to arrest you, but Gary and Denise told them you had already left town and didn't know where you were."

Puzzled as to why I would be arrested, I said, "I think I need to call Captain Williams or Detective Snyder and find out what's going on." "Honey, hand me the phone."

"Are you sure you want to call them?" she asked hesitantly.

"Yes, hand it to me."

Captain Williams was not in but Detective Snyder was available. I told him where I was, and he came over immediately.

"Johnny," he explained what had transpired, "Jimmies buddies filed a complaint and signed a warrant for your arrest." "They claim you came looking for them!"

"You can call the ambulance company and ask them what address they picked those two fools up at."

"I'll do that. I'll get a written report from them. Who called for the ambulance anyway?" he asked taking notes.

"I did," I groaned holding my side as I went to stand up.

"What's wrong with your side?"

"Jimmie got a lucky hit with the poker stick."

"Did you have it looked at?" he inquired.

I told him about the paramedic and what he suggested.

"Where's the captain, tonight?"

"He's gone home. Look, you stay here until Monday and then come in. I'll tell the captain what's happened and where you're staying."

I nodded in agreement.

"By the way, looks like Jimmie and his friends are going away for quite awhile. It seems the three of them have been buying and selling drugs. One of the arresting officers's received an anonymous phone call of vandalism to Jimmie's car. When the officer found the car that fit the description, and couldn't see any outer damage, he checked inside and found ten pounds of cocaine and twenty pounds of marijuana, as well as a thousand dollars hidden under the front seat. The D. A.'s office has them up on charges, but he's looking to get you on assault, and attempted murder."

"Murder!" Sandy screamed.

The detective held his hand up, "Don't worry; he won't be able to make that charge stick. The first charge has already been filed as self-defense, but you should have called me or the captain on the other one."

"Guess I should have, I felt those two would spend a few days in the hospital then they'd disappear."

"Anyway," he added, "Jimmie is saying the drugs belong to the other two guys, and their saying the drugs belong to Jimmie. So we have all three up on charges for drugs, assault with intent to kill with a deadly weapon, and I'll have to see about charging the other two with intent to do bodily harm. They are going to be put away for a long time."

I laughed, "Guess some people just never learn."

He got up to leave, "Johnny, please stay out of any more trouble, okay?"

"I'll try real hard."

"See you Monday morning," and he left.

Part five of my plan came together.

Sandy looked at my tired face, "Johnny, come on, you're exhausted. I'll help you get ready for bed." She helped me undress and fluffed the pillows as I gingerly lay against them. She quickly undressed, curled up next to me and we both fell asleep.

The next morning, Sandy got up and ran a tub of hot water in the whirlpool. I had to admit it did feel pretty good. While I was soaking and letting the surging water soothe my aching body, the door bell rang. Sandy was afraid to answer it but when she found out it was the paramedic, she let him in. He had stopped to see how I was doing, and brought me more tape to re-wrap my ribs, although, I thought it was an excuse for him to see Sandy.

I hated the fact that I would miss Chance's shows, but I was too sore to feel up to anything. I guess I had to finally admit my age was taking a toll on me. I smiled and thought that if I hurt this much, Jimmie and his buddies must feel like they're dying. That gave me some comfort.

Monday morning came quickly. I was beginning to feel much better. After my shower, Sandy drove me to see Captain Williams. He told me the department had an outstanding warrant for me, but if I would give him a statement, he would get the warrant dropped. He took my sworn statement, and I signed on the dotted line. Sandy collaborated my story and signed a sworn statement as well. The captain said we were free to go.

"Johnny," he warned, "the D. A.'s office set a court date for January, 31st."

"Captain, I need to get that date dropped or moved up. Who do I need to see to take care of this?"

He grinned, and rubbed his chin. "Seems to me, I just happen to know of a judge that's not particularly fond of the D. A. Wait one moment," and then handed me his name and number.

I was able to speak to the judge between court hearings. After hearing Sandy's and my story, he had the clerk of courts cancel all his morning hearings for the next day, and scheduled me to appear before him at ten o'clock sharp.

The clerk of courts typed a subpoena and handed it to me to make it official. The clerk was also instructed to make sure that the D. A. was served before the end of the day or there would be hell to pay.

Angered at the whole situation, and for having his orders reversed, the judge said, "Make sure you are on time in the morning. I don't want to give the D. A. an edge in his favor. Do I make myself clear?"

"Yes your honor, we'll be here if we have to camp out at the court house front door."

"I don't think that will be necessary," he finally cracked a smile. "Now get out of here, I'm a very busy man."

We went back to see the captain and told him what transpired.

"Tomorrow morning!" The captain laughed. "The D. A.'s office isn't going to like that," thoroughly enjoying the thought of how pissed the D. A. would be when he received his subpoena. "Do you need me and Detective Snyder for anything?"

"I'd like copies of your reports."

The captain buzzed the office clerk and told her what he needed. "Anything else?" he asked handing me the paperwork.

"This will do for now, thank you," and we left.

The captain sat down, and made two phone calls. The first one to Detective Snyder to have him clear his schedule for tomorrow for the possibility to testify in court, and quickly told him the story. The second call was handled discreetly. The captain shut the door to his office and then dialed the judge's personal number from his cell phone, rather than the office phone in order to have complete privacy.

"Hello," the judge answered.

"Your honor, Captain Williams here," and with a few second delay said, "Thank you."

"You're welcome," the judge replied. The line went dead and Captain Williams smiled as he clicked the off button on his phone.

Sandy and I went back to the hotel to meet our group for lunch. I told them I had a court date set for tomorrow morning at ten o'clock.

"Why is the D. A. so hot on your tail?" Gary asked.

"When I put Jimmie in the hospital the last time, the D. A. thought I didn't deserve to get off without any charges. Captain Williams has released me again of all charges, but now the D.A.'s got the captain in trouble with the chief. I'm not concerned, because the judge is upset with the D. A. for having his orders reversed. I have a feeling it'll be thrown out of court."

"Johnny! Look!" "There's Captain Williams," Sandy said, as all eyes riveted on the captain.

"You stay put, I'll be right back," I instructed everyone, as I went to meet the captain in the lobby.

The captain looked at me, and whispered, "I was hoping you weren't here, because I can't find you."

"What?" I asked, confused by his statement. "What's this all about?"

"The D. A. is pissed at me for releasing you earlier. He called and complained to the chief again, so the chief sent me out to bring you in, and hold you to make sure you appear in court tomorrow. "But!" he said emphatically, looking me dead in the eye, "I looked and couldn't find you, and since I couldn't find you, I couldn't arrest you."

"You're right, I was never here." I went and got Sandy and told her we had to leave right away. I told the others I didn't have time to explain, but that they had not seen me all day.

"To hell with that," Denise declared, "we're all going with you.

We hurried out of the restaurant and went back to Sandy's and drove in through the back gated entrance. We had just walked into the lobby when we spotted a police car parking out front. Sandy went up to her apartment, and the rest of us went into the bar.

The officers knocked a few times on her door, and not hearing anything were about to leave, when Sandy hollered out, "Just a minute."

"It's the police ma'am, open up we're looking for Johnny Raye."

"He's not here right now," she countered, stalling for time as she hid my personal things. "Let me get my robe, I'm not dressed," she added. After a few minutes, she finally answered the door. "How can I help you?" she asked sweetly.

"Where's Johnny?" he asked again, stepping inside without being asked.

"I don't know!" she answered, "I haven't seen him since he met earlier with the captain. He's probably left town by now."

"Mind if we look around?" the one officer asked.

"Be my guest, but you won't find him here," and she let one arm of her robe slip off her shoulder, allowing one breast to be partially exposed.

"Maybe it would be a good idea if I stand by the door in case Johnny would show up," one of the officers said, not able to take his eyes off her voluptuous chest.

The other officer looked through the rooms, and then started poking around in Sandy's personal items.

Afraid the officer would find Johnny's hidden things, Sandy boldly stated, "I thought you were looking for Johnny? I don't think you'll find him in my dresser drawers, and as you've already discovered, he's not here! Now, unless you have a search warrant for something else, you need to leave, or I'll call your captain," she hissed, all the sweetness gone from her voice.

"No ma'am that's not necessary," the officer walked to the door and thanked her for her cooperation.

"As a word of warning, we may be back in the morning, just in case he returns from wherever you say he may have gone," the other officer was saying, but the words were cut off from the sound of the door as it slammed in his face.

Sandy watched as the patrol car pulled out of the lot. She waited a couple of minutes, feeling it was safe, went down to the bar with the others. Sandy found us sitting in the corner booth, and told us what happened upstairs. We had a good laugh at the part of her exposed breast.

"So what you're trying to say Sandy," I teased, "is those guys were just a couple of 'boobs'!" We were laughing so hard I had to hold my side.

When the laughter died down, Sandy said, "Johnny, they also said they'd be back in the morning. They didn't buy my story on you leaving town."

"What are we going to do?" Denise asked.

"Nothing, don't worry!" I said. "Sandy and I will go upstairs, and if they come back, she'll just tell them I'm not there. They'll need a search warrant to come in and check, and if they go to get a warrant, the judge isn't going to issue one. So, the rest of you need to go about your business and act as if nothing is going on."

The guys took the girls back to the club, but before they left they all insisted they would come to court to testify on my behalf. Sandy and I decided to go to bed early to get a good night's sleep and to be up early for the next day's proceedings. We both were tired from the day's activities, and I was still too sore and too preoccupied with everything to make a good bed partner. And Sandy, well in light of everything that had happened to her in the past few months, she was going through a sex breakdown.

We arrived at the courthouse a half an hour early. Both Captain Williams and Detective Snyder were there. Relief showed on their faces as they recognized me coming through the courthouse security. We walked into the courtroom and sat down.

The D. A. abruptly approached me. "You better have a good attorney cause

I'm sending your ass to jail."

"Oh, but I have the best lawyer in town!" I hissed, "ME!"

He laughed and went back to sit at his table, a smile of triumph on his face. "Gloat, you little maggot," I whispered to myself, "just wait till the judge gets a hold of you."

Our whole group arrived and I told Sandy to sit with them. I got up and slowly and deliberately sauntered over to the table where the D. A. was sitting and sat at his table.

Part Six of my plan was about to begin and finalize.

"What are you doing here? This table is for lawyers only, you can't sit here," the D. A. tried to embarrass me.

I sneered in return, "I am an attorney today!" "And besides, this isn't your courtroom," I taunted, daring him to say more.

Not to cause trouble for him self, fully well knowing he wasn't on the judges favorite list, he shut up and ignored me as if I was an unimportant gnat about to be squashed. I chuckled, sat back and relaxed.

We all rose as the judge entered the courtroom. Looking around his domain to take in who was in attendance, and staring a hole through the D.A., he said, "Please be seated."

"Your honor," I asked, before he started the proceedings, "Is there a problem with me sitting at this table?"

"Are you representing yourself?"

"Yes sir, I am."

"Then by all means, stay where you are, unless there's an objection."

The D. A. was about to object, but kept quiet when he saw the glare from the judge. I grinned. Chalk one up for me. With all formalities completed, the judge told the D. A. to present his case.

Seeing where this was headed, the D.A. decided to stall and ask for more time to be better prepared, and hoped to be assigned a different judge. The D.A. explained in graphic detail the two beatings that I had given Jimmie and his two counter-parts. He dramatized the fact that they were beaten so severely that they would need hospital care for the next several months, and wanted a postponement until they could be released from the hospital.

I objected on the grounds that this case shouldn't even be brought before a judge. "Your honor, here are copies of all the police reports," I said, and handed them to him. "As you can see, they clearly show that I was only protecting myself. I have asked Captain Williams and Detective Snyder to be here today to verify the contents of these reports. Also, your honor, the D. A.'s office had a warrant issued over the week-end for my arrest. He acted on his own personal feelings, as he did not have a report of any charges against me, other than the ones he trumped up."

"Your honor," the D. A. spoke quickly, "here are copies of charges filed by two of the victims that state, Johnny Raye, hunted them down and then beat them up. In my years of experience, that's a premeditated attempt to do bodily harm," he said, justifying his charges.

The judge looked at me and smiled, "Do you have anything to say regarding this?"

"Yes, your honor, I'd like Captain Williams to bring you the report he obtained from the ambulance company that picked up these two victims." Once the docket was in the judges hands, I said, "Your honor, to save the court time, if you will look at the address where the victims were picked up by the ambulance and taken to the hospital, that address is none other than Sandy's," and I pointed to where she was sitting. "I have been staying with her and this obviously points to the fact that I did not chase these guys, they came to see me with intent to do me bodily harm."

"Would you two please approach the bench?"

When we stood in front of the judge, he asked the D. A., "Why do you have this man in my courtroom when you have no case against him?"

"I had a signed complaint, your honor, not only from the other two victims, but also from Jimmie Stamps himself," he said, and handed the judge the complaint.

Bingo! I thought, and had I all I could do to keep from laughing.

"As you can see your honor, Johnny went to the victim's girlfriend's apartment with the intent to injure or even kill Mr. Stamps, fully well knowing the victim would be there."

"Is this true Johnny?" the judge asked. "No sir, I'm in town visiting friends that I didn't get to see over the holidays, that being Sandy, your honor, and when I went to her apartment, Jimmie was there and he flew into a rage at the sight of me. The rest is on the report."

"Jimmie Stamps," he sat back in his chair, momentarily thinking, and then abruptly leaned forward. "Didn't I sentence him several months ago to serve time in the county jail?"

The color began to fade from the D. A.'s face. "Yes," your honor, he answered softly.

"What?" "I can't hear you!" the judge's voice boomed loudly.

"Yes, your honor, you did."

"Well what happened? Why is he out?"

"I felt since the jails are overflowing," he stammered feebly, "I had him released."

"Well it looks to me like you made a bad decision. I'm going to let Mr. Raye finish defending his case, and then I'm going to charge your office with a contempt of court fine for over riding my direct decision, in the amount of two hundred dollars, and an additional two hundred dollars for wasting this courts time. The next time you present a case to me using personal feelings to make judgments rather than hard facts, I'll have you removed from office." "Do you understand," he said angrily. "You're lucky that Mr. Raye hasn't filed a harassment counter suit to your office. Now sit down both of you."

By now the D. A.'s face had gone from stark white to blood red from embarrassment.

"Your honor," I said, "I would like to ask for a dismissal on the grounds that the D. A.'s office falsely set a case without any evidence, and totally ignored the police reports given him on this case."

"But your honor, based on the complaint I . . ." the D. A.'s voice trailed off from the loud slam of the gavel. The judge's voice was filled with malice as he told the D.A. that if he heard any more 'buts' from him, he would have him thrown in the county jail for thirty days. "Unless you have a real case against Mr. Raye," the judge was trying to keep his anger under control, "I suggest you leave this man alone." "Case dismissed!"

Everyone jumped at the sound of the gavel once again pounding on the judge's desk. It was surprising to all that it didn't break from the amount of force behind it.

The courtroom was suddenly filled with voices from all the well wishers. As we were all leaving, the D. A. approached me.

Totally humiliated he had to have one last crack at me, "You think you're so smart, don't you?"

"No sir," I flashed him a sarcastic grin, "I think you're stupid!"

The captain and the detective laughed at his chagrin, as he hurried away.

"Good job, Johnny, they both said, patting me on the back.

"No, you guys deserve all the credit, if you hadn't helped me, I wouldn't have had a strong enough case to win."

Captain Williams shook my hand, "Johnny, you have no idea how much this has helped us. The D.A. will think twice before ever releasing a prisoner so quickly, and three thugs will be put behind bars for the next twenty-five years."

I paid the clerk of courts office the court fine, and thought it was the best one hundred and fifty dollars I had ever spent. We went back to Sandy's to celebrate. I reminded every one of the party for Jessie the following week-end. "Motel arrangements will be made for each of you. Limos will bring you out to my place on the lake. The jet will pick you up and bring you to Florida. It will mean a lot to me if y'all came."

"I'm not working next week-end at the club," Chance said, "my last show is

Wednesday." "Michele and I can leave Thursday, stop in Birmingham for a couple of days and then head to Florida. Mr. Steadman closes the club every year at this time and takes a weeks vacation."

"That's right," Denise agreed, "daddy loves to go to the Bahamas, or Hawaii to relax." "He loves the islands, says the salt air is good for him and he loves the scenery, but mom says it's the scenery on the beach that he really likes, if you know what I mean."

"Will there be room for all my equipment on the plane?" Gary wanted to know.

"Sure, there's plenty of room."

"Johnny, if Jessie doesn't have much of a family and she's been sick for awhile, that means she didn't have much of a Christmas?" Denise spoke thoughtfully.

"You're right. She probably didn't even have a tree. I'll call Lisa and have her arrange to have one decorated by Sunday. We'll just have another Christmas together."

I picked up the phone and called Lisa Marie. She told me Jessie's daughter, Doris was there that she arrived that morning and was trying to run the household.

"What do you mean?" I couldn't believe what I was hearing.

"Well, for starters, I'm going to be sleeping on the sofa because she took over your room. She's going around saying this is her mother's house, and soon all this will be hers, so we can all just leave. And, she said she'll take care of her mother herself. I'm only staying because of you, and because I care about Jessie. Besides, she's made me mad enough now that she couldn't pry me out of here with a crow bar."

"Until I get back, this is what I want you to tell her. First of all, the house belongs to me, and tell her I'm on my way home. She can stay at the hotel, and come and visit with her mother in the afternoons. Secondly, get Samuel and Joseph to remove her from the bedroom. If she has any questions, she can see me when I get back, but I want her out of the house. Lisa, the reason I called, is to see how Jessie's doing, and see about putting up a Christmas tree."

"Jessie is holding her own," she replied, "and you're too late about the tree, because we've already decorated one." "Jessie was thrilled when she saw it."

"Good, want more to do?"

"Sure, the party plans are completed, so I don't have much to do."

"Go shopping and pick up gifts for Jessie, Samuel and Joseph. I'll call Carolyn to write you a check. Let's invite her too. In fact, let's make this the best Christmas that Jessie Mae has ever had."

"I'll have a great time with this shopping spree. So when are you coming home?" she inquired, and I could tell she hoped it was right away.

"Tomorrow," I said wistfully.

"Johnny, are you okay? Did everything go alright in Dallas?"

"Everything went just fine, I'll tell you about it when I get back."

"Kitten, do me another favor?" Before she could answer I asked, "Would you call and order another fifth wheel like the one we have, and have it delivered in the morning? Have them hook up to the septic tank. Samuel and Joseph can hook power from the other camper, they know how to do that. I'll let Carolyn know about the camper and she can arrange for a cash payment. I gave her Gary and Chances number in case she ran into any problems. Thanks, Kitten, I'm glad I can count on you. Call me later if you need me," and hung up.

"Sandy you know what? I haven't seen Kristi or called her since I've been here? How is she doing?

"She's great. She went with Frank to visit with his family for the holidays, she'll be back tomorrow," Sandy replied.

"Then I won't get to see her before I leave."

"No, but let's leave her a message to call us as soon as she gets in. Then you can invite her for Sunday. Johnny, you haven't said anything about me coming, am I invited?"

"Yes you are. It wouldn't be a party without you there, but I need you to be on your best behavior. Karen is going to be there, and I want to spend time with her. Promise?"

"For you, I promise."

I made my call to Carolyn and gave her the details necessary to write the checks.

"I'll handle everything for you, don't worry about a thing," she said.

I hung up thinking that Carolyn was going to work out just fine.

We grilled hot dogs and ate chips. Nobody felt like doing anything, especially me. After the past few days, I needed a night of no problems. We called it an early night. Everyone wanted to pack for tomorrow's flight.

I had just climbed into bed when Sandy walked out of the bathroom naked. She took her hands placed them on my shoulder and pushed me against the pillows. She leaned over me rubbing her body up and down the length of mine. I could feel the heat from her body as she straddled me. I really hadn't wanted this to happen, but with her hips moving up and down on me, she had aroused me to the point I didn't want her to stop.

She kissed me longingly. Her breath became labored as the pace of her rhythm increased. I cupped her butt in my hands and enjoyed the feel of her muscles as they tightened and released. As she came closer to bringing us to total culmination, our bodies entwined, thrust meeting thrust, until finally we both cried out, and then we lay side by side, our skin glistening from sweat, our bodies totally spent.

"Thanks," she said, "I needed that." "Do you realize that I haven't made love to anyone since you left?"

"You mean you and Jimmie didn't make love?"

"No," Jimmie had sex with me and satisfied himself."

"In other words," I grinned at her, "you were hungry." "Honey, you need to take charge of your life, find a man who loves you for just you. We've talked about this before."

"I know, but why should I have someone else when we enjoy making love."

"Because I'm not always around, and someday I'll have someone I want to share the rest of my life with."

"Well until that day," she yawned, "I'm content to leave things as they are."

I was too sleepy and too tired to get into a discussion. Sandy curled up next to me and slowly our bodies relaxed as slumber overtook us.

CHAPTER 21

The next morning we showered and finished packing. It was prearranged for all of us to meet in the lobby and eat breakfast before we left for the airport. We sat sipping our coffee when the hotel manager came and told us the limo driver had our luggage in the car.

Chance and Michele walked with us to the limo. "See you Saturday," Michele said.

"Have a safe trip," Chance added.

"You too! Be careful driving, and if you need anything, you know how to reach me."

The four of us climbed in the limo, and once again we boarded Lisa's plane at Dallas airport. I made sure everyone was comfortable, and then went into the cock pit to speak to the pilot. We chatted for a few minutes, and then the pilot asked if I had a nice Christmas.

"Lisa, Priscilla and I spent a quiet day at Graceland. How was yours?" I asked.

"While you and Lisa were in Florida, we went home to our families. It was very nice, thanks for asking."

I explained to him about Jessie Mae, about taking care of her, and why we were in Florida. I then told him about the party on Sunday and asked if he and the co-pilot would like to come and bring their families. They thought it was a great idea and would love to come.

"Johnny, that's really nice of you sir, not very many people these days would worry about the elderly that way or even care how they feel."

"Is your mom still living?" I inquired.

"Yes sir, she lives near Miami."

"Well, you need to look after her while you can. Make life easy for her and let her enjoy life to its fullest, after all, look at the years she gave you."

"You're right. I think while we're in Florida, I'll take her out to dinner and maybe some after Christmas Specials."

"There you go, I'll tell Lisa Marie I gave you extra time off."

"Thank you, sir. I appreciate you reminding me just how much life means to someone who's old and feels life is passing them by. I'm going to take better care of her, and maybe when her time draws near, she'll know how much I loved and appreciated her, and all the things she did for me."

I smiled and placed my hand on the pilot's shoulder. "I'll be in back with the others if you want or need something."

"Thank you again, sir."

"Your welcome."

Gary was flipping through the television channels and stopped suddenly. The news was on, and Priscilla was being interviewed in California regarding the Christmas Special. The reporter was trying to pry information from her as to my whereabouts and where I'd be performing next. I grinned as she brushed him off by telling him that Johnny Raye was hired to perform at Graceland, and where he went from there was his business and not hers, and that she was not his keeper.

"I sure hope he doesn't come to Florida looking for me, especially right now."

"What are you going to do if this reporter finds you, Johnny?"

"I guess I'll have to introduce him to Jimmie or Jimmies friends," and grinned.

"I have a hunch this reporter is going to find you and give us trouble."

"You're probably right, but I'll have to worry about that later, right now I've got to deal with Jessie, and her troublemaking daughter."

"Her daughter?"

"Yes, when I talked with Lisa, she told me Jessie's daughter is causing trouble with everyone, and trying to run everybody off including Lisa Marie, and I'm afraid it's going to hurt Jessie."

"I know you well enough to know you'll do the right thing. From what you've told us about Jessie, she will respect your decision and stand behind you even if it does hurt her feelings, no matter what you decide. So, Johnny, my advice to you is quite worrying!"

"I guess you are right, but I'm not going to let her come in and ruin our Christmas party for Jessie."

We sat back and watched a movie while the girls took a nap. Before you knew it, the pilot flashed the 'buckle your seat belt sign', and we prepared for landing. I told the pilot to enjoy his visit with his mother, and I'd see him Sunday for the party.

I had the driver take us to the motel where Lisa had rooms reserved so Gary and Denise could check in as well as Sandy. I knew Sandy had hoped to stay at the house with me, but I told her the bedrooms were full, and I was sleeping on the sofa. I also explained to her that Karen may come, and I'd like to spend time with her. I didn't want to hurt Sandy, but I had warned her that this could happen. I also explained to her that she would have to be a little less friendly. Flashing that mischievous smile at me, she promised she would be on her very best behavior. Finally getting everyone settled; we left for the cabin.

I had called Lisa from the car phone and told her we were on our way. She met us in the driveway as we drove up, and said, "Before you go in, Jessie's daughter is still here and won't leave."

"What does Jessie want?"

"Jessie told me to leave things as they are for now until Johnny comes home, that he'll know what to do and he'll handle everything, and that's all she has to say about the matter."

I laughed. "Good, Jessie knows I'll run her out and set her straight." I kissed and hugged Lisa Marie, told her how proud I was of her, and thanked her for all she had done while I was gone. "I know it hasn't been easy on you with Jessie's daughter being here, but I'm here now and I'll take over. Why don't you show Denise, Gary and Sandy around while I go in and see Jessie Mae."

I went directly to Jessie's room. She was resting, and I sent the nurse out so we could be alone. She looked even more tired than when I had last seen her. Her cheeks were hollow, and it appeared to me that she had lost several pounds. I bent down and kissed her cheek.

She opened her eyes and said, "Johnny, I'm so glad you're home. My daughter Doris is here. She's causing problems for everyone."

"I don't want this question to hurt you, but what is she here for, to see you or to get what she can from you?"

Before Jessie could answer, Doris walked in and said, "You must me Johnny!"

"Yes, and you must be Doris, how are you doing?" I asked, as we sized each other up.

"I'm doing fine," she replied flippantly, "and so is my mother." "I want you to remove these people from this house. It seems they won't listen to me, and I want everyone out, including you!"

"Excuse us Jessie," and I grabbed Doris by the arm and wheeled her out of the room, and didn't stop until we reached the front porch, all the while she was spitting and sputtering.

"Let go of me," she yelled. "You're hurting my arm!"

Doris's husband hurriedly followed behind. I yelled for Teresa to come outside. Within seconds Teresa appeared.

"Get Doris and her husband's things out of the bedroom, they're leaving immediately."

Doris raised her voice to me yelling, "We are not leaving! You are! This is my house now, and I'll call the police if you don't leave!"

I blocked the doorway preventing her from entering. Glaring at her, I said between clenched teeth, "I own this damn house, I've always owned this house, and you and your husband have worn out your welcome. Now my patience is worn thin, so you have two choices, either walk to your car right now peaceably or I'll have you thrown out of here. Now get the hell off my property!" I stood rigid, feet spread, arms crossed.

Looking at the anger on my face, Doris's husband took her by the arm and said, "Come on, let's go." They picked up their luggage that Teresa brought out for them. But before they left, Doris stuck her head out the window, and yelled, "You'll be hearing from my attorney."

"Good!" I yelled as they sped down the driveway.

By this time, everyone had gathered on the porch, all in agreement that they knew I'd throw them out when I returned. I apologized to everyone for losing my temper, told them the show was over, and to get back to doing whatever it was they were doing before this happened.

I went back to Jessie's room to check on her. I apologized to her and for her daughter's behavior. "Looks to me like she's here with her hand out for the taking, but irregardless, I shouldn't have lost my temper."

To my astonishment, Jessie started to laugh. "I told Lisa Marie you'd handle her when you got home, and you did. Now don't worry about her anymore."

I kissed her cheek again. "Rest for awhile and then I'll take you outside on the deck so you can get some sun."

Betty, the nurse, came in and asked if I needed any help, but I told her we were just fine.

As I wheeled Jessie on the deck, a police car pulled up out front. I told Teresa to bring the officers to the back deck. I settled Jessie onto the lounge chair and had just got her comfortable when the officer's approached us.

"Are you Johnny Raye?" one of them asked.

"Yes, I am. Something I can do for you officers?" I asked, noticing Doris was with them.

"This lady claims you threw her off her mother's property."

I laughed. "Officer this is her mother. Why don't you ask her who owns this property?"

"I apologize ma'am for disturbing you," he could tell Jessie's condition wasn't good.

With as much effort as Jessie could muster, she said, "Officer, this house belongs to Johnny so get these people off his land."

"Yes ma'am, Miss Jessie." Taking Doris by the arm, he said, "You'd better leave." Turing back to me, he said, "Good to see you again, Johnny."

"You too, Pat! By the way," I added, "we're having a party here Sunday for Jessie Mae." "Why don't you come and bring that beautiful wife of yours?"

Doris stopped dead in her tracks. "You're his friend, and you're taking his word!" "I'm going to report you to your supervisor!" she yelled loudly.

"Lady, I've known Johnny and Jessie Mae for years. Now I brought you out here as I was told to do, and if you don't leave, I'll take you to jail. "Now move!" Looking back, he said, "We'll see you Sunday."

"Oh, ah Pat, make sure they leave."

He nodded his head, and taking Doris again by the arm, they left.

Jessie Mae started to cry. I dropped on one knee next to her and took her hand. "Jessie, I don't want you upset by all this. If you want, I'll have her brought back here for you? I feel terrible about this whole situation."

"No," she replied weakly. "You're right, Johnny, she's not here to see me, she's only here to see what I have that she can get her hands on."

"Have you told her you've left everything to me?"

"No, the attorney can tell her after I'm gone."

"Jessie, I'll handle that for you. She needs to know, and besides, there may be something personal that you'd like her to have."

"Okay Johnny, you take care of it, now let's enjoy this day. You have a way of making an old woman feel happy."

I smiled at her. "I love you too! Now what do you want to drink?"

"I'd like some sweet tea," she smiled.

"Sweet tea it is," and I called for Teresa to bring us a each a glass.

Jessie looked pale in spite of the hot sun on her. The past week's constant tension with her daughter being here, and then today's blow up seemed to have weakened her even more. We sat for quite some time together. We enjoyed watching Joseph teach Sandy and Denise how to bait their hooks with plastic worms.

Teresa was cleaning the bedroom where Doris and her husband had stayed, so Lisa could move her things back in.

The nurse came out to check on Jessie, and seeing she was napping, pulled up a chair to sit with us. Lisa joined us.

"Johnny, have you seen the new trailer yet?"

"No, I haven't had the opportunity to look inside yet. "It looks like the other one doesn't it?" I asked, as I got up to go along with Lisa.

"Almost," she answered, grinning.

Upon entering, I noticed right away the difference in trailers. The kitchen had a center island. This one had a slide out in the living room. Three steps led to the bedroom and bath. This fifth wheel was elaborately decorated and more spacious than the other.

I also noticed that the fixtures in the kitchen were in gold, as well as the bathroom. The bedroom was large enough to accommodate a king size bed. I stopped and stared when I noticed a picture of Graceland hanging above the headboard.

"Lisa, how did you manage to get this?"

"I discovered it in a furniture store where I purchased the furnishings. Are you pleased?"

"Pleased! I'm tickled to death with this. It's beautiful. Kitten, I love it, thank you very much."

We sat for a moment and enjoyed the coolness of the interior. Lisa excitedly told me about the gifts she had purchased. She had found a great department store, and bought shirts and watches for Samuel and Joseph, and for Jessie Mae, a very pretty emerald green dress with matching shoes, and a diamond necklace.

"Daddy," I thought it would be a good idea to give Jessie Mae the dress and shoes early so she can wear them at the party."

"You're right. The necklace we'll give to her at the party and make it look like it's from everyone," I said.

"But there's one more thing, and I know she'll like it, and so will you."

"What's that?" I asked, curious as to what my daughter had cooked up.

"I went to a photographer and gave him a picture of you in costume, another one that I found of Jessie Mae, and one of myself. He has a new procedure where he can take the three pictures and make us look like we posed together. I hope you like the antique frame. Its oval shaped and hand carved."

"I can't wait to see it, Lisa, that's wonderful, what a fantastic idea."

Teresa knocked on the door and said Jessie was asking for me. She wanted to go down to the lake and watch Gary and the girls' fish. I scooped her frail body in my arms, carried her to the dock, and sat her in the swing I had built a few years back. Gary was having such a good time helping Jessie with her rod and reel we left them alone and went back on the deck. The nurse asked if I wanted her to go down and sit with Jessie, but I told her no, and just to keep an eye on her.

"I don't want Jessie to feel like she's being treated like an old woman, you know what I mean."

She smiled in understanding, "I agree, I'll go down once in a while, and see if she's tiring out. Forgive me for saying this, but actually, being around everyone and being cheerful is a lot better for her than the tension her daughter brings every time she steps into a room."

It was near supper time when we brought Jessie back to the house. She was worn out by the time she finished eating. The nurse prepared her for bed and within minutes she was asleep. The rest of us were worn out as well. Gary, Denise and Sandy went to the motel, and I was ready to go to the new trailer.

"Daddy, Sandy had hoped to stay with you, but she felt you didn't want her to."

"Was Sandy hurt or just sad about it?"

"Well, I think disappointed was more like it. Why did you not want her to stay?"

"It's complicated. Sandy is a good friend, and I'm afraid she wants us to be more than friends."

"Well, you have slept with her quite a number of times."

"This is a little hard to discuss with my daughter, but, yes, once too many I'm afraid. Anyways, I'm hoping Karen will come down with David and Tara, and I don't want Karen to think that I'm here with Sandy."

"Sounds like you've got a problem."

"I've talked to Sandy about this a dozen times and she says she's okay with things like they are, but I know Sandy's feelings, and she's so sex crazy. You'd think she'd want to find someone her own age."

"She likes you, and age has nothing to do with it."

"Maybe not to Sandy, but it does to me. There's a paramedic in her building who seems like a real nice guy. I've seen him look at Sandy, and I think he kind of likes her, but she hasn't figured that out yet. I think she's infatuated with me and thinks of me as her security blanket. Now that Jimmie's out of the picture, she can begin a new life for herself."

"Gosh, I'm sorry, in all the excitement around here I forgot to ask you about

Dallas. What happened?"

Lisa was all ears. I told her the complete story minus a few gruesome details.

"And now," I yawned, "I'm tired and going to bed."

Lisa hugged me tight, "I'm so glad you're here and safe."

"That makes two of us!" and I kissed her good night.

The following morning Lisa came to get me up, but I was already dressed and sitting at the kitchen table looking out over the lake. "What's up?" I asked.

"Doris is out front with her attorney."

"That's just great, I can see this is going to be a good day!"

Tired of all the problems, I stormed out front. I glared at Doris and yelled, "I told you yesterday not to come back. Don't you listen?"

"I've brought my attorney," she retorted, vehemently. "He'll handle this!"

I glared at him, and asked, "What is it you want?"

"Let's talk calmly about this, Mr. Raye. I've found through the court house records that this property is in your name, and Jessie Mae's name."

"That's right, but if you would have checked further, there's a clause in the deed that in the event of Jessie's death, her half of the house reverts back to me."

"I never saw any clause that states that, Mr. Raye."

"Then you should have looked closer. Wait here and I'll get my copy." I all but threw the copy at the attorney. I was totally fed up with this whole mess.

Doris' attorney checked my copy. "Doris, I'm afraid he's correct about this. Apparently the records haven't been updated yet to reflect the changes. "But," he said, trying to act like he had something on me," there's the matter of one hundred thousand dollars that Jessie placed into Mr. Raye's account that was done this past week."

"Yeah, what about it?" I could barely contain my anger.

"My client feels that she is entitled to that money."

"Now look here," I growled, and he flinched as I took a step closer, "Jessie isn't dead yet, and that was a decision she made. I'm also listed as her sole heir and executor in her will. That entitles me to her old house in town, and her life insurance. If you check the records, you'll see that I've been paying for her medical as well as health insurance." And then I turned back to Doris, "You haven't bothered to come to see your mother in the last twenty years, you couldn't even seem to find the time to call her. Now that Jessie is dying, you come here with your hand out, acting like you own everything. I'm afraid your client hasn't got anything here to claim except to make amends with her mother before she dies. Now unless you want to tell your mother why you haven't come to see her, I suggest you hit the damn road. I'm sick and tired of you wasting my time and everyone else's."

"I'm sorry, Mr. Raye, Doris's attorney said, "I was under the impression Jessie had already passed away, I didn't know she was still alive," and he turned and gave Doris a disgusted look.

Just then, the nurse wheeled Jessie on the front porch. "In a voice stronger than her frail little body could handle, she said, "I'm not only alive, but I've still got all my faculties. You're trespassing on property where you're not wanted. I no longer have a daughter, but I have a son, and his name is Johnny. I don't ever want to hear from you people again, you're strangers to me." And with that said she had Betty take her back inside.

I looked at Doris who was now crying. "I'm sorry it had to come to this, I was hoping the two of you could talk, but all you're concerned with is material things. All your mother ever wanted from you was your love, but because of your greed you'll lose that as well as everything else."

"I'm sorry, Mr. Raye, to have bothered you, but I need to get back to my office," said the attorney. They got back in his car and left.

Teresa had breakfast just about ready when the phone rang. It was David and Tara calling to let us know they were coming to the party, as well as Karen, but that Karen was bringing Judie and driving her own Cadillac. I gave him the name of the motel and the directions and told him to get them to Karen also. I let him know that reservations were made from Saturday through Monday.

"When's Chance coming?"

"He'll be here either Friday night or Saturday morning. Why don't you give him a call? He's at home visiting with family for the holidays," and I explained about Steadman's being closed.

"Great, maybe we can all drive together. I'll call you from the motel when we get there."

"Good, I'll see you then, give my love to Tara," and we hung up.

I went to check on Jessie to see how she was doing after being so upset with Doris.

"Will you have breakfast with me, young lady?"

She wiped the tears from her eyes and said, "I'd love to you old fart."

And with that we started to laugh.

"Johnny, this party you're giving, you don't need to go through all this trouble and expense just for me."

"Jessie, if you'll remember, this year we didn't have our Christmas together, so we're celebrating Christmas this week instead."

Everyone was at the table and I had Joseph bless the food. Gary called right after breakfast to let us know that he and the girls were going to the beach for awhile, and then shopping before coming out to the cabin. I told them to enjoy their day and that nothing was going on at our house.

"It would be good for Lisa Marie to join you. Hold on while I ask her if she's interested," I suggested.

I told Lisa what their plans were and she was excited to go. They were to meet in the lobby of the motel in an hour.

"Do you need the limo, Johnny?" She asked.

"No, keep it with you and have fun," I hollered, as she went out the door.

Joseph asked what I was going to do for the day, and I told him nothing. I wanted a quiet day with no problems. The only excitement I wanted was to catch a fish.

Jessie looked at me and said, "You know, you used to spend a lot of time on that lake. I remember when you went fishing every morning, and fished all day, and only caught one or two for me."

"I know," I said, "You never would eat more than one or two."

"You don't eat fish?" asked Teresa.

"I love fish, but I'd have to clean them and cook them on an open fire. That's what I built that little, rock fire pit. I put an iron grate across the top and it works great. I learned to do that as a boy, fishing with the neighbor kids. If I hadn't done that, we wouldn't have had anything to eat. All this talk about fishing has given me the itch to go."

I went to the garage and came back carrying my rod and reel and headed to my hot spot on the other side of the lake. I kicked back and sat in my fishing chair under a palm tree. The day was sunny and unseasonably warm for this time of the year. I had closed my eyes for a few minutes when I felt the tug on my line. I had a large mouth bass that was mad as a hornet and was putting up quite a fuss. I kept pulling and reeling until he was close enough to net. I held him by the gills, "Mm, looks like a five pounder, sure hope the rest of the day is as good."

There's something about the excitement of the catch. You never know you've got him until he's spread across an open fire. It was close to four o'clock when I decided to call it quits for the day. I really enjoyed myself. No stress. No one hassling me. I relaxed for the first time in days. I gathered up my fishing gear and grabbed my stringers from the water. I counted fifteen fish in all between bass and catfish. Joseph and Samuel cleaned them for me so we could fry them for supper.

"I'm glad you caught some fish," Teresa commented when she saw my stringers.

"Why's that?" I grinned.

"Cause Jessie knew you would and had me make cole slaw, hush puppies, and right now I'm about to fry some potatoes, and all we needed was the fish."

"Is Lisa Marie home yet?"

"No, she called and said they wanted to go out in town for the night, and then wanted to know if you'd like to go with them. She said to call her and she'd send the limo back for you."

I called Lisa's cell phone, and when she answered I told her to enjoy the night, and that I wanted to stay at the cabin. I'd see them all tomorrow.

"I'll come back in tonight if you want me to," she suggested.

"Kitten, you can stay at the motel and come in tomorrow, just be careful and have a good time. Do me a favor, and change your name for the night."

"Okay, you ole worry wart, I love you."

"I love you too, Kitten."

Samuel and Joseph had finished cleaning and cooking the fish. Teresa had the table prepared and we sat down to eat. Jessie was a little more perky, and was able to eat a little of the catfish, and a few bites of everything else.

"How did you catch so many?" Samuel asked. "Joseph and I fished all day and all we caught were three catfish.

"You were using plastic worms, right?"

"Yes, that's all we've got for bait."

"No, at the edge of the pine tree's you can push back the straw and you'll find all the worm's you need."

"Why didn't you tell us that yesterday," Samuel asked.

Before I could answer, Jessie started cackling, and said, "I thought all black men knew that."

I laughed. "Joseph is the one who taught me to use my rod and reel, before that I just used a fishing pole."

Samuel looked at me, "You may be white, but you fish like a black man." He grinned from ear to ear.

We were too full to move, so we sat around to talk for awhile. Joseph mentioned that he invited the crew at the orchard to come on Sunday.

"Johnny, there will be about forty workers that said they would love to come, but they don't have any transportation," he commented. "What about renting a bus? What do you think of that idea?"

"Where can you rent a bus?" Samuel asked, liking the idea.

"I guess the first place we can look is the yellow pages and see what's listed."

We checked and found several listings and decided on one that sounded promising. It was a private touring company who rented out buses either by the day or by the week. I told them we needed one for Sunday from early in the morning to late at night. For the size bus we needed, the charge was only three hundred and fifty dollars for the day since it was local, and that was with a driver. The dispatcher said they needed a credit card or check, so I told them I would have my accountant handle that. "Samuel, you can tell the crew in the morning about the bus."

Jessie was beaming. "What's everyone wearing? I haven't bought anything new in so long, and everything I own is old and worn."

"Don't worry your pretty little head," I said, "I'm sure you have something nice to wear in your closet."

"No I don't," she sounded wistful.

"Well maybe when Lisa's home tomorrow she can go through your things and pick out something nice."

She nodded, and yawned. "I'm a little tired," and asked the nurse to get her ready for bed.

"She'll be so tickled when the nurse gets her ready in her new dress." I whispered. We'll let her open those gifts before the party starts, on Sunday. Until then, no one say a word." I instructed. "I'll tell Lisa in the morning to pick out something nice from her closet, and tell her that's what she'll wear."

"Okay, Johnny," they all agreed. We continued our conversation in hushed tones so Jessie wouldn't hear what we were discussing.

I was tired from being in the sun all day fishing, so I decided to enjoy my evening alone and watch television. I called Carolyn and left her a message to write a check and have it delivered in the morning to the bus company. I went to the trailer to shower as I could smell fish on me. My hair was still wet and dripping when I grabbed a coke from the refrigerator and lay on the bed to watch a movie. I had barely flipped through the channels when the remote fell from my hand and I was sound asleep.

Next morning I felt great after a fun day and a good night's restful sleep. I thought of how nice it would be at Graceland to be sitting in the sun room drinking coffee, and watching the birds play in the snow, if there still was snow. Memphis had another snow storm, but that was a couple of days ago and it could have melted by now. Then I thought of how peaceful it was here by the lake. Feeling content, I dressed casual and went to the cabin to see what was going on for the day.

I no sooner stepped onto the back deck when Teresa came out to greet me, but I could tell before she said anything that something was wrong by the grim look on her face. "Is Jessie all right?" I asked, ready to bolt to her bedroom.

"Jessie's fine, Johnny, it's Doris, she just pulled up out front. She's crying and wants to see her mother, but Jessie refuses to see her."

I went out front, and Doris said, "I'm only here to see my mother, I don't want anything else. I'm very sorry for being such an ass these past several days, but I don't want my mother to die and not be able to explain to her why I never came around to see her."

"Look, why don't you come around back and wait on the deck. I'll go in and talk with Jessie and see if I can change her mind."

"Please," she said, and for the first time since I met her, I truly believed she was sincere.

I had Teresa bring us some coffee, and then asked Doris if she and her husband had eaten breakfast. She shook her head no and told me she'd been crying all night, and how stupid she had been all these years to have let pride stand in her way from seeing her mother. Meanwhile, Teresa prepared a breakfast of fried potatoes, grits, scrambled eggs, sausage and toast.

"Excuse me, but go ahead and eat, I'll be back in a minute and left to go to Jessie's room.

"Don't even ask," Jessie said, before I had a chance to open my mouth. "I know she's here, and I don't want to see her, so just go away."

I could tell by the set stubborn look on her face that this was not going to be easy. "Jessie," I tried to cajole her into laughter, "I know where that daughter of yours gets her foolish pride." "Sometimes we make mistakes," I started out softly, "some are small and some others not so small." "Doris is here and wants to explain things to you. Personally, I think you should hear her out. So what are you going to do?"

Jessie looked at me and smiled, "Your heart is always in the right place, but it's too soft."

"The good Lord made me this way and maybe for a good reason."

Reaching her hand out to me, she said, "Okay, Johnny, I'll listen, but if things get ugly, you get them out of here."

"I promise," I grinned, and Betty and I helped her into the wheelchair and brought her out on the deck. I sat Jessie in a lounge chair and made sure she was comfortable.

"Before we talk, let's enjoy a good breakfast together first."

"Whatever," Jessie grumbled.

I went to help Teresa bring out more food. We poured another round of coffee for everyone. The sound of food being scooped on plates seemed extremely loud from the lack of chatter. To break the silence, I asked if Samuel and Joseph were here. Teresa replied that they were still in their trailer and hadn't been out today. I went to the edge of the deck and yelled for them to come and eat. Joseph came out and said they'd eat later. I told him no that they could eat now. Reluctantly they joined us.

"Do you all always eat together?"

"Yes, but there are more guests in town that aren't here right now, and they won't be back until this afternoon. Now that we're all eating, Doris why don't you tell us what it's like living in New York City?" I asked her, to get the conversation going.

As she was describing New York to us, about the hustle and bustle and skyscrapers, Jessie started asking questions about the department stores, and the traffic. Doris directed the conversation to Jessie to keep her mothers interest. She explained how, at times, the traffic was so heavy that it would take three or four hours to get home. Occasionally, she arrived at home later than ten o'clock and she lived only a short distance from her office.

"It would be bad if you had to go to the bathroom," Jessie laughed, "there's no way I could live like that."

Doris laughed along with her mother. "There are some days that I wished I did live elsewhere, but we live outside of the city and we love it. Especially when it snows, and all our friends get together for wine and eggnog."

"What do you do Bob?" Jessie asked Doris' husband.

"I design and construct large buildings."

"Wow, do you go up to the top while they are under construction?" Jessie was intrigued.

"Yes ma'am," he responded. Bob was obviously a man of few words, but he was polite.

"Man, I couldn't do that," I said to keep the conversation going, "I don't like height that much."

Doris took a deep breath, "Mama, I don't know how to say this without hurting your feelings, but through the years Bob and I have done very well for ourselves. We live in a neighborhood of very well to do people. Here, they would be called snobs. All of our friends came from rich, old established, affluent families. To fit in, I couldn't bring myself to tell them I came from a poor family, and that my father died working in the fields, and that we lived in an old shack in Florida that had more holes in it than you could count. It just got easier to pretend that both my parents were dead. I've always been ashamed of my upbringing all my life, and wanted to belong with people that were educated and well to do."

"I'm so ashamed of myself for how I treated everyone here, and how I treated you. I now realize my life has been empty without you. I love you mama, and I'm sorry for every lie I've ever told about you. I'm proud of you. You worked hard all you life, and if it hadn't been for you giving me the education I needed, and the opportunity to get ahead, I wouldn't be where I am today. I'm still having a hard time with the truth about my life, but I do know that after yesterday, Johnny is right. I don't want you to die. I don't think I can live with myself knowing that you died and I never got a chance to say I'm sorry, and that I love you much more than you'll ever know." By now she was crying unashamedly, tears streamed down her cheeks, but relieved that the truth was out in the open.

"I don't understand how you could go twenty years without once coming to see me, and only calling me once or twice in all those years," Jessie said, still to hurt to offer forgiveness. "If only you would have called to let me know how you were doing or even call to ask if I needed anything. You have no idea how many nights I lay crying, worried sick about whether or not you were sick or still alive. Not even a call to say I love you. I never even received a Christmas or birthday card, and when I'd send one to you, it would always come back with wrong address written on it. Did you think I was so stupid that I wouldn't recognize my own daughter's handwriting? How do you think I felt remembering all the years I did without so that you would have something? Maybe it didn't seem like much to you, but believe me, many a night I was so hungry I would get stomach cramps and I wouldn't eat so you'd have something to fill your belly. I saw to it that you ate a hot meal at school while I'd have an orange for breakfast and lunch just to keep the hunger pains away. I wore shoes with holes so you could have new shoes, and you say you were ashamed of me."

Tears rolled from her tired old eyes, but she wasn't finished yet. "Just how do you think I should feel after all these years? Johnny took me out of that old house in town. He's always seen to it that I was taken care of, as if I was his own mother, and never once did he look at me as some old black lady that was nothing. Just tell me why I should leave you anything. I scrimped and saved for years to put money in the bank so that I could have money to take care of myself when I got to old to work and feed myself. Now I find out I'm going to die before I even get to enjoy my retirement."

Doris sobbed even harder. "I know I don't deserve anything from you, but I want to spend what time you have left with you. I guess that's why I was so hateful to everyone when I got here. I came here to take care of you, and it hurt me to see someone else doing what I should have been doing all along. Please mama, I'm begging you to forgive me, give me a chance to make it up to you, please mama," Doris pleaded.

Jessie cried softly, but she never spoke.

Waiting for a reply from her mother and not getting one, Doris stood up and said, "Johnny, I'm sorry." "It's time Bob and I go and leave you alone."

"Wait," I said, not wanting her to leave on these terms. Somehow I had to figure a way to get those two back together. "We're having a Christmas party for your mother on Sunday, and I'd like for you to stay."

"Are you sure?" Doris was hesitant.

"Yes, I'm sure. Besides, we've got a lot of old farts coming; we need some one younger to help us."

Jessie cracked a smile, and not being able to hold back, she cackled that familiar, old laugh I had grown to love through the years, and said, "It's us old farts that make party's come alive."

"Well one old fart does anyway," I laughed along with her.

"Yeah me," she smiled.

"No, actually I was referring to me. All you do is lie on your butt all day while I go out and sweat in the hot sun to catch your dinner," I grinned, and then winked at her.

She burst out laughing once again. "Well, tomorrow I'll fish all day and you can lie around."

"Young lady, you have a deal."

"Joseph," Doris asked, "do they tease each other like this all the time?"

"Oh yes," he replied.

"Doris, we don't have any room here at the house, but I've got rooms reserved and paid for at a motel on Vero Beach for friends that are coming for your mother's party. Would you like to sleep there and stay here during the day?"

"I'd like that very much, and thank you, for everything."

It was time to end the hurts. I hugged Doris's neck and took her by the hand to stand next to her mother. "Don't you think, young lady," I said to Jessie, "that you should hug your daughter's neck?"

Jessie looked at Doris; tears again slide down her weathered old face. Jessie slowly put her arms up to her daughter. Doris almost flew into them; she responded so quickly. It was quite emotional watching mother and daughter reunite, as both hugged and kissed, and told each other how sorry they were, and how much they loved each other.

"Teresa, why don't you the change sheets on the roll away bed? Bob, would you mind sleeping at the hotel tonight, and let Doris stay here with her mother?"

"No," he said, watching his wife, "I'd be happy to."

"What about the nurse, where will she sleep?" Doris asked, not letting go of her mother's hand.

"I'll check and see if she wouldn't mind sleeping on the sofa for one night. Besides, she really doesn't sleep that much."

"The nurses have given mother excellent care. Johnny, you are the finest man and brother I've ever known."

"Thanks, Doris, you're not bad for a sister either," I kidded back.

About that time, Lisa Marie, and the others came bouncing through the front door. Lisa looked very angry at seeing Doris's car parked out front. "What's she doing here?" Lisa asked, glaring at Doris.

"Its okay, Kitten. Doris is sorry for the trouble she's caused everyone, and she's trying to make it up to her mother."

"Sorry my ass, it's probably an act so she'll get her mother's inheritance," she was not willing to trust Doris.

"No, she's here on good terms, and Jessie has forgiven her, so let's not say anything out of the way."

"She treated me like shit, and now you're asking me to not to say anything!"

"Yes, I am asking."

She studied my face for a moment and then relented. "I'm only doing this for Jessie Mae."

Doris overheard Lisa, and came into the kitchen and looked directly at Lisa. "I'm sorry for the way I acted towards you and everyone else, you have every right to be angry at me, but please accept my apology, I really am sorry."

"Alright, I guess if Jessie can forgive you, then I can too."

"Doris, I don't think you really know who this is."

"Sure, I do, mother told me her name was Lisa."

"Yes, it is, but its Lisa Marie Presley, Elvis's daughter."

Doris's face blanched. "My God, I really am sorry, please forgive me."

"Well, she's really, really rich, and when you go back to New York, you can tell all your friends that your mother has famous, rich people staying at her house," I teased her.

"No, my friends are bigger assholes than me."

"At least now you realize it," I kept teasing her.

Doris laughed. "Yeah, you're right, but I'm going to change."

"Johnny seems to know how things will happen before they happen, it was a gift handed down from his mother," Lisa said.

"What do you mean?" Doris asked.

"Well, he told me you'd be back, and here you are."

"That was probably just a lucky guess."

"No, Johnny knew, trust me, he knew."

We walked out on the deck, and I asked Gary if David had shown up yet at the motel? But he shook his head no.

"Tell me about your night, did you have fun?"

Sandy piped up first, "We went dancing at a club on the beach, and man it was full of good looking men."

"Well did you find one good enough to take home?" I teased.

"Well," she giggled, "for a night, but not for keeps." "Although," she said prancing around for dramatic affects, "he wants me to stay with him in Florida."

"What did you tell him?"

"I told him he was crazy, that I was going back to Dallas."

We laughed at Sandy's antics, and then Denise said, "I think Lisa Marie found herself a boyfriend."

"Yeah, but I told him my name was Kelly and he believed me."

"Good girl," I said, "you don't need anyone chasing after your money."

"Oh, he thinks I'm broke, and that Gary is the rich guy."

"Yeah," Gary laughed remembering the conversations from last night, "but, Lisa, he really did like you."

"Yeah," Sandy said, "but he was only wanting a place to crash for the night." "They were just beach bums," she added.

Jessie, listening to the conversation said, "All you young girls got men chasing after you, shoot, it's been years since I've dated a man."

Denise laughed, and asked Jessie, "What would you do if you had one?" she teased.

"Why, I'd love him all night," she answered emphatically.

"Mama!" Doris said, surprised at her mother's sense of humor.

We were laughing so hard by then, and Jessie still had a good comeback. "After all," she continued, "I'm only eighty six years old."

The rest of the evening we sat around on the deck listening to music. The air was chilly so we wrapped Jessie in a big quilt to keep her warm. The bull frogs croaking was so loud around the lake, it almost sounded like they were having a private party of their own. Little tree frogs hung on windows and glass doors, busily catching bugs that were attracted to the inside lights.

We were getting concerned there still was no word from David, but he finally called to let us know they had just arrived. Apparently they had a late start which totally messed up their schedule, and said they were tired and they would see us all in the morning.

Jessie dozed on and off so we took her to bed. Betty wanted to check her vitals. We noticed that she had drifted in and out of sleep all day. Betty warned us not to excite her too much, as she was growing very weak. Betty tucked her in, gave Jessie her medicine, and then instructed Doris to listen for

300

her during the night, and to waken her if she moaned in her sleep. She told us that Jessie was now in a lot of pain, even though she never complained.

Betty and I were alone in the kitchen. The other nurse had an emergency so Betty was staying round the clock. I asked her if she would prefer to sleep in Lisa's room, and that Lisa could sleep in my trailer, in my bed, and I could sleep on the hide-a-bed.

"This may not be very professional of me, but I could sleep in your trailer if you don't mind?" She suggested.

"No, I do mind, and no I don't think so," and smiled at her bold offer.

"Well in that case, I'll sleep on the sofa," and then grinned at me.

Sandy had come in to see where I was and had overheard the conversation. "Thank you," she mouthed the words to me.

"Your welcome," I mouthed the words back.

The air continued to grow colder, and with Jessie's party tomorrow, we decided to call it a night. Before retiring, I went to Jessie's room to check on her one more time. Bob had left with the group, but Doris was there keeping a close watch on her mother.

"I don't mean to meddle in your affairs, but why does such a famous girl like Lisa Marie Presley do everything you want her to do? I mean you treat her like she was your daughter."

"Well, she calls me dad occasionally. I think she needs a father figure, and because I remind her so much of her dad, she has attached herself to me. Does that make sense to you?"

"Yes it does, it's very easy to get attached to you."

"Well, thank you."

"Johnny, thank you again."

"No need to thank me, I'm just glad that you and Jessie are talking."

Just then Jessie spoke up and said, "Would you two go to bed, I can't go to sleep with you two running off at the mouth."

"Okay." I laughed, "I'm leaving." I bent down to kiss her. "Tomorrow's a big day for you, you get a good nights rest! I love you." I whispered in her ear.

"I love you too." She whispered sleepily.

Teresa was in the kitchen and asked me to join her. She poured me a cup of coffee and asked what she needed to do for tomorrow. I told her there really wasn't much for her to do other than make breakfast in the morning for all of us here, and our guests that are coming from the motel. I told her it would be easier for her to do a buffet setup, and let everyone serve themselves. She didn't need to fuss as there would be plenty of food all day to eat.

"Teresa, the catering service will be here around ten o'clock with all the salads, snacks and desserts. Samuel, Joseph and a few of their friends will rotate cooking the meat on the grill throughout the day. Tents will be set up. Do you know what time they're delivering the tents?"

"No, I don't know anything about the tents, but I'll ask Lisa for you in the morning, and I'll check on the food and make sure everything is replenished as needed."

"Thanks Teresa I appreciate that." I left to retire to my trailer to get a good night's sleep as I knew the next day would be a hectic one.

CHAPTER 22

Morning came early. The clock read eight thirty. Not ready to get up yet, I let my mind wonder. Another year is here and already it's starting out bad. I'm going to be losing Jessie Mae, and somehow I have a feeling I'm going to be having trouble on down the road. I dragged myself from the bed to get ready since it was getting late.

On the way to the house, I noticed a truck pull up with the food and drinks and another coming up the drive-way. Lisa met me and said the place we rented the tents from had arrived and we were ready to set up.

"You're a peach, Kitten, you put a lot of work into this, and I know I couldn't have done it without you."

She kissed me and said, "Thanks, daddy, I needed to hear that from you."

"Honey, I'll always try to remember just how much you do, and I don't mean just for me either."

"By the way, who's handling business for you at Graceland during your absence?"

"There's a full time staff and mother oversees everything for me when I'm not around, but if there's a problem, they call mother. You know mother, if she's there, I'll just be in the way."

"Lisa, I don't want to keep you from your duties."

"Don't worry. You'll soon be leaving for Vegas, and I'll catch up on my work, but for now it can all wait."

The day turned out to be picture perfect. Not a cloud in sky. The sun shone bright, and only a hint of a breeze could be felt. The temperature was supposed to reach between seventy and seventy-five degrees. Maybe my feelings this morning were wrong. The ideal weather was a good omen.

I found Gary setting up his equipment. Chance and David were helping. I hugged them both and told them how happy I was to see them, and so glad they could come. "Where's the girls I asked?" as I looked around and didn't see them.

"They're in town shopping. Judie and Karen found an antique shop that's only open on week-ends for tourist trade, and they were dying to go there," Chance said, and rolled his eyes. "They'll be back in a little while."

"How's everything here?" I asked.

"Sure," David said joking, "sleep all day and come out after all the work is done to ask if he can help."

"No," I kidded back, "I didn't ask if I could help, just checked to see how it's going."

"He's got you there, buddy," Chance said. "You'll never learn will you?"

"Well, you were going to ask," David said to me.

"Okay," I replied, "anything I can do to help?"

"Yeah, you can make us a list of songs for today."

"Why don't we set up for Karaoke, and give everyone a chance to sing. I have something cooked up for them. Then later tonight, the three of us can sing whatever we want. No programs to follow."

I checked on Samuel and Joseph as they were setting out tubs for the ice and beer. The screened tents were up, and tables and chairs were being arranged to make it look festive. We had seating for close to one hundred people and by the looks of the crowd that was already there, it would be close to that many in attendance. The bus had already arrived, and instead of forty people, the count was closer to fifty.

The grills were hot and the cooks were already grilling pork loins, chops, barbequed chicken, Polish and Italian sausage, hot dogs, and burgers to be put on later.

Doris hollered for me to come inside that a reporter was here to see me from a television station in Memphis. Chance heard her telling me about the reporter.

"Johnny, you want me to get rid of him for you?"

"No, I'll take care of this."

I knew which reporter it was. I stormed into the house. He was in the kitchen, along with a cameraman interviewing Teresa, and Betty.

I snarled in anger, "Teresa, Betty, do not answer any more questions!" I turned to the now nervous reporter and cameraman. Anger flashed from my eyes like daggers, as I was truly fed up with this guy. "What are you doing here, and how did you find me?" My voice became louder with each word I spoke.

"I came to interview you," he stammered, "a follow up to the Christmas Special."

I was aggravated for the intrusion on my privacy. This was getting to be too much like it used to be, and exactly what I no longer wanted.

Before the cameraman even knew what was happening, I grabbed his camera and ripped the film from it. Grabbing both of their arms I escorted them to their van. They quickly jumped in and locked the doors. Swearing, at me and then at each other, I noticed they couldn't find the keys to the car.

"Johnny!" At the sound of my name I turned to see Chance, David and Gary coming up behind me, tossing a set of keys between them.

"I think he's looking for these," David said.

I started to laugh when I realized what they had done. I was about to respond when another car came up the drive. It was the sheriff.

"I called him, Johnny," Teresa said, and grinned, "just to be on the safe side."

It was Pat. He got out of his car and casually walked towards us. "Teresa called and said you had two trespassers again, seems to be contagious. The other day it was Jessie's daughter and now these two clowns. You might need to hang a 'no trespassing' sign out front," he grinned.

"I guess they'll be needing these," and I handed Pat the keys.

By now the reporter had rolled down the window. Pat stuck his head inside the car and said, "If I ever catch you two within ten miles of this place, I'll have you arrested." "Here are your keys. I'm going to follow you boys all the way out of town. Oh, and if I was you, I wouldn't speed, run a red light or not come to a complete stop. My wife is waiting for me to pick her up to bring her to this party, and if I'm late because I had to write you a ticket, there'll be hell to pay. Trust me. You don't want to see me get angry!"

"Johnny," Pat nodded, "see you in a little while." They drove off, with Pat riding their tail.

As they left, Karen drove up in her Cadillac with the rest of the girls. Denise jumped out first. "Johnny, are you in trouble again?"

"No, that damn reporter showed up unannounced, and he had to have a personal escort out of here."

Gary, Chance, David and I looked at each other and laughed. Karen got out of her car and I smiled warmly at the sight of her.

"Hi," she said taking my hand. "Have you seen my car?"

"No, I haven't but isn't it the same as the others?"

"Not quite, I have something to show you," she said blushing. Still holding hands we strolled to where her car was parked.

"Look at the seats." Her eyes sparkled.

I grinned when I saw the big letters of J. R. under the initials of E. P.

"Well that was nice of you, but you should have put your initials on instead of mine," I teased her.

She turned and wrapped her arms around my neck, and gave me a long, meaningful kiss. "Thank you," she whispered in my ear, "I love the car. You have no idea how surprised I was when David and Tara delivered it to me Christmas morning. There's only one thing that could have made it more special."

"What's that?" I asked, wondering what I could have done to make it nicer for her.

"You could have been sitting in the front seat with a red bow tied around your neck."

"Oh, if I could have been there, I would have."

"I wanted to call you and thank you, but you don't have a phone and David didn't have Lisa's number."

"I'm planning on getting one soon, but not just yet. I'm not sure I want one."

"Oh, they are so handy. I use mine all the time."

When we turned around, everybody had disappeared.

"Come on," I said laughing, "I want you to meet Jessie Mae."

I showed Karen and Judie around the cabin and we stopped in the kitchen so I could introduce them to everyone. "Miss Jessie," Karen said kneeling next to her, "I've heard so much about you and you look just like I pictured."

Jessie Mae took her hand, and said to me, "She's very pretty, Johnny, you be especially good to this one, I think she'll be good for you."

"And just how do you know that?" I asked teasingly.

"I know, I just know," she replied, nodding her head to confirm the wisdom of her own statement.

306

I left Karen inside to visit with the rest of the group, and I went out to check on how everything was going.

Lisa had thoughtfully ordered netting to be hung from the tents and a screened tent around the food area and where the guys were grilling to help keep all the bugs away. Large tents were ready in case of rain. Even though the sky was cloudless right now, anybody that lives in Florida knows that an afternoon shower could appear out of nowhere.

The guys decided to set Gary's equipment on the deck. They felt it would be a better idea as half the deck was under roof. It would protect the equipment from the sun, and in case it rained, nothing would get wet.

I looked at Chance and David, and asked, "Why don't you two get some Karaoke singers up here, and if you can't get anyone, you two do a few songs and get everyone going."

"I know that guy standing over there in the black, short-sleeved shirt. His name is John and he does a great job singing Johnny Cash songs. I'll bet he'll get the crowd going," Gary commented, "we'll call him up first."

I walked around the grounds. It looked like a little city of it's own with all the tents and people around. Many of the guests complimented me regarding my performance at Graceland for the Christmas Special. One in particular asked, "It must have been awesome for you to have stayed at Graceland."

"Yes, it was quite an honor for me. Does everyone here know that Lisa Marie is here?" I announced.

"Yes, they all said, we've been waiting for her to come out of the house."

"She will in a little while, she's handling some last minute details." I went inside to tell Lisa Marie that she had fans waiting for her.

"You mean they want to see me and not you for a change," she said, teasing me, but pleased that everyone wanted to see her.

"Before you go out there, Lisa, let's let Jessie open a couple of her gifts first."

"Good idea, I'll get them." "Jessie," Lisa said excitedly, "Santa came last night, guess he looked for you the other day and couldn't find you so he had to make a return trip."

"These are for me?" Jessie was surprised.

"Well, these tags read Jessie Mae, and unless there's another Jessie Mae in the group, I think these are for you."

Jessie opened them slowly with a little help from Lisa as Jessie had become very weak. Tears welled in her tired old eyes as she looked down at the emerald green, sequined dress and matching shoes.

"Now that's a party dress," I exclaimed. "I think we need to have Betty get you ready. You have a few people out there that are waiting to see you. What, no words? How do you like that? We buy her a party dress and she's speechless."

Jessie tried to talk but all she could do was take my hand and give it a gentle squeeze. By now there wasn't dry eye in the house, including me.

"That's all right darlin; you'd probably make us take it back."

"No," she finally said, and shook her head. The nurse and Doris took her in to get her changed, and Lisa went out to sign autographs and visit with everyone.

I went outside to join the others, and as I glanced around, sitting at one of the tables was Kristi and Frank.

"It's about time you came over to us and said hello," she teased.

We hugged and kissed and chatted a few minutes about the show I did in Graceland, and then I asked how their Christmas was. "Take a look," and with that remark she stuck her hand out for me to see her engagement ring.

"Wow, Frank, this must have set you back a few paychecks?" I kidded, and hugged and congratulated them both.

It was quite obvious that Kristi was very much in love with Frank with the adoring look she flashed at him, and he with her as he placed his arm around her shoulder.

"Have you set a date yet?" I asked.

"No, not yet, but when we do, we'd be honored if you would sing at our wedding."

"I'd be proud too."

I excused myself as I spotted Doris and Bob sitting on the deck. "Why are you sitting here?"

"I'm on break," she grinned, "I haven't worked this hard in years."

"Is mother ready?"

"All most, she kicked everyone out but Betty, she wants to surprise everyone when she comes out in her new dress. Johnny, mother is very weak today, but she is so excited. Wait until she comes out here and sees how many people showed up in her honor. Thank you for having us stay, these are memories I'll cherish the rest of my life."

"Your welcome," I said, and then asked, "Why don't you sing us a song."

"Me, oh no, I can't sing."

"Sure you can, it's easy."

"Nope, you're not getting me up there."

"Before the night is over, you'll be up there with the rest of them," I kidded.

"Don't hold your breath," she teased back.

I spotted Karen with Judie sitting with a bunch that came from Birmingham. I put my arm around her and asked if she and Judie were going to sing for us.

"We probably will later, but why don't you sing for us?"

"I will, I'm going to sing one especially for you," I said, tapping her on the end of her nose.

Just then I glanced up and saw Sandy standing off by herself by the lake, "Excuse me Karen for a minute, will you?"

"Sure, we're enjoying all this delicious food; you may have to roll me out of here before the nights over if I keep eating like this."

"That's what it's for. Enjoy it, because I don't want to be eating leftovers for the next week."

I went and put my arm around Sandy's shoulder. "Is there something wrong?" I asked tenderly.

"Yes there is!" she said emphatically. "I miss being with you, and when you're this close and you don't notice me, I feel like I'm being left out."

I smiled at her pouted expression, which I'm sure was meant for me to feel guilty. "Sandy, I love you very much, and you are my best girl friend, and I'm not avoiding you. I just want you to let loose and feel free to have fun without anyone around to threaten you. You knew I wanted to be with Karen. I was afraid this would happen. I told you from the beginning not to get sexually involved with me, but you said you could handle it, and now you're in love with me, but I'm not 'in' love with you."

"No, I can handle it. It's just that you aren't talking to me, it's like you're avoiding me."

"I am?"

"Yes you are." she replied. "Do you realize you've introduced Karen to everyone except me?"

"I didn't?"

"No you didn't."

"Well I'm sorry, come on, I'll introduce you to her right now!" And I kept my arm around her shoulder as we walked in the direction of where Karen was sitting.

"Karen, I'd like you to meet a very close friend of mine, "Karen this is Sandy."

"Hi, Sandy," she said, "you work at the supper club where Johnny performed at in Dallas. He's told me all about you."

"I hope it was all good."

"Well, he told me he almost went to jail fighting with your ex-boyfriend."

"Yes, he did."

"But," Karen said, "I'm glad he won't be around to bother you any more."

"Yeah, Sandy agreed, not for a long, long time, if ever."

"You should have had him arrested a long time ago."

"I should have," Sandy said, as she sat down, "but sometimes you're too scared to do anything."

I left the two of them chatting to check on Jessie Mae.

Lisa Marie stopped me, and looked in the direction where Karen and Sandy were sitting, "Your kettle of hot water may boil over, and you could get burned."

"Maybe it'll just stay warm and not boil over."

Just then the nurse and Doris brought Jessie out on the deck. Jessie looked absolutely beautiful in her new dress. At the sight of her, everyone stood and gave her a standing ovation. The clapping of hands and whistling was so loud that the following day people said they could hear it several miles down the road.

We had prepared a lounge chair with a banner that read, "For the Guest of Honor." Jessie couldn't stop smiling, tears of joy streamed down her wrinkled face. Not a woman there looked as beautiful as Jessie did right then. We made sure she was settled comfortably in her chair, and then asked if there was anything she needed.

"Well there sure is, get me a plate of food, I'm starving."

Doris quickly got up and prepared her mother a plate. She piled as much food on it as she could manage.

"My goodness child, I hope there's some left for the rest."

Pat and his wife arrived, as well as the pilots. Carolyn came and jumped right in to help. Everyone we had invited had come, and some had brought friends and family members. The day was passing with Karaoke in full swing. The guests were enjoying the food. Well wishers spent the day visiting with Jessie. All the while, Betty stayed at Jessie's side, watching her and making sure she was okay.

"Mother, you look so happy."

Jessie replied, "I am very happy, but I'd like it if Johnny would sing my favorite song to me."

"Hearing her request," I asked, "Which one is that?"

"Amazing Grace," she replied.

"You'll get your wish, but first we have a few Christmas gifts to distribute. Samuel and Joseph, would you two please come up here?" I announced taking the microphone. "These gifts are for you for looking after this place and taking care of Jessie."

"Harrumph! Jessie said. "More like me taking care of them."

Lisa took the microphone and announced, "And now, if everyone would be silent for a moment, we'd like to have Jessie open her Christmas gifts from all of us to her."

"Taken by surprise, Jessie said, "I've already got my presents."

"Not all of them," and Lisa handed her the picture of the three of us to Jessie.

"Oh," she squealed, "this is wonderful."

The picture the photographer did for us turned out perfect. He had arranged us so that it looked like Jessie Mae and Lisa Marie were sitting side by side while I sang to them. It turned out so much better than I had ever imagined it to be. The frame Lisa picked out seemed to enhance the effect the photographer had achieved.

Jessie unwrapped her next gift. She cried openly when she held up her diamond necklace and said she wouldn't live long enough to wear it. I took it from her and placed it around her thin neck.

"Wherever you go, you'll always look lovely wearing this."

She squeezed my hand in appreciation.

"You know Jessie," I said, "that's twice today you've been speechless."

It was getting close to evening, and the party was still going strong. Lisa had purchased his and her diamond rings. We had planned a Karaoke contest for the best male and female singers with the audience as the judges. Of course, Chance, David, Gary and myself were not allowed to enter.

While the contestants were signing up, Jessie and I sang "Silent Night" together. I then sang "Amazing Grace" to her, as she requested, and then as a special request from Lisa Marie, I sang "Holly Leaves and Christmas Trees. For Karen, I had decided to do "Angel" and dedicated it to her.

I introduced David and Chance and they each did a few Christmas songs as well as standard tunes. The crowd was having a great time, and no one wanted to leave, especially with the contest about to begin. Couple after couple came up to sing. Several were good, but most of them were terrible. No one cared as they were having too much fun. Finally, the last couple finished their song and the audience voted. The couple that won did a country and western duet, and had sounded pretty good together considering it was their first time they had sang together as a couple. They were thrilled with their rings, and I thanked Lisa again for the good idea.

Gary sang and people danced wherever they could find room. When he finished, I was asked to sing several more songs. I looked at Jessie's smiling, peaceful face, and I knew my next choice would be "Peace In the Valley." I'll never forget the happiness on her face when I began to sing. She gave me the biggest smile, and ever so slowly closed her eyes.

Jessie passed away mid-way through the song, her face softened by the peace she found and her smile remained even after she drew her last breath. Tears ran freely down my face. I couldn't remember crying that hard since the passing of my mother.

Somehow I managed to finish singing to Jessie. Doris and Betty were going to remove her, but I stopped them. "Let her be, her night isn't over yet." I announced to everyone that Jessie had passed away, and asked that we raise our voices in song to sing "Swing Low Sweet Chariot" for her, as she had requested me to do several days ago.

I asked the crew from the orchard that I used to sing with to start the song and that we'd all join in on the chorus. The sweet blend of the deep bass, baritone and tenor voices filled the air. The richness of everyone singing from their hearts would have made Jessie proud. After that, I sang "Green, Green Grass of Home." Everyone cried as I finished. I asked Gary, David, Chance and Doris's husband to carry Jessie to her room. The nurse had already called the coroner to come and take her.

Doris and the nurse stayed with Jessie. I asked the guys to join me in prayer. I started by saying the smile on Jessie's face told me the angels came for her during her favorite song, and to please bow their heads and join me in prayer.

"Father, you sent your angels and took a very sweet lady from us. We ask that you give her all the riches of heaven as she was a very poor lady here on earth, but was rich in love and friends. We ask that she walk the streets of purest gold, and that there be peace in the valley where she may live forever and ever. Amen."

The coroner arrived and carried Jessie's frail little body away. Lisa held me tight, her body shook uncontrollably from crying so hard. "Daddy," she said, not caring if anyone heard, "I only knew Jessie a short time, but during these days I spent with her, I grew to love her."

"I know Kitten, she loved you too."

"Johnny," Doris cried, as she came over to where I was sitting, "What are you going to do with my mother's body?"

"Jessie and I discussed this the other day. She has a will and it stipulates that she is to be cremated. She wants her ashes to be placed on the mantle for one year, and then one year from the day of her death they will be spread over the lake. If you want, you can meet me here one year from today, and we can spread her ashes together."

That brought on another bout of tears, and she finally said, "I'd like that very much. Will you have services?"

"No, Jessie didn't want anything special to be done except be put to rest. She told me that this party gave her a chance to share her last moments with those she loved, and for them to rejoice with her in her finest hour. I'll honor her wishes in that regard."

"Johnny, thank you for letting me spend the last few days with her."

"Your welcome, I'm glad you were here, it made Jessie's last moments of her life more meaningful."

We stood in silence for a moment, and then I said, "Doris, in the event that something should happen to me, I want you to carry out her wishes. Samuel and Joseph will remain here to maintain the property, and Teresa will live here to keep the inside of the cabin clean and ready for guests as needed. Before you leave to go back to New York, I want to discuss the house with you, but not tonight. Tomorrow we'll go through her things and talk then. Doris, the diamond necklace that we gave her tonight will be kept for your daughter."

"My daughter, how did you know I was pregnant?" she asked, confusion written in her expression. "I only found out myself the week before we came here. Other than Bob, I haven't told a soul. Not even mother. I thought I had more time with her to tell her, but now it's too late."

"That's where you're wrong. Jessie told me the other day when she and I spent the day together that she had a premonition you were pregnant with a little girl."

"A little girl," Doris spoke softly." "Mother always had the ability to predict things, and she was always right. Bob and I had almost given up the idea of having a child. I thought I'd never conceive, especially this late in life, but this is truly a blessing from God. You know Johnny, I always said if I ever had a daughter I'd name her Anne, but now I think I'd like to change that to Jessie Anne. I think mother would like that."

"Somehow, Doris, I think she knows."

She nodded and went off to find her husband.

The guests were leaving. The bus was pulling out with the crew from the orchard to bring them back into town. Samuel and Joseph made sure they took food home with them. For those that remained, I announced that there was still plenty of food and refreshments left, and to help themselves. I went into the kitchen and asked Teresa for a cup of coffee, and went to sit at the table when Karen came in and sat next to me.

Laying her hand gently on my arm, she asked, "Johnny is there anything I can do?"

I shook my head no. "Thank you for your concern, I appreciate that."

Teresa looked at me and asked, "Johnny, have you eaten yet today?"

"Not since breakfast."

"Let me fix you a plate. Doris, would you like a plate too?"

"Please," she nodded.

"I'll be right back."

"Samuel, Joseph," I said, as they got up to leave. "Before you go, I want you to know that you can remain here at the house. Teresa will look after you two, and you can maintain the outside, while I'm away. So help her out as much as you can, and I'll be home from time to time to see if you need anything."

Samuel said, "You don't need to worry about us, we'll be fine. Miss Teresa will watch over us."

"Just remember," I grinned, "there's still a lady in the house, and she's the boss."

"It'll be like Miss Jessie was still here."

"Well, maybe her spirit will be around for awhile until she knows you two will be okay."

"She looked after us for years, Johnny," Samuel said, fighting back tears.

I nodded, momentarily unable to speak. When I regained my composure, I said, "Samuel, Joseph, I want you to know that Jessie Mae had saved one-hundred thousand dollars for her retirement, and she stipulated to me that she wanted you two to have it. Oh, I almost forgot. She said to make sure you didn't spend it all in one place." That brought out another bout of tears.

Teresa returned with our food, and I asked Karen if she wanted some. She rolled her eyes back and patted her tummy. "If I eat another bite, I swear, I'll have to exercise everyday for the next month to get rid of what I ate today," and then added, "but boy, it sure was good!"

After eating, I stood on the deck to talk with the guys. Tara, Michele, Sandy and Kristi came and hugged me and offered their condolences.

Sandy asked if I was okay, and I replied, "Jessie had an old saying, *when you or I are gone, the living must go on.*" I saw that she was happy when she passed away by the smile on her face. That told me she saw the angels coming to take her. Doris told me Jessie's last words were, "*I'm ready,*" and then went to sleep."

"She was a very sweet lady," David said.

"Well, I'm going to miss her, and like my mother, I'll miss her too, but I'm going on doing what I set out to do or I know Jessie will come back and whip my ass."

"You know, I believe she would," Gary said, laughing, and then softly added, "I kind of took a shine to her myself."

"Chance," I asked, "Did you get enough to eat?"

"Johnny," Michele answered for him, "He ate enough for two people."

"Good, I hate to see a growing boy go hungry."

It was after midnight when we finished cleaning up and bagging the trash to be ready to be hauled off tomorrow. We stacked all the chairs in rows to make it easier for the rental company to pick up. The girls were packing up the rest of the food to eat for leftovers. I told Samuel and Joseph to keep the rest of the beer and whiskey.

The only people who now remained was our group, and I asked Samuel and Joseph to quit working and join us. We sat around on the deck and talked about how happy Jessie was, and how thrilled she was with the party.

"It really was nice of Pat and his wife to lead the ambulance in his squad car with his lights flashing to the funeral home," David said.

"Yeah," I agreed, "Jessie would have liked that."

I began to tell stories of when Jessie used to wash and press my clothes, and then chew me out for wearing them in the fields to pick oranges.

"You used to pick oranges?" Karen asked.

"Yes, I picked a few."

"Yeah, he picked a few is right, Jessie used to make us throw a couple into his basket to make it look like he was picking as many as us," Joseph laughed, as he remembered the early years.

"Miss Jessie used to tell us his hands were made to play music, and not for climbing trees picking oranges," Samuel said grinning, and then added, "she said he'd probably fall out and break something, so she'd get Johnny to sing, and we'd fill his baskets."

Karen was laughing so hard at our stories, as well as everyone else. Then to add to the humor, Sandy piped up with more of her humor. "I'm glad you didn't fall down and break something."

"I'm glad I didn't break something too!"

Gary laughed so hard he fell backwards off his chair. Chance was going to help pick him up, but said he looked better that way than he did sitting upright.

Denise said, "I'll vouch for that."

Samuel asked, "Johnny remember the little green snake?"

"Oh brother, do I. It was one of those hot sultry days, the humidity was as high as the temperature, and I was soaking wet so I decided to take a break under one of the orange trees. As I sat down, I spotted a little, green grass snake crawling by, so I picked it up and put it in my pocket. Now Miss Jessie wasn't afraid of snakes; I've seen her kill several in the orchards, but she sure didn't like them. So I walked over to Jessie and pulled that green snake out of my pocket, and laid it in her lap."

"What did she do they all asked?"

"Let me tell it," Joseph said laughing. "Miss Jessie was mad as a hornet. She went and broke off a branch to use as a switch, and she chased Mr. Johnny, here, all the way down the road to the main highway, all the while cussing him out. Johnny was laughing so hard it only infuriated Miss Jessie all the more. Well, we all got to laughing at the sight of them and a few of us fell off our ladders, one of the girls broke her arm falling from the tree."

"Yeah, I remember that. Jessie made me fill her basket and mine until the cast came off."

"So Jessie was the overseer for the company?" Karen asked.

"Yes, Jessie worked there for forty-five years."

Doris had been sitting quietly listening and then said, "I remember when I was about six years old, my mother and father were working the fields that paid about five dollars a day and a place to stay. Back then it had dirt floors and holes in the walls and the roof leaked. Those were some hard times, that's why I left when I was sixteen and only came back a few times after that."

"What happened to your father?" Judie asked.

"Father," Doris said, shaking her head, "well my father had an eye for the women, and he ran off with one of the workers when I was about twelve years old. Mama changed then, she didn't laugh anymore and she had to work harder to put food on the table to make up the shortage of my father. The overseer, at that time, liked mama, and he let us stay in the house. Well father returned about a year later. I came home from school one day, and there he was sitting at the table just like he'd come back from the store. Now, father was a big man, and mama never said a word, but that night when he was asleep, she beat him with a two by four. He left after he got better, and we never heard from him again."

We all were laughing at the stories, and it felt good, as it lessened the sadness of Jessie leaving us. "You know," I said, "Jessie was the kind of woman who'd love you to death, but you didn't want to cross her, cause if you did, you'd wish you were dead."

"Sounds like she had a really hard life, David said.

"Yes she did, but no matter how hard she had it, she'd always go out of her way to help you, and I know one thing for sure," I said, "I'm really going to miss her. I'll bet right now she's looking down on us and saying, "Get off your ass and get on with it, because I'm where I want to be, with my Maker.""

"Amen to that," Doris said.

"When will they have her ashes back to you?" Lisa asked softly, as she hadn't spoken a word since she cried in my arms.

"It takes about a week," and then I explained to everyone what Jessie's wishes were. "I'm thinking of having a little head stone made and have it put down in my favorite fishing spot. Like a small memorial. She loved it here."

We were all yawning and everybody was trying to stay awake for my benefit. "Look, it's late, why don't we call it a night."

Without much protest, they got up to leave and said they see me in the morning. Karen asked if she could stay. I responded with a definite yes. I had hoped she would. She told Judie to take her car and drive back to the motel with the rest of the group. Kristi and Frank had left earlier as both needed to get back to work by Tuesday.

I was happy for Kristi and Denise. I just wished Sandy could find someone who would treat her nice, and love her for the sweet person she is.

Karen and I went to my trailer, and she asked if I wanted anything to drink. I told her no, but if she wanted a soda the refrigerator was full. She fixed us a glass of ice water as I walked into the bathroom to freshen up. While I was still in the bathroom, Karen got undressed and was already in bed under the sheets when I returned. I chuckled to myself at her bashfulness and then I undressed and crawled into bed and pulled the sheets over me.

"Let's just talk awhile," she suggested.

I agreed as I didn't want to sound too anxious, but all I really wanted to do was make love to her.

We talked about me going to Vegas, and the question of pretty women came up, but I brushed it off by asking her what she thought of the Christmas party for Jessie. She thought it was great, and she hoped that when she dies, someone cares enough to make her life a little more comfortable before she passes away. Vegas was brought up gain, and when I said I wanted to take her with me, she didn't answer. She had curled up next to me and had fallen asleep. I pulled her closer, and drifted to sleep, content with the feel of her body next to mine.

The next morning I awoke early. Karen was still sleeping. I went into the kitchen and made coffee and then took my shower. As I was getting dressed, Lisa knocked on the door. She had seen the light on in the kitchen and since Teresa was still sleeping, she thought she'd see if I was awake.

"What's the matter, Kitten, are you having a hard time sleeping?" I asked, looking at the dark circles under her eyes.

"I've been up most of the night worrying about mother. I guess with Jessie passing away, it got me to thinking of how much work I left for mother to handle in Memphis while I'm gone. I should really be there to help her with all the book work, especially after the Christmas Special. I packed my bag and I'll be leaving for the airport in a little while." It was a hard decision for her to make, she wanted to spend more time with me, but she knew she belonged at Graceland.

We talked about me stopping in Graceland before I left for Vegas. I told her I was going to Birmingham first to pick up my car, and then I'd stop in to see her. Then she asked how Karen and I were doing, and if I was taking her to Vegas with me. I told her no that she was not ready for that yet, even though I was.

"Give her time," Lisa sounded mature for her young age, "she just needs her space until she decides she's ready and she know what she wants."

"Yeah, maybe you're right."

"I thought I heard voices," Karen walked into the kitchen wrapped in my bathrobe. "Good morning, Lisa," and then asked if I was going to come back to bed.

"No," I'm going to the airport with Lisa. Why don't you go back to bed and I'll wake you when I return."

"Maybe," she replied, sounding disappointed.

"Whatever," I responded to her, and turned to Lisa. "Let's go before everyone returns for the day," and we left.

At the airport, Lisa said, "Daddy, I think you made Karen a little mad not going back to bed."

"I may have, but if she cares, she'll get over it. I'm not going to play games with her. I think she wants to get involved, but she's not ready to make a commitment. Kitten, I owe you a lot for these past several weeks and maybe one day I can repay you for all that you've done."

Holding me tight, she said, "Daddy, you don't owe me anything, I've had the best time of my life just being with you. Thank you so much for coming back into my life."

"Lisa these past weeks I'll treasure always." I had a hard time letting go, and finally I said, "You need to go now, have a safe flight, and I'll see you at Graceland." I stood and waved to her as she waved back at me from the window until the plane was out of sight.

I instructed the limo driver to take me to the funeral home to pick out an urn for Jessie's ashes. The director was very helpful as this was so difficult for me to do. I chose a white marble box that was embossed with red roses on the lid.

Across the road from the funeral parlor was a small company that engraved headstones. I ordered a rectangular, flat, gray granite headstone with the words, "In Loving Memory, Jessie Mae. May The Fish Be Plentiful In Heaven."

With that accomplished, I went back to the cabin, and on the way, I told the limo driver I wouldn't be needing his services any longer. I handed him a one hundred dollar tip and told him I'd call on him the next time I was in town. He thanked me and said he enjoyed the party, and said it was a pleasure driving us around and looked forward to my return.

318

Instead of going to the trailer, I went into the house. I was surprised the rental people were through taking down the tents and loading everything onto their trucks. David, Chance and their wives, and Sandy, Judie, Gary and Denise, as well as Bob and Doris had all arrived.

I asked Doris to come into Jessie's old bedroom. Betty had returned Jessie's green dress, shoes and jewelry while I was gone, and laid them on the bed. I told Doris to take whatever she wanted.

I chose a few pictures of Jessie with Lisa and myself, and some old ones of us all working together in the orange groves. I told her whatever she didn't want we'd leave and let Teresa distribute things to the needy. I then told her I was going to change the will stating that if something happened to me, the cabin was to be left to Samuel, Joseph and to her with the stipulation that it was never to be sold as I wanted it to be handed down from generation to generation.

"Johnny, it's hard to believe she's gone."

"I know, but I still feel her presence."

"Me too," she smiled, and all of a sudden said, "Oh my gosh." Placing her hand on her abdomen, she smiled, "I just felt my first flutter."

We both looked at Jessie's picture sitting on the dresser and smiled. No longer feeling sad, I left Doris to finish her packing and joined the others in the kitchen.

"Johnny, we've been talking, and all of us want to discuss what your plans are as we'd like to get on the road," David said. "We need to decide who is riding with whom, and who's going where."

"Michele and I need to get back to Dallas before Wednesday, and we're all packed and ready to go," Chance commented.

"Me too," Gary said, "I've got all my equipment packed and ready to load into the u-haul trailer when it arrives. Joseph went to pick it up. With Lisa gone, I didn't know exactly what to do about getting my equipment back to Dallas so I rented a trailer, and Chance said he could haul it behind his car."

"I agree with all of you, I really don't need to stay here, there's nothing left for me to do. I ordered Jessie's headstone and urn this morning, and Samuel and Joseph can bring them here."

"Chance, can you take Gary and Denise back with you as long as you're hauling his trailer?"

"No problem, big guy."

"Hey, what about me? Am I supposed to walk home?" Sandy asked.

"I'm sorry, honey, I just have a lot on my mind, and I'm just trying to make sure everyone gets home. Chance, can you squeeze Sandy in with all of you, since you're all going to the same place?"

"We'll make room, even if we have to put Gary in with his equipment," he agreed.

"David, can you and Tara follow me in Karen's car as I need to go to Birmingham to pick up my new car. It's ready. I think that takes care of everybody. Is everyone all packed and ready to go?"

"Yeah, we're all ready, we're just waiting on you," David said.

"Judie," Karen asked, "Did you bring all my things?"

"Yes, I packed your bags, and put our luggage in the trunk."

"Karen I'll meet you out front, give me a few minutes to get my things packed, and say my farewells."

Joseph returned with Gary's trailer. They packed Gary's equipment while I finished mine. It didn't take me long, so I called Carolyn and thanked her for coming to the party, and told her I was leaving early, but I'd keep in touch. I called the home care office and told them what a remarkable job the nurses had done taking care of Jessie Mae. I hugged Samuel and Joseph's neck and kissed Teresa on the forehead. I thanked them for everything and told them if they needed me to call Carolyn.

"Teresa, as soon as I get to Vegas I'm going to buy a cell phone, and I'll call you with that number."

Chance, Michele, Gary, Denise and Sandy had just left and David and Tara were in their car waiting when I walked to where Karen's car was parked.

"You're mad at me aren't you?" Karen asked.

"No," I answered, "disappointed maybe, but not mad."

"Well, I really did want you to come back to bed. I had decided to make love this morning, but you were too busy for me, I guess."

I laughed. "No, not too busy, I'm just not sure what it is you want me to do, and when I should do it."

"I'm sorry Johnny, I'm afraid I'll make a commitment and it won't be the right thing for me, at least at this time. I've explained to you before, I have my dress shop. I've had to work hard to get my business established to where it is today. I hope you understand. I'm just not ready to give up that part of my life."

"I do understand," I agreed. "I'm not ready for you to give up your life style just for me, but I need to know that when the time is right, you'll be there."

She thought for a moment, grinned impishly, and replied, "When you give up your life style, *and* you are ready to retire from the entertainment field, *and* young women, *and* ready to settle down, then I'll be ready, but not until then."

"That's what I needed to hear. This way we can take our time and not be pressured into decisions we'll both regret later."

"Hey you two, are you going to stand around and yak all day? We really need to get going," David and Tara said, laughing.

I put my things in Karen's car. "Are you driving or am I?"

"You!" and she handed me her keys.

CHAPTER 23

We took our time getting to Birmingham. It started to rain and everything looked drab and dismal. Karen, Judie and I followed David and Tara. To break up the monotony of driving, we sang songs. We picked out a few from our high school years, and since we couldn't remember all the words, we started to make up our own, which put us all in good humor.

Karen drove me to David and Tara's and dropped me off there as she still had to take Judie home. I told her I would see her tomorrow at her shop, after I picked up my new car. I kissed her longingly and she drove off.

David, Tara and I sat around conversing for a few hours. Tara decided to take down her Christmas tree. As she was putting away the ornaments, she asked, "Johnny is it going to work out between you and Karen? She seemed a little angry in Florida, if you don't mind me asking."

"Well, let's put it this way, neither of us got our way last night, or this morning.

David shook his head and said, "You mean you slept together and nothing went on?"

"Yes, David, that's exactly what I'm saying."

"Hell," he said, "I'd forget her."

"No, it'll happen when the time is right, and if it doesn't, life will go on, but

I'm trying to make it happen."

"Don't give up, Johnny, I like her and I think you two can make it, just take your time." Tara replied.

Both David and Tara were yawning and trying so hard to stay awake for my sake so I told them both to go to bed and that I'd see them in the morning. I went back to my bedroom, laid across the bed thinking of Karen and fell asleep.

Tara cooked breakfast for us. There's nothing better in the morning to make your mouth water than the smell of coffee perking and bacon frying. I kissed Tara good morning, and sat at the table with David. I told her when she got tired of David to let me know, I was available.

"Someone's going to tie you down one of these days," David laughed, "but I'm going to keep mine, I've got her trained right."

"Johnny, it may be soon if someone keeps talking smart like that," she threatened David with the spatula, waving it in his direction.

"David, when are you closing on your bar?"

"Tomorrow." He then asked Tara, "What time anyway?"

"Nine o'clock at the bank so we need to be up early."

"Can one of you run me over to the car dealership today?"

"I can," David volunteered. "But first, why don't you call and make sure everything is ready?"

I called Zeke, and he was in. He confirmed that the car was now waiting on me to be picked up so I said I'd see him in about an hour, and to make sure he had all the paper work prepared so all I had to do was dot my I's and cross my T's.

We ate a leisurely breakfast and chatted non-stop about the Christmas Special and Jessie Mae's party. I patted my stomach, as I'd had enough. I glanced at my watch anxious to get going.

"Hey, slow down big guy," David said, and then added, "it'll all come together."

I grinned at his paraphrase, "Quit stealing my lines."

"Well, I imitate almost everything else you say; I may as well steal that line too!"

"Wow!" David exclaimed when we pulled into the car lot. He spotted the car parked on the show room floor. "Johnny, he's added chrome wheels and exhaust pipes."

I raised the hood and looked at the engine. "David, come here and see this, that's not all he's done, he's added chrome valve covers, and a chrome air filter cover."

The engine glistened under the bright florescent lights. Zeke came and stood next to us, grinning like a possum. "Like her? I thought it gave her a little more class. Come on, papers are over here and ready for your signature." He went over a couple of things with me, insurance, etc. Carolyn had already transferred the funds so within a few minutes, I was handed my keys.

David left to go home. I told him I'd see him back at the house after I visited with Karen. It was only a twenty minute drive to her shop. I found her busy in the back room sewing. She didn't hear me come in. I snuck up behind her and grabbed her around the waist. She screamed from fright at first, and then laughed when she discovered it was me.

"Gee, you sure do spook easy," I grinned.

"You scared me half to death," she scolded and then grinned. "I didn't expect you till later."

"I thought I'd like to take a pretty little lady to lunch, but if you're too busy," I teased, waving my arms at all the material she had around her.

"I'm starving, but I don't know how I can be with all I ate this week-end. Let me quick freshen up and I'll be ready."

We walked to a local restaurant near her shop. On the way, I apologized for the fact that we didn't make love while she was in Florida.

"Well, you aren't gone yet, maybe later," she said, her eyes looked directly into mine.

"Mmmm, I'd like that very much." We continued our walk; she smiled contentedly, and placed her hand in mine.

At the restaurant, a number of people recognized me and wanted autographs. We were seated in a corner booth and the waitress brought us two sweet teas. Winking, she asked Karen, "Is this the one?"

Embarrassed at the direct question, Karen nodded yes.

The waitress wanted my autograph, and after writing her a short note, I asked Karen, "What did the waitress mean when she asked if I was the one?"

Answering slowly, she stated, "Well, everyone saw you on television and I told my friends I was there with you, that's all."

"Oh," I teased, "Did you also tell them you slept with me."

"No! I didn't!" And then thinking for a second, replied, "But I'm going too!"

I smiled at her teasing, "Well you better not tell them everything or we both might be embarrassed."

"Hey, I'm not crazy; I'm going to tell them you were great in bed."

I enjoyed the easy banter between us.

While we were eating, two other waitresses came to our table and asked for my autograph. One of them told Karen when she was finished with me, she wanted me.

"Okay," Karen laughed.

"Damn," I said, "I feel like a piece of meat ready to be passed around."

"Oh no, in this town you're mine and I don't share. Elsewhere is your business, but not here," she teased.

Without any more interruptions, we finished our lunch, but neither of us ate very much, as both of our thoughts drifted to the possibility of what was to come.

"Johnny, is that your new Cadillac?" She asked on the way back to her shop.

"Yeah, I was wondering if you were going to notice it."

"I guess when we left my shop, I had my eyes on someone instead of something," she laughed softly. "Gee, she really is a beauty with all the chrome trim," she commented. "I'm so happy for you. After this past week, it's nice to see you smile again."

It was a quiet afternoon in Karen's shop. She placed the 'Out For Lunch' sign in the window, locked the door behind us, and said, "Follow me."

In her sewing room was a day bed that she used when she stayed late to finish a rush order. She turned, looked at me and without saying a word, slowly removed her clothes. Standing naked before me, she did a slow pirouette. Age had intensified her beauty. Her breasts and butt were still firm, her long legs still shapely. Her hair hung loosely around her slender shoulders, but it didn't hide the rapid pulse beat in the base of her neck.

Following her lead, I quickly removed my clothing. Shyly she came and wrapped her arms around me. I pulled her close and buried my face in the sweet scent of her hair. I kissed her passionately and gently laid her on the daybed. Passion consumed us both. As we made love, it was as if we'd been waiting a lifetime for each other. She cried out as she reached the top of her peak, and I moaned loudly, as I reached mine. I realized then for all the preaching I did with Sandy, Kristi, and Denise what it meant to have a meaningful relationship.

I lay next to her, cuddling her in my arms, not able to move. I was so relaxed; I didn't want to get up. I just wanted to stay there forever. Unfortunately, the daybed was too small to be comfortable for very long. Laughing at our scrunched position, I regrettably got up pulling her with me. Neither of us spoke as we held each other tight. Gently she pulled away saying she needed to re-open her shop and reaching for our clothes, we quickly dressed. I told her I was very glad we had the opportunity to make love before I left for Vegas. It gave me something to look forward to and something to build on.

"I know what you expect of me, Johnny, my feelings for you are very strong, but I'm just not ready to give up what I have and follow your dreams. I still have my own. But, like you, I want to retire someday and settle down with someone I truly love for the rest of my life. What we have right now is special, and if it's meant to be, we'll find a way to make it happen, just not now."

"You're right, Karen, I find in you what I once lost by my negligence. When I'm settled in Vegas, I'll call you and let you know how to reach me." This time she reached for me and kissed me long and hard. "Keep that up and we'll have to take another trip to that back room." Giggling at the memory of her passion, she kissed me again, and I left.

Judie saw me leaving Karen's shop. She yelled for me to come and get my hair cut and meet some of her friends. Excited at seeing me, her customers asked for autographs and told me how they enjoyed the Christmas Special. They all believed I was the real Elvis. "You just never know," I teased the ladies.

While Judie cut my hair, I had to sing a song for her clients as they all stood around me. The smell of perm solution filled the air. I laughed at my audience. Color ran down the face of one. Aluminum foil wrapped in sections, stuck out like a sputnik on another. Women under dryers shut them off so they could hear. A manicurist smeared nail polish on her customer. But in spite of it all, a better audience I couldn't have asked for. Judie finished and I left. Little old ladies lined the windows waving as I got in my car and drove away.

Back at David's, I found Tara trimming rose bushes. I asked her if it wasn't a little to cold to trim flowers.

"No," she informed me, "this is the season to trim roses for spring, and why I'm doing it, I don't know. I won't be here to see them bloom."

"Are you happy following David around? Now tell me the truth."

"Yes, I'm so happy just being with him, and I can't tell you how happy you've made us both. Johnny, sharing your life with us has been a great experience and a dream come true. I'm happy to be David's wife."

"You're quite a remarkable woman, and David is one of the luckiest men in the world."

David came out to join us. "Yes, and I know it too, so don't you go worrying about me letting things get out of hand."

"If they do, I'll kick your ass all the way back to Alabama, and that's a promise."

He laughed. "I hope you never have to."

I loaded my car, this time it took several trips, as my wardrobe had increased. I was to meet Gary on the road and told David I'd call and let them know when I arrived in Vegas. After kissing Tara good-bye and hugging David, I once again was on the road.

CHAPTER 24

I drove until I reached Mississippi and decided to take a break. I called Gary and he and Denise were packing clothes. Gary was having a hard time trying to figure out where he was going to put everything. He said Denise was bringing every outfit she owned, and the car was already packed full, and she still had a half a closet to go. He laughed at the look of frustration on Denise's face as she started to unpack to repack.

"I'm in Mississippi," I informed him, "I'll meet you in a day or two at the Casino on Highway 40 in New Mexico. I'll be staying at their motel. I've already booked two rooms for us."

I wanted to be in Vegas by the week-end, but I decided to take my time driving, as I had never traveled through the western states alone, and I wanted to take in some of the sights. I figured this would be a great experience to remember, so I figured I'd make the best of it.

Within a few hours, I arrived at Graceland and found Priscilla with Lisa Marie buried in paperwork, and with a full schedule of meetings. Rather than stay over night and distract them from their duties, I decided to take them both out to eat.

Lisa said she missed me, especially the excitement. Priscilla was happy to see me again, but was anxious to get back to work. They both wanted to finish early, as they each had plans for the evening with friends.

We ate a quiet, peaceful meal. Several people recognized Lisa and Priscilla, and stared openly at me whispering among themselves, but left us alone. I was grateful for that. I wanted a few minutes to chat with them privately without being disturbed, as I didn't know when I'd see them again. I told Lisa I'd call her as soon as I was settled.

The meal ended all too quickly. The limo driver brought us back to Graceland. Priscilla hugged and kissed me good-bye, and wished me the best. She whispered to me that she still loved me and then walked away, leaving me a few minutes alone with Lisa.

I took her by the hand and we strolled around Graceland. Everything was back to normal. Tourists were staring and some were trying to approach us, but Lisa signaled for security, and they were blocked from getting any closer.

"Kitten, this is very difficult for me. I have so many mixed emotions flowing through me. I miss this place more than you'll ever know. It's hard to explain. I was king here at one time. It's hard for me to be here and not claim all this as mine, yet wanting it, but on the other hand, I could never go back to living in a prison again. Tourists are traipsing around freely, and I have to schedule a time for a tour." I shook my head at my own confusion.

"Daddy," she said softly, "I never gave all that a thought; I never realized you felt this way."

"That's all right," I answered. "Listen, I need to hit the road and you need to get back to work."

"I love you so much daddy."

"I love you very much too, Kitten. Tell Joe, I'm sorry he was out of town, and I didn't get to see him, but tell him I'll call him when I'm in Vegas. Tell George I'm sorry I missed him on his day off."

"I will, call me when you get to Vegas," she hollered, as I drove through the gates of Graceland, wondering if this would be my last time.

I reached Fort Smith, Arkansas, and stopped for dinner and fuel. From there I drove to Oklahoma City, and drove around for awhile. I found the Civic Center where I had once performed and the hotel where the guys and I had water balloon fights. When that had become boring, we had ordered a tub of Jell-O and pudding to be brought in. Whew, you want to talk about a sticky mess. I thought it was funny at the time, but now it's embarrassing to think we did all that.

I was enjoying everyone looking at my car, and giving me the thumbs up sign. I felt good to show off and drive freely on the main street. Figuring I had wasted enough time, I drove back to Highway 40, and continued heading west.

I stopped at a motel in Amarillo, Texas, to get a few hours of sleep. It was mid-morning when I awoke. I found the motel's restaurant. It actually felt good that no one knew who I was, and no autographs to sign. I finished my Mexican breakfast, and did a little sight-seeing in a few old western shops and tourist traps. Seeing what I wanted to see, I continued on my journey west.

From Amarillo, I drove until I reached the "Lucky Star Casino," in New Mexico. Once I was checked in at their hotel, I called Gary. He told me he was on the outskirts of Amarillo. I gave him the phone number of the hotel and my room number in case he needed me. He said he'd see me some time tonight or tomorrow. "Did you get everything packed?" I inquired.

"For the most part," he chuckled. "Denise had to leave half her clothes and she had a fit, but I told her we were packed so full that if she put in one more outfit, I'd strap her to the front of the car and use her as a hood ornament. She thought I was kidding until I brought out tape and a rope."

I laughed as I pictured his car with barely enough room to sit. Knowing Denise, she brought enough clothes to last six months without having to wear an outfit more than one time.

At the Casino, I thought I'd try my luck at cards. I played for a couple of hours, and was ahead by two hundred dollars. I quit the game to play the slots, and settled on a "Five Times, Wheel of Fortune" machine. I played with the money I had won at the card table. I had close to one hundred and fifty dollars in the machine when it hit a double, double red seven. The payoff was eight hundred and fifty dollars. Lights started flashing and bells started ringing.

The attendant that came to give me my payoff, looked at me strangely, and then asked, "I don't mean to be nosey, but are you Johnny Raye, the Elvis Impersonator that was on television?"

"Yes," I responded softly, "but do me a favor and keep your voice down, okay?"

"Sure," she whispered, "but can I have your autograph?" I signed her note pad, collected my money, and then went back to the card game.

While I was waiting for a spot to open at a table, the floor manager approached me and asked how long I planned on staying at the hotel. I told him a day or two depending on how much money I lost and wanted to know why.

Sitting next to me he asked if I'd be interested in doing a show for them. Quickly explaining that the attendant told him who I was, he stated that the Casino was interested in me performing for them either Saturday or Sunday night or possibly both.

I countered back by telling him it all depended on how much the casino was willing to pay. I decided to play cat and mouse, and this time I definitely decided to be the cat.

Rising from his stool, he said, "Let's go talk somewhere privately, shall we?"

"I'll follow your lead."

He escorted me to a room where two gentlemen were already waiting. I raised my eyebrow in question, but didn't speak until I was introduced. One of the gentlemen was the manager for entertainment, and the other was a heavy investor/owner. I remained quiet.

"May I call you Johnny?" the entertainment manager spoke.

Nodding, I shook his hand. He introduced himself as Tom and the other as Gene.

"Would you be interested in doing two shows for us, two on Saturday and two Sunday night?"

"Mmmm! I'm willing to do two shows, but that's four show's you're asking for. I guess it depends on how much you're willing to pay."

"That depends on what your asking price is!"

I leaned forward in my chair and said, "Let me be up front with you. This isn't Vegas, but I know this Casino does real well. But, I'll let you off easy. This is what I want, two hotel suites, one for me and one for my assistant for three nights, and three thousand dollars for each show. That's twelve thousand for both nights."

Relief showed in their eyes. Tom drew up a contract, and all we had to do was fill in the blanks. We shook hands and Tom said he would get with me first thing in the morning. The other man named Gene never spoke, he stared at me all the while we negotiated and only nodded his head as I left.

I stood outside the door for a moment and heard Gene say to Tom, "I never forget a face, and I saw Elvis live in concert in Hawaii. He walked right past me within five feet of where I was standing. If this man isn't Elvis, it's his double."

Oh, oh, guess I need to be careful of this one. No matter, I thought as I walked away, he'd have a hard time proving it. I went back to the tables to see if a spot had opened up. On the way I found Gary and Denise, or they found me.

"Hey big guy, leave any money in the machines for us to win?" he laughed.

"I can do one better than that," I grinned.

"Oh! Oh!" Sounds like you have something up your sleeve for my guy," Denise smiled.

I told them first about my winnings, and then about the shows.

"By the looks of how much business this place gets, it should be a good audience. And we need to meet with Tom, in the morning. He's the entertainment manager for the Casino."

Gary nodded in understanding. He and Denise wanted to play the slots and I headed to the tables once again. I played poker for several hours and ended up breaking a little ahead of even.

Tired, I called it a night and went to the front desk to find out which room I had been reassigned. The reservation desk clerk informed me that my things had been moved to suite 406, and that Gary had the adjoining suite in room 408. I thanked her, took my key and went in search of my room.

The following morning, Gary and I met with Tom. Tom presented us with a schedule, and explained how they advertised.

"How did you advertise so quickly?" I asked.

"That's easy. This casino owns their own radio station, and we started advertising already last night. You'll be performing in the concert hall on the second floor."

"Concert hall?"

"Yes. It will cost patrons thirty-five dollars a person if they want to see you perform live, but first let's discuss the rest of the items on the agenda.

"I think we've been had," Gary was amused at my expression. "What's the matter big guy?" he asked, grinning his usual grin.

"I thought I was the cat chasing the mouse. Instead, I just discovered I was the mouse eating the cheese, and the cat swallowed me cheese and all. Well, they got me this time. It was a good learning experience, but I bet it won't happen again."

The shows went extremely well. The concert hall was filled both nights. The front marquee flashed, "Saturday and Sunday night only, live and in person, the number one Elvis Impersonator, Johnny Raye." Disappointed people had to be turned away due to over capacity. I received standing ovations for each show, and did numerous encores. Gary and I talked about the money, and to make us feel better, we passed our earnings off as chump money while we were passing through on our way to bigger things.

Monday morning the manager came to my room to pay us, and said, "We decided to give you a little extra."

"Good, I didn't know you wanted us in concert, I thought you wanted us to do a show on the casino stage."

"You never asked, and we never said. Anyway, we would like to hire you again in the future so we decided to be fair with you. How about forty percent of the door?"

"That would be good from the number of people I saw in the audience, but normally, we get seventy five percent of the take at concerts."

"I can't go that high. Can we round that out and make it sixty percent? How about twenty-four thousand? This is not a large casino, but the crowd was double what we expected and all machines and tables were filled with people lined up waiting to play. Our profits in the last two nights brought in more than the last two week-ends put together. Thanks, Johnny, the next time you're going to be in our area, let us know ahead of time, we'd love to have you back here again," he said, counting out twenty-four, one thousand dollar bills that his security man handed him.

"You're welcome, and I will," I replied as I shook his hand.

I called Gary as soon as they left. He brought Denise with him. "We got paid, but there's been a slight change," I said, trying to be serious.

"Don't tell me they don't want to pay us after the crowd you drew. How much did we end up with?"

"Only twenty-four thousand dollars." I had to force myself not to smile.

"That's totally ridiculous, we. . . . What did you say?"

Not able to contain myself any longer, I repeated the amount, and told him what Tom said.

"Hot damn, the pot grows sweeter all the time," he sat shaking his head.

"You know we need to set payment amounts and if casino's can pay, we'll play, if they can't meet our demands, then we won't." I stated.

"If you make it a flat twenty-five thousand per show at the casinos, and seventy five percent of the take on concerts, you'll come out okay," Denise did some figuring.

"Hey, good business head on this girl."

"Yeah," Gary agreed, "she could be our business manager."

"That's a good idea. We need someone we can trust. Alright, let's set up our income percentage now. How much for our new business manager?" I directed the question to Denise.

"I'll want, oh let's see, ten percent."

"Okay Gary, what about you?"

"I'll take thirty percent, leaving you sixty."

"Sounds like a deal I can live with. Are we all in agreement?"

"Yes," they both answered simultaneously.

"Be right back." I took some of the money and went to a window cashier and asked for hundred dollar bills. Going back to my room, I gave Gary and Denise their share, leaving me with a balance of fourteen thousand, four hundred dollars. I then went to one of the business financers in the casino, and had them wire ten thousand to my account in Florida. The balance and what I already had on me to start with, left me with enough money to survive on for quite a while, in case we didn't find work right away.

We left the casino together and hit the road. We drove all day and part of the night, stopping in Kingman, Arizona. I didn't want to get to Vegas until the following morning. We stayed at a motel to get a good night's rest and met for breakfast around ten o'clock. We had just finished eating when an RV coach parked outside caught my attention. It was an Eagle model, top of the line. I went to look at the exterior when the owner saw me admiring his RV, and offered to show me the inside.

The sitting area had two tan leather chairs with a matching sofa. The end tables were solid oak, hardwood, tile, and carpeted flooring of the finest quality throughout. A large screen television with surround sound was encased in solid oak cabinets, as well as the kitchen with a bar that separated the kitchen from the sitting area for four. The bedroom had a king size bed with storage underneath and a desk area for a computer. One wall was all closet, and above the bed were built in cabinets. The bath was solid tile with porcelain fixtures. The shower was enclosed in etched glass trimmed in polished brass.

We chatted for awhile, and then he said, "You look so familiar. Pardon me for asking, but are you the Elvis Impersonator, that did the Christmas Special at Graceland?"

"Yes sir," I replied, "I am."

"Well then you definitely need one of these little beauties to travel around in for your concerts. Here's a card with the salesman's name on the back from the dealership in Tennessee where I purchased this one. Talk to Doug, he's a personal friend of mine, and he'll take good care of you."

Gary and Denise were waiting for me, and asked if I was going to purchase 'us' a coach.

"No, I'm going to buy one for myself; you can get your own."

Denise laughed. "Gary doesn't realize he's rich now, it still hasn't set in."

"Well, 'darlin' he definitely needs someone like you to remind him."

"Yes I do!" Gary gave Denise a big hug.

CHAPTER 25

Tired, we arrived in Vegas and found the Silver Dollar Hotel and Casino. We checked into our rooms and then later we met in my room. I told Gary I didn't want to say anything to Gus, the general manager, of the casino, just yet. I wanted to check things out around town.

"Who knows? Maybe Denise can find us a better deal, and remember Denise, we're a pair, I work with Gary only."

"That's the only way," she smiled.

"Okay, you two, get busy on your end and check out the casino's in this area. I've thought this over Gary, and I'm going to call a realtor about finding us a house while you're our scouting casinos."

I called a local real estate agency and within an hour a realtor was calling me from the lobby of the hotel. She asked me to meet her in the bar. A gorgeous looking girl was sitting on a bar stool sipping a diet drink. Her shiny blonde hair hung long and straight down her back, just reaching the top of her cute little butt. She was wearing a light tan suit and when she turned around to face me, she exposed a pair of shapely long legs. I asked her if her name was Beth from the real estate office. She told me she wasn't, but she wished she was, as she got up and sauntered seductively from the bar. The scenery in Vegas seemed to get better all the time.

I then felt a light tap on my arm. Turning around was a short, brown-haired girl about five feet-four inches tall and probably weighed no more than one hundred and fifteen pounds.

"I'm sorry," I apologized, "your agency said you were blonde and tall."

She laughed, "That's the other Beth. She was already booked this afternoon so I came instead. Is that okay with you?" She sounded a little insecure.

To ease her doubts, I replied, "That's fine with me, I'm looking for a house, not a wife."

"I left my briefcase over there in that booth. Let's sit there where it's quiet, and I can show you printouts of some of the houses on the market, and the necessary paperwork to get you contracted with our agency."

When I had called her office earlier, they had asked me questions up front, which helped Beth select the houses to meet my needs and interests.

"You said your name is Johnny Raye?" she inquired, beginning her portfolio on me. "Occupation?" she was all business.

"Entertainer!"

"My office said you were looking for a very large house, is that correct?"

"Mm, hmm!"

Flashing me a pleasant smile, "I take it that was a yes?"

"Yes, I want something in the eight to ten bedroom range, all with their own private baths. It has to have a very large kitchen, a large family area and a large great room. A swimming pool is a must, and it needs to have tropical landscaping. A waterfall would be nice. I want it to look like Elvis Presley lives there or some rich or famous celebrity does. You get the picture."

"Wow," she exclaimed writing furiously. "My office told me that you were hoping to find something outside of town."

"Well I do want some place out of town, about thirty acres would do! I'd like to purchase a few horses, and a barn would be great, but if it doesn't have one, I'll have one built.

"Yes sir," she finally quit writing.

"I know this isn't going to come cheap, but I'd really like to keep the price down as low as possible."

"What exact price range are we looking at?"

"Tell you what. You find the right house with these qualifications, and I'll tell you what I want to offer."

"I have a few printouts, but I now know that they will not be what you are looking for, and I won't waste your time showing them to you." I signed an agency agreement locking me in with her real estate agency, along with numerous forms and disclosures. "Will you be staying here at this hotel, for me to reach you?"

"Yes, just leave me a message at the front desk."

"Sure thing, Mr. Raye, I'll call you later today," she offered me her hand.

I hung around my room, watched the news to see what was happening, and around five o'clock the phone rang. It was Beth, the realtor, but her voice sounded different. She was downstairs, and she wanted me to meet her in the bar. I walked in, looked around, but didn't see her. I sat and waited, thinking she may have stepped out for a minute.

After several minutes passed, a very attractive woman approached me. "Are you Mr. Raye?

"Yes, I am," I smiled at the gorgeous, blonde. "Are you Beth?"

"Yes, then glanced at her watch as if she was in a hurry to go somewhere. "May I call you Johnny?" But I noticed as she spoke to me her eyes were looking around the room and her attention was definitely not on me.

"No, you may not, and you can call and tell your office that I want to see the other Beth or I will do business elsewhere," and I got up and left.

About a half hour later, the other Beth called and said she was surprised I asked for her after seeing the other realtor.

"Why, do looks make her a better agent?"

"No, Mr. Raye, they sure don't, but all the big deals go to her."

"Well it looks to me like that needs to be changed. You struck me as a person who is efficient and very organized. I like that in a person."

I asked her to meet with me around eight thirty in the morning, in my room. She responded right away that she'd be there at eight-thirty sharp. I knew I was dealing with a new agent in the real estate business after what had just transpired, but she was energetic and really cute in a pixie sort of way. This might be the way to build up her confidence. I thought back on Kristi and how she changed her way of thinking after I met her.

I called Gary's room and he and Denise had just come in. We met in the dining room twenty minutes later so as to give them time to freshen up. I had changed into my dark blue pants with a light blue shirt, and my white sports coat. The hostess escorted us to a table, and it wasn't even ten minutes later when Gus approached our table and instructed the waitress to give us anything we wanted 'on the house'.

"It's good to finally meet you, Johnny, and how have you been Gary?" he asked, shaking our hands.

"Good," Gary responded casually, and how's business?"

"Very good, and I'm looking to increase business now that you're here," Gus glanced in my direction.

Gary introduced Denise as our business manager.

"She handles all our negotiations for us," I said, winking at Denise.

"Well I'd rather deal directly with you, Johnny."

"Sorry, Gus, I have a contract with Denise for the next five years, you know how it is."

"Sure Johnny," he sounded a little disappointed. But being the business man he was, he turned to Denise and asked, "So little lady, when can I talk to you?"

"Not to be taken lightly, Denise said very businesslike, "Tomorrow morning will be fine with me, let's say around nine o'clock, over breakfast, here in the dining room!"

"Nine o'clock it is! Enjoy your meal." Excusing himself, he left to handle other matters.

"Johnny," Denise was all business, "I've talked with two casino managers today, and they want you to do a couple of concerts then play their casino's three nights a week, and they are willing to meet our demands."

"Great, while we're eating, you can tell me the details," and then added, "we may need to ask Gus for more."

"Well, I'll tell him what we've been offered by the other two casinos, and ask if he can do better."

"Denise, when we're done here, do you think you could go with me and help me pick out a dress for someone?"

"Johnny, you've only been in town a few hours and already your planning to transform someone. Who is she?" Denise laughed.

"The real estate lady. She's down on herself, low esteem."

"Like Kristi?"

"You might say that."

The casino's hotel had several novelty shops, as well as women's and men's clothing shops to choose from. We found one that carried a petite section. I spotted a gray sleeveless, knee-length dress with a matching jacket that could be used for business attire or a night on the town without the jacket.

The sales clerk was very helpful as she was almost the same size as Beth. "How about matching underwear?" the sales clerk was working her sales pitch.

"That sounds good, Denise, can you help with that?" I then found a light blue pants outfit that was form fitting that would be flattering to her little figure. I picked out a silver pair of earrings and a necklace to match. I paid for the purchases and turned to find Denise and Gary. I found Gary sitting in a chair with his arms crossed. "Where's Denise?"

"In trying on some new clothes. She said if she's going to be a business manager, she may as well look like an expensive business manager."

"That's right," Denise said, laughing as she joined us.

"She doesn't need clothes to make her look sexy," Gary grinned, "she's sexy no matter what."

"He loves it baby, and so do I. You just buy whatever you want, honey, you're making your own money now."

"That's right. I like looking sexy and I like new clothes. Besides, I have plenty more in my bank account in Dallas. Daddy always adds to it every month. He makes sure his little girl is well taken care of. She grinned, knowing she was spoiled and always had been, but her parents raised her to appreciate a dollar. Denise never flaunted her wealth to anyone; she was a good and kind hearted woman, and never thought of herself as being any better than anyone else. In fact, she loathed snobs. Most of her friends were not from affluent families.

We brought our purchases to our rooms, and I told them I wanted to play cards with my winnings from New Mexico.

"How much did you win?" Denise asked.

"Oh, about a thousand dollars."

"Well I lost about two grand, but that's okay." she laughed. "It was Gary's money I was playing with."

I managed to find an opening at a table for eight, playing Texas Holdum. After a few hours I was up about thirty thousand dollars. I had bluffed a few hands, but for the most part, I was lucky drawing winning hands. It felt good winning, as I was playing against several professional gamblers. One gentleman said he'd been playing cards all his life. When he was young, he had only worked for a few years. Disgruntled at not being able to get ahead, he started playing cards at a local bar, and decided to make a career of gambling. His wife held a management position with a well known firm and he earned his own money at the tables.

Because I was doing so well, one of the other players asked if I was wearing a four leaf clover around my neck. "No," I responded politely, "I think the gods are smiling down on me tonight, and before I lose what I've won, I think I'll call it a night. Gentlemen, it's been a pleasure." I cashed out my chips and was surprised that they totaled out to forty-six thousand. Not bad, considering I started with five thousand.

It was after one o'clock in the morning and on my way back to my room, I found Gary and Denise playing the slot machines. Denise was winning and Gary wanted to try his hand at Black Jack for awhile. I was tired and said I'd see them later in the morning.

"Let me know how your meeting with Gus goes," and wished them both luck. I didn't need the money I had just won. So I stopped at the cashier station and had a manager wire forty thousand of my winnings to my bank account. I enjoyed being in control of my own money, and being wiser with finances. I really enjoyed watching my nest egg grow.

Even though I still had a flair for spending, I knew how to make money and how much to spend. I had talked to Carolyn the other day and the interest on my earnings from the Christmas Special was accumulating quite nicely. Considering what I would be making this next year, I knew I could retire and live very comfortably. This style of living is great if you're young, but at my age, it was very tiring, and retirement sounded better everyday. I thought about Karen, and as I undressed and crawled into bed the last thing I remembered was her smiling face, as I drifted into a peaceful sleep.

I woke to the sound of my phone ringing. It was Beth. I told her to come on up. I quickly called the front desk and asked them to send a hair dresser to my room. Still in my bathrobe, I answered the door. Beth was wearing a green flowered blouse and green slacks, which would be fine for casual, but not when you are selling million dollar real estate. Her short hair was cut cute, but needed to be styled.

"Come in," I offered politely.

Leading her by the hand, she halted part way into the room. "Mr. Raye," she hesitated, and looking at my appearance said, "I don't make it a practice to sleep with my clients."

Looking at the distress on her face, I burst out laughing. "I'm sorry for my appearance, but I'm not out to seduce you. Just relax. I have a surprise for you. I have a hairdresser on the way up here now. I felt that if you're going to sell million dollar houses, like the other Beth, you may as well look the part."

Embarrassed by what she thought, she said, "I'm sorry, please forgive my accusation. I can't afford a hair dresser right now. This place is a little out of my league."

"Not anymore, I'm taking care of this."

A knock at the door ended any further discussion. It was the hair dresser. I explained to her that if she could do Beth's hair, re-cut and style it right away, I'd give her an extra hundred.

"No problem," the stylist said, but I need to bring her downstairs with me. Come on honey, you come with me; I already know what color and style that would work. We have a make-up artist that can give you a few pointers on accenting those cute features you have."

Not knowing what to make of all this, Beth looked back at me and seeing my smile, shrugged her shoulders and followed the hair dresser.

While Beth was downstairs, I showered and dressed in a gray suit with a black shirt and gray and black tie and black boots. I sat around waiting on Beth, and about an hour later there was a knock on my door. Not knowing what to expect, I opened the door. "Beth, you look sensational."

The hairdresser didn't have to cut much of my hair. She re-shaped it to make it look fuller and frame my face. I love the new color. It's so warm and soft looking, instead of my mousy brown. They showed me how to apply make-up and to enhance my features with different shades," she babbled.

Pleased at her new look, she smiled gratefully and said, "We need to go or we'll miss our appointment with the bank manager at the property I want to show you."

"Not yet," I said, "Call the bank manager now and tell him to meet us in about an hour. If he wants to sell us that property, he'll wait."

Beth made the call, and I was surprised at how professional she handled herself and assertive she had become. I knew it, I thought, there's a lot of talent hidden beneath her lack of confidence, all she needed was to have someone guide her. Maybe I'm in the wrong business, I grinned at my thoughts.

I handed Beth the packages I had purchased last night. "Try these on. You can use my bedroom."

"Oh Mr. Raye, I couldn't, I definitely can't afford these."

"But I can. The sales clerk thought you would like the matching undergarments to go along with it. By the way, what size shoe do you wear?"

"Six narrow, why?"

"Get dressed and you'll see," and I shut the bedroom door behind her.

I called one of the shops and had them bring up several pair of shoes in black and gray. By the time Beth dressed, the shoe's had been delivered.

"Mr. Raye," she spoke softly as she stood in front of me. "I don't know what to say."

"I do, you're a knock out."

"You think so?" She blushed.

"Beth, I know so. Men will turn their heads twice when they see you coming."

She blushed again, and then tried on several pair of shoes and found one pair to match the gray dress she was wearing and a black pair for the pant suit. The jewelry accented her slender neckline.

"We need to go. The limo driver is waiting on us."

"A limo?" She just shook her head, totally befuddled with the transformation of her and her new status.

Once we were in the limo, I asked, "Now tell me about this house and how did you find it so fast?"

She explained that a millionaire had it built a couple of years ago, but he had passed away. His only heir to the estate was a daughter. It had taken the estate attorneys six months to locate her. The owner had already paid out well over five million for the house, but still carried a mortgage of two point six million.

The law in Nevada states that foreclosure property can be sold, but not for a profit, only what's owed.

The daughter had taken the two million her father had in his savings and disappeared. From what Beth had been told, the daughter had been a problem child all her life, and a big disappointment to her parents. His wife had died several years ago, and they had no other living relatives, as both parents were an only child on either side.

"My theory is," Beth said, "the daughter wanted to grab the money before the bank could acquire it to pay off the mortgage, and that left her free from having to make expensive payments on the house, and ending up with nothing to live on in the long run. Granted she could have sold the house and got more for it, but in the meantime she wouldn't have any money, and if the house didn't sell right away, she could lose it all. So now the bank is trying to sell it and re-coup what's owed on the balance."

"The problem is, the bank has had the expense and up keep of the estate and the feeding of the horses, and were in the process of preparing to sell them as it's now a liability of the bank. They've already auctioned off all the furniture to help defer costs. When I called the bank and inquired about the property and told them I had a prospective client that would be interested in a package deal, the bank manager said he would come out personally to meet us and would put a hold on the sale of the horses until I could show the property to you. That would save the bank a lot of time, work and expense"

"Why hasn't someone else bought the house?"

"It's new on the market. There are two couples that have looked at the property, but neither wife liked the idea of living this far out of town. So neither are that interested. I think they had the affordability to buy, but not the income to maintain it. From what I understand from my records, we are talking one big, huge house. I'm as excited to see it as you are."

We were running a little late, and when we arrived the bank manager was just getting into his car and was about to leave.

Shaking the bank manager's hand, as we stepped out of the limo, Beth said, "Thank you for meeting us here, and I do hope you received my message that we would be arriving later than scheduled, as my client opted to look at another property before I showed him this one."

In the same breath, and without giving the manager chance to respond, Beth said, "Mr. Carlson, I'd like you to meet my client, Johnny Raye. Mr. Raye, this is Mr. Carlson, the bank manager I told you about on the way over here."

We shook hands, and I kept grinning at the devious, but professional way Beth was handling everything. She didn't let the bank manager get the upper hand first. She was taking the lead and letting him follow her.

We opted to look at the exterior of the house before checking the interior. It reminded me of Graceland, but on a much larger scale. It also was a two story, but had separate wings that extended from the center on each side. Four huge ornate posts supported the front entrance which was done with European stone. The rest of the exterior was in white brick.

The driveway leading to the house was paved in cobblestone. Two lions, one on each side, adorned the private gateway of white bricked and concrete platforms. Flowering trees lined each side of the drive and were now in full bloom. Mr. Carlson informed us that a professional landscaping company came twice a week to service the lawn and trim the exotic shrubs that seemed to be everywhere. I was happy to see several palm trees, which reminded me of Florida, as well as numerous different shade trees.

To the back of the house, a concrete drive-way was poured that extended from the house to the barn. The barn was painted red with white trim and stood out from the stark white of the house. White fencing extended for almost as far as the eye could see, and at least a dozen or more horses could be seen grazing contentedly.

Beth whispered to me, "Originally there were only ten acres that were listed that went with the property, but after checking further into the court house records, I discovered there are one hundred acres, not ten acres that are included in this deal. I was able to acquire a copy of the original survey. I was right. Someone did a big typo, and I'm hoping no other agents caught this yet in case you decide you want to purchase the house. Otherwise, there will be a big rush of agent showings for purchase, if nothing else, for a resale."

Unlocking the house for us, the bank manager escorted us inside. We entered into what Beth said later, was a dream come true.

Stepping into the center of the foyer, a curved, marble staircase, trimmed in polished brass, gradually wove its way to the second floor, balconied walk-way. Two six-foot in circumference, hand-blown glass chandeliers hung from recessed, vaulted ceilings, immediately caught our eye.

Mr. Carlson led us into the center of the house that was the main living area. This room had a white marble fireplace that took up most of one wall. It opened into another room separated by white column, hand-carved, support posts, and a wall of glass windows from floor to ceiling with French doors. This design allowed a see through view from the back to the front of the house, but when closed off for formal affairs or different parties did not obstruct the view.

The second room was used as the family room or den, and another fireplace adorned one wall, but this one was all in stone that the owner had shipped in special from Italy. The back wall was also enclosed in glass with French doors that opened to a court yard, which separated the house to the pool area and pool house.

Half of the pool house was glassed that encompassed a work out room, and the other half had an enclosed steam and changing room. And, of course, a waterfall gently flowed recycled water from its pump area into the swimming pool. The pool was surrounded by various shaped boulders, shrubs and water plants. Later I was to learn that the boulders were not real, but actually were formed into different shapes to look like authentic boulders, and then poured with concrete.

Off to the right was the formal dining room with a rounded bay window, beyond that was a huge kitchen all with stainless steel fixtures, and a center island with a Jen-Air grill. A sun room extended from the kitchen that could be used as a nook.

Mr. Carlson brought us back into the main room and we then entered the other wing of the house. This wing had eight large bedrooms all with their own private bathrooms and enough room for separate sitting areas, four downstairs which we viewed first, and four up which we reached from a private stairwell.

What's across the walk-way?" I asked.

That's where the master bedroom is located," Mr. Carlson boasted, "and just wait until you see it."

Both Beth and I stood in awe. The master suite was built over the kitchen, dining, and sun room. One wall had a fireplace like the one right below it in the family room. An alcove entrance opened into an office and the other a sitting area. The master bath had three steps that led up to a whirlpool tub, large enough for two to fit very comfortably, that was surrounded with gothic posts. A separate double shower, all in marble, matched the countertops as well as the flooring.

We couldn't find the closets until Mr. Carlson picked up a remote, pressed one of several buttons, and another room opened up, behind a mirrored wall, exposing two revolving shelves, one for 'him' and one for 'her'. Built in shelves and drawers covered the back wall.

Mr. Carlson left us alone so Beth and I could do a walk-through of the house and discuss things in private. We took our time admiring all the large crown molding in each room and intricate designs and extras that were added.

"Beth, I really like this house, it's exactly what I want. Make the deal. It will be cash, and I want the closing set for the end of the week."

"Grinning from ear to ear, Beth said, "Mr. Raye, let's find Mr. Carlson, and tell him the good news." We found him waiting in the kitchen.

"Mr. Carlson, do all the lighting fixtures and chandeliers remain with the house, as well as everything we have viewed here today, as well as the twelve horses in the corrals?" Beth inquired, to confirm what went along with the deal.

"Yes, everything you see right now stays."

"Also," she asked, "I understand that there is one hundred acres that belong with this property according to the courthouse records, is that correct?"

"Yes," he replied, "that's correct.

"In that case, Mr. Carlson, we have a deal. Mr. Raye and I will be writing up the contract, and I'll have a copy to your office and all disclosure forms before the end of the day. Mr. Raye will write a check today for the full amount of the asking price, and will have his accountant transfer funds by tomorrow to cover the check. He requests the closing to be done by the end of the week. Friday before noon, to be exact! Since your bank handles in-house closings, let's set the time to finalize the deal at ten o'clock."

Mr. Carlson agreed and shook my hand once more. "Everything is up to date on the house. All we have to do is prepare the paperwork and have your client sign the papers. I'll tell my secretary to let me know when you deliver the contract. Thank you, Mr. Raye, Beth. I'll be seeing you on Friday." He relocked the house and Beth and I walked towards the barn so I could see my 'soon to be' new horses.

A worker named Manuel that the bank paid to care for the horses was in the barn stacking hay. We chatted for a few minutes and I then asked him if he would like to continue to work here. The bank was paying him three hundred dollars a week and I told him I would pay him three hundred and fifty if he would stay. I explained the duties that he would be required to do, and he said he was already doing all that and more.

"Sir," he said, "my wife is a maid at a cheap hotel in town and is looking for a better job."

"How much does she make now?"

"Two hundred and fifty dollars a week," he boasted.

"One rule you need to learn up front is do not lie to me." I said sternly. "Now, how much money does she make a week?"

"Seventy-five dollars," he answered, looking very sheepish.

"Then bring her out Friday afternoon, as of that time you will both be working for me."

A smile lit up his face.

I then asked, "Can she cook?"

"Yes sir, she is not only a good housekeeper, she is an excellent cook, and that's the truth."

About that time a white Arabian stallion came and nuzzled my arm. I scratched his nose and then behind his ears. He kept nuzzling me. Manuel said that he was looking for a sugar cube. He told me the horse would keep bugging me until he got his sugar, and he handed me two cubes.

I hid them in my hand, but the horse was watching and knew he was about to get his treats. Growing impatient, he held his proud head high, stamped his feet and whinnied loudly, as if to say, "Give me those." I laughed at his antics and opened my hand for him to nibble on his treats. Satisfied with his find, he let me rub his neck a few more times before wandering off to join the other horses.

"Looks like you've made a friend, Mr. Raye," Beth said, happily.

Beth and I left, and on the drive into town, we filled out all the necessary papers she brought with for me to sign. I wrote her a check to hold and called Carolyn to wire the funds. When we finished, we stopped at Beth's office so she could make copies of everything. It only took her a few minutes, and from there I had the limo driver take us to the bank. Beth delivered the papers and said Mr. Carlson was surprised we had prepared them so quickly, as he had only returned from lunch a few minutes before. I then brought Beth back to the hotel with me so she could pick up her things and get her car.

"Mr. Raye," she said, "I'd like to leave the jewelry here for a while if you don't mind."

"Let's get a few things straightened out first, starting with Mr. Raye. Please call me Johnny, okay! And another thing, I gave you that jewelry, that shouldn't be a problem for anyone."

Looking embarrassed, she said, "My husband is a gambler and he loses a lot." "To support his habit, I'm afraid he'll hock or sell the jewelry. It wouldn't surprise me if he tried to sell the clothes too."

"Seems you're full of problems. Why don't you change into your other things until I think of something?"

"No, I'm going to take them home with me, and if he even thinks of touching them, I'll threaten him within an inch of his life!" She gathered her new as well as old things together and gave me a kiss on the cheek.

Looking somewhat embarrassed by her boldness, she said, "Johnny, I don't know how to repay you, not just for the clothes, but for you believing in me. It's been a long time since someone trusted my abilities. I had been down on myself, but as of today, never again." With that she left and I smiled at how happy she looked.

Gary asked who the adorable lady was that just left.

"Never mind," Denise said, gently slapping his arm, "It's none of your business."

"That was Beth," I laughed.

"The girl that was here yesterday? She really turned out to be quite a looker."

"Yeah, but she has husband trouble."

"Oh no, not another Sandy."

"No, this one is an addicted gambler, and loses a lot of money or so she says. What did you find out about our deals," I asked Denise, getting back to business.

"I found a number of places who would love to have you perform in their casinos, but Gus seems to be the one who want us full time. The Imperial

Palladium, Joker's Wild, the Palace Royale and the Fitzpatrick could only afford to have you perform on week-ends. Gus wants us three days a week and will pay what we're asking, and he wants to draw up a contract for a year."

"Well then, I guess we need to show them how much Gus's business will increase and put us in a little more demand. What about a casino for David?"

"Gary helped me with that one. The Celebrity is interested in him, but not for the money you'll be making. He can make seventy-five hundred a night to do shows on Friday and Saturday nights. So I guess it'll be David's call, but I'm sure he'll take it. The Celebrity wants to advertise before he starts and Gus wants you to start a week from next Wednesday. He's putting your name up in lights on the casino's marquee, and will be advertising on billboards, and on the radio, as well as television."

Gary asked, "How was your day, did you find us a house?"

"Yes, I'm closing with the bank on Friday," and explained to them about the house. When I was finished, I told them I would be hiring an interior decorator to help with the furnishings.

"Don't do that," Denise pleaded. "You said you talked with David and Tara earlier, and that they will be here tomorrow. In that case, I'll call Michele and she can come here early. Let the three of us women pick out all the furniture. We can save you a ton of money by not hiring a decorator. Besides, Michele is schooled in this area and the three of us will have fun doing it. It'll be a way for us to have a part in this. What do you say?"

"I'd say I think the three of you are pretty darn terrific, are you sure Tara and Michele will want to do this?"

"Positive! Johnny, we'll all be living under your roof, we need to contribute somehow? You've done so much for all of us already."

"I've been thinking about that myself. Would you agree to splitting the expenses four ways, like the utilities and helpers? Now if you guys think this is too much, we can work something else out, or hell, I didn't even ask, maybe you two want a place of your own?"

"No," Gary said, "That sounds like a fair deal, we'll stick together."

I loved the closeness of our friendship. We called it a night, and I told them I'd see them sometime tomorrow.

I called Carolyn the next morning to find out if the funds had transferred, and she informed me the money was wired and should reach the bank in Vegas before two o'clock.

I decided to take a drive out to the property. Either the bank or Beth placed an additional sign out front that read, "Under Contract." That would discourage other people from going through the house. Legally it wasn't mine yet, but I didn't want any strangers going through 'my' house.

I found Manuel out by the barn talking with two women.

"Senor Johnny, this is my wife, Carmen, I was telling you about her, and this is her sister, Juanita."

"Ladies, pleased to meet you. I told Manuel yesterday that I was looking to hire two women to do the cooking and cleaning."

"Si!" Carmen said. "We quit out jobs this morning and came out here to see the house. It is very beautiful, no?"

"Yes it is."

I explained what their duties would consist of, and they both nodded in agreement when I told them I would pay them each two hundred and fifty dollars a week.

"Thank you, Senor Johnny," they said. "We only made seventy-five a week at the hotel plus tips, but the tips were very little."

"Manuel, I see there is a horse trailer here but no truck."

"That's right, Senor Johnny. The daughter that came for a few weeks sold the vehicles for quick cash."

"Well, we'll need a truck to pull the horse trailer, so if you're finished here we need to find a dealership in town that sells trucks."

"I know of one who will give you a good deal."

Manuel was right. The dealership we went to was trying to clear his inventory to make room for next year's stock. I looked at several trucks and then found one I liked. It was a heavy duty Silverado, fully loaded, four hundred diesel engine, four door, with towing package. We made the deal and once more, Carolyn handled the finances. I handed Manuel the keys and told him his first job working for me was to drive the truck back to the barn and park it and I'd see him later. He was thrilled that I trusted him to drive my new truck and swore he would be extra careful not to let anything happen to it. I went back to the hotel to wait for David and Tara.

My phone was flashing when I got back to my room. I called for messages and there was an urgent from Beth. Better not be any problem with the purchase of this house. Beth's office put me through to her right away.

"Johnny," she said breathlessly, "I've been trying to reach you. The bank has all the necessary paperwork ready. We can close this afternoon at four o'clock." It was only one o'clock now, so I told her to go ahead and confirm.

"I'll pick you up at the hotel," Beth said, "around two thirty." "That will allow us time for traffic problems."

"No, I'll have the limo driver pick you up at your office. A deal of this magnitude requires us to arrive in style."

I was disappointed when we stopped to pick up Beth. She looked nice, but she wasn't wearing either of the outfits I had bought her, and decided to mention it to her. She told me that, Ronnie her husband, threw a fit, that if she needed any new clothes, he'd be the one buying them for her.

"Well, maybe he was right, maybe I was out of line, but you didn't look like someone who was selling million dollar houses. I was only trying to help your self esteem."

"Johnny, don't worry about it, he talks like a big shot, but all he'll do is try to sell them for money. I know they were expensive. The boutique you purchased them from only caters to the elite clientele. Well, we're here, and this should take less than an hour if the bank has all the paperwork ready."

Mr. Carlson's secretary escorted us to the conference room. Since we were a little early, they were still putting the paperwork in order, but it would only be a few more minutes. We sipped fresh coffee and ten minutes later the closing attorney and Mr. Carlson had everything they needed, and forty-five minutes later, I was handed the keys to my property. Beth was excellent and thorough in making sure everything was correct.

Back in the limo, Beth said, "Johnny, getting back to what we were discussing earlier, I've rented an apartment, I'm leaving my husband."

"Are you sure you want to do that?"

"Yes, Ronnie is a good man, no, was a good man, but his gambling is a sickness. He refuses to get help, and I can't go on this way any longer. I've decided that I'm going to pick up my new outfits and jewelry right after I drop you off. I only have a few personal items I want to take. My brokerage made in excess of over one-hundred and eighty-two thousand dollars from this sale, and I will receive seventy percent of that. I'll be just fine."

"Do you want me to go with you in case there's trouble?"

"No, it's high time I learned to stand on my own two feet."

"Open yourself a new account, in your name only, and when you get your check you can deposit it in there."

"I already did, I opened one yesterday, and tomorrow when I receive my commission check I'll have it deposited in my new account. Thank you again for having so much faith in me, I now know I have what it takes to be a good agent."

"I already knew that. I sensed that when I first met you. All you needed was a little encouragement."

She smiled in appreciation. "If you ever need anything or have a problem with the house, call me," and she gave me her card with her cell phone number, that way I could reach her day or night.

I told her to come and see my shows and she said she'd like that. We wished each other good luck and I left to meet with Gary and Denise. They were waiting for me in front of the hotel with another limo. I was surprised when I climbed in and discovered David, Tara and Michele were already sitting in the back seat.

Excited at seeing them, and after hugs and kisses from Tara, and Michele, I asked, "What's up, where are we going?"

"To see 'our' new house," Denise said.

Once we pulled up front and I unlocked the door it was total chaos. The girls were squealing with delight and the guys stood in awe. They were running in every different direction trying to see it all at once. Denise brought a tablet and the ladies were busy writing down all the things they would need to buy.

After looking the house over, the guys headed outside. Manuel had parked the truck next to the barn as I instructed, and by the looks of how spotlessly clean it was, he must have wiped it down when he returned. We walked around and then checked on the horses. I couldn't find any sugar cubes but I did find apples. Cutting one in quarters, the white Arabian trotted over to the fence to see what I was holding. Looking at me after sniffing for sugar, and realizing he'd have to settle for something different, he nuzzled my hand and contentedly ate the apple. Petting and talking with him, he stayed longer this time and rested his head next to mine so I could scratch him behind the ears. Grabbing the curry brush that was hanging nearby, I opened the gate.

The white Arabian stood in the same spot eyeing me suspiciously. Walking slowly towards him, and talking softly all the while, I gave him another piece of the apple and started brushing him. When I was done, he whinnied softly, turned and trotted off. Half way to the other horses, he turned and looked to see what I was doing. Laughing at him, I knew he was looking to see if I had anymore apples. Satisfied that was all he was going to get for the day, he trotted to the other side of the corral.

"Looks like you've made a friend," David said.

"Yeah, I love the intelligence in his eyes, and he's already showing me his personality. I've been trying to think of a name for him, but I don't have one yet."

"I wonder if he likes music." Gary chuckled. And we all laughed.

The girls were ready to go, they had prepared a list a mile long. Each had already selected their rooms, and were excited to get started decorating.

Riding back to the hotel, Denise asked, "Johnny, we know that you wanted to buy all the furniture, but we've been talking among ourselves *and* we want to buy our own bedroom suites. That way it'll seem more personal to us, *and* we can choose whatever style we want. Is that all right with you? Besides, it'll cost well over a hundred thousand just for the bedroom suites, and at that rate, and what you're spending on us, you'll be broke."

"Don't worry about that, I'll be making good money, as will all of us. We'll be fine, but if you want to buy your own, that's fine. I'll take care of the rest."

I left everyone at the hotel, and I went to play the slots as I was tired and not in the mood to play anything serious. I wanted to relax and have fun. I selected a ten times a dollar progressive machine. I had been playing for several hours, and was down over two grand. I was about to quit when I hit all three tens. With the two thousand I lost, my winnings totaled over two hundred and forty thousand dollars. The casino held my winnings in a special account that I had previously arranged with them. I figured I could use that money to purchase items for the house, which saved me from wiring money from my Florida holdings.

Everyone met for breakfast early the next morning, as we had numerous stores to go to according to Michele. She had several in mind, and with her decorating knowledge, would be able to bargain and get us better deals. The girls had stayed up half the night scourging the papers for sales. Knowing who had what on sale we first went to Klein/Meyers, who were noted for their fine line of hand crafted furniture.

Denise and Gary walked in the store ahead of us and a sales lady asked if she could help them. Denise told her they were with me.

Looking me over, she said, "Oh, another Elvis Impersonator, if you see anything you can afford, let me know," and she walked off to help someone else.

"Gary, do you believe what just happened?"

"No. Maybe we need to look somewhere else."

"No, we need to find someone who's interested in making a damn good commission, and then rub it in that bitch's face."

Infuriated, I found the customer service department located at the rear of the store. A sales manager saw us approaching. He extended his hand to welcome us to the store, and asked if he could be of service. Liking his attitude, I told him what we were here for, and what had just transpired. Apologizing for the sales lady's attitude, he told us to follow him and he would personally take care of us. Bringing us to the second floor which housed all the bedroom suites, I found exactly what I wanted.

I chose a four poster, cherry wood, king size bed, with matching armoire, and night stands. I tried several mattresses until I found one that felt the best. I then chose furniture for my sitting area and office, all in cherry wood. Because of the volume of furniture we bought, we were given an additional forty percent discount.

The women were finished choosing furniture for their rooms, as well as the spare bedrooms. Having all the bedroom suites completed, the manager brought us to the third floor for dining room and living room furniture, which I left for the girls to select. I took the guys with me to find den and game room furniture.

We spent the entire evening shopping and selecting specialty items from store to store, but with the girls having everything organized, we managed to pick out all we would need.

The guys were chomping at the bit, their patience with shopping worn thin.

Deciding not to push them too far, the ladies said they would finish up tomorrow with the bathroom, and kitchen accessories. The window treatments remained with the house, and it's a good thing, after what I had spent.

We ate a quiet meal together since we missed lunch. Michele left immediately after she finished eating so she could try to call and catch Chance between shows. David, Tara, Gary and Denise went to Gary's room to discuss David being hired at the Celebrity. I wanted to call it a day and went to my room to relax.

I was getting ready for bed when the phone rang. I had left word with the hotel manager that if a seat opened at a card table to call and let me know. It was him, and he informed me that there were seven poker players and they were asking for me to be the eighth. I hesitated for a moment, and thought, why not, I've been lucky so far, maybe my luck would continue.

At the table, I recognized several players from the other night. It seems I had taken thirty thousand of their money, and they were anxious to try and win it back. The cashier brought me twenty-five thousand dollars worth of chips. They again wanted to play Texas Holdum, no limit, and I smiled.

I dropped out of the first three hands, having lost only two thousand. The fourth hand I caught a pair of nines. I stayed in and called the bets until there were only three players left. The first three cards on board were king, jack, and nine. The guy on my left bet ten thousand dollars, the guy on my right dropped. I called, not knowing whether he had three kings or three jacks, or was bluffing. The street card showed another nine. I hesitated for a few minutes and then decided to check. The other player bet twenty-thousand. I called and raised ten thousand. He called, thinking I had a full house jacks high. I knew then he held kings high.

The river card was drawn. It was an eight, no help to either of us. Sure of himself, he went 'all in'. I only had eight thousand left. I called. I showed my four nines. He was stunned. I won the pot of over sixty-thousand dollars.

"Well played, very well hidden," he said, shaking my hand as he got up to leave.

The next hand I drew a pair of aces. The bet was five thousand. I was last to call with five others remaining. I raised the bet to ten thousand. Four people called. The first three cards were ace, six, and three. It was my bet. Deciding to see who had what, and to sweeten the pot, I only bet five thousand. It was quickly raised to twenty thousand. One more player dropped out. I called. The street card turned a queen. The bet came around to me at twenty thousand. I figured one player had three of a kind and the other two pair, but possibly all three of us had three of a kind. By the cards showing on board, there was no way for anyone to have four of a kind. The river card turned a six, again, no help to anyone.

Now it was a bluffing game, and it was my turn to bet, so I checked. The bet now was twenty-five thousand with a raise to forty-five thousand. I raised the bet to sixty thousand. Now in for too much money, each player called. I showed my three aces. Two players were now out of money. Leaving only three players, I folded the next four or five hands, letting them battle it out. Finally it was down to just two of us.

A crowd had gathered of twenty to thirty people to watch. No one said a word. It was as if everyone was holding their breath, not even a whisper was uttered. My opponent had sixty thousand. I had one hundred eighty thousand. I needed to end this fast. I drew a six and seven of hearts. He bet ten thousand. I thought for a moment and then bet forty thousand. He folded with a pair of three's. The next hand I drew a jack and queen of clubs. I bet ten thousand, this time he only called. The first three cards were a nine and ten of clubs, and an ace of hearts. He had three aces. I had a possible straight flush. There was no way I could drop, but I needed him to go 'all in.' The next card, the street card was a king of clubs. I had my straight flush. He bet twenty thousand. I told him to count his money. I was going 'all in'. He knew I had a flush, and he needed another ace or the board to show a pair. He hesitated, but thinking he could beat me with his hand, he called. We both stood. I showed my hand. There was no way for him to beat me. The river card was shown, it was a king. He had his full house. But I had the straight flush.

"Damn," he shook his head, "With your luck tonight, you could fall into a bucket of shit and come out smelling like a rose."

We shook hands, each of us telling the other how well we played. Those still around us gave me a toast, "To The King," they cheered. I collected my winnings, and again placed them in the hotel safe.

I lay in bed that night thinking my luck wouldn't hold out much longer. I needed to keep my mind on my upcoming shows. Tomorrow I knew I'd be busy getting things organized at the house. The utilities were to be transferred to my name, without any interruption of service. The phone company was coming out to connect to the main box.

I rose early, skipped breakfast. Instead I grabbed a cup of coffee and a doughnut from the lobby. The furniture trucks were already there when I arrived, and so were Denise and Michele. They were directing everyone and in a few minutes the rest of the gang arrived. Tara, David and Gary had gone grocery shopping, and then picked up coffee and doughnuts to eat.

The girls kicked me out. "We'll handle everything here. If we need you, we'll yell."

I strolled down to the barn to check on the horses. Manuel was already there cleaning out the stalls. He handed me a couple of sugar cubes. The big white stallion sauntered over to where I was standing.

Nuzzling me to get his sugar, I said, "Not yet big fella." "I think I'll take you for a ride."

The previous owner had named him, "Kings Choice," Manuel said. "He won him in a poker game."

How ironic, I thought. "The King," is riding "The King."

Holding the bridle in my hand and letting him sniff it, I gave him his sugar cubes. When he finished, I slid the bridle on, this time singing to him softly. His ears twitched at the new sound. I gave him a hand full of oats which he munched happily. As I saddled him, he turned to look at me but never resisted. Still singing to him softly and rubbing his neck, I climbed in the saddle. Giving him a moment to get used to my weight and handling, I walked him towards the lake. The other owner must have ridden him often as he seemed like he was enjoying this, and wanted to run. I gave him his head and barely tightening my thighs, with a gentle nudge, he quickly responded and opened into a full gallop. I rode for about an hour, letting him choose his own pace. Riding back to the barn, I brushed him down, singing to him once again, and gave him a bag of oats, and his sugar cubes.

Standing by the fence, I looked at the other horses. A pretty little Palomino filly pranced playfully in the distance. That would be a horse for Karen to ride when she comes, I thought. Speaking of which, I needed to call her and tell her I bought a house, and had my own telephone number for her to reach me.

I found Manuel cleaning out the pool. He thought that we might want to go for a swim this week-end after moving in. I thanked him for being so thoughtful. His wife and her sister were coming later, and bringing a big pot of chili. I told him not to make it so spicy that no one could eat it. I told him to Americanize it, as I had tasted spicy chili in Texas. It took me a week to quit sweating.

I stayed around for awhile, and after answering fifty questions, was pleased with the way the furniture was arranged and how nice everything looked. I went to check on the progress of my bedroom and was amazed that everything was already in place. All it needed now was personal touches. That could all come later.

We took a break, and ate the chili. It was a little spicy, but very good. By now everyone looked tired.

"Why don't we call it a day and finish tomorrow, we'll be ready to move in, and the personal things we'll finish while we're here." I suggested and was offered no resistance.

I left to go back to the hotel. Beth had called me so I returned her call. Her husband answered. He was upset because she was leaving him. I explained to him that I told her to give him a chance, but that he would have to go to a clinic to get help for his gambling. Frightened this time because Beth was actually leaving, he said he was willing to check himself in on a six month plan, but Beth was leaving him anyway. He wanted me to talk to her.

"Just out of curiosity, where are the two outfits I bought her?"

"In her closet. I need her. I just want to get our lives back to the way they used to be," he cried on the phone.

"When you check yourself into the clinic, call me and I'll talk with Beth, and I will do my best to convince her to be around when you're through with treatment."

About an hour later, Beth called. She agreed to come to my room and we'd talk. She told me that she was tired of her husband and his problem and had wanted to leave him for a long time. She didn't know if she loved him enough to give him another chance, and was tired of his lies and false promises to get help. Although, she said this was the first time that he admitted he had a problem and needed help.

"Beth," I asked, "if he checks himself into a clinic would you give him another chance?"

She thought for a moment before answering. "Johnny, I loved my husband very much when we married. If I could get that same man back, yes, I'd stick around and give him a chance."

"He's checking into a gamblers clinic tomorrow morning. It might be good for him if you drove him there, and if he really means to change, then you could give your marriage another try."

She started to cry. I believe mostly from relief that their marriage had a chance of making it again.

I took her hand, and said, "There are people out there who can help you deal with your husband's problem. It might be good for you to enroll in these classes. You'll have to change too, be firmer and know the right answers if you see him start to falter."

"Thanks, Johnny, you're right, I'll go home and talk with Ronnie tonight." She gave me a big hug and left looking happier than when she arrived.

Sitting around I began to feel cramped in my suite. To hell with tomorrow, I'm staying out to the ranch tonight. I couldn't pack fast enough. I practically threw things together, and had my car loaded in half an hour. Going back to the room to check to make sure I had everything, I called the house, unsure if anyone was still there, and when David answered, I told him I was packed and on my way home.

The girls had already brought their personal items and wanted to stay too. The rest they would pick up tomorrow.

Relaxing from a long day, we sat around talking about our upcoming shows. David had called the Celebrity and would start performing next week. Gary and I were anxious to get back to performing, and after the chaos of moving, it would feel like heaven.

. . .

The month few by quickly. Chance finished his job at Steadman's. Michele had decorated their room, and all they had to do was move their personal things. Denise found him a job at another casino for the same amount of money that David was making. Our little business manager was doing a good job for all of us. Gus was extremely pleased at the increase of business to his casino. To keep us from leaving and going to another casino, he gave us an extra ten thousand a week.

Denise came up with an idea that it would be good for us to do benefits for cancer patients and fund raisers for different charities. We became well known throughout Vegas. People even came to eat at the casinos just to see our shows.

Denise convinced me to build a marriage chapel, and have 'Elvis' sing at your wedding. She said several had been built so why not capitalize on a good thing. In our spare time we could sing there, if we so chose, or use other Elvis Impersonators. Tara, Michele and Denise handled the bookings, and in no time at all, the chapel was paid for and showed a profit. My nest egg was multiplying fast.

Everything was going great for me. When I first bought the house I thought I may have over done things, but seeing the joy I brought to all my friends, it was well worth the investment. We were living like one big happy family, everyone was getting along great. For the most part, I was happy, but I still had a void in my life.

The guys helped fill the void by playing cards at the house, shooting pool, swimming and riding horses. We gambled from time to time in the casinos. We worked, we played.

Gary was happy being with Denise. David and Tara were planning a family. Chance was happily married to Michele. So what was my problem? With everything I had, I was still missing the love of a companion. Sensing my loneliness, 'my family' talked me into taking a trip to Alabama.

CHAPTER 26

I took a few days off in July, and excited about my trip, I paid Karen a surprise visit. I walked into her shop and instead of scaring her like I did last time, I stood and watched her in the back room.

Her little bell above her door rang, and she hollered out, "Be right with you!"

I could feel her body, and smell the scent of her hair as I remembered our making love in the back room of her shop. It felt like an hour had passed, but it was only a few minutes before she looked up and realized it was me standing there.

"Johnny," she squealed with delight as she rushed into my arms. We kissed and hugged and hugged and kissed, each telling the other how much they were missed.

"I was hoping you'd come for a visit. Why didn't you let me know you were coming? I must look a mess. You didn't say anything about coming when I talked with you last week."

I kissed her again to stop her from babbling. Finally, holding her at arms length, I said, "I've come to take you to Vegas with me. You can open a shop there if you want, but I want you to come and stay with me."

"But you aren't retiring yet, are you?"

"No," I shook my head, "Not yet, but I'm tired of being alone." "I want to wake up every morning and see your face, and again the last thing before I go to sleep at night. I haven't been with another woman since you and I made love here in your shop. Sell your shop, Karen, come with me."

"Oh, Johnny," she said, pulling away. "Let me think about it for a couple of days, this is so sudden, and it's such a big commitment."

"Okay," I said, "I'll be here until Friday, and I intend to spend all my time with you." "But for now, I'm starving, how about we eat lunch at the restaurant we ate at the last time I was here?"

Arms around each other, we strolled casually toward the restaurant. We each ordered a hamburger steak and fried green tomatoes with a tossed salad. Waiting on our order we sat sipping sweet tea, and filled each other in on what was happening. She told me she was still singing Karaoke at a couple of clubs in town with Judie. She admitted it wasn't near as much fun as it was when our group was all together.

Our food arrived and we ate silently for a few minutes. "I haven't had fried green tomatoes since I was here last time. I sure do miss southern cooking."

She asked how things were going in Vegas. I told her about our shows and David and Chances as well. We talked about the ranch and that we all were living there quite happily, except for me, I grinned.

"All of you are under the same roof? You always talk about them being there, but I guess I didn't realize you were all living together," she asked, with a little dismay in her expression.

"Yes, it actually works out great. No one is in each other's way. The house is huge, and offers everyone their own privacy, which we all respect. Everyone chips in on the daily expenses. We have a system that works to the satisfaction of all of us."

"I don't know, Johnny, that's an awful lot of people under the same roof. No one fusses or disagrees on anything?"

"No, everyone is busy and when we are at home together or all at the same time, which is rarely, we swim in the pool or play games. I believe you'll be happy, and after a couple more years I should have enough saved to settle down and retire in Florida if you'd like. I'll have to find myself another hobby then," I grinned at her.

But Karen wasn't grinning. "Don't you think we should wait until then for us to get together?"

"Karen, I'm asking you now, I'm not going to ask you again," disappointment dripped from every word. "Tell you what, I'm leaving tomorrow. You can reach me at the Carriage Inn." I stood up.

"But you just got here," she said, hurt filling her eyes.

But I didn't see that for the hurt I felt in my heart. "I guess I've wasted my time coming here," and stormed out of the restaurant.

I had rented a car, and drove back to the Inn. Angrily I paced the floor of my room, and stopped short when the phone rang. I thought it would be Karen, but it was from Judie asking me to give Karen a couple of days to make up her mind. I told her I didn't know what I was going to do and hung up the phone.

I thought about our conversation for a moment and decided the best thing for me to do was to go back to Vegas. I didn't think it would do me any good to stick around as the answer would be the same. Making my decision, I called the car rental agency and told them I would be keeping the rental longer than expected, possibly as long as a week.

I grabbed my bag and threw it in the back seat of the rental. I had talked with Lisa Marie, the other day and she said she had been thinking of spending a week at Graceland. Needing to feel loved, I wanted to see Lisa Marie so I drove to Memphis.

I was too hurt and disappointed to stop and think of the short notice I was giving Karen, and what I was asking of her. I didn't realize I hadn't even asked her to marry me, just live with me, my way. I didn't realize any of this until much later.

CHAPTER 27

Arriving at Graceland, Joe told me Lisa Marie was still in California, but Priscilla had returned yesterday to check on things.

"Is she alone?" I asked.

"Yeah, she's staying in the guest house, Johnny. We've had record breaking tourist business since you did your Christmas Special. Everyone is checking out the grave sites and speculating about your death. It's really been great for business," he laughed. "Anyway, big guy, how's Vegas?"

I told him about the shows and how well we were doing. I asked him to come and stay out to the ranch as we had plenty of room. He said he'd love to the first good vacation he could get. He left to get back to work, and I went to find Priscilla. I was stopped by many tourists to sign autographs. I signaled for security, and I was finally able to reach the guest house.

Priscilla was asleep on the sofa when I walked in. I gently kissed her cheek, and sat down to watch television. The last tour of the day was over so I walked to the main house to my music room to record a new number, and was singing "Funny How Time Slips Away," when Priscilla walked into the studio.

"Something wrong, Elvis?" she asked, hesitantly.

"Why do you ask?" I answered with shortness to my tone of voice.

Picking up on it immediately, she said, "Because every time you had a problem or had a lot on your mind, you'd come in here and play all night. Just like now. So do you want to sing or talk?"

"You know me pretty well, don't you?"

"I used to think I did, but most of the time you were too busy making movies in California, and chasing women."

"I know I was a bad ass back then, but I've changed, Cilla. Really changed. Back then I didn't realize I had everything a man could want, but wasn't settled enough to appreciate what I had. I'm really trying very hard to not be the way I used to be."

"Let me guess, you're having a problem with Karen?"

"Yes, I am. She's still not ready to settle down and I'm in Vegas alone."

"There's a lot of pretty woman in Vegas. I can't believe you're alone."

"Well believe it. I've not been with a woman all the while I've been out there."

"Tell me what happened."

"Well, I went to Birmingham and asked Karen to come to Vegas with me, but she doesn't know yet what she wants. I mean, I haven't seen her since the first part of January. I thought she would be happy to see me."

"Have you told her yet that you're Elvis?"

"No, I can't tell her right now, it's not the right time."

"Look, you might go by the name of Johnny Raye, but you're still Elvis Presley, and you shouldn't have to beg any woman to come with you."

"Priscilla, I'm not begging her," I said, in Karen's defense.

"Sounds like it to me."

We left the studio and went to have coffee in the sun room. The tourists were all gone for the day, so we sat back and relaxed.

"Are you staying the night?"

"No, I'm just passing through. I need to sing awhile in the studio, it relaxes me and helps me make the right decisions." I sang for several hours, but my heart wasn't in it.

"Well did you decide what you're going to do with Karen?" Priscilla had rejoined me.

Wearily, I answered, "Yeah, I'm going to go back to Vegas, and just go on doing what I'm doing now, I guess. I'll give Karen a little longer to come to a decision before I move my life in another direction."

"Stay the night. Tomorrow's another day. Besides, I haven't made love since Christmas when I was with you," she hinted.

I chuckled, knowing that wasn't true. "Thanks for the great opportunity, but I need to pass."

Trying not to hurt her feelings, I told her I had to get back to Vegas. Thanked her for the coffee and the talk, kissed her cheek and told her to come and stay at the ranch so and we could go riding together.

"Sounds like fun, maybe someday I will," she replied politely, as I drove away from Graceland, once again.

I drove through the night and into the next day. When I reached Flagstaff, Arizona, I booked a motel room. Rather than continue onto Vegas, I took a few hours the next morning to see the Grand Canyon. I sat on the side of the road and admired the beauty around me. Mountains of every color imaginable spread out before me. Catching my attention below me were tiny specks that moved ever so slowly. Barely able to discern what they were, I finally realized it was a caravan of tourists riding donkeys to the bottom of the canyon. I watched a park ranger taking pictures of a family with their children.

Shoulders slumped, loneliness engulfed me once again. I needed and wanted so much to have someone to share all this beauty. Thinking the last few days over, I made the choice to give Karen until December when I would go to Florida to spread Jessie's ashes.

Pulling into my drive-way, I realized how blessed I was. I loved being out here, and again the ache to have Karen swept over me. Inside, no one was home. Thinking everyone went to see David or Chance's shows, and being tired from the long drive, I went to bed.

Unable to sleep, I thought I heard Gary and Denise come in. Donning my robe, I followed the sound of voices in the bar room. It was Gary and Denise, and Sandy. She was standing next to the pool table, and ran and to give me a big kiss.

"What are you doing here girl?" I asked, with little joy in my voice.

In all her excitement she didn't notice the sadness in my voice. "You're going to be surprised. I need to borrow your house for a few days in October."

"Tell him why," Denise exclaimed, noticing my expression.

"I'm getting married," she squealed, bubbling with excitement. "Johnny, remember the paramedic in my building that helped you?"

I nodded.

"We've been dating steadily, and he popped the question. He's going to night school to be a doctor, and by this time next year, he'll graduate med school."

Her excitement contagious, and not wanting to spoil her fun, I finally laughed. "I knew he was more interested in seeing you than helping me."

"Well anyway," she giggled, "he loves me." "Johnny, you were so right, he loves me for me, not for my body," and then rolled her eyes, "but he says he doesn't have any complaints in that department." "That's why I'm here, I was having a hard time deciding where we should get married when Denise called and told me about the house. I knew then that this would be the perfect place. I didn't want to ask you over the phone, so I came personally to ask if we could be married in your house."

Wrapping my arms around her, and tweaking her nose, I said, "Sandy, our house is your house, of course you can have your wedding here, I wouldn't want you to be married anywhere else."

"Thank you, Johnny," her eyes sparkled with happiness. "By the way," she teased, "you still look damn good!"

"Johnny," Denise asked, "where's Karen?"

"She's not ready yet," I retorted.

"Oh hell," Sandy said, "she's got to be out of her mind."

"I'd rather know she's sure of what she's doing then have her jump into something she's not ready for and us end up being a big mistake. I'm too damn old to worry about it now. I should have settled down a long time ago, when I had the chance. So until someone claims me, I'm available."

Now you tell me," Sandy teased. "Last year ago I'd have given you the moon if you'd have asked for it."

"Uh, huh, and you wouldn't have met the 'doc'."

"As always," she grinned, "you're right, but you're still good in the sack."

"Thank you baby, I needed to hear that."

"Look, I know you're going to stay up late talking, but I'm bushed, and I'm going to bed. See you all tomorrow."

Sandy stayed for a few days. She loved riding and swimming in the pool. She tried her luck at the casino and won a couple hundred dollars. To my surprise she behaved herself; guess she really is in love. After she left, the house seemed empty and quiet without her bubbly personality. Though I was never in love with her, I do love her dearly.

Three months passed quickly, and it was October. Sandy's wedding was on Saturday, and we were decorating the house inside and out to make this day special for her.

I rented a platform and trellis from a bridal boutique to be set up near the water fall. Denise ordered all the flowers, and Michele and Tara bought all the decorations, and had all the guys standing on ladders hanging crepe paper from every nook and cranny. The housekeepers were busy cleaning and polishing and cooking enough food to feed an army.

Friday night we had a bachelor/bachelorette party at the house. Sandy's hubby-to-be was nervous as a cat. He was trying not to drink too much, but ended up drunk enough that he fell in the pool. It was a sobering experience when he hit the cold water. You couldn't help but laugh at the shock on his face.

"Someone hollered, call a paramedic, man over board."

"Real funny," he said climbing out of the pool. Which made us laugh all the harder.

Sandy's and the doc's parents arrived early the next morning. Both parents were happy with the marriage, and it appeared there wouldn't be any in-law problems. Kristi and Frank arrived within a few minutes of Sandy's parents. They announced they were planning on getting married next year. "Looks like we have another wedding to plan," I laughed.

Gary was handling the music. Sandy held me to her promise to sing at her wedding. I chose "Crying In The Chapel," "Don't Cry Daddy," "Memories," and "Can't Help Falling in Love."

All morning the girls kept Sandy from seeing doc. Finally it was time for the ceremony to begin. The minister was waiting patiently. Denise was the maid of honor, and Tara and Michele were bride's maids. Doc had his brother as best man, and David and Chance as groomsmen.

The girls looked lovely in their apple green dresses. But all eyes were on Sandy. Sandy's father was a rather large man and Sandy looked little and fragile as she clung to his arm. Tears trickled down his cheek as he kissed his only daughter before handing her to doc. Sandy's eyes never left doc's face or his from hers when he saw his lovely bride. She looked absolutely radiant.

Her dress was all satin that was form fitted to the waist with a slight flair to the floor. Her train was scalloped in three layers with beaded edgework that flowed gently behind her.

Sandy had been paranoid for the past several days. She had nightmares of Jimmie coming and spoiling her wedding. As much as we tried to convince her Jimmie was locked up and nothing would happen, she still jumped every time the doorbell rang.

During the service, when the minister asked if there was anyone who felt this wedding shouldn't take place, please speak up now, Sandy's heart started to pound. Holding her breath, with a look of fear on her face, she slowly turned around. Doc, seeing her distress, took her hand and squeezed it gently. Placing his arm protectively around her, he whispered, "I'll never let anyone ever hurt you again. That's a promise."

Looking at the love in his eyes, her face once again became radiant, as the minister said, "I now pronounce you man and wife, you may kiss the bride."

We partied all day into the evening. Carmen and Juanita had prepared enough food to accommodate an army. Sandy and Doc were packing to leave as they had planned a honeymoon in the Grand Canyon. "It's supposed to be so beautiful this time of the year," Sandy exclaimed.

"Yes, it really is, and I think after a couple of days there you should go to Paris," and handed her two air flight tickets. Sandy squealed with delight and hugged and kissed me profusely.

"Hey, save some for me for later," doc laughed and then said, "Johnny, I can't thank you enough for all you've done for us."

"Just take care of her, and I mean that from the bottom of my heart."

"Or you'll break my legs?" He teased. "Sandy told me all about Jimmie."

"Doc, if you ever need anything, let me know." "Now my dear," I handed Sandy back to her husband, "your chariot awaits you."

Before they left, I told Sandy to open the briefcase that I had placed in the limo earlier. She started to cry when she realized it contained a hundred thousand dollars.

"That's for spending money and a help to get a good start with your marriage," I said.

"This day is a dream come true," Sandy, said, and now doc was crying too.

The guys had tied beer cans to the bumper of the limo, and Denise wrote Just Married in bold letters on the back window. Dodging all the rice throwing, the happy couple waved until they were out of sight.

We partied until dawn. I told Carmen and Juanita to leave everything until later and we'd all help clean up.

I lay restless in bed that night going over the wedding and wished it was me. It was then that realization sank in. All along Karen had tried to tell me in a gentle way what I wasn't able to see for myself. I had fallen back into my old ways of arranging everything and telling her what I wanted. Not once did I ever ask her what she wanted. And when she finally confided in me about her dreams, what did I do but get angry because she didn't drop everything for me right then and there. We hadn't spoken since the day I left her sitting in the restaurant. It wouldn't surprise me any if she never spoke to me again. And then, it came to me, starting tomorrow . . . and I drifted off to sleep.

. . .

Before you knew it, it was December. I had made myself a promise that if I didn't hear from Karen by Christmas, that it was over between us and I'd move on with my life. Everyday, since Sandy's wedding, I had one single red rose delivered to Karen with a card that said, "I miss you."

Lisa Marie came and stayed with her boyfriend for the holidays. His father was an actor in Hollywood and they both loved Elvis music.

Gary and I took two weeks off as was stated in our contract. It was a relief for me as I was getting tired of the demands. He and Denise flew to Dallas for a few days so Denise could enjoy time with her family, but they came back to spend Christmas at our house.

Chance and Michele flew their parents in to visit for a few days, but their parents left early to visit with other family members.

David's last show finished early and Chance was doing a late performance. We were all able to get together to see them perform. Afterwards, we celebrated by going out for steak at a well known restaurant, and then went clubbing. We had a great time watching other clubs private shows.

I went to the casino, but there wasn't any card games going on so I played the slots, winning and losing, winning and losing. Guess my luck had run out, I thought.

It was six thirty and the sun was peeking through the clouds when I pulled into my driveway. I left a note stating I was not to be disturbed, and slept peacefully until three o'clock that afternoon.

Hungry, I got up and went to the kitchen.

Lisa was there, and asked, "How much did you win?"

"Only a couple of grand, my luck seems to have run its course."

I looked around and noticed everyone was standing around grinning. "Well you're a happy bunch, mind telling me what's so enjoyable?" my voice trailed off, as I noticed a vase of a dozen red roses on the kitchen counter. "Who got the flowers?"

Then for the first time since entering the kitchen, I noticed petals of roses in a path on the floor leading to the game room. Opening the card to the roses, it read, *"I Miss You More!"*

From the shadow of the game room came a voice, "If you plan to retire with me, we're going to need that money."

My heart skipped a beat, "Karen, is that you?"

Stepping from the shadows, and walking towards me, she said, "I thought you were going to sleep the whole day away."

"How did you get here? And hesitating, I asked softly, "Why are you here?"

Taking a deep breath, she responded, "I've sold my dress shop, and decided you needed me to keep you straight until you're ready to retire, that is, if you'll still have me."

Reaching my arms out to her, she all but fell into them.

"I wish you had called me first, I would have left those two girls in my bed back at the hotel," I teased.

Wiping the tears from her eyes, she looked at me and said, "Just tell them to call a cab and go home, you won't be needing them anymore."

"Is that a promise?"

"Yes Johnny, that's a forever promise." "Mmmm," she said, snuggling deeper in my arms, "if you're ready to take a shower, I know someone who would love to scrub your back."

"Looks like you met your match," Lisa laughed.

Walking with arms around each other, we ascended the stairs to my room.

Looking around and laughing, she said, "Okay, where are they hiding?"

With a smile, I teased her. "They must have heard you were in town and disappeared."

Untying my robe, she said, "It's a good thing, because we won't need an audience for this performance."

CHAPTER 28

Prior to our wedding, I knew it was time to tell Karen the truth. I saddled my horse, and her Palomino, which she lovingly named 'Rosebud'. Together we rode out to the lake to our favorite spot. Knowing something was on my mind, Karen quietly rode next to me. Helping her down from her horse, I led her to a grassy spot next to the waters edge. Taking her hand in mine, I opened a box with a five-carat diamond ring and slipped it on the finger of her left hand.

"Will you marry me, and be mine forever?"

With tears in her eyes, she answered, "Yes, now and forever."

Looking into her eyes, I said, "Karen, there is something I must tell you. Once we marry, your name on the marriage license will read Karen Raye, but your real name will be "Karen Presley."

Waiting for some reaction, I was shocked when she said, "I know." "I figured that out when you did the Christmas Special, and from the love Lisa Marie has for you." I held her close to me and looked at the love that shone brightly in her eyes.

Karen and I married December 25th, Christmas Day. It was a quiet wedding ceremony at our house with only Lisa Marie and our family of friends in attendance. Karen couldn't have looked more beautiful when she appeared wearing a white satin pant dress, trimmed in small diamond clusters across the bodice that she had made prior to her coming to Vegas, in the event should we marry, she told me.

As I promised, after our wedding I called Doris and arranged a day to meet her at the cabin in Florida. Karen, Doris and I held hands as we spread and watched Jessie's ashes blow in the wind, some falling to the water. We all felt Jessie Mae's presence, and then suddenly, a tiny cry broke the silence. We turned and smiled at Jessie Anne as she squawked from her baby stroller.

EPILOGUE

We know Elvis as the greatest performer of our time. For years we have visited Graceland only to mourn him. How great it would be if we could believe he was alive today. We know his life style today would be so different from the way it was.

The next Elvis Impersonator that you see that's in his seventies, will you wonder? I know I will.

I guess we will never really know the real truth, but this is one writer that would like to think it happened just this way.

"Long live the King!"